Sleb

ANDREW HOLMES

Sleb

SCEPTRE

Copyright © 2002 by Andrew Holmes

First published in Great Britain in 2002 by Hodder and Stoughton
A division of Hodder Headline

The right of Andrew Holmes to be identified as the Author
of the Work has been asserted by him in accordance with
the Copyright, Designs and Patents Act 1988.

A Sceptre book

3 5 7 9 10 8 6 4 2

A CIP catalogue record for this title is
available from the British Library

ISBN 0 340 82361 5

Typeset in Sabon by Palimpsest Book Production Limited,
Polmont, Stirlingshire
Printed and bound in Great Britain by
Mackays of Chatham plc, Chatham, Kent

Hodder and Stoughton
A division of Hodder Headline
338 Euston Road
London NW1 3BH

For Mum and Dad

ACKNOWLEDGEMENTS

I am indebted to the following for their help and support: my wife Claire (happiness really is Claire-shaped), Lucy Fawcett, Andrew Gordon, Antony Topping, Katy Follain, Toby Tennant, David Taylor, Rob Waugh, Alex Simmons, David Granger, Andrea Storey, all at *Muzik*, *CVG* and *Mondo* (R.I.P.), Dr James Barlitt, Eric Frank, Hazel Orme.

CHAPTER ONE

'Bloody hell, it's lucky neither of us is diabetic,' said the well-known soap star Aaron Bleasdale to his girlfriend.

Actually, he sort of nuzzled the words into her neck as they took their turn before a huge bank of news photographers, many of them standing on short aluminium step-ladders in order to get a better vantage-point.

'Aaron! Aaron!' they shouted, even though only roughly half of their rank knew his name, and they were the half who knew he was just shutter practice before the proper stars arrived. Still, the girlfriend was wearing a very revealing dress.

'What?' she nuzzled back to him, as they posed before the snappers, who acted excitable but were actually bored.

At the celebrity couple's back were more people, members of the public who were kept from spilling on to the red carpet of the entranceway by rounded metal barriers with peculiarly comforting feet, really stable-looking. These barriers had been erected towards the middle of the afternoon and people roaming Leicester Square at that time had wondered idly, 'What's all that in aid of?' as they passed. Phil Yorke, whose friends called him Yorkie, had said to his girlfriend, 'Bet there's a première on tonight. Wonder what it is . . .' But his girlfriend had been miles away, not really listening. You know how couples are sometimes.

Thing is, Yorkie was right. There *was* a première and lots of well-known faces were expected to attend. In order to capture their attendance, breakfast-television crews had set up not long after the metal barriers arrived. Their purpose was to record the stars arriving ready for broadcast the next day, when the viewing public could monitor what the stars were wearing and how they reacted to the crowds bellowing for their attention. They were essentially puff pieces, a bit of glamour to slot between the troubles in the Middle East.

The same viewing public could catch up on all the *really* juicy gossip by diving into the tabloids to find out who had got drunk at the after-show party, who had snogged whom, and who mysteriously disappeared into a toilet cubicle with whom. The red-top tabloids would dutifully pass on all the dirt while the others – the *Mail* and the *Express*, in particular – considered themselves above such tittle-tattle, leaving their columnists to comment on gossip of which readers would only be aware if they'd been reading another paper.

So, really, the whole palaver did not exist within its own time-frame, and the red carpet was merely where it started. In reality, it was held chiefly to benefit the following morning, and then, to a lesser extent, for the columnists later in the week so that they could extract pithy put-downs from Caprice's dress. After that, it was for the Sunday papers, with their supplements, picture spreads and witty captions of which the subs desk were rightly proud. Given the correct circumstances its ripples might be felt for years. Who, for example, has not heard of 'that' dress worn by Elizabeth Hurley to the première of *Four Weddings and a Funeral*?

On this particular occasion, though, it would all be different.

There would be no gossip. No tittle-tattle. No 'that' dresses or witty captions. There would be only one story.

And it would centre on *why Felix Carter was not there*.

'What?' she said again. And her name is not recorded. She was simply Aaron Bleasdale's glamorous partner, a 'Mystery Blonde'. Good-looking, though.

They made sure their body language was right as they stood for the hissing Nikons. They stood leaning into one another, and even as she repeated her 'What?' she was sure to make it look as though they were sharing a private moment. Such a dear couple, so close and together even in public – even when caught in the incessant magnesium pop of the camera flash.

So he said – again, 'Bloody hell, it's lucky neither of us is diabetic.' And all the time he kept up that private-joke-sharing smile. They were only there for a second or so.

But bless him.

'What do you mean, diabetic?' The Mystery Blonde's voice was quizzical, but her face stayed faithful to the whirring cameras.

'You know, what with all the flashing. Like a whatsit, like a strobe light.'

'Oh, aha.' And she started to laugh, even tippy-toed to give him a kiss (click-click), using it to smother her guffaws and saying, as she did it, 'You mean *epileptic*.'

'Oh, God.' He slapped his forehead dramatically because he liked doing things in a slightly dramatic fashion. He was, after all, an actor. But inside he was seething. When he'd said to his new girlfriend – who was, admittedly, very sexily dressed for the night, 'Bloody hell, it's lucky, etc., etc.,' he had been doing it purely to draw her attention to the . . . well, to the *attention*. He'd been meaning it as a kind of code for, 'Hey, babe, check out the glamour on me. Don't get paparazzi bawling at you when you step out with your "civilian" friends, do you?' So really he was just bigging himself up, the stupid great insecure lunk.

Abigail was the PR girl who ticked off their names on a specially decorated clipboard as they passed into the door of the cinema. (Odeon West End, by the way. Good cinema, bit pricy.) Abigail had looked at herself in the mirror before she left home that evening, as the mini-cab beeped impatiently in the street, and she'd thought she looked great. She was wearing a black dress she'd bought at Oasis in town, and the thing was, she'd been to a lot more upmarket shops than Oasis in search of her perfect première attire. She'd been all over, in fact. But in the end it was good old medium-priced, dependable Oasis that had come up with the goods and she would tell that to the girls next time she saw them all.

Clearly, Abigail knew her place in the whole première/breakfast TV/tabloid/columnist toboggan run, which was why her dress was carefully planned so as not to upstage any of the visiting guests yet still to provide exactly the required amount of glamour and style. She looked good. She even momentarily caught the eye of Aaron Bleasdale as he flicked on his 'You know who I am?' smile, and she responded with a smile and theatrical tilt-and-tick on her clipboard. And with that the celebrity couple passed into the foyer of the cinema, which was already half full and buzzing with the anticipation of a group of people knowing that their betters were surely soon to arrive.

As a PR girl, Abigail was used to exalting that which was otherwise average, and she would have likened her current position to a kind of celebrity airlock. Just a couple of feet in front of her, beyond the doors, the barriers separated the herd from the guests who approached her along the red carpet, pausing and posing, depending on their importance, for the cameras who relied on B&Q ladders for their stature. Look, she thought, there comes someone who nobody recognises. He could be the film's producer and nobody would notice. No cameras. The photographers do all but study their nails as he wanders nonchalantly past, sporting a deliberately bemused look, like he wants everyone to believe that he's somehow above this celebrity circus. Whereas behind her were gathered the great and the good, relieved to have escaped the gauntlet of clicking cameras and panting fans, pleased at last to be among their own where they could establish their own air-purified hierarchy. Yes, she thought: a celebrity airlock. It was a good analogy. Worth mentioning to the girls next time she saw them.

Truth be told, she wasn't that pleased to welcome Aaron Bleasdale and his Mystery Blonde. After all, Aaron was strictly

B- to C-list. The kind of familiar face you might expect to see on a quiz show hosted by Paul Ross. The people she really wanted to see were the A-listers, and she only wanted to see them to have the *experience* of seeing them, which would only gain momentum in the retelling. Like the event itself, Abigail only stood to benefit from its ripples. Her participation in it would only accrue resonance when she held court in the *faux*-sincere surroundings of All Bar One as she and her friends loudly interrupted one another with snowballing tales of celebrity encounters.

So, no, she wasn't *that* delighted to allow Aaron Bleasdale into her celebrity airlock. What she really wanted to do was meet and greet the big guns: 'Enjoy the film.' Flirt when flirted with: 'We've had a very good reaction from the journalists who have already seen it.' Gush: 'This is my *third* time! And to be honest – really – I get something different out of it every time I see it.'

And of all the big guns, Felix Carter was the biggest – the .44 Magnum of big guns. After all, he was the country's biggest pop star. He had emerged from the rave scene and his days with the band 24/7, graduated to massive solo success and had since launched an acting career. He was impossibly handsome and charismatic. He was the one the girls would be really impressed by.

But he wasn't there; his name remaining frustratingly unticked on her clipboard. And as the Odeon's day staff busied around her and closed the doors, and two went outside to tell the crowd, 'Show's over, folks,' she had to accept it: he wasn't coming. With a final, hopeful look into Leicester Square, she turned and consulted her specially decorated clipboard to check which screen she'd put herself in. As she did so she suddenly felt dowdy and slightly embarrassed by the Oasis dress, which now felt like skimping instead of a canny buy.

Where was he?

*   *   *

Exactly half an hour earlier, the model Saffron Martyn was standing in the lounge of her Fulham flat, watching the road through her bay window, waiting for her car to arrive.

She always had butterflies whenever she was waiting for a car or a cab. There was something about the waiting that made her nervous – the lack of control, probably. But on this occasion her stomach was doing more flips, lurches and curtsies than usual. So much so that she wondered if she might be sick. She hoped not. Being sick was something she particularly didn't want to do since she was terrified of marking or creasing her dress. Plus, there was nobody around to hold her hair out of her face.

The dress had been made, especially for her and especially for this occasion, by her designer friend Tom DeBute, which was correctly pronounced *der-boot-ay*. She was his favourite model, his 'pet model', he liked to call her. And he was her favourite designer, mainly because she always looked fabulous in his clothes. DeBute was not a particularly well-known designer outside fashion circles, and Saffron had not broken out of the catwalk circuit and into the celebrity and gossip-column one. But both unspokenly knew that – providing the dress was right – all this could change after tonight. They were, after all, guaranteed the camera's kiss. She was being taken to the première by *him*: Felix Carter.

So she stood and waited nervily for the car, which was due to pick her up first and then him. Not such a gentle-manly arrangement, but that's the way things were. And she smoothed the dress, noting with renewed horror exactly how little of it there was to smooth. That, of course – still unspoken – was the plan. Maybe it should have made her sad that she was gift-wrapping herself for the morning's tabloids, but it didn't. She was just playing the game.

When the car arrived and she stepped in daintily, she watched the driver's rear-view mirror like a hawk, checking for any looks he might cast while thinking she wouldn't notice. He didn't; just drove, silent and professional. That was a bad start, she thought. But then, he was a professional, and professionals don't bat an eyelid. Not eyelid-batting is a skill essential to those in the service of the stars, and that thought relaxed her, made her think she was in good hands now. Whisked, by an expert, to the première, showered with attention, then whisked home again, like walking on air, above the ordinary folk.

The car pulled up on the street in Kensington outside his house and she arranged herself carefully on the back seat, crossing her legs first one way then the other. She laid an arm on the elbow rest, then thought, Too casual, and took it off again. She pouted, smiled and finally settled on an expression somewhere in between.

With the engine still purring, the driver stepped out of the car and closed his door, softly and without slamming it. He folded his hands in front of him and stood straight, ready to open the back door for his new passenger.

Saffron watched him, thrilled afresh at his professionalism. Then she turned her attention to the front door of the house, musing that it would be funny to watch this huge star come hurrying out. Would he be patting his pockets to check for his keys, the way normal people did? Would he stand and lock his front door, check it was locked just to be on the safe side? Or hesitate, then let himself back in with a small, apologetic wave, 'Oops, sorry. Just forgot me fags . . .'

But she waited, and rearranged, and the driver waited with his hands clasped in front of him, his face expressionless but probably thinking about the football or a little DIY job that needed doing at home. And the door didn't open.

After a moment or so, the driver looked round to her and raised his eyebrows, quizzical. She returned his look, but said nothing. Then he walked across the road to the house opposite, climbed the steps to the front door and pressed the bell.

And waited. Nothing. He turned to look back at the car,

as if to say, 'Tried him. I'll try again,' then pressed the bell a second time, waited patiently on the doorstep, hands clasped as before. Perhaps another two minutes went by before the driver returned, opened his door and peered at her in the back seat.

'Perhaps a telephone number, ma'am?' he suggested.

'Er, yes.' She dug in her tiny purse for her tiny mobile phone. She'd entered his number just three days ago and had experienced a rush of excitement every time she'd scrolled through her telephone book since. Now, though, she tossed her hair elegantly away from her ear and called his house.

No answer.

She lowered the phone and seemed to wither with disappointment. The driver looked at her expectantly, waiting for directions, a command to relieve him of the burden of her expectation. In return she smiled queasily back, wanting him to decide for her, willing him to suggest . . .

'Shall I try the bell one more time, ma'am?' he said. 'Just to be on the safe side?'

'Yes. Yes, please. If you wouldn't mind,' she replied. And the driver tipped his head in a yes-certainly, wishing the stupid cow would accept defeat, and trotted back across the road and up the blasted steps for the third time.

She watched. On the doorstep, she saw for the first time, was a bottle of something she couldn't quite make out in the light of the streetlamps – something golden-looking – but she was too tense to wonder what it was. And then – thank God! – the door finally, miraculously opened, but only an inch or so. She squinted her eyes to see as the driver and the person behind the door – was it him? looked like him but she couldn't tell – seemed to exchange words.

They spoke for a moment before the driver reached into his jacket then pulled out something he gave to the person behind the door. A beat, and the person passed whatever it was back to the driver, who indicated the bottle of golden liquid on doorstep, then turned and crossed the road to the car. Again, her rampaging nerves prevented her questioning what she had seen.

Then the driver was back, opening his door, leaning in to speak to her.

'Ma'am, I'm terribly sorry. The gentleman passes on his most humble apologies, but he's awfully unwell and will be unable to make it tonight. It seems we had previously disturbed him at an inconvenient time, if you get my meaning. He was otherwise engaged in the bathroom. He wonders, can he perhaps call you tomorrow, or when he's feeling a little better?'

She absorbed the news, her mouth twitching, a facial tic she had acquired at school when other girls, jealous of her beauty, had taunted her mercilessly. With a little of that anguish returning, she said simply, 'Thank you. Perhaps you could take me home?'

He nodded in sad confirmation, stepping into the car and feeling very pleased with himself all told. Just two days ago he had been a minicab driver, and look at him now. He was talking the chauffeur-talk like an old pro. As a reward to himself on the return journey, he let his eyes wander to the rear-view mirror so that he could fully admire the model's dress – or, rather, the lack of it.

He knew one thing: squits or not, there was no way *he* would have passed up the chance for a night out with *that*.

Of course, the driver had no way of knowing that the last thing Felix Carter had been planning to do was pass up the chance of a night out with Saffron Martyn.

In fact, Felix had been planning to take Saffron to the première, then to the after-show party and then back to his house, where he intended fucking her brains out. He would have done it too, if he hadn't been dead.

But the driver would find out in the fullness of time, and

then he'd wonder whether the killer had been on the other side of that door when he stood on the step. Had he been a mere door's width away from the man the world came to know as Christopher Sewell?

CHAPTER TWO

Is it going?

Yes, thanks. Um, Christopher—

Call me Chris.

OK, thank you. Chris, would you mind clipping this to your collar?

I certainly don't mind. Jack, is that allowed? Can I clip this to my collar? It's just a little microphone, how much damage am I going to do with that? Jack nods yes, it seems that's allowed. Let's see . . . how's that? Testing, testing . . .

That's fine. We're set.

Great. Where would you like me to start?

Well, I'd like all of our time together to be your memories of the events leading up to the . . .

Murder?

Yes.

So . . .

So start with a memory and let's go from there. Try to keep the events as chronological as you can. You might find it helps to imagine you've been hypnotised. Talk me through what you see, what you feel, what you hear . . .

My, we're quite the professional, aren't we?

I assume that's why you allowed me to see you.

Hmm . . . Right, I'll start with my father's funeral. It's as good a place to start as any, I suppose.

OK, um . . . OK, I'm sitting at my father's funeral and I find myself becoming aware of my body, slowly letting me down. The traitor. Typical, I think, as I feel rivers of sweat darting from beneath my armpits and racing towards my waistband. *Bloody typical* that I'm sweating freely on the day we send my father into the furnace. And that in a moment or so, when the vicar's finished with his bit, I'm going to have to stand in front of the family and friends, deliver my eulogy and worry about whether or not they can see my nerves spreading slowly and wetly across the chest of my white shirt.

Then there's my face, it's burning like I've got one of those Freemans catalogue heat lamps directed on it, the kind you shine on a pulled muscle. Beside me, Sam squeezes my hand, which is resting on the pew between us, and then she strokes my arm with her other hand. Squeeze. The first squeeze says, I'm here for you, Chris. The stroke: the stroke says, Babe, don't worry about the nerves and sweat and such, you'll be fine.

Will I, though? Will I be fine? I wonder . . .

Four days before that, Sam arrived home from work. I was standing in the lounge of our flat smoking a fag, taking stock of my feelings like you check for blood after a fall.

I'd just finished speaking to Auntie Jean on the phone. She had had the pleasure of telling me that my father had died, without warning but peacefully, and in his sleep. It would have been sort of weird to ask, 'How did he look when he was found?' but I'd have liked to verify the picture my mind's eye formed: Dad, eyes closed, looking for all the world as if he was slumbering like a hibernating grizzly, his striped-pyjama arms pointing at his toes, the sheet – not a duvet, 'too faddy' – pulled up to his chest and neatly folded over. I remember the first time I watched *The Silence of the Lambs*, seeing Hannibal Lecter and thinking, God, he's just like my dad. And then I saw *The Remains of the Day*, the one where Hopkins plays the butler – repressed, buttoned-up, stern, super-organised. And I thought, That's more like my dad. I don't recall – did we ever see Hopkins in his pyjamas in *The Remains of the Day*? If we did, I bet a week's wages they would have been a blue-striped pair. Just like my dad's.

'What's up?' said Sam. She tossed her handbag on to the sofa and wormed her way out of her coat. She couldn't be bothered to take it one arm at a time so the sleeves turned inside out. 'I tried your mobile. We needed milk. Not to worry, I got some.' She tugged at the sleeve for a bit, trying to get it outside-out but thought better of it.

I was thinking, This is a good excuse to get very drunk. Then I was thinking how shameful it was that I was going to use my father's death as an opportunity to take advantage of Sam's sympathy. The thoughts of a rat. Not a 'love rat', but a 'drink rat'.

'You OK?' she said at last, coat finally forgotten.

'I suppose not, really. Dad's, um, died.'

Sam looked as if she'd been stung. 'John? Oh, no. Chris . . .' She moved towards me, embraced me for a moment in which she rested her head on my shoulder, said, 'I'm so sorry,' then stood away, but holding me still.

I felt all sort of prickly and wriggled away from her.

'How do you feel?' she said. 'Oh, baby, it's so sudden. Was he ill? Was it . . . ? Where . . . ?'

'He died in his sleep last night. Natural causes – whatever, you know, that means.'

Dad was too young to go dying in his sleep like that: slowing down and going, like a battery. Knowing him, he simply willed it. Decided to go in a dignified manner, cancelled the milk and the *Daily Mail*, put out the rubbish and lay down to die.

'How are you?' she said into a silence during which I mused about my father, idly wondered where the draught was coming from, noticed that *Top of the Pops* was on television and decided I wanted a drink.

'I don't really know,' I answered, and I was almost surprised to hear the truth when so much of my time is normally taken up with deceiving Sam, keeping her in the dark.

'How do you feel?' she said.

'I don't really know,' I told her for the second time, and I was just as surprised to hear the truth again.

In the silence I turned to look at the telly in the corner of the lounge. The credits were scrolling across the final performance on *Top of the Pops*: Felix Carter singing his latest single. Singing the chorus, 'I lo-o-o-o-v-e you'. He was wearing a sleeveless knitted top, all the better to show off his muscles, shining and oiled under the studio lights.

'It's you,' said Sam – softly, almost to herself. She said it out of habit, because that's what she always says when we see Felix Carter – I look a bit like him. Except, of course, I don't, really: I don't have the muscles, or the looks, the money, the women, the fame or the talent. I just look a little bit like him.

You'd be forgiven for wondering how I keep Sam in the dark. OK, a normal evening might go like this.

I arrive home, usually about ten minutes ahead of Sam, take off my coat, have a piss and feed the cat. Then I go to the fridge and pull open the vegetable drawer, which holds two cans of Stella Artois or a similar premium-strength lager: Red Stripe, perhaps, or Kronenbourg. I take both cans from the fridge and place one in my coat pocket, open the second and pour half of it into a glass, necking the rest in one go. Then I start on the glass with short sips. Sam arrives home, looks at the glass and purses her lips slightly disapprovingly, but I smile sweetly and drink in short, civilised sips while she tells me about her day before announcing her decision to go and change, at which point I sigh, say casually, 'I'm off down the shop. Need anything?' and she says no, or yes: gravy, please. She goes through to the bedroom to change and I let myself out of the flat, immediately whipping can two out of my pocket. I drink the contents in three – perhaps four – long gulps, I deposit it carefully in a litter bin, hold my hand to my mouth, silently burp boozy gas, and enter the shop. On the door is a biro-written sign that says, 'Two Schol Children Only At Once'. Inside, they continue to offer an excellent deal on Stella Artois: eight cans for six pounds. I make two trips to the chiller cabinet for eight cans of Stella, unless they've been left in their plastic neck holders, in which case I manage the lot in one. I pay the woman shopkeeper, who stands behind an insanely high counter, which makes me feel five years old every time I shop there. We are all schol children in this shop, I think. Then I hoist the plastic bag, which they 'double up' for me after a prompt on my part, and leave the shop, bidding them farewell. They don't say farewell back, they never do. Outside the shop I rummage in the bag, pull out can three and drink it in three – perhaps four – gulps on my way back, depositing it carefully in the wheelie bin outside the house before letting myself in. Sam's still changing so I shout a hello and proceed quickly through the lounge and into the kitchen where I open the fridge door, put four cans in the top section and three in the bottom in the plastic drawer where the vegetables are kept. I cough loudly to disguise the *kik-kk-fssh* of can four's fizzy birth. It lives a short but fruitful life before I polish it off quickly and tuck it, empty, into the bottom of a bin bag. I burp silently and copiously into my hand, take stock, breathe deep, deep breaths and find that – great – I'm pissed and ready for the evening ahead. Work dissolves into the past and with it go the annoyances and grievances I've collected during the day.

'Sam?' I call.

'Yeah,' and her voice is small from behind the bathroom door.

'Fancy a beer with me?'

'Um . . .' She pauses behind the door. A beat. My question, so innocent. She wants to say, 'Chris, do you think you should? You've just had one, and you're supposed to be drinking less, remember?' Or, 'No, Chris, and I don't think you should either.'

But instead she says, 'I'll share one with you.'

Which is the answer I'm expecting, so I open can five without worrying about the noise it makes and pour half-and-half into glasses, which I take through to the lounge.

We're outside the funeral—

Sorry, am I jumping around too much for you?

This is fine, really.

You wanted me to do it like this, but it sort of means I'm jumping around. You know, in time.

This is great. Try to keep it chronological if you can, but whatever suits you best.

OK. Fine.

We're outside the funeral and one of my aunts has spotted a dog turd lying like a comma on the gravel outside the crematorium. Sentry-stood over it, she directs the mourners away, saying, 'Mind your feet, love, mind your feet. There's a nasty down there.' Pleased to have something to say and do, something useful.

'Who would let their dog do that?' tuts someone else. 'Really.'

I agree. Who would let their dog do that on the crematorium gravel? But, then, the Midlands is a weird place. I remember Terry Hall of the Specials said that once. He was right, the Midlands is a weird place. It's the sort of place where people let their dogs shit at funerals and men barely out of their fifties give up the ghost and follow their wives into the afterlife. Where a twenty-nine-year-old man is suddenly orphaned and stares into the breeze, registers his wife gripping his hand, wonders how he feels.

The day after the funeral we're back in London. Sam returns to work and I sit and watch television. I could go to work. Should go to work, really. I sell ad space for a magazine, and without my help the nation's females might never know which products help them to live their life, or give them frizz-free hair or refined skin or full-volume lashes, but I have just cremated my dad, and it's not often that I have the opportunity to sit and get blind drunk by myself. So I stay at home. The nation's females will have to wait for a day.

After *GMTV*, but before *This Morning*, they show *Trisha*. It's the English version of *Jerry Springer*, where guests with car-crash private lives are ferried on to make the rest of us feel happier about ours. As I watch, a girl with multiple earrings and blonde hair pulled back in a ferocious ponytail has just delivered an ultimatum to her twitching boyfriend: '*stop seeing your ex or it's over.*' The boyfriend's mouth is moving and some words come but he can't form whole sentences. He's not the sharpest tool in the box, but even he's aware that he's in a tight spot here: if he refuses, he gets no pussy. If he agrees, he looks like one.

Holding the microphone towards his twitching mouth, Trisha's saying, 'You've heard what Altea's said, Nathan. How does that make you feel?'

Nathan doesn't know how he feels because he already has too much information in urgent need of processing. If his brain had an in-tray, the manilla folder marked 'feelings' would have been prioritised downwards. So instead his mouth continues to work, and odd, disjointed words continue to come out of it. Though I despise earrings, and Nathan has one, I can't help but feel some sympathy for his plight. I'm sitting wondering how I feel myself, only the camera isn't here to record my doubt. Thank God for small mercies.

From next door I hear the baby crying. Three years we've been here and not once has the baby stopped crying. Not once. It's not quite loud enough to warrant a potentially confrontational trip next door to complain, but still, loud enough to chisel sadistically at our nerves. Sometimes, in darker moments, I wish that the baby would die.

I wait until exactly eleven a.m. before I go to the shop, because that's what I do. I tell myself I'm stocking up on lager because a couple of work colleagues are coming over for drinks this evening, and I buy a large packet of dry-roasted peanuts so the shop assistant will know that too. Thirsty work colleagues, obviously. The kind of work colleagues who enjoy guzzling large quantities of premium-strength lager. The only work colleagues to have.

Back at home I do the fridge thing and hunt out my *Star Wars Trilogy* box set from the spare room, which looks less and less like a spare room and more like the aftermath of a bric-à-brac explosion. It's exactly eleven fifteen by the time I get settled with the first of my tins and the first of three *Star Wars* films, a fitting tribute to my father who took me to see it at the Leicester Odeon in 1977. When we returned my father joined my mother in the kitchen and I skipped happily into the lounge brandishing an imaginary blaster (not a light-sabre – I wonder why?) and settled down to watch *Happy Days*. I got a sore bum later that night. How was I to know that a trip to the cinema was in lieu of time in front of the TV?

Funny, really, me remembering my mum in the kitchen like that, frozen in time. Just six years later she was dead.

Anyway, at about three thirty I go back to the spare room to fetch a video called *Danny Baker's Own Goals and Gaffs*. *Danny Baker* isn't in the box, but a video called *Sandy and the Students* is instead, and I put that in the video-recorder then pull down my trousers and pants to my knees and lie on the carpet in front of the TV, the video remote in one hand, a strip of toilet paper in front of me.

At about three fifty I realise I am very drunk. I have already seen Sandy have sex with two men in a dormitory and two of Sandy's friends have sex in a locker room, and I still haven't come. At about three fifty-one I close my eyes.

At about four thirty Sam arrives home from work early to find me asleep in front of the television with my trousers around my ankles and a strip of toilet paper carefully laid out in front of me. On the television a man masturbates into Sandy's face and comes on her stuck-out tongue, going, 'Aaah, yeah . . .'

Sam has left work early to be with me in my grief. To see how I am.

CHAPTER THREE

London (Reuters) –
POP star Felix Carter has been found dead in his west
London home this morning.[1]

Fifteen words. And as far as anybody knows this was the first
public announcement of the Carter death. At this point the
news was simply that: death, and could have been via suicide,
an overdose, a heart-attack, or an accidental fall. The fact that
he had been murdered would come later.

There are some stories – the resignation of Margaret
Thatcher, for example – over which news agencies squabble:
Ceefax claims first broadcast, PA News disagrees, Reuters
contests. Other stories – the death of Princess Diana, say –
they leave to the news ether, respecting the sensitivity of the
event, even though they almost certainly argue privately over
ownership. With the death of Felix Carter, it was Reuters who
broke the tape ahead of the rest.

London (Reuters) –
POP star Felix Carter has been found shot dead in his London
home. The 31-year-old singer's body was discovered by a
maid who raised the alarm at about 8 a.m. this morning. A
second man, also found at the house, has been arrested and
is in police custody.[2]

More words this time: a grand total of forty-seven working

---

[1] The first report, transmitted by Reuters at 8.41 a.m. on Wednesday,
5 November 2003.
[2] The second report, transmitted by Reuters at 8.57 a.m. on Wednesday, 5 November 2003.

words. And an extra layer to the story had been added. It appeared that Felix Carter had been murdered, an assumption rooted in the fact that another man was found at the house, the man we now know to be Christopher Sewell: a twenty-nine-year-old advertising sales executive from north London, married to Samantha Sewell, a twenty-eight-year-old conference organiser.

These were merely the first tentacles of information – fifteen and forty-seven words respectively. Nothing. Teeny-tiny-weeny molecules of data in comparison to the hundreds of thousands of words that were to follow. And they came via Reuters, a news agency – in fact, the *first* news agency – set up in 1851 by Paul Julius Reuter, who adopted that name from his given name, Israel Josephat. Reuter was made a German baron in 1871, but not before he'd set up a London-based telegraph office aimed at providing national newspapers with international news. Nowadays, and with the right Internet browser, members of the public can log on to the Reuters website at Reuters.com. However, it tends to be a statistics-based site, so the casual user would prefer to consult the BBC site or Ananova.com, which is a division of PA News, another news agency and one that was almost as swift to send its own details of the death to the media.

Given the nature of the Internet, and that the above trio of agencies all have a substantial presence, it's possible for a member of the public to receive national and international news at almost exactly the same time as the mass media. As only a tiny percentage of the population will be sitting in front of computers logged on to news websites at 8.41 a.m. on a Wednesday morning, the mass media retains its importance, thanks to the resources it can deploy at even the most fact-starved story.

Thus, even as Eamonn Holmes on *GMTV* shot his cuff and touched a finger to his earpiece – always a telegraph of some import – and said, 'Ah, we're just getting some news in . . .' newsrooms were mobilising and teams were being dispatched: to the police station where Christopher Sewell had been taken, but primarily to the site of the death. From there they broadcast the pictures to which the world awoke, of a quiet, very upmarket – obviously – but otherwise unremarkable Kensington street: one house decorated with the fluttering plastic of a police line (do not cross), and what looked like a makeshift polythene porch erected around the front door; expensive cars with their numberplates blurred out; policemen standing around keeping guard, others wearing white disposable overalls ducking into the polythene porch.

This was the scene the bleary-eyed nation saw when they reached for the remote control and opened their window to the world.

It's always more difficult for journalists reporting stories in well-to-do areas. The bystanders and eye-witnesses they rely on for story-filling quotes are in shorter supply. They tend to guard their privacy with a little more care and are less interested in appearing on television or seeing their names in print. They mark their achievements in different ways.

So the TV, radio and newspapers found different ways to report this story. They found psychologists prepared to comment; dug up music journalists happy to analyse the pop phenomenon of Felix Carter, and broadcast endless archive footage of Felix in concert, or Felix performing at Prince Charles's birthday and meeting the heir to the throne afterwards. All the while they were waiting for more 'proper' news to arrive, to flesh out those tantalising forty-seven words.

Just for a start, they would have liked to know about the discovery.

It was the cleaning woman, Martella, who made it. She was not, it's worth noting, a 'maid', as reported by Reuters later in the morning. She was a cleaning woman, and there is a difference. Not to most people: to be fair, that small detail took a subservient role compared to the sensational death of Felix Carter. And not to Carter, who himself was variously

21

referred to as 'singer', 'pop star', 'pop singer', 'rock singer', 'singer/actor' and 'superstar' during the reports of his death. But it did to Martella.

The way she saw it, in the grand Venn diagram of music you could be a superstar, singer, pop singer and rock singer all at once. What's more, if any one person characterised the central intersection of these circles it was her employer, Felix Carter.

She, on the other hand, was employed to visit the house three times a week – fewer when he was on tour – and rid it of the considerable mess he left. That made her, as far as she was concerned, a cleaning woman. Later, after spending endless hours in a police station and finally being allowed to leave, she ignored the ringing phone for a moment and looked up the exact meaning of the word 'maid' in a dictionary.[3] What she read clarified her initial thoughts. She was not a 'young, unmarried girl; maiden', she was a woman of advancing years, just on the outposts of sixty. And neither was she unmarried. She had married once, almost exactly thirty-four years ago, a man named Jack who ended up preferring the company of a girl who worked in Woolworth's, and after that disaster, well, she never really saw the point of doing it again.

Neither was she 'a spinster', not in the accepted Miss Havisham sense anyway. She didn't have a 'partner', as they say these days, but she had never been short of gentleman company, friends and admirers. Her backgammon nights saw to that.

Which left, last but most pertinently, 'a female servant', which, clearly, was the point of confusion for the news writers. And no, she wasn't a female servant either: she was not full-time and she was not employed to be at the beck and call of her employer, whom she hardly ever saw anyway, even though she felt she knew a lot more about him than most. She. Was. Not. A. Maid. And if there was one thing she took away from the

---

[3] *Collins English Dictionary*, Millennium edition, (Harper Collins).

whole experience, it was that bad-taste-in-your-mouth feeling of having been misrepresented. Yes, it was such an insignificant mistake that she knew any attempt to set matters straight would be met with derision, but to her it was important. She felt then that she had some inkling of the way that, at times, her recently deceased employer must have felt.

Had he been alive, Felix would have taken Martella's anger over this editorial error as a positive sign. A vindication of his decision to hire her. It proved that Martella was concerned with different things. She didn't care whether or not she got into the papers, and she didn't care what he got up to and was similarly unlikely to go spreading his secrets around. All she cared about was cleaning. And backgammon. Although she did not know it, Martella's irritation at being called a maid made her a better cleaning woman.

Those who passed Martella in the street would often assume subconsciously that they'd just seen a Turkish lady, or a Spanish one, or maybe a redoubtable matriarch of Greek origin. This was because Martella, who had been born in 1941 in Reading by way of an English/Scottish coupling and named in homage to the beverage of choice during the night of conception, had a somewhat exotic look. A comforting, weathered appearance, perhaps. Indeed, friends often remarked upon her resemblance to the film star Miriam Margolyes, a respected English actress who has enjoyed a successful career playing women of varying nationalities: Welsh in *House!* (2000), American in *Magnolia* (1999), Austrian in *Immortal Beloved* (1994). Small, but pivotal roles.

Perhaps, if they ever decide to film this story – of Felix Carter and his killer – Miriam Margolyes might consider taking the part of Martella, the cleaning woman who discovered the body. A small, but pivotal role.

Martella's role began that morning when she arrived at the house, not really knowing what to expect. Or, rather, to expect the unexpected. She knew that her employer had planned to attend a film première the night before and that meant one of three things. Either Mr Carter would be absent, whereabouts unknown, or he would be tucked up sound asleep in bed – perhaps by himself, more likely with a female friend, identity unknown – and stay there while she worked. Or she might find him asleep on his sofa, TV on, still in his clothes, as she had done on a number of occasions.

She shrugged off a light drizzle and let herself in at the front door, quietly in case of either of the latter eventualities. Damp from the rain, her fingers slipped on the doorknob slightly as she closed it softly behind her, but even so, forensic teams were later able to take fingerprints from it, and hers were among them, left just moments before she told the world that Felix Carter, the pop star, was dead.

It was dark and silent inside, but that was usual, and she paid it no mind. Most people she knew would be up and about at eight a.m., but Mr Carter was not most people. He had a unique job with unusual hours, and that meant she could have no preconceptions as to how she might find things. There was a smell, though. And had she ever worked in any kind of medical capacity, she might have identified it as that which accompanies death. The smell, they say, sticks to you even when you've shed your work skin and you're sitting around a table at a dinner party, feigning interest in the FTSE index to keep your partner happy.

But she hadn't worked in any medical capacity, she was a cleaning woman, so it was not an odour Martella recognised. To her it was simply . . . *new*.

The next thing she noticed, and this did strike her as odd, was that his tuxedo was hanging in a doorway at the far end of the dusky hallway. Hanging as if he'd fetched it from a cupboard ready to wear, but never got round to putting it on. It was still in its plastic.

And that was followed very quickly, as she took a step into his front room, by the sense that something here was very wrong. She couldn't say what, it was more of a feeling.

And then she saw the sofas.

Felix's two white leather sofas were his pride and joy. They occupied the middle of the front room, standing opposite each other, two fine additions to the room's other boyish decorations: an almost complete collection of *Star Wars* figures – from the original trilogy, not the badly received prequel *Episode I: The Phantom Menace*. Not from that one, because Felix didn't like it. He'd wanted a lifesize stormtrooper, of course, but had decided against it, perhaps because both Robbie Williams and Gary Barlow owned one and he wanted to forge his own path. That was always his way.

And, with the exception of two men, who sat facing each other in the sofas, everything else seemed to be normal. Except, of course, it wasn't. The two men made sure of that. And she realised that something *bad* had happened here. Something she would not be involved in tidying up.

She stood, her large frame filling the doorway, and took in the men and the blood that spotted one of the white leather sofas. Never get that out, she thought vaguely, then slowly became aware that the two men in the room appeared almost identical. There on one side was Felix, lying back in the sofa, looking asleep to all intents and purposes, apart from the blood that seemed to have spread from his back, a stark red on the white leather. And apart from the purple hole in his chest.

And there on the other side of the room, facing him, was also Felix. But this Felix was sitting slumped, with a bottle of whisky held to his stomach, looking at her carefully. Watching her.

Martella was not one of those people who sat in front of the TV of an evening pouring scorn on the characters, as her husband had done: 'As if!' and, 'There is *no way* she'd just stand there like that in real life.' She didn't do it, first, because she'd never felt the need to put the world to rights as her ex-husband had done, but second, because she knew instinctively that there was no such thing as a predictable human response; no way you could say with any certainty how you would react to any given situation. Especially those situations that were so far outside the envelope of everyday experience. The kind of situations you expected to see on the television. Or the one in which she found herself now.

So, in this instance she simply stood stock still in the doorway, rooted so firmly to the spot she found it impossible to move. She didn't notice, but her fingers relaxed and the plastic carrier-bag she'd been carrying (contents: a blue tabard and that day's edition of the *Daily Express*) dropped smartly to the floor.

It was the only sound in the house as Martella and Felix number two studied each other.

But then, as her eyes continued to adjust to the gloom, she registered that it wasn't Felix at all. At first glance you might easily be taken in, as she had been. But it was definitely not her boss. The face was different. Similar, but different. And the build was wrong.

It was, of course, the first time she'd ever seen Christopher Sewell, but it would not be the last, not by a long, long chalk. He looked in his late twenties, dressed in jeans and a T-shirt, untucked at the waist. His hair was dark and cut short, like her employer's but without the styling. He was good-looking, but not handsome. In many ways, she supposed, he was quite unremarkable. He certainly wasn't the kind of man to whom she would have given a second look in everyday life. The cleaner in her noted, with some satisfaction, that he had an orderly face: all the bits were in the right places but there was nothing particularly special about any of them. Except, of course, that they were currently sitting on a sofa in Felix Carter's house.

Perhaps her eyes had taken some time to adjust to the gloom inside, for it was only after what seemed like an age that she realised he was not looking at her after all. His eyes were shut. And on closer inspection, as she let out a long, slow breath she didn't even realise she'd been holding, it dawned on her that the man was slumped – sleeping, or perhaps unconscious.

'Hello?' she said at last, still cautious. And the word dropped like a stone in the silent room. The man showed no sign that his peace had been disturbed. He simply continued the illusion of his silent contemplation and finally she relaxed. Her prairie instincts at last told her, 'No threat. This man is no threat,' and her shoulders dropped with relief.

It was only when she tore her eyes away from the sleeping man that she cast her gaze back to the other sofa where, she realised, the *real* Felix sat. But this Felix was not sleeping, or even unconscious. He was dead, she thought. He could perhaps have been sleeping, but no: the smell, the blood, the *feeling* in this dark room. He was dead. She looked at him for a moment, thinking that she had never seen his face so serene. He looked like an angel.

At last Martella took a step back and out of the room. She felt calm, thinking now of the detective programmes she watched and the lessons she'd learnt from them. Her favourites were the Inspector Wexford mysteries, written by Ruth Rendell. From those and from the others – *Taggart*, *Cracker*, *Silent Witness*, *Inspector Morse* and *A Touch of Frost* – she knew that a disturbed crime scene was the enemy of an organised investigation. So she merely took a step out of the doorframe and into the hall, never taking her eyes from the two men in the room, and reached into her coat pocket for her mobile phone, which she drew close to her face in the gloom. When she pressed the red rubbery 'on' button she found herself secretly pleased: first, that she had a rare opportunity to use her mobile phone, and second, that she'd remembered to reach for it in the first place – she so rarely used it that it was hardly second nature to her. It was, she thought, an example of her composure.

Then she dialled 999 and told the world what she'd found. And after that she walked back down the hall towards the door, let herself out and stood on the doorstep waiting for the police to arrive, buttoning up her coat against the drizzle. All the while she thought not of Felix Carter, but of the man in the armchair, and of the look on his face.

Only now did she realise that it was a look of complete contentment.

CHAPTER FOUR

How do you feel, Chris?

How do I feel? I feel great. I have Jack to look after me. Have you met Jack?

I have, yes.

Then you'll know I could hardly be in better hands. And the other prisoners give me a lot of respect. I'm not exactly top dog, that honour belongs to somebody else, but I'm given a lot of respect. I'm probably the most famous person most of them have ever been in contact with. I give autographs, you know. It's so the wives and girlfriends can sell them on the other side, bit of pin-money. I don't mind. Plus I have lots of letters. Lots of people want to see me. You're very privileged.

Thank you.

No need. I'm enjoying myself. Shall we do more 'visualising'?

You're happy with that approach?

Absolutely. Let's see . . .

OK, here's me, coming through the door to our flat. I've had a couple of quick Kronenbourgs after work, so Sam's home first. I drop my briefcase to the lounge floor, use one hand to open my shirt and loosen my tie; enjoy the image of a weary man returning home from work I've just created, and call, 'Hello?'

'Hi,' says Sam brightly, walking through from the kitchen. She's holding the cat, which is upside down in her arms but watching me, always wary the way cats are.

'It's a little baby,' coos Sam, 'come to see her daddy.'

I'm not the cat's daddy. That falls to another cat, blissfully unaware of its paternity somewhere else in north London. I'm also slightly irritated that Sam hasn't asked me how I am, or offered her lips for a kiss, or even enquired about my day. Instead she snuggles baby words into the cat's stomach while it fixes me with a stare that might be saying, 'See, I couldn't care less about all this attention. That's the difference between you and me. Loser.'

'Take her,' says Sam.

'No, you're all right,' I say. 'I've got to have a piss.'

'Go on,' she insists. 'Take her. She likes you.'

Why, I think, can she not see that the cat doesn't like me? It doesn't even like her. It treats us both with an indifference that *Big Issue* sellers would find insulting. If it really was a child, and I was its father, I would have sired a sulking, pierced, obnoxious teenager with a special form of clawed Tourette's. And here is this furry injustice, nonchalantly swiping the affection that rightly belongs to me.

'Take her,' says Sam again, holding her across to me as though passing a baby over the font. 'Just hold her for a second or so.'

So, to keep the peace, I take her and hold her awkwardly for one, two, three and four seconds. Then I hand her back, at which point I feel something wet on my hand, which I instinctively raise to my nose.

'Shit!' I say. 'There's shit. The cat hasn't wiped its arse!'

'Only a bit of poo,' says Sam, with the tone of somebody quietening a hysterical child. But still she plops the cat down to carpet and it trots through to the kitchen, away from my wrath.

'Oh, fuck! I don't want shit. I've just come home from bloody work and I've got shit all over me.'

'It's not all over you, it's on your hand. It's just a little. Wash it off is all.' But she says this with tiredness in her voice, and the look she has, which I ignore as I stomp angrily to the bathroom, is of someone whose bubble has been burst. As if the moment has failed to live up to her expectations.

Ah, I'm sorry. I've jumped again, haven't I?

You have, yes. I didn't want to stop you, but . . .

You should have done. My mistake, I'm sorry.

It's not really a problem. Just if you could, you know, keep it as chronological as you can.

Certainly.

Perhaps we should go back to the bit where Sam walked in while you were, er, masturbating?

Well, I wasn't 'er, masturbating'. I was asleep. Had I been awake I would have heard her key go in the front door and I would have taken some form of preventive action. As it was, I was asleep, so the first I knew of Sam's early arrival home was the rustle of a Sainsbury's bag – she'd brought me home something nice to eat. And then I was aware of her standing over me with that dogshit-shoe look, the video playing and the bloke going, 'Aaah, yeah . . .' like the beginning of a new nightmare.

When she woke me I was in exactly the same position as when I fell asleep. I must have looked like one of those figures they found preserved at Pompeii, but a wanking one. And instead of bursting out crying and blaming this outbreak of self-gratification on the sudden and almost inexplicable death of my father, or perhaps adopting an ashamed look and taking my punishment like a man, I decided that attack was the best form of defence. So we argued, and there was a lot of shouting, some crying too, I think, but not me.

The next thing I know I'm waking up on the sofa with a blanket over me, obviously put there by Sam to keep me warm. And Sam is putting a piece of paper on to the coffee table in front of me and she straightens upright when she sees me stir. 'Do you remember what happened last night?' she says, from a position of such moral high ground she must be oxygen-starved. She looks nice all done up in her work clothes. She always does. 'Do you remember calling me a cow?' she asks, before I can answer. 'A *fucking* cow?'

I don't remember. But to confess to amnesia seems like rubbing salt into the wound, so I stay quiet. I'm still trying to remember who I am and what I'm doing on the sofa; why

I'm not dressed and ready to go to work since Sam obviously is, and I usually leave for work a quarter of an hour before she does.

'And my crime,' she continues, 'was having the audacity to take a couple of hours off work with the aim of cooking my poor bereaved husband a nice meal. Only to find my husband as drunk as – as . . .' she wants to say skunk, but realises it's not quite appropriate, so she searches for another word and eventually abandons it, '. . . I don't know what, fucking *wanking* in front of – of – *porn*.'

This is useful information to me. Like a rusty screw, my memory needs a couple of wrenches to budge and I begin to recall some of last night's events: shouting (both), crying (hers), indignation (mine), recrimination (hers). Bad stuff. All of it. Bad, bad stuff.

'I'm sorry,' I manage, wincing at how poorly the words suit my behaviour. 'Sam, what time is it?' And if I'm hoping for sympathy there's no way it's on the menu.

'You're going to be late if you go in, but I suggest you don't. You're in no fit state. Your uncle rang.' She points at the piece of paper she placed on the coffee table earlier. 'He wants you to ring him. He's the – whatsit? The executor of your father's estate.' And with that she shoulders her handbag and leaves, slamming the door behind her.

I groan. Next door the baby starts crying. Outside, a minicab beeps, waits, then beeps again.

It sounds like peacocks on the lawn and the distant sound of shotgun fire, but my father's 'estate' actually consists of a semi-detached house along the Groby Road in Leicester. That house might have seen a few people come and go over the years, but for the last thirty it was the Sewell family mostly who came and went. And for the last ten of those years my father had lived alone, only in a not-living kind of way, a consumed-with-something kind of way.

He loved my mother, I'll go to my own grave knowing that.

He loved her in such a deep and fundamental way that when she was killed his anguish would have been too much for his son to bear so he kept it hidden away. Only he kept it inside, where it squatted in his soul and spread cancer through his heart.

God, he was hardly Funboy Three when she was alive. The pair of them were a lone moral outpost of war-time values in Leicester's shifting landscape. They kept a tight ship, had standards. We ate breakfast together, as a family. And when my father returned from a day mending people's gas central heating to what surely must have been a frighteningly high standard, we ate supper together as well, as a family. I called it tea, or dinner, because that's what my friends called the meal they had when they got home from school. But I was always corrected. It was supper. And after supper we ate dessert, not pudding – Ski yoghurts.

It was hardly an act of cruelty not to provide me with a little brother or sister to play with, but it was so *them*. There was not enough room in the semi-detached house on the Groby Road, so one child was all they had, but they did their damnedest to make sure that that one child was a well brought-up child. I was steered away from the faddy crazes of my playground friends but never neglected. I was taken to Norfolk for seaside visits, bought one ice-cream a day but never more than one because one's enough – you don't want to end up looking like him over there. I was taken to the cinema, to suitable films: *Star Wars*, yes; *Grease*, no. I was bought good clothes. Not the right clothes, but good clothes. It makes me laugh now when I see the stylish adverts for Clarks shoes that fill the space I sell. It makes me laugh to think of the times I wriggled away from the Clarks' shop foot-measuring machine, begging my mum to buy me Doc Martens instead, like the ones my friends wore.

Listen to me, moaning that I had the best instead of the most fashionable, forgetting the other days. The days of countryside and making kazoo noises with blades of grass held between the thumbs. Coasting along sun-splodged country lanes beneath an umbrella of foliage singing my times tables from the back seat – I could never do my nine times and I still have difficulty now. The days when, looking back, it felt like everything we did or talked about was somehow for my benefit, as part of a gentle campaign of ongoing nurture and education. So easy to forget those days when you have the nagging hurt of a never-bought pair of Doc Martens hanging sullenly around in the back of your mind.

And even though I'm only – what? Twenty-nine. Yes, twenty-nine. Even though I'm only twenty-nine, and that hardly puts me in the 'good old days' bracket, I remember my childhood as being a safe place to be. Where playing cricket and football on the street or cycling madly up the pavements with my Raleigh Grifter swinging beneath me wasn't a dangerous thing to do, wouldn't get you picked up by a pervert, or knocked down by a car. Even without Doc Martens the Leicester of my growing years was a happy and safe place to be.

Until, of course, the screech-bump thing happened to my mother.

The night she was killed she had gone to a WI meeting. I'm grateful that I've never encountered the WI since I moved to London, except on the news, booing Tony Blair. But then the quaint, slightly claustrophobic environs of groups like the WI are what people move to London to escape. I'm sure the WI is still going strong in pockets of rural Britain, where its members hold crisis meetings in a bid to modernise their image, where lack of membership means the permanent threat of closure. To be honest, I hate the WI, and even its staunchest supporter would have to admit that's a fairly understandable reaction, especially when you consider that my mother hated it too. She would much rather not have been walking home from the WI that night. She went to forge good relations with our neighbours. She went out of a sense of duty so that the family would slot that little bit more easily into the cosy world of Groby Road, Leicester.

I was reading a Paul Zindel book by the light of a bicycle torch when it happened. I was eleven.

I was not supposed to be up, or even awake at that time. It was about ten-ish so I read by the light of the only torch I had, which happened to come off the front of my Raleigh Grifter. A sensible thing to have, but unnecessary since I never rode my bike after dark anyway.

The idea was that if one of my parents came up the stairs I would hear them and switch off the torch thereby extinguishing any tell-tale light creeping from beneath my bedroom door. It was a precaution I took not only because it was past my bedtime, but also because Paul Zindel books were slightly above my reading age and I was terrified of being caught with this one. It was called *The Undertaker's Gone Bananas*.

And then I heard the screech-bump. The screech: brakes being applied sharply, familiar from films and television, rare but not entirely unknown in everyday life. Then the bump, which was a noise like thumping a pillow really, really hard. A solid, but cushioned blow.

It must have been loud. Really loud for me to have heard it. My bedroom was at the back of the house, overlooking a well-kept garden that boasted a slide, which was probably due for a trip down to the dump, and one of those rotary washing-lines that squeaked softly in the breeze. I crept to the window anyway and pulled the curtains over my head to look outside and into the garden. Nothing but the slide, the washing-line and a square patch of light from the kitchen window.

If I'd been at the front of the house I would have looked out and the streetlamps would have shown me a car stopped in the middle of the road. And on the road in front of it, some way ahead, where she had been thrown by the force of the collision as she crossed to our front door, my mother.

If I'd been at the front of the house, I would have seen the car reverse slightly, perform a U-turn with a second screech of tyres, and speed back in the direction it had just come from, leaving my mother the solitary occupant of the road. I might even have been able to read the numberplate, or at least take a description of the car. But I didn't see any of that. As I say, my bedroom was at the back.

From downstairs I heard my father run to the front door, which he opened but did not close behind him. He would have been expecting her back at exactly that time and she was never late. And when you love someone that much, you must just know.

I wonder what he thought in those brief moments before his world stopped turning. I wonder if he hated himself for hoping that she had been delayed, perhaps caught chatting to one of the members about Rice Krispie cakes, for praying that it could be *anybody else but her* lying like litter in the middle of the road.

Not long later there were sirens, but I did not stray from my bedroom. And although I felt fearful, I never knew what was going on outside in the road. Eventually I fell asleep, and when I woke up my father was standing over me, his face frozen.

When I finally went back to school the other kids ignored me. I told Sam, one drunken night, blubbing into her lap, that the kids at school had ignored me, and she stroked my hair, telling me that they hadn't really ignored me, that it had been me who felt different, adrift and alone. Maybe she was partly right. Maybe they hadn't actively and spitefully sent me to Coventry. After all, they would have been told by teachers and parents to be extra-specially kind to me. But this was almost twenty years ago, and twenty years ago eleven-year-olds living in Leicester had two parents who lived together. Divorce was as rare as death. Except eleven-year-olds don't have much concept of divorce. But they know about death. So when I returned to school, I had deadmum disease, the screech-bump lerg, and touching me might mean catching it and everyone knows you can't tig your butcher so you just pass it on until, suddenly, all of the mums are dead. And there are no more frozen lollies, no more packed lunches and clingfilm and cake bowls to lick – just dads who tell you to quieten down and are only really good for mending punctures.

So maybe they didn't ignore me. They weren't nasty eleven-year-olds, just frightened ones, but they might as well have ignored me. And when I went home – well, he didn't ignore me either, but he might as well have done. I wondered then and I still wonder now what he felt. He must have missed her like you miss a limb, but the part of him that wasn't grieving for her would have been burning with injustice and hatred for the man or woman who left her dead in the road outside. And that left no part of him for me.

CHAPTER FIVE

A cleaning woman named Martella – like the Cognac but not – stepped out of a house and into a drizzly day. And the world gradually became aware that Felix Carter was dead.

'Bloody hell,' said the well-known soap star Aaron Bleasdale to his girlfriend. And he felt a shiver of something that wasn't shock, sadness or grief, but excitement. Felix had been due to turn up at the première last night, and briefly a connection story passed through Aaron's mind, one that ended with the words, 'And the thing is, that could *so easily* have been me.' Just as quickly he dismissed it.

He'd heard the news from Channel Four's breakfast programme which returned after a news broadcast – the team clearly in a state of dazed confusion.

'Well,' said a presenter, pulling himself together for the cameras, with the floor manager and the producer jabbering into his earpiece, 'we've just had the same news as – as you have, and I can tell you we're all a bit, er, *shocked* here . . .'

'I can't believe it,' chipped in another presenter, her hand to her mouth. 'That is terrible.'

'Well, erm, obviously we'll keep you updated with any more news as we get it,' added the first, 'but for the moment all we can do is send, well, our deepest condolences to the family. Um, Felix was a great friend to the show, as I'm sure you all know, and we're all a bit – we're all a bit – well, I think shocked is the word. Obviously, er, this is breaking news. Perhaps, God willing, it won't turn out to be as bad as it first sounds, but at the moment, it does seem as if Felix has died, although we're not sure how.'

And with that they went into a item called MWA, Moggies With Attitude, in which members of the public are invited to bring aggressive and belligerent cats into the studio in a bid to outdo the reigning 'sourpuss', a tabby called Liam from Braintree.

'Bloody *hell*,' repeated the well-known soap star Aaron Bleasdale to his Mystery Blonde.

Even though she knew the difference between diabetic and epileptic, he had decided not to dump her after the première. Following a lousy film but decent aftershow party, several glasses of champagne and one and a half lines of coke, he'd decided to do the exact opposite. He'd brought her back to his flat where he'd failed to stay erect for long enough to have penetrative intercourse. Aaron Bleasdale was good at playing the dastardly but charming nightclub owner Jack Trent on *Town Affairs*, but he wasn't much cop in bed. He blamed it on the coke.

'What is it?' mumbled the Mystery Blonde into a pillow, her mysterious blonde hair a blonde aura around her head. She wished that she'd put on her bra, or at least a T-shirt. She didn't want him staring at her breasts when she got up to dress. Already she was composing an e-mail to him in her head. In it she'd subtly massage his ego by claiming that the pressures of his celebrity were too much for her to bear. She thought that if she worded it correctly she could even make it seem as if he was doing the dumping, not her.

But inquisitiveness eventually got the better of her and she raised her head from the pillow. Just a little, the blonde hair dropping to form a silky cage around her head. Then a little more, and she blinked at the stark bachelor white of Aaron's walls and peered at him through a veil of her own blondeness.

'What bloody hell?' she said.

'Set your face to stunned,' said Aaron. He was quoting *The Simpsons*, a line that, because he was also a committed – but secret – *Star Trek* fan, had made him laugh for about a week. And still made him laugh whenever he thought of it.

'Felix Carter is dead,' he added, his eyes bright.

'Really?' she said, suddenly alert, thinking: Mobile phone. 'God. When? What happened?'

'I dunno. It's just come on the news. All they know is he's been found dead in his house. Oh, but there's someone else there and he's been arrested.' As he finished saying this he realised he'd said it a bit straight, and cursed himself for not adding more drama. But Mystery Blonde wouldn't have noticed: she was already swinging her legs out from under the covers and dabbing her feet on the carpet to find slippers, which weren't there because it wasn't her flat.

'I've got to get to work,' she said, explaining the sudden activity.

'Why?' said Aaron, who'd been hoping a blowjob might be on the morning's agenda before he left for the set. 'You're not a newspaper.'

'No, we're a celebrity-based style magazine and a recent survey showed that Felix Carter is our core reader's favourite singer, her biggest object of desire, her best-dressed male *and* the man she'd most like to be stranded on a desert island with. So if the guy dies, we kind of owe it to her to pull out the stops a little.'

'You owe it to your circulation, you mean.'

'Whatever.'

She found her mobile phone on the carpet, scooped it up and scrolled to a number to dial. Aaron propped his head on his hand to watch her in action.

'Tania,' she barked down the phone, pronouncing it the posh way, 'Tarn-ya', rather than the common way, 'Tan-ya'.

Tania Jenkins was the magazine's picture editor, and not due to get out of bed for another ten minutes. She was, therefore, somewhat on the bleary side.

'Yeah?' she said, the word sounding more like a groan to the Mystery Blonde.

'Tania,' she said, more business-like than Aaron had ever seen her before. He marvelled at this new side to her. 'You'd better get into the office as soon as possible. Felix Carter has been shot.'

'I know,' groaned Tanya, exasperated. 'We shot him three weeks ago, remember?'

The Mystery Blonde raised her eyes heavenward. 'No. Not shot for the magazine. Shot, as in shot dead.'

'Jeepers,' blurted Tanya, slightly more awake now. 'Really? Like, shot? With a gun?'

'Real bullets and everything. Listen, can you give your lot a call? We'll be wanting to do some kind of picture special on him. And we'll need to get onto it straight away.'

'Right,' said Tania, although she seemed a good deal less galvanised by the news than the Mystery Blonde was. 'Will do. See you at the office, hon.'

Mystery Blonde ended the call, musing that hers was surely one of the few vocations where staff needed an early-morning phone call to get them to work before ten a.m. And then she looked around for her clothes. Happily, the night had been so passion-free that she'd had the opportunity to fold them and put them over a bedroom chair prior to Aaron's limp attempts at love-making.

Nevertheless, as she dressed, Aaron leered shamelessly at her from the other side of the bed. His head was propped on his arm and he was clearly trying to flex his muscles at her. Pathetic, she thought.

'This survey of yours,' he preened, 'where did I come in it?'

She shouldered her handbag and looked him over, her lip curling. 'You didn't figure,' she said.

And with that she left, setting off to work. To *Sass* magazine.

In Matching Green, a carpenter named Tim turned away from the television and called to his wife, 'Oi, Cath! You hear this?

You still got that whatsit he signed? It'll be worth a mint now.' In the kitchen his sobbing wife finally decided that she'd had enough of him.

In Leeds a father's heart broke as he watched his twelve-year-old daughter absorb her life's first loss.

In Braintree, the Seymour family, owners of Liam, the breakfast TV 'sourpuss' champ, celebrated another week of victory.

In London, a prostitute called Colette Carew rolled a joint as she watched the news, not really interested. She would have been a great deal more interested had she known that the man arrested was Christopher Sewell: she had tried to fuck him just four days earlier.

In Rochester, a Marilyn Manson fan, who sang with a band of his schoolmates called Infinite Doom, clenched his fist and cried, 'Yesss!' with what he hoped was loud enough spontaneity to convince his mum how much he *really hated* manufactured pop stars. His mum, who owned one Felix Carter album and a single, was suitably scandalised, so he took a plain white T-shirt from his drawer and used a black marker pen to write 'Good Riddance' across it. There were arguments when he tried to leave the house in it.

In London, psychiatric nurse Tony Simpson stood in front of his television, his eyes wide with shock. Hanging on the wall above the television was a framed cutting from the *Sun*. He had only put it there yesterday. It showed a headline saying, 'Nice one, *Sun*!' with the *Sun* part of the headline done in the paper's masthead. Below that was a picture of Tony, holding a paperback book and his CD Walkman, grinning at the camera.

It was thanks to this appearance in the paper that, just

two days before, Tony had appeared on the Channel Four programme *Happy Monday*. Felix Carter had been on it too and he'd made a bit of a fuss of Tony. For that, Tony had liked Felix. Had liked him a lot.

In another part of London, a man named Brian Forsyth sat in bed and watched the news thoughtfully. Scattered around him on the bedspread were his Felix Carter scrapbooks and pasted to the walls of his room were his Felix Carter posters – pictures spanning his early 24/7 period to the present day. Sitting on top of a chest of drawers opposite him, his television formed the centre of what could only be described as a shrine, with Felix videos and CDs neatly stacked around it, their artwork to the front. He was always very careful when he opened a drawer, in case the shrine toppled.

Looking around, it was exactly the sort of bedroom one might expect a stalker to live in, which was apt since Brian Forsyth was a stalker. He was Felix's stalker. For three years he had pestered Felix with escalating frequency until the star had been forced to take out a restraining order, which Brian had greeted with a mixture of satisfaction and outrage. Now, he bit a fingernail as he watched the news, his other hand feeling around him on the bed for the remote control. He located it, held it before him and pointed it at the video, ready to pause his recording of the news once the adverts came on. Nothing worse than having bits of adverts on the tapes.

In Edinburgh, Alex Salter, the lead singer with a band called the Grobbelaars, whose single, 'Kiss You To Death', was at number one in the independent singles charts – just as Felix's 'Love You (To The Nth Degree)' topped the official charts sponsored by Worldpop.com – was moved by a kind of kismet. And he sat down to pen a tongue-in-cheek tribute song, 'Felix, Ah Ken Ye'. He intended the song to appear as an extra track on their next single release, 'Mile High Waves'.[4]

In London, Abigail the PR girl was slowly roused by the sound of footsteps from the flat upstairs. She said, 'Urgh,' long and slow into the empty room, partly to hear herself speak and partly because the sound accurately represented how she felt. She leant over to squint at her bedside clock and in her line of vision was the dress she'd worn last night. That, and the clipboard she'd carried around all evening, hanging on to it at the aftershow party held at the Café de Paris, just a short hop, skip and jump away from the première.

The clipboard, she could see, was covered in what looked like hieroglyphic scribbles and she struggled to remember why until – Oh, my God, she thought. All those autographs! She'd decided at some point, after one or two wines, and one too many at that, to use her clipboard as a souvenir of the night, asking stars of the film to sign it for her. She dimly remembered two men who'd laughed, said they had nothing to with the film, but signed it anyway, at her drunken and flirtatious insistence.

'Urgh,' she said again into the room, which was silent but for the tick-tock of the clock, which told her she was fifteen minutes late.

She pulled herself from the bed and went to sit on the toilet, rubbing sleep from her eyes and pissing as she tried to recollect the events of the night before. That bit – no, not too bad. That – well, a bit embarrassing, perhaps, but hardly something to get into a froth about. The signatures – a clever way of networking with those who, after all, were her clients. A subtle bit of ego massage for egos that were always in need

---

[4] The song never made it on to the CD. The Grobbelaars' record company, Chrysalis, opted instead for a Perfecto remix and the band's own 'Brucey Bonus Mix' to back up the title track.

of a thorough body rub. Nothing to worry about. She had merely been vivacious and bubbly, an asset to any party. She had been doing her job.

She wiped, stood up and let her 'Slooping Beauty' nightshirt fall to just above her knees, imagining she was a post-op lobotomy patient being led through her ablutions. She felt like one, anyway.

Avoiding the contemptuous gaze of the mirror she padded flat-footed through to the kitchen, her night's stock-taking almost complete.

One thing nagged, though, a tiny worry loitering at the back of her mind. She had said that it was *such a shame* Felix wasn't there. Had said it to quite a few people, now she thought about it. Over-egged the pudding on that score, perhaps. OK, so she'd said it to just about everybody she'd spoken to at the party, which made just about everybody at the party. And that included people whose presence really should have been sufficient for her – the stars, for example. Would they have been nettled by her insinuation that really the night was not complete without a singer who had no connection whatsoever with the production? Maybe. She tried to put herself in their position. Those in charge of their insecurities would have laughed and thought, Bless her, of this slightly tipsy star-struck PR girl. What a sweetie. But it wasn't them she was worried about. What about those with more fragile egos? Would they have gone away composing an indignant phone call to Vanessa, her boss, a legend in the world of film PR? You got to be a legend in that world by treating the Abigails of this world like shit. Hadn't Vanessa famously met a misbehaving employee at the door one morning with a box of the girl's belongings? 'I cleared your desk for you,' she is supposed to have said, as the girl stood forlornly on Wardour Street. 'The job centre's that way.'

And then her waking, hung-over mind formed the theory that by drawing attention to his absence she'd compounded a failure on her part. After all, was it not her mistake that he'd failed to turn up? Perhaps she hadn't PR-ed the event successfully, hadn't sold it convincingly to his agent.

So the fact is, when Abigail heard the news, the first thing she felt was relief.

She heard it on the radio, which she had switched on with one hand as she flicked the kettle clicker with the other.

'That was the Grobbelaars. And now, if you're just tuning in . . .'

She listened to the news with her mouth hanging open, her hands resting on the worktop in front of her, but thinking (oh, the shame), Thank God, thinking of his name that she'd never crossed off her clipboard (and how valuable would that be now?), thinking of the girls in All Bar One, rapt at her small but significant role in the unfolding drama. For the first time in her life she found herself if not exactly at the epicentre of a national tragedy, then at least close enough to feel the breeze. She decided she liked the world of PR, *really* liked it. The news put a spring in her step, which got her to work on time, although she was careful to adopt a wide-eyed look of shock when she entered the office.

Also in London the model Saffron Martyn awoke with a hangover of her own – an emotional one. She woke with eyes puffy from crying, and she woke to the sound of the telephone ringing.

'Oh. My. God,' said the camp voice at the other end of the line. It was Tom DeBute, who ranked last but one on the list of people she wanted to speak to at that moment. But when they'd got over the initial confusion of why he was so shocked, and when he'd told her what had happened, she hung up with a feeling similar to Abigail the PR girl: relief. For her own reasons, of course. Well, some were her own, and some were the same.

*   *   *

Again, in London – but not such a nice part – Phil Yorke, whose friends called him Yorkie, tapped his girlfriend's shoulder as she brushed her teeth. He was fairly unschooled in the ways of women so he was not to know that they don't like being watched while they brush their teeth, and dislike being disturbed at it even more. When she whipped round, with toothpaste all over her mouth, snapping, 'What?' he recoiled sharply, saying, 'Nothing. Doesn't matter . . .' and went about getting ready for work. You know how couples are sometimes.

And finally, in Luton, a girl called Lindsey woke up on the second day of a lay-off from work because of the flu. She thought she caught the news on the radio, but because she was blowing her nose at the same time she couldn't be sure what she'd heard. She knew something was up because the DJ came back, simply said, 'This is very sad,' and went straight into a record, 'Tears In Heaven' by Eric Clapton. Too slow, too maudlin for this time of the morning, surely? She dragged her duvet off the bed and pulled it to the sofa in the lounge, wondering what had happened and simultaneously thanking her lucky stars that she lived in the age of the duvet, when bedding could so easily be moved from one location to another. What was it they used to be called? Continental quilts? When she heard the news properly, she wriggled even deeper into the sofa and pulled her duvet really comfy around her neck, thrilled that she could spend the whole day in front of the TV, get the news as it broke. Would she remember where she was the day Felix died? She thought so.

That day, at a little after midday, the Metropolitan Police issued their official statement. Moments afterwards, the information had been reprocessed and was posted on news Internet sites.

Police have confirmed that Felix Carter has been shot dead in his west London home.

The pop singer was discovered by a maid fatally wounded early this morning. He never regained consciousness and was pronounced dead at Charing Cross Hospital at 8.25 a.m.

The singer – whose 'Love You (To The Nth Degree)' single is currently at number one – died from a single gunshot wound to the chest.

A second man was arrested at the scene and is in police custody.

There was no sign of forced entry at the 31-year-old singer's house and police believe the shooting happened sometime last night. Mr Carter was due to attend a film première and a limousine service has confirmed a driver was despatched to collect the star, but left after being told he was ill.[5]

'Has he been charged?' asked the journalists covering the story. 'Has this Sewell character been charged yet?' And the press officer, pleased to lord it over the breathless reporters, spread his hands, saying, 'Look, all I can tell you at the moment is that Christopher Sewell is in police custody. You'll have more news as soon as I get it. All right?'

---

[5] From Ananova.com, posted at about midday on Wednesday, 5 November 2003.

CHAPTER SIX

Chris, would you like to stop?

No. Thank you, but no. I'm OK.

That must have been difficult, talking about your mother's death like that?

It was and it wasn't, really. It's nice to have someone to talk to about it. Sorry, we digressed. Do you want to continue?

Of course. Do go on.

Where was I?

Sam has just walked out.

That's right. She walks out, the door slams behind her. Bad feeling hanging in the air like a nasty smell.

So I lie on the sofa and listen to the flat settle: the boiler struggling to meet the demands of the thermostat, the kettle filament clicking, fridge humming, the walls and floors relaxing after Sam's morning of bath, tea, makeup, clothes and recrimination. I groan again, say, 'Sorry, Sam,' into the empty room, try to imagine how she must be feeling and fail. What would I think if I returned home from work to find her smacking the pony in front of a George Clooney film, *The Peacemaker*, say? Well, I'd be delighted obviously. But men are different from women. Women take a dim view of their menfolk's masturbatory habits, men positively encourage it. And, anyway, the whole *Sandy and the Students* thing. That was only the half of it. Perhaps if I'd leapt up all apologetic and humbled, she'd have turned a blind eye to the locker-room sex on the TV, put it down to taking the rough with the smooth. It was the shouting and swearing, the drunkenness. That's what did it. That's why she'd gone to work wishing she had a better man, and why I'm lying here, wishing I was one.

She watches me now, peering from the mantelpiece in a framed photograph of our wedding day, smiling and beautiful on the happiest day of her life. Next to her on the mantelpiece are our porcelain busts of Darth Vader and Darth Maul – Beauty and the Beasts. That sounds a bit grand, 'busts'. In fact, they're moneyboxes, which were once filled with chocolate coins and are now stuffed to bursting with coppers. They were both presents from Sam who's always thinking of me, even when I'm drinking away her respect, wanking on the floor beneath our wedding photograph.

When I'm done with groaning and feeling sorry for myself and for Sam, I eventually peel myself off the sofa and get ready for work. And because I'm shaking hands with Doctor Guilt I make an extra-special effort with the people at the shop when I go in on my way to the tube, like paying war reparations to the day. I'm also feeling unexpectedly good. Not mentally, obviously, but physically I'm still buoyed by the alcohol from last night – I've yet to get a hangover in other words. So when I go to pay for my bottle of Purdey's I amp up my hellos and goodbyes, with alcohol my jovial bodyguard. But I get nothing in return. *Nada*. Not hello, or thank you or goodbye. Not even when I say, 'Keep the change,' which I've been saying more frequently of late in a doomed attempt to break the ice, to forge some kind of local-shop/valued-customer relationship. There's a sign I notice for the first time. Perhaps it's new, or perhaps its familiarity has rendered it invisible before. 'Do not ask for credit,' it says, with not even the usual '. . . as a smack in the mouth often offends!' to sweeten the pill. Not even that from this shop.

'I will break them,' I announced to Sam once, waving a tin of lager in the air for dramatic emphasis. 'I will bombard them with so much politeness that eventually they'll have to give in. You mark my words. One day I'm going to go in there and they'll say hello and ask me how I am, and they'll double up a bag without me asking and probably hold the door open for me when I leave.'

'Bless,' said Sam, not really listening to me. 'You go for it, babe.'

'Mock all you want. The day when me and the shop are best pals is fast approaching.'

Maybe I won't break them, I ponder, as I carry on towards Manor House tube, glugging from my Purdey's. Maybe they will break me. Perhaps that's the whole point. Anyway, I think, I've got bigger things to worry about: Sam and – more pressingly – my hangover, which has appeared on the horizon and is heading towards me like Omar Sharif in *Lawrence of Arabia*.

Here's a tip for the heavy drinker: love your hangover. It sounds strange, but the way I look at it is that each hangover, while unmistakably a hangover, takes on a life and personality all its own. It's how you deal with it that determines your success as a heavy drinker. You can, of course, attempt to stave it off with a drink the next morning, but this isn't always practical and can lead you quickly from 'heavy drinker' to 'alcoholic'. Or you can try to decrease its ferocity by drinking a pint of water the night before, but that depends on you remembering to do so. And there is no such thing as a heavy drinker with a memory.

So, in order to survive you have to welcome the hangover into your life as a friend and enemy. And, it's true, it can be a two-faced little git. One day it'll be lounging around with its feet up, whistling 'Sympathy For The Devil' by the Rolling Stones and making your life a severely unpleasant place to be. Other days it makes an effort. It'll give you good ideas, or the courage to look at the world in different ways, or it'll help you raise your game to compensate for the shortcomings of your physical state. It forces you into a single mind-state by narrowing the day into a simple test of survival.

Fight with the hangover, and you will always lose. It absorbs water and bananas and fry-ups and Lucozade and Purdey's and vitamins and comfort-buying and little dropper bottles of Rescue Remedy, and it throws them back with twice the shit.

You can't fight the hangover, you have to make friends with it, warts and all; enjoy it, even.

I know all of this – my own advice to me – in my heart of hearts. But how can I make friends with my hangover when he summons such demons?

Trisha pushes the microphone towards me and I wonder whether to make like one of those babies you see on *It'll Be Alright On The Night*: grab the foamy bit, or start chewing on it.

'Chris, now, I know this must be very difficult for you – and take your time – but try explaining to us how you feel . . .'

'About what?' I say, looking out at the *Trisha* audience, who sit watching me. Their expressions are different from earlier, during the section 'My daughter dresses like a tart.' They look at me the way you'd watch a news report on an earthquake in India. How awful. Thank God it's not me.

To the viewers at home I'm introduced with the caption: *Chris: suffers from deadmumanddad disease.*

'Most of us, thank God, are fortunate enough never to go through what you've been through. To be orphaned by the age of twenty-nine. Tell us, how do you go about coping with something like that? *How do you feel?*'

'I don't fucking know, Trisha. I really don't fucking know.' But they bleep out the fucks.

'Tell us about Sam,' says Trisha, this time taking a different tack. A man in the audience is picking something off his tracksuit top. I realise that every single member of the audience is wearing a tracksuit top. And when I look down I, too, am wearing a tracksuit top. A top I know instinctively that I bought at JD Sports in the Bluewater shopping centre – even though I've never been there. It's a good top, too: it goes with the baseball cap I'm also wearing.

'How do you think she feels when you do things like you did last night, calling her an effing this and an effing that?'

My mouth works but nothing comes out.

'You say you love Sam. Do you tell her you love her?'

'S'pose not,' I manage.

'Well, perhaps you'd like to tell her now. Because I think I'm probably right in saying that, at this very moment, Sam isn't feeling very loved at all.'

Sam comes on to applause from the audience, and she takes the seat next to me, but neither of us looks at the other. There's a short silence, which Trisha lets hang in the air as we get used to the idea of each other on the stage. Somewhere in my mind I think that there must be better ways of sorting out private domestic problems than on a morning chat show, but the thought quickly goes.

'Chris?' says Trisha, pointing the microphone my way again. 'Have you got something to say to Sam?'

'Yes,' I say, and I turn to Sam, who looks towards me. I should take one of her hands – I've seen this kind of thing done on TV before. But I'm embarrassed to, so instead I just come right out with it: 'Sam, I luvyer, aneye wanna be a good husband to yer. An' if that means cutting down on me drink then that's what I'll do to try and make it right.'

There's a small ripple of applause from the audience, which Trisha lets die down before turning to Sam and pointing the microphone at her. 'Sam? What do you have to say to that?'

Sam looks at me and takes one of my hands. She's doing it properly at least. Then, looking deep into my eyes, she says, 'Mind the doors. Mind the closing doors . . .'

Shit. I wake up to see the U and the S of the Oxford Circus sign disappearing along the wall as the tube train pulls out of the station – and I realise I've fallen asleep and missed my stop. I'm going to be even later.

Thanks, hangover. Some friend you turned out to be.

When I walk into the office, on Broadwick Street, thirty minutes late, a beautiful woman is winking at me in Reception.

Before I see her I see the uniformed security guard, who nods at me as I enter. I nod back, wondering why others in the building seem to be on first-name, how-was-your-weekend? terms with him, while I've never progressed any further than the briefest head-duck, even though we see each other every day and have done – excluding weekends and holidays – for the three years I've worked there. Not for the first time I wonder whether he sees straight through me. Does he know that I think he's a useless security guard? An obviously past-it excuse for protection whose only real purpose seems to be turning off the odd fire alarm? My hangover tells me that's exactly what it is: he *knows*. And he hates me.

I suddenly remember that my father is dead and the thought hits me like a stabbing pain through the kidneys that HURTS, hurts, hurts, hurts, and then I turn to look at the beautiful, winking woman.

As well as winking one perfectly eyelashed eye, she also has her tongue poking slightly from the side of her mouth – cheekily. The look tells me that she's a fun-loving girl. Not tarty, but likes a night out; enjoys a laugh with her friends. She has a bit of the devil in her, not quite the dreaded 'ladette', but a mischievous edge all the same. Nevertheless, there is a serious side to this woman. She is clearly in control of her own destiny, no doubt successful in whatever field of endeavour she chooses. She's confident with the opposite sex, happy with her looks, content with the choices she's made in life. If she's with someone she's happy but, hey, there's no harm in looking, right? And if she's single she's looking – but, hey, what's the hurry, right?

She's Bridget Jones without the cracks; Ally McBeal minus the analysis; the *Sex and the City* girls without the lubricant. She's what I sell, what advertisers want to be associated with. She's mine and I love her and I pimp her every day. Or does she pimp me? Miss Brand Value Embodiment staring down at all of us, workers and visitors, winking below the masthead. She's *Sass* magazine.

CHAPTER SEVEN

The breathless reporters, the ones who enquired of the police press officer, 'Has he been charged?' did so for a reason. In many ways they asked the question reflexively, because that's what they always did and because it was required of them, but the question had an underlying purpose required by an Act of Parliament, specifically the Contempt of Court Act of 1981: '*A journalist can fall foul of the law of contempt in a number of ways. The greatest risk is in the publication of material which might prejudice a fair trial, such as extraneous information that might tend to sway a juror's mind.*'[6]

The main principle of justice in any democracy is that you are innocent until proven guilty. It's one of the doctrines that keeps tyranny from the door and the contempt of court laws are there to see it upheld. Even if someone is found at the scene, holding the handle of a knife, the business end of which is embedded in the victim, they're still presumed innocent of any wrongdoing until a jury of their peers decides that they're not.

And in order for a jury of their peers to decide *fairly* whether or not they're the guilty party, the jury must be provided with only the facts relevant to that particular case. A defendant might have been in and out of jail all their life, a career burglar, but the jury won't know that when they are next up in court. The fact that they are a career burglar would, after all, influence the jury's decision; it would 'prejudice a fair trial'.

This makes life difficult for journalists. They're in the

---

[6] From *McNae's Essential Law for Journalists*, sixteenth edition (Butterworths).

business of reporting the facts and the news, and whatever people might think of journalists, it's undeniably the case that the vast majority are committed to reporting the truth. But providing *too much* information might find them in contempt of court, which is a crime, and next in the dock.

In order for contempt to be committed, there are two criteria, both of which must be met: first, if publication creates 'a substantial risk of serious prejudice or impediment to particular proceedings', and second, when proceedings are 'active'. Of interest to Christopher Sewell's arrest is the second point: when proceedings are active.

'The Act says criminal proceedings are deemed to be active from the relevant initial step – if a person has been arrested, or a warrant for his arrest has been issued, or a summons has been issued, or if a person has been charged orally.'[7]

And that is why the journalists asked the press officer, 'Has he been charged yet?' They might have asked, 'Are proceedings against him active?' but it doesn't sound as cool. Still, that is what they needed to know: 'Is the case against Christopher Sewell active? Are we likely to be in contempt of court if we publish information likely to prejudice a fair trial?'

In this case, of course, they were. Sewell had been arrested and journalists knew they were severely limited as to what they could report. They could attend the scene of the crime, interview witnesses, chat to the bobbies, listen in to paramedics chin-wagging – fill a whole notebook full of elegant shorthand all about the crime. But in reporting it, their hands were tied. Hence the brevity of the news bulletins.

'Once proceedings become active, the crime can still be reported but the story must be carefully worded lest it should suggest in any way that those in police hands are indeed the culprits . . . One can report a post office robbery and say that later a man

---

7 As Note 6.

was arrested, but not that the man was arrested. It would also be prejudicial after an arrest to describe the appearance of three men who raided a bank as being tall or dark-haired or bearded, lest those arrested answered to that description.'[8]

That initial flare-up of facts followed by a sudden dearth of information is common to almost all headline-grabbing crimes. Take the Fred and Rose West murders, for example. When the atrocity was discovered, all that was reported was the barest facts: Cromwell Street, bodies, man and woman arrested, man and woman appear in magistrates' court and are committed for trial at Crown Court – all the time, just the tiniest details.

But were the journalists sitting around enjoying a break thanks to the Contempt of Court Act? Of course not. They were hunting out the story in readiness for when the Wests were imprisoned. And then and only then did the information floodgates open. Rosemary West gets sent to jail and next day it's 'Turn to pages 2, 3, 4, 5, 6, 8, 10, 11 and 12'; it's special reports, documentaries and books about the crime, the best of which is *Happy Like Murderers* by Gordon Burn.[9] It's more information than the public can possibly stomach but it's only at that point that they get to find out. Because the trial is over and there's no fear of prejudicing it.

So, thanks to the Contempt of Court Act of 1981, the public had to wait for some time until they found out more about the man who killed Felix Carter.

---

[8] As Note 6.
[9] (Faber and Faber). Burn also wrote *Somebody's Husband, Somebody's Son* about the Peter Sutcliffe murders.

CHAPTER EIGHT

Where was I?

You arrive at work.

Yes. So, inside the lift I briefly enjoy the image of a hung-over man and his briefcase arriving at work and then I remember my father. Or, rather, I remember that my father's died, and that the last time my work colleagues saw me I was leaving work as usual.

The lift opens straight on to the sales floor and the first person I see is Geoff, my boss, my *line supervisor*.

'Chris,' he says, to the man who steps out of the lift with his briefcase banging against his leg, 'it's good to see you back. Er, say, ten minutes in my room for a catch-up?'

Ten minutes is longer than Geoff would normally give me. Usually, he'd say, 'As soon as you've dumped your stuff,' or, 'When you're ready.' Ten minutes is a concession to the fact that I'm recently fatherless (an orphan, actually, but he doesn't know that) and I wonder whether he's told the rest of the team, like the headmaster at school. Like, 'Now children, Christopher's daddy has died and gone to heaven. This will make Christopher sad and we must all make a special effort to be extra-specially nice to Christopher. What was that, Adam? . . . No, just because Christopher's daddy has died that doesn't mean yours will too. And I don't want any of you to worry about that.'

The staff who occupy this floor make up the sales teams for the Young Women's Group. Since *Sass* is sold to young women that makes us part of the Young Women's Group too. And the four of us – the display-ads part of the team; Classified sit on another level altogether – have a corner of the floor from which we persuade advertisers to spend their money with us rather than with another of the hundreds of young women's magazines on offer. I'm head persuader. Ad manager of *Sass* magazine. And if that sounds grand, well, it's not really.

When I arrive the *Sass* display-ads department is hardly a hive of activity even though, with me there, we've got what counts as a full team. Just one chair remains empty (and that'll be one of the things Geoff wants to see me about: interviews for a new sales exec). That one spare seat aside, the department is at capacity, and Graham and Adam look expectantly at me as I approach.

'All right, Chris?' says Graham, and wades straight in – sensibly, I feel – with, 'How did the funeral go?'

So that's it, the news is out in the open, and it's all I can do not to kiss the boy. 'Thanks, Graham. You know how these things are. It went as well as can be expected.'

'Great. Pleased to hear it,' says Graham, with Adam chiming, 'Cool, cool,' at the same time. 'Well, listen, I've got some exciting stuff to tell you when you're ready . . .'

That's the trouble with Graham: good at his job but a bit too businesslike at times. It doesn't sit well with a hangover. And I should know.

'That's good to hear, Graham. I'm doing catch-up with Geoff and then we'll talk, yes? You all right for tea?'

Of us all, Graham is the one who was born to sell like other people are born to kill, or born to become nurses. The thing is, with selling you either embrace your job wholeheartedly or you hide it away bashfully like a zit you hope nobody will notice. Graham's an embracer. He sees the job as a balls-out incursion into other people's wallets. He looks in the mirror each morning and the face that greets him says, 'You're a maverick, dude.' For him, it's a lifestyle choice.

This makes Graham sound like a wanker, which he almost certainly is. But I don't hate Graham: quite the opposite, I love him. Simply because he's very good at his job, and if Graham's good at his job, that makes me look as if I'm good at mine, which I am to a degree but not as good as Graham makes me look.

But when I look in the mirror, I don't see a Graham looking back at me. What I see is an older Adam.

Adam's a different kettle of fish, Graham's polar opposite. He came to us through an agency, and to that through an advert in the Media *Guardian*, which is the ad-sales equivalent of the old naval press-gang. But instead of clubs and boozy threats of death, they use the word 'media' to entice new recruits.

Like me, Adam came out of university with vague hopes of doing something creative and was promptly coshed by the Media *Guardian*. No doubt he thought that any job in the media was better than none, and probably assumed that if you were in at ground level you had a chance of progressing into the job you really wanted. He was wrong, of course, but there was nobody around to tell him that, and if he thought Geoff and I were going to give up the truth in the interview he had another think coming.

Adam had to learn the same hard lesson that all of us (except the embracing/maverick likes of Graham) have to learn. And that is that ad sales has about as much to do with media glamour as *Sass* magazine's Shampoo of the Year award has to do with the Oscars. On the odd occasion we see the exalted Prada-wearing members of our editorial team it's in the lift, arriving about two hours after we have and clutching three-pound cups of double *latte*. They all but hold their noses as they pass our floor, not wanting the taint of our mundane monetary concerns in case it should infect their reserves of precious creativity.

Thus, each day the calamity of Adam's career move is drawn more clearly on his face. The poor boy. And the increasing gulf between his dreams and reality also makes him the weakest member of my tiny team, much to Graham's contempt. Still, his is the most genuinely sympathetic face to greet me as I thump my briefcase on to my desk and reach to switch on my computer.

'We'll talk later too, Adam,' I say. 'In the meantime, how's it been going?'

'Um, OK, I think,' he says uncertainly.

'We'll make a salesman of you yet,' I say. And remember how the *Beano* used to have a story called 'The Numskulls?' They lived in this man's head and all had different tasks concerned with controlling him. Well, at the notion 'We'll make a salesman of you yet', three of the Numskulls in the Shame Management department of my own head are sacked for gross misconduct. Unsurprisingly, Shame Management has the largest staff turnover, just ahead of Guilt Control, which is currently working overtime in the light of last night's events. I pray that the members of the Hangover Administration Unit are doing their jobs to the best of their abilities and make my way to Geoff's office.

On my way, I decide to use the rest of Geoff's ten minutes' grace time to make myself a cup of tea, and detour to the kitchen, a poky piece of floor-space separated from the rest of the open-plan office by free-standing panels.

It's only Monday morning, and the area looks a disgrace. I feel hangover anger bubbling within me. Someone has put the kettle on to boil and left it, but looking into it I discover they've selfishly put in just enough water for one cup. The sink is already playing host to two bowls with the remnants of cereal and at least three teabags floating in them. In the end I take the one cup of water for myself, but before leaving I fill the kettle to the brim and leave it boiling for the next person. I'm sure to put my used teabag into the bin. And instead of chucking the spoon into the sink I rinse it and put it with the other spoons. Not too difficult, is it? Now, if only we all did that . . .

Another top tip for the heavy drinker: garlic capsules.

Garlic, they say, is very good for us. Indeed, TV adverts selling Mediterranean food tell us that the leathery-skinned inhabitants of sunnier climates live longer, not because they spend half of their lives asleep but because they eat a lot of garlic. I've booked the print version of these very same adverts into *Sass* many times. Women, in particular, it seems, go for garlic in a big way. Hardly surprising when so much of the magazine is based on affairs of the heart.

Garlic is also a friend of the drinker. Not neat: even the hardiest hangover veteran can't scoff a clove of the stuff the next day. Instead, the humble garlic capsule is the drinker's saviour.

Instructions for garlic capsules warn that you should always take them with a cold drink and preferably with a meal. My theory is that this is because they're sprayed with some kind of slow-acting coating to stop you smelling like you've eaten a vindaloo the night before – they just dissolve slowly with your food, gradually releasing all that Mediterranean goodness into your bloodstream.

But we don't want that. We *want* to smell of exotic food-stuff, no matter how unpleasant that might be for those around us. Because the alternative is to stink like the morning after a New Year's Eve party. And while it's OK to reek of booze every now and then, people ask questions if you smell of it daily. One garlic capsule, then, taken – like a little brown submarine – with a cup of coffee (melts the coating) and on an empty stomach should produce the desired effect, which is, if not completely to mask the scent of alcohol then at least to mingle with it in a more socially accept-able fashion. You can simply chew the capsule, of course, and I've tried, but it tastes unpleasant and the odour's too strong. The coffee method's best. That way you get the effect just right: like a man who's enjoyed a hearty curry and a few pints with his meal. What could be more civilised than that?

One last thing: you have to burp. It helps you get a really good head of breath-steam up. And that's what I do, discreetly into my hand as I sit opposite Geoff, making sure my next huff goes directly into his face. He blinks as his senses misinform him of the contents of my stomach. If he asks, I had chicken tikka masala and a peshwari naan.

'It's good to see you back, Chris,' he says, for what feels like the second time that morning. I sit with my back to the closed door of his office. He normally leaves it open, the very literal expression of some learnt-on-a-course management philosophy.

'How was the funeral?' he asks, and for what is definitely the second time that morning I say, 'Thanks, you know how these things are. It went as well as can be expected.'

It's funny how these big life events bring out the repetitious in you. I seem to remember saying the same things over and over again at my wedding, and at the funeral itself. 'I'm glad you could come' (both), 'I think he would have liked it' (funeral), 'I think she would have liked it' (wedding).

Only, of course, it's a big fat lie that the funeral went as well as expected. Because didn't I get drunk at the wake? And didn't everyone feel slightly embarrassed for Sam as she herded me, stumbling, towards the door and home, saying, 'I'm sorry, this is very emotional for him. *He's not normally like this.*'

'Well, I'm glad,' says Geoff, and for the first time I notice that he's thinning a little on top. He's only thirty, just a year older than me. Does that mean my hair's got a scant twelve months left? 'And we're pleased to see you back.'

And with the funeral subject as quickly and neatly disposed of as my father was, he pulls a stack of papers from his in-tray.

'While you were away, I took the liberty of grading some of these applications for the ad rep's job.'

'Great, great,' I say. 'Being a man down is putting a strain on our resources. Obviously I'm not saying we can't cope, but we're certainly asking a lot of the existing team members to pull the weight of one missing body.'

Four Numskulls in Shame Management are put to the

sword. Two in Hangover Management are asked to clear their desks.

'Absolutely,' says Geoff slowly, looking at me strangely.

I cobble together a garlic huff in response.

He flinches and passes me an application form, filled in with black biro. 'Take a look at this one,' he says. 'Let me know what you think.'

I take it and read. It's two pages long, but here are the highlights.

Name: Luke Radley

Sex: Occasionally, when the lighting is right.

Desired Position: Girl on top. Oh, you mean in the company? Yours, but I'll take Ad Sales Rep as a starter for ten.

Desired Salary: Big enough to keep me from starving, small enough to moan about. Am I right?

Education: Intermittent. Enough for me to able to spell 'intermittent'.

Last position held: 'man in queue at supermarket' for twenty minutes.

Reason For Leaving: Approaching security guard.

Where Do You See Yourself In Five Years?: Fending off the multiple advances of sexually frustrated Page Three models while simultaneously plotting my hostile takeover of Microsoft. Actually, I'd like to be doing all that now.

Sign here: Capricorn.

The first time I filled in an application form was for a Saturday job at the local Leicester branch of Kwik Save when I was sixteen. I took the form home and my father and I sat for what seemed like hours at the kitchen table. We took the dictionary from the bookshelf. We dissected each individual question, asking ourselves first what the question meant, and second, what we wanted my reply to say about me. First we wrote it out in rough, and only when we were certain that we had it right did I sit and commit my answers to the form itself. In my best, *best* handwriting. I got the job, and my father deferred all of the glory, simply saying, 'Well done, son. Well done. I knew you'd do it.'

You'll forgive my French, then, if I say I think of Luke Radley as something of a cunt.

And it's with my most derisive harrumph that I lower his excuse for an application form to the desk.

'Ha ha. Comedian. Shall I file it in the bin?'

'What do you think?' says Geoff, and he's wearing a smile I don't much like the look of.

'I think I'd like to see some of the others. I think this application is a joke we've all heard before. And Mr Luke Radley thinks the punchline is that his freshness and honesty eventually lands him the job, but in fact the punchline is "try Burger King".'

'I think you're being a little harsh.'

'Oh, come on, Geoff . . .' Hangover anger almost boils over and I take it off the heat. 'What I mean is, really, there's nothing here we haven't heard before. You can't tell me that you haven't gone to fill in one of these forms in the past and thought of writing joke answers like these. "Sex: occasionally" – really!'

'It made me laugh, Chris.'

'At how pathetic it is.'

'No. It just made me laugh. It's got a directness I like. This is someone who's determined to make an impact. Perhaps this is someone who'll go out and make a similar impact on the clients. Maybe that's what we're lacking here.'

He's been on a course. That's what it is. He'll have been on a new management course while I've been away, the sort where you have to fall into each other's arms to learn teamwork and reveal stupid secrets about yourself to learn trust. He's come back inebriated with management zeal, probably determined to 'make a difference', and it's this Luke Radley's luck to have caught him at a time when his defences are down. The Force is weak in Geoff now, but give me a day or so and I'm sure I can talk him round.

65

'Anyway,' says Geoff, like, 'subject closed', 'I interviewed him on Friday. I'd like you to give him a call. Introduce yourself. Offer him the job.'

Later in the day, I go to the kitchen for the second time and find it even filthier than it was on the first occasion. This time I leave it, march straight back to my desk where I concoct what is hopefully a funny but mildly scolding 'Rules of the Kitchen' notice.

It goes like this:

Rules of the Kitchen

For all those hard of thinking, please remember this when preparing yourself a nice cup of the 'old Rosy Lee'

1. The first rule of the kitchen is that you must not talk about the kitchen.
2. Strange as it may seem, there is only one 'bin' in the kitchen, and it is that black thing in the corner. That is the only place you should put your used teabags, condoms, tampons and such.
3. You know that thing you do at home when you've had some breakfast cereal? Washing-up? Why not try doing it here as well? It's a crazy plan, but it might just work.
4. Now, here's a revolutionary idea. Since there's more than one of us working on this floor, when you're boiling a kettle, why not fill it up? Chances are someone will want a cup of tea in the meantime, and who knows? You might get a friend for life.
5. Even more revolutionary. When you've made your cup of tea, why not start the kettle boiling for the next person who wants to use it? You may get no thanks for this, but imagine how good it'll make you feel.

Thank you, and enjoy your tea (or coffee!)
Chris Sewell, *Sass* Mag Saddo

I'm pleased with it, all told. It may be born of hung-over intolerance, but nobody else is to know that. It's quite amusing (I'm especially pleased with number one, and the reference to condoms and tampons is quite funny) but it also serves a more serious purpose.

It crosses my mind to e-mail it to Sam before I stick it up. She could tell me if I've got the tone right or not. But contacting Sam doesn't seem like such a good idea at the moment, and if I do, probably best to do it with a sorry, rather than asking her to check over my kitchen-rules list. But then again, maybe she'll think, Bless, and it'll help win her back on-side.

I toy with the idea a moment more before deciding not to, and instead I e-mail her with a simple, 'Sam, I'm so sorry about last night. You deserve so much better. Things have been a bit of a strain lately. Please, let me take you for a meal tonight – your choice! – to help me make it up to you. Love, Chris xxx'.

And then I go and stick up my Rules of the Kitchen. Right above the sink, where everyone can see it.

CHAPTER NINE

FELIX CARTER [10]

Pop wildman Felix Carter, born in 1972, was cruelly taken from us on Tuesday aged just 31 – we won't ever see his like again.

His success – millions of record sales, a promising film début – were only matched by his excess: the well-documented drink problem; his legendary sexual appetite. But in a musical landscape dominated by bland, battery-farm pop outfits and po-faced rock stars with political agendas, Carter stood out as a true original. Only fame in America continued to elude him.

Carter began his career in the underground 'rave' scene of the early nineties, playing PAs at illegal warehouse parties with his band 24/7. Here he developed a taste for the wild behaviour that characterised his career from then on, but these lowly beginnings also taught him the stage mastery that provided the key to his future success. Having taken 24/7 into the charts, the group split, leaving Carter to launch his solo career on little more than a smile and a lone Top 10 hit.

Nevertheless, his first solo single, 'Take Me,' marked a sharp departure from the dance-oriented sound of 24/7 and was an early example of the genre-hopping approach to music that was to define his work, confounding critics but delighting audiences keen to embrace a larger-than-life musical personality.

---

[10] Obituary of Felix Carter, taken from the *Daily Telegraph*, Saturday, 8 November 2003.

Further single success and million-selling albums followed, as did a failed marriage, tales of bad behaviour at awards ceremonies, stories of bed-hopping and rumours of cocaine abuse. He was tortured by his inability to reform and plagued by guilt after drunken misdemeanours. More than once he was admitted to rehab and never shied from discussing his addictions in public, always with the self-deprecating humour that was his trademark. It was this element of his personality, his almost pathological hatred of being taken seriously, that endeared him to fans and gradually won over his critics. Carter never saw himself as anything but an entertainer – he despised the word 'artist' – and this simple ambition, coupled with his very human failings, enabled him to vault normal musical barriers with ease. Of his peers, only Robbie Williams can be said to have achieved the same feat.

It was inevitable that film work would follow his musical success, and just last month he made his début in the low-budget UK thriller, *Enemies*, playing the part of an East End hitman alongside Jeremy Irons. Though the film has not been well received by critics, his contribution was praised and it seemed certain that more film work would follow. Latterly he had also taught himself to play guitar, though typically made light of his burgeoning skills in this department.

Though the details of his death at the hands of an intruder have yet to be made clear, one thing is certain: Felix Carter was a true original. He entertained us, he allowed us to live the rock'n'roll lifestyle vicariously through him. He was at once a warning and an advertisement for its perils. The world is a greyer place without him.

FELIX? YOU TURN IF YOU WANT TO. THIS LADY'S NOT FOR TURNING[11]

I was never a fan of Felix Carter. And though I've always maintained that there's no better reason for a spectacular opinion *volte face* than a sudden death, in this instance, you turn if you want to. This lady's not for turning.

Now before you put pen to paper, I mean no disrespect to the recently deceased. I am, however, being paid (and very well, I might add) if not exactly to analyse this week's events then at the very least to comment upon them, add my froth or my wrath, depending on my feelings on the matter. Equally, I would be failing myself, not to mention my reputation, if I were to add my voice to those who simply moan, 'Another great talent lost,' as they always do; or, worse, if I was to trot out some fabricated story about a meeting with Mr Carter during which he revealed something rather wonderful and vulnerable about himself.

Indeed, I fear the latter scenario might involve a feat of imagination beyond even my talents – my single experience of him, hands-on, as it were, involved quite the opposite of both wonderful and vulnerable.

It occurred at a time when I must admit (your honour) I was not exactly at my intellectual peak. This was a time shortly after my first novel, *Kitoff Gunshot Wound*, had unexpectedly catapulted me to fame, thanks in no small part to the film version that followed it. In my defence, I was a younger, more frivolous version of my current self then, and more vulnerable to the temptations of celebrity. As a result, I had succumbed to the kind of pressures facing a young,

---

[11] Novelist Lorna Curtis, writing in *The Times*, Saturday, 8 November 2003.

talented and celebrated novelist, and instead of beavering away on a follow-up my nights were spent holding court at the Groucho Club, and my days merrily watching publishers' deadlines come and go. Despite rumours to the contrary, I was not fond of constant nose-powdering trips to the toilet, as were many of my followers, and I offer this in defence also. On this particular night I was in total control of my faculties. No, sorry. Wrong inflection. *I* was in total control of my faculties.

Unlike Mr Carter. As he staggered into the Groucho (accompanied by a minder: physique, burly; charisma, non-existent), there's no doubt that there was a marked contrast between how Mr Carter thought he looked, and how he actually looked. If he was later to become something of a substance bore, constantly trying to atone for his past chemical indulgences like a pleading beagle, then he was at this time clearly in the throes of narcotic discovery. How else but with the dignity-draining combination of celebrity and drugs could you explain the sheer arrogance that sweated off the man as he made his grand entrance? Unfortunately for me, I happened to be crossing the floor from seat to bar, or perhaps back again, when the pop star made his entrance. No doubt he was celebrating yet another number one, or perhaps the millionth Felix Carter doll sold, but that hardly excuses his behaviour when, on encountering a lady (i.e., me), he enquired loudly, 'Didn't you used to be cool?'

Now, like the rule in relationships that dictates it is acceptable for you to spend hours ranting unkindly about your own parents, but unacceptable for your partner even to question the quality of their tea, so it goes that what you say into the mirror each morning remains profoundly yours. And for somebody else, especially a worse-for-wear poster boy, to point out your deficiencies – however right they may be – is unforgivable.

Sadly, of course, he was half right, and what threw his observation into the harshest interrogative light was that I found myself utterly unable to reply. Not only was I struck by the sudden withdrawl of rapier wit, I was bereft of a single word. Not a sausage. And, frankly, squeezing out the word 'sausage' would have counted as a major victory in that particular situation. As it was, I simply fixed him with what I hoped was a withering look (that's a laugh: it was me who was withering) and returned to the comfort of my adoring court.

The next night I didn't return to the Groucho. Neither have I been back since, nor to any of the watering-holes that have since replaced it in the favour of the fashionable. In fact, that very night I rapidly upped sticks home where the very next morning I began work on my next novel. It's called *Rattlesnakes* and it's currently available from all good bookshops.

Because – and forgive the sudden jump on to the Hornby train-set here – I learnt something about myself that day. It shouldn't really have required a googly-eyed pop star to teach me, but in the event it did. The 'cool' person he referred to, the hip young Julie Burchill-style gunslinger, would have left him like mulch on the Groucho floor. The cool person would have died rather than settle for a withering look before scuttling back to the safety of 'other people', exactly the kind of 'other people' the cool person had despised for their eagerness to hang on. The cool person's brain had slipped into neutral and was putt-putting along when it should have been tearing up the fast lane and leaving rude, uncouth pop stars in its wake.

So, no, I was never a fan of Felix Carter, and a great deal less so after that particular incident. You may be thinking I owe him a debt of gratitude for setting me once more on the path to righteousness (indeed, *Rattlesnakes* eventually outsold *Kitoff Gunshot Wound*), but I've got no time for that kind of sentiment. Life's too short, and I'm too cool.

CHAPTER TEN

'Do you want to end up like the men on the benches, is that what you want?'

Sorry, this is Sam speaking now.

Got it. Do continue.

OK. So she says, 'Do you want to end up like the men on the benches, is that what you want?' and I know what she means, but I pretend not to. You do, don't you? It's human nature to try to delay confrontation, even if it's only for the time it takes someone to say . . . 'The men who drink on the benches, up near the station. Do you want to end up like them?'

As she says this, she looks up at me from her position on the sofa: me, standing opposite her, like a schoolboy summoned before the headmaster, a blonde, determined, woman headmaster. One who has clearly spent the day making a searching inventory of her marriage rather than arranging conferences as she should have been doing. And who has, at lunch-time presumably, collected some leaflets on alcohol abuse, which she has spread out on the otherwise empty coffee table in front of her, in readiness for my arrival home, slightly late, two pints of Kronenbourg after work – and don't I regret those now! Even the television's off. The television's never off. I look forlornly at it in the hope that it might switch itself on, divert Sam's attention with a new series of *Changing Rooms*, perhaps a Julia Roberts film.

There's a steely look about her that unsettles me. When I see the leaflets, fanned out neatly on the table, I feel doubly uneasy, decide to try to head off the inevitable at the pass. 'Sam,' I begin. 'Look, about last night. I'm really, *really* sorry . . .'

'Of course you are. You're always sorry. You were sorry

the last time, and the time before that.' She says this with a resigned, is-that-the-best-you-can-do lack of emotion.

She's right, of course. How many times have I grovelled my way out of yet another drink-related offence?

Sorry – after the time I got drunk before a performance of *Closer*, needed to leave to go to the toilet, and decided not to return.

Sorry – after my WWF wrestling impression at a friend's dinner party left her antique table in ruins.

Sorry – after being deposited back home by the police early one morning: previous whereabouts unknown; Sam almost frantic with worry.

Sorry – after smashing the gravy boat in a fit of alcoholic rage.

Sorry – after calling her friend a fat bitch. At her wedding.

Sorry – after telling the bride's father he was a boring cunt when he asked me to calm down, at the same wedding.

'You can't just sorry your way out of this one, Chris,' she says, that probing look never leaving her eyes. 'There are only so many times I can heard the word "sorry", OK? I hear the word "sorry" come out of your mouth, I think, Yeah, until the next time.'

'But – what else can I say? I mean, I *am* sorry.'

'I'm sure you are. But this time I want you to show it.'

'Please, Sam, I'll cut down.'

'Heard it before.'

Of course she has. After each gravy boat/WWF/*Closer*/bride's-a-fat-bitch-and-her-dad's-a-cunt episode, all of those and all the ones like them – 'Sam, I'll cut down.' Every time, promises to cut down drinking, which were never empty but had always proved to be. Old habits die hard, they say. It's too easy to slip back into the bad old ways. And, of course, I always did – even more than she knew: while I'd appeared to be drinking less, in fact I'd been hiding it more effectively.

Until now. Once more I've let things slip to such an extent that I face another day of reckoning. And realising that, I look into Sam's eyes, prepared to take whatever solution she offers me, just wanting this conversation to end.

That headmaster comparison suddenly seems more appropriate than ever: you want to take your punishment and leave, grinning with relief that it's all over. Except, of course, that isn't where the punishment ends, it's where it begins, but I don't have the foresight to see that right now.

Outside, in the street, voices are raised. Two people arguing, or perhaps it's just one person shouting into a mobile phone. Whoever it is seems to have stopped outside our window.

'For God's sake, do you hear that?' I start.

'Forget that, please. Ignore that. Concentrate on *this*.'

There's a moment or so of silence. Silence inside the room, at least.

'Sam, look, I will cut down this time. With your help, I can—'

'I will help you. I want to help you. Which is why I've been out and got these.' She indicates the leaflets spread out before her. 'These people can help. Help you. Help you stop.'

I open my mouth to speak, to say that I don't want to stop, and let's not overreact. It was an unfortunate incident. Unpleasant. But it hardly makes me an alcoholic, not like the men on the benches. Just a bit out of hand, that's all. I don't *want* to sit in a smoky room full of smelly men in donkey jackets 'sharing' my problems. I don't want to go anywhere, or actually *do* anything. I just want to cut down. Why can't I do that? Why can't I cut down and you trust me to cut down, and I'll get things sorted? After all, I'm not an alcoholic. I don't wake up gulping Scotch, don't spend my days drinking from the old purple tin and insulting passers-by. I just, you know . . . drink a bit too much every now and then. Regrettable, but not irreparable.

But as I'm thinking this, and as my brain is attempting to work my thoughts into an acceptable and cohesive sentence, which somehow incorporates the concepts 'I don't want to stop' and 'I'm sorry, things will change, trust me', Sam holds up a not-finished hand, saying, 'I'm serious, Chris. You have to do something and you have to do it now. And that means stopping drinking. As of now. I've been in the fridge and I've dumped all the lager and all the wine. I'm prepared to join in too. I think you know that this isn't a friendly request I'm making here. I don't have to spell it out for you, do I?'

'No,' I offer, penitent, but wishing I could be outside this room right now. Wishing, in fact, that I could be in a car running down whoever is standing shouting outside our window.

'Look,' she says, stretching in front of her. 'Read this.'

She holds out a small blue leaflet with the words 'Who, me' and a large question mark on the front, opens it to the middle pages and passes it over to me. I take it, grateful, actually, to be given something to do that doesn't involve having either to promise to give up drinking or trying to talk my way out of it.

'Are you an alcoholic?' it asks, and below are twenty questions, each with a yes or no tick box beside it. They are not particularly penetrating questions, I hardly need to look deep into my soul to answer them. They're things like, 'Have you ever felt remorse after drinking?' Well, yes, of course I have. Who hasn't? Who hasn't woken up the morning after, feeling like they've let themselves down the previous evening? A slip of the tongue. A bit of accidentally boisterous behaviour.

'Do you drink to build up your self-confidence?' says another. Well, er, yes. Isn't that the whole point? Isn't that why people drink in the first place? They don't call it a social lubricant for nothing, after all.

'Have you ever had a complete loss of memory as a result of drinking?' asks a third. And, again, I'm sceptical: name me one person who hasn't.

But I keep these thoughts to myself, dutifully adopting a

concentrated expression as I read, when in fact I want to snort contemptuously.

'You can answer yes to almost all of those questions, can't you?' says Sam at last, after enough time has passed for me to work out that, indeed, I can answer yes to at least eighteen of the twenty, and that, well, they weren't all so stupid after all. Not every single one.

'Not all.'

'*Almost* all, I said.'

I don't know which approach to adopt. Do I play the wounded soldier – break down and fall upon her mercy? Or do I fight my corner? In the end I choose neither option, feeling besieged, just wanting this 'talk' to end, for new-formula resolved and determined Sam to go away and old, cuddlesome, playful, loving Sam to return. I make an indeterminate noise in response.

'And what does it say at the bottom?' she presses.

I've already read it, I know what it says. 'That if you can answer yes to three or more questions then you are almost certainly an alcoholic,' I reply, the resignation heavy in my voice.

'Chris, this isn't a punishment.' Her eyes soften, as though the words on this leaflet were my own admission. 'I'm not docking your pocket-money here. I really feel you need help. And look,' she picks up another leaflet, which she passes to me, 'here's a list of meetings in our area. There are loads. There's one almost every night. Look, I've circled one. It's for tomorrow night at Holloway Road. You can go on your way home from work. See? I'm serious about this, Chris. I'm not a doormat. I'm not one of those women you see on TV, on *Jerry Springer* or something. This is your last chance. And I know that it's coming at a bad time – your father and everything – but I think that just makes it even more important that you do something now.'

I take it with a heavy heart. Holloway Road. Great. I'm really going to bump into a better class of alcoholic there, aren't I? If she was going to insist I joined a group, couldn't we at least have moved to Chelsea first? My mind races as I search for the right thing to say. I can't think of anything, but that's OK because anything I could say would only prolong the conversation and, right now, that's the last thing I want to do. I want to do it even less than I want to join a group of alkies in Holloway Road tomorrow night – which is a lot.

'Do you promise?' she says, looking searchingly at me. 'Do you promise to go?'

'Yes, Sam. I promise.'

Two photographers had a fight at Felix Carter's funeral, which was held a fortnight after the murder, on Wednesday, 19 November.

It wasn't a full-on *Raging Bull*-style punch-up. It was more of a scrap, a handbags-at-dawn affair. One pushed another, aggrieved that his space along the procession seemed to have been taken, and even though it was the tiniest little push, it caught the second photographer on a canister of film he was carrying in his top pocket and caused more pain than was intended. In the heat of the moment, photographer Number Two failed to make the distinction between intent and effect and lashed out, open-handed, at photographer Number One, knocking his glasses skew-whiff on his face. Number One had always had something of a hang-up about the necessity of wearing glasses, and in hitting them out of sync, Number Two had unwittingly tapped into a deep wellspring of psychological hurt, therefore unintentionally provoking a level of violence that was similarly out of proportion to the original offence.

For a moment or two, the pair of sparring photographers slapped ineffectually at one another, each regressing further and further playgroundwards until photographer Number Three stepped between them with a few well-chosen words. They were so well chosen, they might almost have been from a film.

Apart from this minor fracas, however, Felix Carter's funeral passed off with little incident. Visiting celebrities cried on cue, his family looked at once stoic and resentful, and hordes of his adoring fans lined the funeral route with their own farewell messages: from the hastily assembled 'RIP Felix' painted on a sheet, to the more tasteful floral bouquet with one of his own song lyrics acting as the message on the card.

As public outpourings of grief go, it was a good few notches short of Diana (and let's face it, we'll never see her like again), but a few above Jill Dando, probably because Felix's audience was younger and more prone to unchecked emotion. The nearest equivalent was after the suicide of Kurt Cobain. But, then, that happened in America, where they do everything on a grander scale. Teenagers killed themselves in the wake of Cobain's death; nobody was so rash after Felix was murdered. You could hardly cite it as a glowing example of the famous British reserve, but still.

We in the western world like to be able to say where we were when a famous person died. It's almost a tradition. Those old enough to remember will happily recall that they were doing the ironing when they heard of the JFK assassination, or that they were washing the car when news broke of Elvis's demise. Closer to the twenty-first century, most people remember what they were doing when they became aware that Princess Diana was no longer of this earth.

Wherewereyouwhenfelixdied.com was hardly the snappiest dot com title ever, neither was it the most sophisticated idea, but it was here that Felix fans came to remember their idol – a virtual remembrance garden.

Cumbrian schoolgirl Kate Sutton was the curator of wherewereyouwhenfelixdied.com. Prior to this Internet venture she'd had a smaller concern, simply, katiesutton.com, which she'd used mainly as a photographic gallery depicting the growing stages of the family cat, which her older brother had named Swervedriver in honour of the band of the same name.[12] As a devoted fan of Felix's solo career, the idea for wherewereyouwhenfelixdied.com came to her immediately

---

[12] Swervedriver was formed in 1990 and signed to Creation where they gained a name for themselves as part of the 'shoegazing' wave of bands, also including My Bloody Valentine, Ride, Lush and Chapterhouse.

after his death and she soon found herself the custodian of one of the Internet's biggest resources for bereft fans. In the early stages, visitors to the site left simple messages: 'My friend Beth told me at school that Felix was dead and I couldn't believe it. I love him and I will always remember him. Jenny, Market Deeping.' Kate was sure to prune the more distasteful ones, usually variations on a theme of 'Where was I when Felix died? Standing over him with a smoking gun! Chris Sewell, jail,' or just plain nasty ones like 'Celebrating! Felix hater, Worthing.'

But as the popularity of the site spread, and she found herself spending more and more time on the site, editing and sorting comments, correcting her visitors' atrocious spelling, the messages themselves grew more sophisticated. Soon she had to devote a section of the site to poetry, another to those who had stories of meeting Felix face-to-face (which she had never done, although she felt she knew him well). Still another section she named 'My Inspiration' for those who felt Felix's life and work had spurred them on to do things they would not otherwise have done. Tending this collection of odes to Felix's death made her feel as though he was somehow part of her life, and it was not lost on her that being the owner of wherewereyouwhenfelixdied.com made her an extra-special fan. As a result, she cultivated an air of self-righteousness that her family soon found tiresome.

If Kate Sutton's site was one side of the Internet coin in the wake of Felix's death, there was another too. It was inevitable that there would be, especially in light of the fact that this was probably the first sensational pop-star death to occur in the era of the Internet, with all its promise of total information democracy.

Felixisnotdead.com was equally bald in its statement of intent, but a good deal less reverential in execution. Here, people whose friends described them as wags, and their enemies as wankers, left occasionally amusing messages about having seen Felix buying plasters in Boots, or lager in Oddbins, or cocaine from a dealer in Stepney.

Then there was Meejahaw.com, a long-established forum for media gossip. Here visitors, usually work-experience people on magazines, used the message board to discuss the murder in a suitably flippant manner, thus:

>Has anyone got any Feelin' Carter jokes, then?[13]
(NoShame@nonuts.com)

>You're a shick, shick puppy, Moneypenny. But, yeah, I got one for ya. What does it take to get 24/7 back together?
(Bondboy@nickcottonsmumis.com)

>Heard it
(Blakeseven@virgin.net)

>Best I could do at such short notice . . .☹
(Bondboy@nickcottonsmumis.com)

>Are we swallowing this theory about Feelin' Carter's death then? Can I smell fish?
(garybarlowsteeth@flob.com)

>You people are scmu
(Felixfan@aol.com)

>Now he's dead, can we say what we like about him?
(tinkerbelle@madasafish.com)

>Yeah (gets serious) that's the way of libel. Once they die you can say what you bleeding well like (puts away law book). I hear he was hooked on crack . . .
(NoShame@nonuts.com)

---

[13] Excerpt from the message board of Meejahaw.com, taken on Friday, 14 November 2003.

>What's the Frankie Dettori (sp?) on Feelin' Carter?
  (ChrisJ12@talk21.com)

>He *was* hooked on crack. But not the drug kind.
(tinkerbelle@madasafish.com)

>You're all scum!!!
(Felixfan@aol.com)

>Shurely shome mishtake? I though we were 'scmu'??
(garybarlowsteeth@flob.com)

Their conversations were the twenty-first century equivalent
of scrawlings on a bog wall, left with exactly the same design:
to provoke, to outrage. Just as Felix's life was acted out in the
public eye, so was his death.

CHAPTER TWELVE

Turns out it's not full of smoking men in donkey jackets at all. Oh, no, it's much, much worse than that.

What's not full of men in donkey jackets?

The group. The group Sam makes me go to.

I'm sorry. Of course. Do go on . . .

I considered not going, of course. In fact, I'd cruised through most of the day thinking I might go but on the other hand I might not. And by giving myself that choice it became easier, when the time finally arrived, to decide that, yes, I was going to go after all.

See? I tell myself, as I step off the tube at Highbury and Islington. It's really not that difficult. Mind you, that's all I've done so far – step off the tube with the intention of going. That's not the difficult part. The tricky bit will be sitting in a room doing—

Doing what, exactly? It occurs to me, walking down Holloway Road, that I've given zero thought to what's expected of me at this meeting. My preconception is that a group of grizzled men looking old beyond their years will sit on plastic school-type chairs (I already know it's held in a church hall), looking slightly embarrassed and coughing more than is absolutely necessary.

But, of course, it won't be like that at all, will it? It'll be all about 'sharing', and 'opening up' and all the other things that Trisha advises her morning guests to do. Not the kind of thing I'm used to. Certainly not the kind of thing that ever occurred in the Sewell household, where the only opening up my father ever did was to a tricky jar of Branston.

And after the opening up and sharing, of course, comes sobriety. Abstinence. And I'm even less prepared for that.

If I'm honest with myself I'd half thought that when we'd done with the sitting round and coughing, we'd go for a drink. Walking along now, thinking about it properly for the first time, the idea seems ludicrous. But, yes, at the back of my mind, that's what I'd expected; looked forward to it, even. After all, I don't have many friends – none, really – so the idea of being thrown together with a new bunch of people held a certain appeal for me, the possibility of reinventing myself a little, projecting a different image. But that could only happen over a drink. Opening up, even, could only possibly happen over a drink. Again, they don't call it a social lubricant for nothing.

The upshot is that by the time I arrive at the church hall and follow the Blu-tacked signs indoors, I've completely revised my preconceptions so that in the end I'm not at all surprised that there are no donkey jackets in evidence, just two ladies in their mid-forties offering me a cup of tea.

'Hello,' says lady one, cardie and everything, 'would you like a cup of tea?'

I feel incongruous, betrayed by my work clothes and brief-case, as if I've come to sell them insurance rather than talk about a drink problem I don't even think I have.

'Hello,' I say, dazzled by the double glare of their smiles, like the twin suns of Luke Skywalker's home planet. They have the spacy, seen-the-light smiles of the converted. So much so, that I hardly need to ask, 'Is this the . . . the meeting for . . . The alcoholics' meeting?'

'Yes,' says lady two, an almost carbon copy of lady one. 'It's through there. It's about to start, actually. Is this your first time?'

'Yes,' I say.

'Have you had a drink today?'

I have had a drink today. Of course I have. I took a sales report to the George at lunch-time and read it over two pints of

Kronenbourg, glad that it wasn't a Friday lunch-time when you tend to get the weekend drinkers in. But lying about drinking tends to come as second nature to me so the words, 'No, I haven't,' are already out of my mouth before I've had a chance to reflect that the truth might have meant immediate expulsion.

'OK,' says lady one, taking over from lady two. 'Why don't you take a tea through there? Ask for Bécca, she's leading the meeting.'

'Thank you,' and although I have a fear of handling cups and saucers in front of groups of strangers I take the tea because it seems like the polite thing to do. Then I walk through to the other room as directed.

Inside there are more people with 'converted' smiles – about six of them, four women and two men. Fittingly, there's a low, church-like hum in the room, small pockets of conversation that die then pick up again as I enter, teacup rattling gently on its saucer, my briefcase hanging self-consciously by my knee.

They're not quite what I expected. For a start, the mix is more female than male, which is my first surprise. And second, they seem better dressed that I had anticipated, and happier. To all intents and purposes it might be a meeting of people who run health-food shops. Where are the boozy seen-everything veterans, with a regretful twinkle in their eye? This lot don't look as if they could drink their way out of a brown-paper bag. And, for some reason, that realisation makes me feel even more uncomfortable as I hang about by the door, unsure where to sit, what to say, what I'm even doing there.

They steal glances away from their conversation, and cast smiles in my direction. Smiles of warm benevolence aimed at making me feel welcome. They've all been me at one time or another, of course, all taken their first step and hung about awkwardly by a door; they know what it's like and they've got sympathy written all over their faces. So I should be put at my ease, but instead I feel the exact opposite and I'm just about to turn, say I've made a mistake and that I thought this was the book-keeping class or something, when a woman at the far end beckons me over, a spare seat by her side.

'Hello.' She smiles as I shuffle across, seem to make too much noise in putting down my tea and briefcase and rearranging my coat as I sit.

'Hello.' I smile back. 'Are you Becca?'

'I am. And you are?'

'Felix,' I fib, the lie coming too easily.

'OK, Felix. This your first time?'

'Yes.'

'And have you had a drink today?'

'No.'

'OK. I think the best thing for you to do now is just to sit and watch the rest of the group. In a moment or so the meeting will start and we'll say the serenity prayer. Then, as I'm leading the meeting, I'll say a few words and after that it's open to group discussion, which you're welcome to join in if you want. But if you don't, don't worry.' As I listen to her, I realise why they're all so keen to establish whether or not I've had a drink. It's because alcohol is poison to them. They've drawn strength from fighting the common enemy, it's given them a brotherly glow. And if I was to bring the enemy into their Holloway Road hidey-hole, well, that just wouldn't do. It's also because sobriety is a way of life for them; they're disabled by it as effectively as if they'd lost an arm. Sobriety for them began here, and by asking whether or not I've had a drink today they're implicitly suggesting that sobriety begins here for me, too. And I don't want that. Some helpful tips on how to control my drinking, perhaps. A bit of moral support. Not the whole giving-up deal.

As I look around the room, despite their health-food shop appearance, I know that within each of these people is a horror story where the bogeyman lives in a bottle. It'll be a story that ends with them losing their jobs, their families, their loved ones, their self-respect and their sense of self-worth, and they'll probably cry a little as they tell it. Am I like this? I don't think so.

Suddenly I have a strong urge to leave. Right now. A sense that I don't belong for so many reasons. Because I'm not worthy of them – my problem is a hacked-off wife, it hardly matches up; because I don't want to stop drinking, and by coming here I must; because their smiles make me nervous; because they are weak, and I am not. Christ, what would my dad say? A son so morally pitiful he cannot stop pouring lager down his throat? He'd be turning in his grave.

OK, Sam, I think. Like Scrooge's ghost, or Doc Brown in *Back to the Future*, you've shown me what lies ahead, and I'm suitably chastened. No, I don't want to end up like these people. Now can I go?

I pick up my briefcase and stand to leave. But just as I do, at exactly the same time, Becca says, 'OK, everybody. Shall we begin—'

She stops short, having seen that I've stood up and taken a step towards the door, bringing myself into the centre of their circle. I freeze, my Ninja-like exit thwarted.

'Felix?' she says. Her voice is low and sweet but questioning. She says it the way you might correct a naughty child. All eyes are on me, beaming sympathy rays into my cranium.

'Sorry,' I say. 'I really need the toilet.'

Her eyes move deliberately down to my briefcase then back to me. 'Could the toilet wait until after the meeting perhaps?' she says. 'Or until the break? We do have a break in about half an hour.'

'I'm bursting,' I offer pathetically. The briefcase is scalding my hand.

'Felix, I can't stop you going to the toilet, but I would ask that you wait. I'm sure the rest of the group would like you to wait as well.'

And now the image of Nurse Ratched from *One Flew Over the Cuckoo's Nest* has just popped into my head and that settles it. 'I'm sorry,' I say, doing a little need-a-wee dance for the benefit of my audience. 'I really do have to go,' and with my briefcase shouting, 'Liar!' beside me, I make a dash for the door, and hurry not to the loo but outside, to the safety of the street.

Where I do a quick look left/right, locate the nearest pub, and head straight for it.

In the pub I meet a man who calls himself Catweazel. He sits next to me as I'm finishing my second pint and enjoying its restorative warmth. He's just in time to be offered a drink, so I get him a pint of cider along with my third and we get chatting, not about anything in particular, just sounding each other out. I tell him about my father and he gets all over-sympathetic the way strangers in pubs do, repeating, 'Bummer, man,' *ad infinitum*.

Catweazel's not a bad bloke, really. With a name like that I hardly need to explain what he looks like, and we must make an odd couple at our table: me looking like I should be selling insurance; him looking like he should be selling dope cakes at Glastonbury.

He's using me for free drinks, of course. That becomes apparent when our glasses are empty and, even though it's his round, he doesn't offer to buy. Part of me minds, and at one point I consider mashing my pint glass into his grasping, manipulative face, or reaching and tearing his nose-ring from his nostril. But it's only a fleeting angry spell, and after a time I realise I'm glad of his company. It's nice to have someone to talk to. Someone who's not Sam, or work colleagues or converts with angelic smiles and soothing voices. So I buy another. And another. I buy cigarettes, because he's smoking all mine, and again, that angry flare-up, which is dampened when he shows me a trick with matches that he calls 'old man's erection'.

At one point Catweazel suddenly points at me over the table, saying, 'Got it. Got it, man. Like, I thought I knew you. I thought we'd met before or something, but now I know what it is. You look like that pop star, man. You look like Felix Carter.'

I laugh, not sure whether that's altogether a good thing in Catweazel's eyes. He is, after all, wearing an Ozric Tentacles T-shirt. But since we seem to be hitting it off I come right out with it: 'Well? Is that a good or a bad thing?'

Catweazel seems to consider, takes another gulp of cider thoughtfully. 'I don't know, man. Like, on the one hand he's pop-star scum, a paid employee of the man. But on the other hand he likes a party, he likes a booze. He's got a wild side, you know? He's scum, but kind of cool scum.'

After a while, I become aware that I'm getting quite drunk, but when I make vague noises about needing to get home, Catweazel persuades me to stay, slurring, 'But we're just getting to know one another, man.' And because I'm enjoying myself, and enjoying the smell of booze and fags, and the welcoming cocooned warmth of the pub, I decide to stay for another. And another. All the time getting the feeling that this is better therapy than any group can offer.

It's gone eleven by the time I finally bid farewell to Catweazel – thinking I've found a new friend – and walk out into the chill of Holloway Road. I stand there for some moments, swaying and getting my bearings. It's beginning to rain. Not large plops but a sweeping drizzle, like standing near the foot of a waterfall. I see a bus, but decide against it: my faculties are too impaired to risk getting on the wrong one or missing my stop. I need the certainty that only a tube can give, so off I go in the direction of Holloway Road station, ducking into an off-licence on the way and picking up a couple of cans for the journey home. I don't worry about Sam. I'm too drunk. The kind of drunk where your mind tells you everything will be OK, that people will understand. When, in fact, everything will not be OK at all. Not by a long chalk.

CHAPTER THIRTEEN

'Are you coming over tonight?' said the well-known soap star Aaron Bleasdale to his girlfriend. Only he said it via a text message that bleeped its arrival, slightly inconveniently, on the Mystery Blonde's mobile phone.

No, she thought. Not tonight, and not ever. And she scrolled the message downwards, past 'reply' and on to 'delete', pressing the rubber key firmly, satisfyingly.

Over the past few days, Felix Carter's murder had kept her busy. On the downside it had prevented her dumping Aaron, who was using all the technology at his disposal to pester her. On the upside she had been motivated and inspired by a story for the first time in years. She had the urge to uncover facts that she'd previously assumed belonged only to newspaper journalists. And her investigations had made her something of an authority on the case, motivating her to dig even deeper. Which was what had brought her here.

On the other side of the table three young men, wearing suits bought from either Burtons, Next or, at a pinch, French Connection, sat watching her silently as she attended to the affairs of her mobile phone. Although they were sitting in the meeting room at her behest, it did not occur to them how rude it was that she put the bleepings before them. She commanded patience – if not because of her position as features editor of *Sass* magazine, then because she was incredibly, strikingly beautiful. And though they'd all seen her before – in the lift, in the corridor – they'd never previously been so close. Close enough to study the beautiful pores on her beautiful face, to admire her mystery blondeness in detail. In fact, they were glad of the mobile-phone interruption: it gave them time to let their eyes linger on the other side, where the grass was not only greener but wore Prada and smelt of Chanel. Like Aaron Bleasdale's favourite *Simpsons* joke, their faces were set to stunned.

This was the thing with the Mystery Blonde. She lived her whole life in the cosy bubble of her own good looks, sheltered from the world by her beauty. Like the way men in everyday life do not regularly look behind themselves, but Mystery Blonde thought they did. In the street, men saw her blonde hair, quickened their step to walk past her and, once safely in front, threw back a casual look, just to check her out. And they always liked what they saw. Neither are men as naturally attentive in real life as they are in the artificial world of the Mystery Blonde. Men don't ignore her, and their eyes don't glaze over when she begins speaking. Mystery Blonde is always served promptly at the bar; she has never been turned down for a job; people give up their seats for her on the tube. Men, that is. Just so they can have the briefest moment of contact with the most beautiful woman they will see that day.

At last, she put down the phone, reached and pressed the record button on her dictaphone and watched to see the little wheels begin to turn.

'Thanks for coming,' she said, and sized them up.

On the left was . . . Adam? Yes, Adam. He seemed the most timid of the trio. His eyes never met hers. His arms hung down at his sides and he looked hot, possibly at the beginning of a really good sweat. It was November, and the offices of *Sass* magazine had efficient but not overbearing heating – hardly hot enough to make a young man perspire.

Next to him, in the middle, was Graham. Graham was the most professional-looking of the three. He looked as if he should have had a telephone tucked into the space between his head and shoulder. His tie was secured with a fancy knot, perhaps a Windsor. Graham was unafraid to meet her gaze, but he wore a listening look, as if he imagined himself her peer and they were at a meeting together.

Finally, there was Luke, a different kettle of fish altogether. Luke didn't sit, he lounged. His arms were folded across his chest, insolently. And when he met her eyes, it wasn't with the polite professionalism of Graham, it was with the predatory, fancy-myself look of the pub Lothario. A look he'd no doubt unconsciously copied from the likes of – ironically – Felix Carter. And, yes, Luke was good-looking, probably had no trouble pulling the girls in the Slug and Lettuce. The smile that played around his lips hinted at a cheeky, attractive charm, and she found herself amused by him and by the fact that, even here, he was on the pull and she was in his sights. Careful of him, she thought. He might be a handful. And with that in mind it was to him that she directed her first question. 'So, how well do you know Christopher Sewell?'

'Well,' said Luke Radley, 'every time I saw him, he was . . .'

Drunk, I sit on the tube, bent over, moving with the rhythm of the train and only just focusing on the sign that says Manor House when we arrive at my stop. I get off, groggily, thankful for the escalator that allows my legs time off for good behaviour as it takes me to ground level.

Where a disgusting thing happens.

I'm sorry. Hold that thought. Let me change the tape. OK. Ready. The disgusting thing?

Yes, the disgusting thing. It happens as I'm staggering home, slowly but surely, the second of my two cans in one hand, briefcase in the other, watching my feet taking uncertain steps along the route that leads me home – a shortcut through an estate.

Drunk or sober, I don't like this route – Sam never takes it, she goes the long way round – and not because poor people live there. We're not snobs. It's because of the noisy youths who hang around at the gates and the cars that roar up and down the road, teenagers in baseball caps hanging out of the windows.

From time to time the cars are abandoned, and sit forlornly by the side of the road, falling prey to vultures wearing Tommy Hilfiger. The hub caps go one day, next morning a side window's smashed, and the day after that the boot is jemmied open. And all the time people like me hurry through. People pleased to use the estate as a shortcut but keen to get to the sanctuary of their home turf.

During the day-time, on my way to and from work, I hasten through and hope the gangs of kids don't stop talking to stare at me as I pass. I always wait until I get to the end of the road before I light a cigarette in case one of them asks me for a fag. My liberal urges pity them their filth and hate the scum who make their lives ever more miserable, but self-preservation speeds me through as quickly as possible.

Tonight, the estate is a portrait in hardship grey, an image reinforced by the pitiless drizzle. The late hour means the kids are in bed, or off burgling old people. And there is nobody around but me.

Only, there is.

I look up from the hypnotic movement of my feet and see a man walking towards me. He sees a shambling drunk bloke, concentrating too hard on walking in a straight line, looking like a fatter, sadder Felix Carter, his briefcase banging against his leg. He sees a victim.

I see a strutting, rangy white man ambling down the pavement towards me; a hips-front, balls-out walk. One arm is swinging casually, rapper-style, the other is thrust deep into his jeans. I hear him too, noisily hawking up phlegm, which he gobs expertly and proudly on to the pavement.

Even pissed, I can see that he's life's scrag-end. A self-important scumbag stoned and as drunk as I am, but intoxicated by his own menace. He's like the benign Catweazel gone wrong, fuelled not by cider but by hate, by the desire to turn all he touches into shit so that only he can feel better.

We're about two hundred yards apart now and he's already fixing me with a stare that I notice but affect not to, pretending indifference to his finely honed act of intimidation, trying to straighten myself from drunk and vulnerable to some kind of imposing stature. Unsuccessfully, as it turns out.

A hundred yards away, his head has tilted up, his mouth screwed into contempt.

Fifty yards, and I feign interest in nothing that's happening beside a block of flats.

Just a couple of steps away now, he raises his hand suddenly to his nose, pushes one nostril flat – like you see footballers do – and then, as we pass each other, blows snot all over the shoulder of my coat.

I stop, sway, grab at a wall to stop myself falling. Shocked, my brain is trying to process the information: I've been attacked, it says, but I'm unharmed. And perhaps that apparent contradiction explains why those fight-or-flight impulses we hear so much about lie dormant, overridden by the self-same shock that means that instead of taking off down the street in fear of my life, I do nothing but stand in a state of hazy bewilderment, trying to understand what's just happened.

He carries on past. I look at the brown-green gob of mucus on my shoulder, the streetlight bouncing off it almost prettily, and vomit. Puke rains down on to the pavement and over my shoes. From behind me, I hear him give a short, barking laugh as he continues towards the tube.

And that is the end of our contact. He walks away with his scrag-end victory – one more person's day destroyed – and I'm left with snot on my coat.

Controlling the urge to vomit again, I wheel round, suddenly sober, and take a few quick strides after him, calling, 'Hey.'

He turns with a look of surprise, which he masks with a come-on-then smile. 'Yeah?' he says. Like that – a what-do-you-want yeah. And I make to punch with my left hand, which he moves to block, leaving himself open for my right, which is holding my briefcase.

The force of my forward impetus helps the metal frame of the briefcase slam extra-hard into the side of his head, opening his ear, which spurts blood, a burst of primary colour in the grey night. He stumbles and I follow with my left, a good hard punch – harder than I've ever hit anyone before. Pain shoots up my arm but it's worth it to see his nose split and crunch under my fist. More blood, and he falls backwards grabbing at air to try to break his fall, saying, 'Eurgh,' as he does so.

I kick him as hard as I can in the balls. He shrieks like a schoolgirl and curls to grab at his wounded groin, leaving his bleeding head vulnerable to a second kick. And then a third. And then – oh, go on – a fourth.

Now one hand is protecting his balls and another's wrapped over his head. Since his stomach is the only place I can reach, I kick him twice in the guts, causing him to curl into an even tighter ball, muffling his sobs, his vain pleas for mercy. As he lies wounded on the street, all remnants of his previous arrogance bleeding on to the concrete slabs, I slowly remove my coat and casually but carefully wipe the snotty shoulder on his hair.

Naturally, that's what *should* happen. Indeed, it's what will happen, over and over again in my head as I continue to lurch my way home, booze, anger and frustration jostling for position in my brain. More violent versions include the use of a piece of scaffolding, which happens to be lying handily on the pavement. The less popular PG-rated alternative involves me letting fly with a volley of deft, cutting remarks, which leads to us facing off before he turns and walks away, intimidated.

All feature me leaving the scene with some semblance of pride intact. None ends with me doing what I do, which is to stagger on to the end of the road through the estate, almost crying with the anger and shame.

When I turn the corner I grab at the nearest tree for a leaf. I miss and lose my balance, almost fall and grab again, swiping a leaf angrily from the branch. But the leaf is small, thin and weak, and my finger pokes through it when I try to wipe the snot from my shoulder. Retching, I dump the briefcase, grab a handful of small, thin, weak leaves and bat away frantically at my stained shoulder, squeezing my eyes shut to ward off the crushing humiliation, the stares of drivers as they pass, the invading thought that if my father could see me now . . .

Eventually I leave the tree alone, and though I can hardly bear to touch anything with the same hands that have wiped this man's snot, I pick up my briefcase, trying to shake my head free of the shame that threatens to overwhelm me. And then I continue home where, my drunken brain tells me, Sam will give me lots of sympathy.

'Oh, my God.' She sits bolt upright in bed, and reaches for the bedside lamp. The room is flooded with light. What she sees is me, standing before her, moving backwards and forwards, working my mouth with no words coming out, lots of industry but no product. A sorry, *sorry* state.

'Oh, my God.' Her hand flies to her mouth. Tears are already welling in her eyes, because everything about me betrays the fact that I've taken her warning and wiped my arse with it. That's the way with drinking: nothing's real until it's actually happening, and vaguely I wonder how I didn't see this coming, ask myself what I had expected.

She drags herself to the front of the bed, pulling herself from the foot of it, bending down and grabbing her dressing-gown in one flustered and furious movement.

'Sam,' I manage at last. And I want to tell her about the snot thing. I want to tell her so that she will feel sympathy for me, as though that will excuse me.

But she's bustling past me to the bedroom door, pulling on her gown at the same time.

'God, what have you done?' she says, wheeling around in the doorway to face me. 'After everything we said last night. Look at you!' Her voice has risen to a screech. Mistily, I hope the old lady upstairs won't hear her.

'Sam, listen,' I try again. But she won't. She turns and marches out, shouting, 'You're sleeping in the other room. Get your stuff and get out of the bedroom,' like she can't stand to be near me, like even being in the same room as me is worse than mustard gas to her. Something inside me rises. Anger. Groggy thoughts, like: I'm not sleeping in any other room, it's my bed too, I'll sleep where I like. And: Why won't she listen?

'Sam, please,' I start, for the third time.

She's in the hallway now, as if she doesn't know what to

do with herself. Animated to pointless action by my betrayal. 'You promised,' she shouts over me. 'You *promised* to get help. Where have you been?'

'Sam, I dildo. I mean, I *did* go, but—'

'But what? What, when you promised? Didn't *anything* I said get through to you? Do you know what you've done? *Do you know what you've just done?*'

And why won't she listen?

'Sam, please . . .' I take a step forward, into the doorway of the bedroom.

'No!' She moves back, keeping the distance between us. 'Don't you come near me. Don't you even *think* about touching me.'

What, like I'm some kind of infectious disease now?

'I did go. It was just—'

'You're unbelievable,' she interrupts. 'Look at the state of you. Look at yourself, Chris. LOOK AT YOURSELF!'

And why won't she fucking listen?

The bubbling anger suddenly rises to the surface and I move towards her, my hands outstretched, wanting to hug her. No, wanting to grab her, wanting her to listen to what I have to say. But she twists away, screeching 'Get off!', dives for the bathroom and locks the door before I have a chance to stop her. The door in my face only makes me angrier and I bang away at it, not giving a fuck if the old bitch upstairs hears us or not. On the other side, Sam's crying now, that muted mewling sound that either dampens your anger or stokes it. Guess what effect it has on me?

'Open the fucking door!' I shout. 'I can't speak to you like this. Open the fucking door!'

'Go away,' she says, from the other side, her voice taking on the echo of the bathroom. 'Go and sleep it off, go and sleep it off, go and sleep it off,' like a mantra, and then, as if a bubble of anger has burst within her too, like she's disgusted by her attempts at placation, she screams, 'YOU MAKE ME SICK!'

Which, I suppose, is what does it.

And I take a step back, raise my foot, and with all my weight behind it, kick at the door.

Thunk.

It should break and open, like they always do in films. Except it doesn't. There's the definite sound of splintering wood, but the door stays shut.

'GO AWAY!' she screams, frightened and angry from the other side.

But I'm in my stride now, and I kick again, then again, until finally the door opens and there is Sam, cowering on the toilet seat, her hands over her head as though she is waiting for a bomb to go off.

No bomb goes off, though. The violence of kicking down the door has stopped me in my tracks, and I stand in the doorway, trying to make sense of it all. She looks up at me, wet-eyed, red-faced, speaking through a mouthful of anguish: 'Oh, you're the big man now.' Still, a kind of calm descends over us. But for her part, it's a mind-made-up calm, the calm of the inevitable.

'Sam, I'm sorry,' I say, knowing that she's right. Where was the man who breaks down doors in front of frightened women when the dog-end who snotted on my coat was about? Where was he then, eh? Eh?

I can't reach the toilet because she's sitting on it, so instead I puke into the basin.

Funniest thing, after a night of heavy drinking, you wake up feeling great. Not only that but, for a period of, oh, about five minutes, it seems as though nothing is wrong with the world.

And then the clouds begin to form, and your memory returns, and you realise you're not feeling that great at all.

In my case, I wake up on the sofa and it takes me a few minutes to realise that there's something naggingly familiar about this scene. Sam isn't here, though. She's gone. Just as we both understood she would be. She's a woman of her word is Sam.

Of course, I know what I'm supposed to feel. Initial sadness with an exhilaration chaser. Get through this awkward Sam's-gone phase and I can skip straight to the excitement of new beginnings. Watch *Stars Wars* whenever I want. Put up a huge poster of Princess Leia in the lounge (the one from *Return of the Jedi*, you know the outfit I mean), not in a frame either, just Blu-tacked straight on, and probably not straight at that. What's more, I can forget all about hiding tins of Stella. I can make myself a Stella tree if I want, one that I can topple over with a boozy burp, just like Burt Reynolds does at the beginning of *The Mean Machine*. I can let *Sandy and the Students* run free, watch it at my leisure, lounging on the sofa in my dressing-gown with a can in one hand and a fag in the other – a fag that tastes extra great because nobody's there to say, 'That's the *fourth* cigarette you've had tonight . . .'

But, like everybody else, I've read *High Fidelity*, like everybody else, I've had women leave me before (usually because of my heavy drinking, funnily enough). And I know that the cold, hard reality is the enormous hole that opens up in your life. And anyway, here and now, lying on the sofa with the dreadful, dawning realisation that my wife has left me, that last night I *kicked down* our bathroom door, that I broke my promise, none of that boy-stuff seems at all attractive.

Because it's not me that I feel most pity for. It's her. Of all the men in the world she could have married – and she could have had her pick of quite a few – she chose me. And she did it on the basis that I was a good bet for the future. Someone who would love, respect and nurture her. And I turned out to be – what? I don't know, but I know that I tricked her into loving me, I tricked her up the aisle and then it turned out I wasn't quite the product advertised. Batteries were required, or contents had settled in transit.

Whatever, when you look at it that way, she'd been the victim of a big con. She had dreams, and I shattered them. Me and my tins of Stella. And that's not fair. Of all people, I can understand that.

It can go either way, of course, now that she's gone. Either I stop drinking entirely as the first step to winning her back, or I go to town: get pissed and stay pissed.

In the end I don't decide on either option. But by not taking the former, the latter becomes a foregone conclusion.

What I do decide is to take the day off, and when eleven o'clock rolls around, I go to the shop to buy beer. Of course. And at the shop I tell the woman to keep the change as brightly as I can and ignore the way she ignores me in return, don't let it bother me at all. It doesn't even leave a nasty taste in my mouth.

On the way back to the house I pop into the newsagent where the people behind the counter are far more obliging, and for some reason I buy a copy of *Phonic* magazine with Felix Carter on the front. 'His most revealing interview yet!' says the coverline. I'm not sure why I buy it. Maybe it's because I look a bit like him. Because he likes a booze. Because he's got a wild side.

CHAPTER FIFTEEN

THE MAN WHO WOULD BE CLEAN[14]

When Felix Carter tells you he'll answer all of your questions, he's not joking . . .

We meet one side of Felix Carter on the first day, a period set aside for photographs, general pre-interview chitchat and a chance to hear his fourth album, *No More Lies*,[15] which he proudly produces on CD-R, announcing, ambiguously, 'It's just a rough cut, or maybe it's not . . .'

He's in fine fettle. Full of the joys of spring, you might say. With minimum prompting he whips off his T-shirt to reveal the famed Carter bod beneath, a toned and tattooed testament to the chasm of difference between the artist who waddled out of rehab a year ago and the man currently enjoying good notices for his film début, *Enemies*, and who stands on the cusp of his fourth solo album. An album, he's fond of saying, that 'farts all over the other three'.

Since all we have to go on is a rough CD-R, it's a little early to say whether the tentatively titled *No More Lies* will, indeed, be directing air biscuits in the direction of its predecessors, but the signs look good. 'Planet Of The

---

[14] Excerpt from an interview with Felix Carter in *Phonic* magazine, cover-dated November 2003, a copy of which was found by police in the home of Christopher Sewell.

[15] The album was subject to a last-minute name change and released as *About Time Too* on Monday, 27 October 2003.

Gapes' is this year's 'I'm With You, Babe', a rousing anthem destined to elbow its way into the public consciousness in much the same way. Then there's 'Love You (To The Nth Degree)', the imminent first single, in which Carter savagely deconstructs the love song, leaving it sounding exactly like a love song. Having his cake and eating it? That's the Felix Carter way: the housewives' choice who can kick it with the kids. The rock'n'roller taking guitar lessons. The in-the-wings actor. The pub-rocker who can fill stadiums and have audiences pogoing one moment, crying into their beer the next.

And, of course, the damaged sex symbol. His *Smash Hits* good looks may have matured into the kind of fizzog that has him pegged for big film stardom, but the demons that have famously accompanied him in recent times have still to exit stage left. Booze and, to a lesser extent, cocaine continue to be responsible for most of his less salubrious tabloid outings. Nevertheless, today's sunny demeanour is, he says, a product of the latest bout of exorcism: two weeks off the sauce and counting. He knows there have been such dry periods before, of course: all-too familiar 'new-me' pronouncements. And after countless, very public plunges from the wagon and various trips to assorted clinics, it's too early to begin talks of a reformed character, despite his own zeal.

'My trouble is, I want to be Keith Richards, but really I'm more like Penelope Keith,' he says. 'When I'm drinking, I'm like this live-fast-die-young rock'n'roller, but next day . . . Someone once said Felix Carter is a man who really should get out less, and I think I'm beginning to agree with them.'

Not long later, the photography is complete, Felix Carter has worked his mojo on a weak-at-the-knees makeup girl and the day is over. We bid Felix goodbye. He's off to a photography exhibition being held in his honour, he says, grimacing, 'orange juice only', as he skips out of the studio, promising to meet us tomorrow when we'll conduct the full interview.

The next day, just two hours before we're due to begin the interview proper, the phone rings. During the briefest of conversations, a strained and obviously under-the-weather Felix Carter explains that today is 'not good' for an interview, and could we make it tomorrow when 'I'll answer any question you want.'

And so it is that a scant forty-eight hours after proclaiming, 'Things are going too well to let booze mess it up,' Felix Carter is in something of a state. A terrible state indeed.

The vision that greets us today is in direct contrast to the buff pop star of two days ago. Looking bloated, unshaven and hunched with shame, all traces of his earlier effervescence are gone, replaced by a powerful and painful-to-watch visitation of guilt.

Things were going well, he explains. Following the photoshoot, he'd attended a photography exhibition held in his honour where the strongest thing he'd had to drink was an orange juice. But, somewhere along the line, the walls filled with photographs bearing his image had got to him, and, instead of heading for home and an early night as he'd promised himself, he'd gone in search of a drink, a 'proper' drink. And then to another, and then to . . . Well, he doesn't quite know.

One thing he does remember. 'I saw Terry Hall – you know out the Specials and Fun Boy Three? I was the biggest Specials fan when I was at school. God, I don't know where it was, but I was going up to him, pestering him all night, getting him to sign something, and then something else, introducing people to him, stuff like that.

'God, I can't believe I've made a cunt of myself in front of Terry Hall.'

And with his promise to answer 'anything you want' still fresh in our minds, we begin.

Did you hurt your head, falling off the wagon?
Oh, very good, mate. I'll have to use that one meself. Yes, I

did hurt me head, but I can't show you the bruises, they're on the inside.

Let's put it another way. How are you feeling this morning?

I feel like an old alkie. No, I feel like a young alkie. Either way, I feel alkaline. An alkaline battery, that's me. Goes on for ever. Shouldn't really mix with an acid battery, might be a bad reaction. Don't throw me on the fire. Next question, I'm rambling.

Is that how you think of yourself, as an alkie?

[Sighing heavily] I don't know. I really don't. I don't know what an alcoholic is. Well actually, I do. You're an alcoholic when you admit you're powerless under alcohol – that's what they'll tell you at AA. I don't know. Sometimes I think having a drink problem or a drug problem goes against every kind of work ethic I was ever brought up on, you know? It's like the most self-indulgent, weak thing you can ever be. Me dad had a drink every day of his adult life, but he didn't have the fucking time to be an alcoholic, it wouldn't have occurred to him. So sometimes I just think it's a big luxury for someone – especially for someone like me – to go, you know, 'Oh, I'm an alcoholic. I need help.' And expect the whole world to be saying, 'The little lamb.' It's like, how can you not control what you pour down your throat? Get a grip, man. So, no, I'm not an alcoholic.

OK, do you have a drink problem then?

I have a problem with drink. I start. I feel good. Sometimes I even think of stopping. But then there's this kind of white-heat lust to take it all the way. You know, just to let the booze take you where it wants. And the thing is, I have this amazing capacity for drink. I'm not saying I can hold my drink, not in the sense that I can drink a lot and not get drunk, but once I am drunk I can carry on drinking. I don't have that cut-off point that other people seem to have. I don't get sick or any of that shit. And somewhere along the line my conscious self just kind of abdicates, puts its feet up and leaves my drunk self to get on with it. Blackouts, man, they're the most frightening thing in the world, but when you're drinking that's exactly what you're chasing. It's like you're giving yourself the night off. And then you wake up the next morning with the shakes and you're shit-scared for what you got up to. And that guy last night, the guy who you were, he's a complete stranger to you. You don't know him; you don't want to know him, but you're thinking, 'Fuck, it's me. I wanted to get like that.' There's got to be some kind of deep-rooted self-hatred at work to want to get like that. But I don't even want to go there . . .

You mention AA. Do you attend?

I think there's been pictures of me attending, hasn't there? The one time I go to AA – and I could have been going to help out a mate, for fuck's sake – some cunt's standing outside with a camera.

Were you there with a mate, then?

Ha! What do you think? But that's not the point. I *could* have been helping a mate. It just so happens I wasn't.

Did you participate?

The whole thing about AA is that you can take part or you can just sit and listen. For me, it was the sitting and listening that helped at the time. I don't know, I came out of it, and I just thought that I shouldn't have been there, that I didn't deserve to be there, because these are people who have reached rock bottom. They're there because life's got the better of them and nine times out of ten, booze isn't the cause, it's a symptom. And then you've got me sitting there. This kind of pampered pop star. I felt like an interloper, you know? Like I was watching them having sex or something. I don't know that I'm going to do the AA thing again.

Does being a celebrity make it easier or harder?

Christ, I don't fucking know. I think being a celebrity makes it easier to be a cunt. OK, right, I made a nuisance of myself with Terry Hall. And if I'd been a regular person annoying Terry Hall, chances are someone would've sorted me out. And maybe – I dunno, maybe that would kind of make you stop and think and you'd think, Right, Felix, you're being a cunt, now's the time to get your coat and go. But because you're famous, nobody stops you, nobody tells you off. So in a way it's worse. I mean, you get pissed and you wander around going, 'I demand to have some drugs!' And someone gives it you. And you get away with that because you've got a single in the charts. Do that without a record deal, or a film out or something and you'd get your head kicked in. Being famous automatically makes you a wanker. Being pissed and famous makes you the Wanker of Wankers.

But on the other hand, being famous: it gives whatever you do this kind of mythical sheen. I'm just a pisshead, but because I'm Felix Carter, I'm a hellraiser and people think I'm cool. And, you know, I'm under no illusions about that. If I wasn't me, I'd be thinking I was cool. Does that make sense?

If you could magically 'unfamous' yourself, would you?

Sometimes I would. I would now. Now the phone's ringing and people are telling me the stuff I got up to, and I'm wondering if it's going to be all over the papers [as it turns out, it's not]. And then, of course, you get, like, the weird fans, which means I do have to have a bodyguard, which can be a bit freaky, this guy hanging around all the time . . .

So there's that. But at the end of the day, when you're famous, you're in this bubble. OK, I've got a stalker, but then so have thousands of people who aren't famous. People who can't afford minders. See, you're protected from all the shit that people have to go through. You hear famous people in interviews going, 'I have to pay my bills like everybody else,' and that might be true, yeah, you might have to pay your bills like everyone else, but so what? Do you ever have to queue at a bar, pay for your own drinks, even? Wait for a bus? Get trampled on the tube? When was the last time a shop assistant was rude to me? Or a waiter ignored me? I can't remember . . .

But the media attention?

It comes with the territory. One day you'll hate the media because they make up so much shit and you're too tired to kick up a fucking stink about it. But the next day the media are like a mirror, but a really truthful one. Like today. My phone's ringing, but none of these people are going, 'Look, Felix, you made a show of yourself, you acted like a twat.' It's all [assumes Cockney wide-boy accent] 'Wa-hey, you naughty boy! You coming out tonight?' It's the papers that tell you when you've been a cunt. You know those 'bystanders' they have? That's the papers talking to you, telling you you've made a wanker of yourself. It's not like they care or anything, they just don't have a vested interest in licking your arse most of the time.

So, fame. Curse, or cool as fuck?

Cool as fuck. No, curse. Tell you what, it's a curse. But it's a pretty cool-as-fuck curse.

CHAPTER SIXTEEN

Would you like a tea?

I'm fine, thanks.

Really? Jack will get us a tea, won't you, Jack? Jack looks after me, he protects me.

It seems you're quite at home in here.

I am. Of course I am. All the shit I had to go through before, I don't get any of that in here. Out there, I was Chris Sewell, sweaty bloke you ignored on the tube. In here, I'm still Chris Sewell, but Chris Sewell that you know. Someone people like you want to speak to. Not many people can claim that, can they?

I suppose not.

So, no tea, then?

No, thank you. Please, continue.

You've presumably been in long-term relationships before?

I have, yes.

Then you know that one of the things you find yourself saying and hearing in any long-term relationship – marriage especially – is the sentence, or variations of: 'We're going to spend the rest of our lives together.'

You hear it in moments of tenderness, as a validation of your love. It pops up during arguments to underline the transience of whatever you might be bickering about. It surfaces during moments of hesitancy and self-doubt. It's a big old life, it may seem short but, still, there are a lot of hours and minutes to fill, and the thought of sharing the whole thing with someone else, well, it's a commitment, all right.

It's also a big fat lie. Leaving aside the fact that you're a heavy drinker and your wife will leave you as a result, the bald truth is that you're not going to spend the rest of your lives together – not unless you're both killed in the same car, by the same bus at the same time. At best, you get to spend the rest of *one* of your lives together. And that's hardly the same thing.

Magazines like *Sass* devote endless pages to the exploration of the simultaneous orgasm, as if that were love's ultimate expression. But what they should be doing is offering handy advice and tips on simultaneous suicide – 'Noose Knots For Beginners!', 'Know Your Own Overdose Limit!' – because that's where you get to find whether your love really cuts the mustard. Marriage, coming at the same time, agreeing on the same design of curtain – it's all the wuss's option compared to shuffling off this mortal coil together.

Unless, of course, there's someone else to think about, and in my father's case there was. Me. So maybe he bided his time, waited until I was set up, happily married and with a career, then lay down to fulfil his part of the contract. Like some angel bowing out at the end of a film, whispering, 'My job here is done.'

If that's true, I wonder what he'd make of my botched attempt at a higher, grander love with Sam.

This is what I think about on the train back to Leicester.

I'm due to meet Auntie Jean and Uncle Ted and the three of us will go to Groby Road where I can survey my father's estate. It's a salvage job: I have to decide what I do and don't want from his remaining possessions. What I don't reserve for myself will be included in an auction.

And, in normal circumstances, Sam would have come with me as moral support. But clearly these aren't normal circumstances because Sam has left me, so I have to make this journey alone.

It's now been three days since she departed and in the meantime, I've done this:

1. Walked around the flat feeling its emptiness, picking up her things and reminding myself what I love about her. What do I love about her? The fact that I can smell her socks and not know if she's worn them. The mysterious tubs, pots and tubes that litter the bathroom. The smell of her that's getting fainter by the day. Just her . . .

2. Spoke to Luke Radley, begrudgingly offering him the job of ad sales rep with *Sass* magazine and requesting that he start as soon as he's able. Became annoyed at his *laissez-faire* approach, when he told me casually he'd 'be in touch' to let me know if he wanted to accept.

3. Received a phone call from Luke Radley accepting the job and telling me he could start the following Monday.

4. Visited the supermarket and had a brief flash of that elusive sense of exhilaration when I bought myself some Matey handwash. (I'm sorry if you're expecting a load of amusing 'coping by myself' anecdotes, but there aren't any. I can use a washing-machine. I know how to cook. I can find my way around an iron. I pay bills. I feed the cat. Being a man doesn't make me a domestic retard in much the same way as being a woman didn't prevent Sam from programming the video or putting a CD on. I don't miss her for her ability to sort the whites from the darks before a wash, I miss her because she's my wife.)

5. Texted Sam, saying, 'I love you, I miss you, I'm sorry.' Received no reply.

6. Called Sam's mobile. It rang but there was no answer, her mobile telling her 'Home'. Walked down the road and phoned her from a callbox. She answered. I hung up. It told me all I needed to know.

7. Spoke to Uncle Ted and arranged to meet him at Leicester railway station.

8. Drank a lot of Stella, cried a lot, watched detective programmes on TV: *Taggart*, *Wexford*, but not *Silent Witness* – not that one because the lead character's called Sam and, yes, it really is that bad.

9. Lost a minor argument with Geoff Clarke over the appearance of my Rules of the Kitchen list. He felt the tone was patronising. Aside from that, a couple of girls in the department had taken exception to the reference to tampons. And anyway, he didn't feel it was quite, er, *appropriate* for a team leader to be getting hot under the collar about conditions in the staff kitchen. That was more of a cleaners' issue. Somebody removed the Rules of the Kitchen list from the wall and, just to take the piss, they put it in the sink.

10. Received a cold phone call from Sam telling me she was fine, and at her mum's and needed time to think and, oh, you're going back to Leicester on Sunday? Well, since I was going back to Leicester on Sunday could she use that opportunity to come and collect some of her stuff? And maybe I shouldn't have shouted at her that she could *take the fucking cat* while she was at it. And it would have been better if I hadn't been so drunk. Obviously.

11. Sprayed some of my aftershave on Sam's dressing-gown because I knew she'd be collecting it, and I wanted her to smell it and be reminded of me.

12. See 8.

13. Left an emotional note for Sam, promising to change. Ensured note was suitably tear-stained.

14. Dithered in the shop over whether to buy a half-bottle of vodka or tins of lager for the train journey. Eventually decided on the lager, reasoning that a man drinking vodka on the train is an alcoholic. A man with tins is simply a man whiling away his journey in a civilised manner.

Briefly I feel like Gary Lineker when I step off the Intercity at Leicester, only because there was once a Walker's advert where he arrived there by train, wandering along being greeted by everyone he met. Me, I'm greeted by Auntie Jean and Uncle Ted who, it occurs to me for the first time, are just about my only close relatives now. We make small-talk and I do my utmost to hide that I'm drunk, and if they notice they're too polite to say anything, dropping me off at the house and promising to return in a couple of hours, after they've had a Harvester and a wander around the shops.

The last time I was here was for the funeral, when I didn't really notice the place, just the people filling it with sympathetic faces. Now I stand at the doorway, like one of those teenagers in stalk-and-slash films – feeling the same sense of queasy dread. It's all I can do not to call out, 'Hello? Is anyone at home?'

It's cold, of course – who heats the home of a dead man? – and dark, so I switch on the hallway light, registering how familiar that small act of acclimatisation feels. Then I fish a can of lager from my coat pocket and pop the tab, standing at the doorway until I've finished it.

The house is just as I remember it from my childhood, obviously. Up the hallway and on my left is the lounge. In there is a set of bookshelves, a TV and video, a sofa that must be over a decade old. Straight ahead is the kitchen, but before that is a flight of stairs, and it's those I head for when the can's finished, placing it on the doormat to throw away later.

Ironically, it's my father's philosophy that propels me up the stairs, the get-it-over-and-done-with ethic. The last thing I actually *want* to do is root through his personal effects. In fact, I can't think of anything worse. And if it wasn't for Dutch courage I'd be sorting through spoons just now. But it has to be done, and it's best that it's done by me. The alternative is to have Auntie Jean and Uncle Ted struggling to make sense of his life and death. I don't think he would have liked that. So it's with his words ringing in my ears that I mount the stairs, the stairs that were known once upon a time as 'the wooden hill to Bedfordshire'.

'Get it over and done with, son.'

I begin crying when I'm about half-way up, but I put that down to the drink.

It takes me all of ten minutes to find the gun. Not that I

was looking for it: up until now I'd been blissfully unaware of the existence of any kind of firearm in the house where I grew up. But my father was a methodical man, insanely tidy, a fervent organiser, a big one for throwing things out, so there isn't really a great deal of stuff to go through. All there is are three shoeboxes and one of those home-organiser things. It's not a huge amount to show for a life.

The home organiser is neatly filled with the kind of documentation that life pulls along in its tow: passport, bills, guarantees, instruction manuals, and warranties for anything in the house with a power cord. All of them filed under the correct, biro-written heading.

Of the shoeboxes, one is filled to bursting with photographs, and I put it to one side for later, unable to cope with a tidal wave of memories. The second box seems devoted to my mother. I catch sight of what looks like a letter in her handwriting, and wipe away tears as I place it on top of the photographs box, wondering when, if ever, I'll be able to bring myself to look at them. Not for the first time I wish that Sam was here. To help me look, to help me be strong.

The third box is heavier, and emptier. Inside it is the gun.

Apart from the fact that it's a pistol, it's not immediately obvious what kind of gun it is. Wrapped in what appears to be an oily once-white tea-towel, it simply lies in the bottom of the box like a manta ray at rest.

I stare at it, realising that my hands are shaking. I know very little about guns, but I know that they require a licence by law, and that licence requires its holder to keep the said firearm in some kind of safe, lockable cabinet. Not a shoebox.

And I don't know what's more surprising: that my father owned a gun, or that he was breaking the law in doing so.

Awestruck, I use two hands to lift it out, like the high priest in an Indiana Jones film. It's heavy. I jog it gingerly, feeling its weight, and then I lay it down on the carpet in front of me, rearranging myself into a comfortable cross-legged position for a full inspection.

Have I ever seen a real gun before? I've fired air pistols, of course, using tins of pop for target practice. But even in its dormant, wrapped-in-a-tea-towel state, it's obvious that this is a different kind of weapon altogether. It smells different – oily, like they tell you in books. It's bigger, too, about twice the size of the airguns I handled as a kid.

It occurs to me that this could, indeed, be the first time I've ever seen a real, proper this'll-kill-you gun up close. Funny, really, you see them used thousands of times in films and on TV, they become as familiar as milk, yet your actual contact with them turns out to be zilch. I laugh – it's almost like finding a movie star in your room.

I can't help but be a bit disappointed when I finally, carefully, unfurl the tea-towel to reveal the pistol beneath. It's a gun all right, but not a very cool one. It would have been a bit much to expect an up-to-the-minute Glock that won't show up on airport metal detectors, but this is virtually an antique. Like my father, it belongs to a different era. True, I recognise it from films, but from films set in the desert during the Second World War. It even has a large loop fixed to the bottom of the butt. A lanyard, I think it's called, which – if I recall correctly – is used to hang the gun around your neck like a pair of sunglasses.

Nevertheless, aside from its age, there's nothing about it to suggest that it's in anything but working order. Clearly it's been well kept: the oily tea-towel is testament to that. It's clean as well. Not that I expected it to be blood-stained or anything, but you'd have thought a gun this old would show some signs of wear and tear, a little rust perhaps. No, this gun has been regularly and lovingly attended to.

By my father.

I lift it up and hold it by the handle, almost as if I'm about to use it in anger, but keeping my finger well away from the trigger. Then I turn it over, looking for the safety catch, which I locate where a right-handed person can use it with their thumb. I may lack hands-on experience with guns but a lifetime slouched in front of the TV is doing me proud now. This is the sort of gun that 'breaks' so you can pop the bullets into the chamber and sure enough, towards the front of it is a catch, which if I was to pull it, would open it. I leave it as it is, though – and since I can see daylight through the holes I deduce there are no bullets in it, but I'm not taking any chances: I lay it down again gingerly, wrap it up in the tea-towel, put it carefully back into the shoebox and replace the lid.

I turn my attention back to the other two boxes, and swiftly find what I'm looking for: a box of bullets in a crinkled, ageing brown-paper bag, looking just like boxes of bullets do in the films, pushed to the bottom of the Mum box. Feeling like an old pro now, I examine the bullets, which, again, look no worse for wear, before carefully replacing them in the box.

A gun. Bullets. My father.

Of course, if Sam was here she could explain to me why my father owned a gun and bullets. A keepsake, she might say. A curio. She'd chase away the thoughts I'm harbouring now, the ones involving my mother and the man who ran her down. She'd put her arms around me again, assure me that everything was going to be all right. But she's not here, so those thoughts go wandering unchecked.

Then I do a quick but methodical search, just in case there are any other surprises lying in wait for me. Under mattresses, beneath cupboards, behind drawers. I pull up stray carpet, I try loose floorboards, I poke my head into the loft and I even tap along the walls, listening for hollow bits. Nothing. So I take the three shoeboxes, stuff them into a carrier-bag, and then, for the sake of appearances, I randomly collect books, records and family photo albums, stacking them by the front door for sending on at a future date. Lastly, I look into my old bedroom. I don't know why, he redecorated it as soon as I left. Not out of spite, just because. Still, I walk into my old bedroom and I spend a few minutes looking out into the back garden, wondering exactly when it was that he took the slide down to the dump.

'All set, son?'

Me, my uncle and auntie stand at the front door of the house. I'm carrying a plastic carrier-bag full of three shoeboxes, one of which contains an illegal firearm, another with bullets for it.

I should say, 'Uncle Ted, did you know Dad owned a gun?'

To which he'd reply, 'Gosh, did he keep that old thing? Blimey, that was given to him by blah-blah. Must be blah-blah years old. Better hand it in to the blah-blah, I suppose. Must have been quite a shock coming across that, I bet . . .'

But I don't, because I have a feeling – and it's a feeling of disquiet, if I'm honest – that Uncle Ted would have no more idea of the gun's existence than I had two hours ago. And that my thoughts are right: that it wasn't an antique, or hand-me-down or family heirloom; that my father hadn't kept it clean and in good working order simply because he was an orderly man. He had had that gun for one of two reasons, and the fact that he died without the aid of a bullet pretty much rules out one of them.

So instead I say, 'Did you have a nice lunch?'

'Yes, thank you,' replies Auntie Jean. 'We found a Harvester. I think it's where the old Berni Inn used to be.'

'Well, they took them over, didn't they?' says Ted, and for a moment we all furrow our foreheads, trying to recall the commercial to-ings and fro-ings of the catering industry.

We give up. 'So that's what you're taking, then?' Ted gestures at the hastily assembled pile of belongings behind me.

'Yes. That's all. And I'm taking these now.' I raise the carrier-bag: gun inside. 'Just a few photographs and whatnot. Some of Mum's stuff . . .'

They look embarrassed. 'You sure you don't want it sending on with the rest?'

'I'll take it now, if that's OK. Sam would like to see some of the pictures.'

'How is Sam? All right?' says Auntie Jean. She beams as she says it. Both she and Ted love Sam. Of course they do, everybody loves Sam.

'She's fine,' I lie. 'At her mother's this weekend.'

'Ah.' They both do a penny's-dropped look. 'We wondered.'

'Right. Yeah. With her mum.'

There's a pause. I try to think of something to say, but everything that comes to mind seems inane. Finally, Ted saves us, says, 'Not much to show for a life, is it?'

'No,' I reply.

'Shall we make a move, son?'

They drop me at the station some twenty minutes before my train, so I've got time for a drink. And when the car's out of sight, I head for a nearby pub. It's always been a notorious pub, this one. Its proximity to the station guarantees a steady stream of dodgy characters. In normal circumstances I'd probably give it a wide berth; walk the extra few hundred yards to another. But these aren't normal circumstances. And I think you know why.

CHAPTER SEVENTEEN

Erotomania was not a word people knew particularly well before Felix Carter was murdered. However, following his death – or, to be exact, following the trial and subsequent imprisonment of his killer, Christopher Sewell – it was a concept that gained entrance to the public consciousness in much the same way as vCJD, cybersex, compassion fatigue and air rage had before it: ushered in by the media.

Some years before, the self-same media had introduced the world to the concept of stalking, a crime that preceded the popularisation of its name by some centuries, since it involved systematically pestering a victim and making their lives unpleasant for them. Previously, however, stalking had been simply a crime, more properly known as harassment. But in the nineties it had earned phenomenon status, largely because of a series of high-profile celebrity stalking cases.

In 1989 the American actress Rebecca Shaeffer was killed by her stalker in west Hollywood; the singer-and-sometime actress Björk was sent an explosive device by her stalker, who later committed suicide; in 1999 television presenter Jill Dando was shot and killed on the steps of her home in Fulham, London, again by a stalker, Barry George.

And these were only the most sensational cases. Stalking soon became ubiquitous among those in the public eye, the joke being that to have one was a measure of your celebrity. Simultaneously, it became a byword for fan worship, helping to explain the acute unease that accompanies the truly obsessive. No longer were committed fans the cornerstone of a star's popularity. Now they were stalkers, an object of both fear, contempt and no small measure of ridicule.

Because the laws against contempt of court prevented the media openly describing Christopher Sewell as a stalker before he was found guilty and sentenced, there was no discussion of the phenomenon until then – not in relation to Christopher Sewell and Felix Carter, anyway. But when he began his life sentence for first-degree murder, the information floodgates opened.

Only, they didn't. Not really.

From the moment that he was charged by police on Wednesday, 5 November, Sewell had refused legal counsel, announcing to police his intention to plead guilty. Psychological evaluations pronounced him fit to stand trial and he duly appeared for committal at a magistrates' court, minus a solicitor as promised. More than one commentator mused that he appeared almost to enjoy the brief time he spent in the court, and the trip in and out, shepherded and protected from the media and public by police officers.

Inside the court he stood before three magistrates who seemed nervous and overwhelmed by the attention, more used to dealing with low-level, less newsworthy cases, and he answered the clerk to the court's questions. He confirmed his name and address, said the one word, 'guilty', when asked to enter his plea, and with that, the first phase of the Crown against Christopher Sewell was closed, the magistrates ordering that a date for a Crown Court appearance be set.

His appearance in Crown Court, early in the New Year, was almost as perfunctory.

Sticking with his pledge to plead guilty, Sewell continued to refuse legal counsel, asked that nothing be said in mitigation and declined to defend himself in any way. The jury, who, to a man, had been panting with expectation for the case, were not even asked to retire.

Thus, what should have been one of the most sensational court cases of modern times was over in the period it took for the prosecution to make their case and for the judge to pass sentence. Christopher Sewell was led from the dock to begin his life sentence, and although 'enjoying himself' was perhaps overstating the case a tad, he certainly seemed in no particular distress. He showed no remorse or fear: he smiled at members of the jury. If anything, he appeared content, at ease with both the attention and his fate. He was a natural at the stardom game.

In the meantime – in fact, from the moment Christopher Sewell had been arrested – the press were digging. Contempt laws may stop newspapers printing damaging and prejudicial information, but they don't prevent them hunting it out, and when it comes to unearthing background information there are few organisations as proficient as the British media.

Who drew something of a blank.

Friends and associates of Christopher Sewell were tracked down and interviewed wherever possible, but it quickly became crystal clear that Sewell had few associates and even fewer – precisely none who ever cared to admit it – friends. And those the media did manage to find had little to say about Christopher Sewell – it turned out that he was not a particularly memorable man. And if journalists were hoping to excavate clues as to the root of his aberrant behaviour, there were none. 'Slightly odd' was the general consensus, which hardly ranks up there with 'unhinged', 'sexually dangerous' or 'clearly homicidal' in the circulation wars.

What they found was that, while he might have been an 'outsider', in the sense that he had few social connections, he was not the classic, accepted example of one: no combat jackets, large pornography collections (just *Sandy and the Students*), Sven Hassell novels or an unhealthy interest in death. He didn't make people – especially women – nervous, he didn't spend hours playing *Quake III*, and he wasn't in the habit of downloading precise instructions on how to make bombs or hack into the White House computer system. True, he was fond of the occasional drink, and there were many accounts of embarrassing drunken episodes, but otherwise precious little in the way of revealing background information.

They tracked down the wife, of course – Samantha.

She tried running to ground. In an attempt to avoid the media's rheumy gaze, she rented a home on a housing estate in Bedford. But finding her was an early-morning yawn for the likes of Britain's tabloid newspapers, and they had soon located her. Getting her to talk, however, was another matter indeed and, seemingly impervious to the increasing sums of money offered to tempt her, Sam refused – and continues to refuse – to speak to them.

Of course, the lack of revelatory detail at the trial, coupled with the shortage of background interviews, meant the media had to do what the media always does when it finds itself with a dearth of hard facts: analyse the ones they had. They wheeled out the experts, and what they wanted the experts to talk about was stalking. And because the public was already comfortable with the concept of stalking as a social phenomenon, experts were able to discuss it in terms of its component parts: erotomania, obsessive delusional behaviour.

Writing in the *Spectator*, Dr J. B. Hawkins said:

From the little we do know of Christopher Sewell, we are nevertheless able to form a picture of a man with an authority problem; an alienated individual who believed – and probably still believes – that the social fabric holding us all together has let him as an individual down . . .

By focusing on someone in the public eye, someone with whom Sewell clearly felt a great deal of affinity, he might have found a comprehensible target for his rage and frustration. Feelings which until that point would have been internalised were able to find an external expression . . . .

In describing him as a 'stalker', we may be guilty of ascribing to him an all-too-quick and easily understandable classification. Obsessive behaviour in stalkers tends to ger-minate for a period of up to three years, and mostly, at least initially, within the bounds of the law, until their behaviour escalates in tandem with a rising sense of frustration at their inability to penetrate the world of their victim, reaching some kind of 'flashpoint' where a transgressive act is likely to occur. In the case of Christopher Sewell and Felix Carter, it seems the germination period was highly accelerated, since to the best of our knowledge, Sewell only began to fixate upon the pop star some two weeks prior to his 'transgressive act', in this case, the murder. Thus, Sewell can hardly be thought of as a classic stalker, and is therefore either a psychological anomaly, or not a stalker at all, simply an enraged man seeking an outlet for his anger . . .[16]

Meanwhile, writing in *The Times*, novelist Lorna Curtis provoked controversy, saying:

If we accept that stalking – erotomania, delusional behaviour: whatever we're calling it in the name-it noughties – is an expression of love gone wrong, then surely celebrities must be prepared to concede a degree of provocation? When their entire existence is based around a strategy of persuading the general public, nay, pleading with them, to love them unreservedly, unequivocally, flaws and all, doesn't it seem somewhat churlish to complain when that self-same strategy works? What a surprise it must be to discover your adoring public are not all worshipping automatons capable of regulating their admiration in a manner most convenient to you, that there may be a murderous maverick in their midst. But why not? After all, if you create and inhabit a hyper-real world of love and emotions writ large, how can you complain when your public tailor their response accordingly? And, to paraphrase Dennis Hopper in *Blue Velvet*: what is a love letter, but a bullet from a gun? . . .

But this national obsession with celebrity stalking, doesn't it miss the point? Why, for example, do we blindly accept that stalkers are in love with their chosen victim? Because

---

[16] From the *Spectator*, Monday, 5 January 2004.

to do otherwise would be to chip away at the very values that provide the foundation of our celebrity culture, that's why. Stalkers may represent the dark side of fandom, but at least that's what they are: fans. And for an ego-obsessed celebrity, it's much more palatable to believe that the man – note: hardly ever 'woman' – behind your discomfort is a warped lover, not simply someone who hates your guts. God forbid. Maybe, just maybe, stalking is not love as we're so eager to believe, but purely an expression of displeasure as large and grand as the lives celebrities lead? Wouldn't that be a turn up?[17]

---

[17] From *The Times*, Saturday, 10 January 2004.

CHAPTER EIGHTEEN

The first thing I notice when I walk through the door is the cold. The second thing I notice is that the cat doesn't immediately impede my progress by wrapping itself around my legs and miaowing imploringly up at me.

Good, I think. The furry cunt has gone.

Oh, you look shocked.

You hate the cat that much?

Not really. I'm just describing my state of mind. I'm quite pissed at this point and I'm thinking, Good, she took me at my word, the cat is gone. But when I walk through to the bedroom, it's evident she's taken much more besides.

The hairdryer's gone, and the carpet seems bare without it sitting there, picked up, used and dropped every day as it was. Also missing are the hundreds of mysterious tubs and pots and tubes that reminded me of her. Where once they cluttered the bedroom windowsill, now it is empty, announcing its need of a coat of paint.

And those are only the ones from the bedroom. In the bathroom, just my shaving gear, a bottle of shampoo in the shape of C3-PO and my Matey handwash remain. The bath that this morning groaned with hair conditioner, face masks, bath oil from the Body Shop, tiny bottles of gift-set gels from Boots – all lined up along the sides – is now naked. She's taken the mirror, for fuck's sake. She's also swiped the little makeup mirror I used for shaving, which effectively leaves me with a mirrorless bathroom . . .

As I walk back to the bedroom I register the hollow, echoey feel of the cupboard even before I've looked inside. Sure enough, just my clothes are left, taking up barely a third of the original space. It seems futile, but I sweep them across the rail where they clank and dangle, no doubt enjoying their new-found freedom. The drawers are similarly empty. Gone are her knickers, socks, tops and scarves, and I find myself yearning to be able to touch and smell them. I didn't think the point could be driven home more emphatically than it already had been, but here's the evidence.

In the kitchen I locate the source of the cold. She's left a window open and I can almost hear her muttering, 'Hmm, smells disgusting in this flat, better let some air in . . .' as she does it. She's done it to make a Sam point: don't let yourself go just because I'm not here. I slam the window shut and light a fag. Point taken.

I could put my tears down to the drink but, really, should anyone have to go through what I have today? How can someone who snuggled so close, requesting love and giving it in return, who promised to stay in sickness and in health, for richer and poorer, and everything in between, suddenly turn out to be so merciless?

If I had mates, the kind of mates you go for a drink with, they'd tell me, 'That's women for you, mate,' and they'd be right. Even Sam, who I never doubted I would go to my grave loving. Even her.

It's the note, of course, that I study for any signs of regret, compassion or hints at reconciliation. Before I even read it I hold it up to the light, inspecting it carefully for tell-tale tear-stain wrinkles. If she cried when she wrote it, and judging by the new emotion-lite Sam, I doubt that she did, there's nothing on the paper to prove it.

The note says:

Chris,
    Your note was lovely, but I'm afraid it doesn't change things. Please use this time to try to take hold of your life,
    Sam

PS Please don't phone again. And that aftershave stunt? I thought you were above that kind of thing.

I try reading it with the emphasis on different words. I read it using her voice. I read it slowly, and then I read it very quickly.

But however much I read it, nothing about it changes. In fact, the more I read it, the starker it becomes. Only the word 'lovely' betrays any kind of feeling. The lack of Xs as kisses, the absence of 'Love, Sam' or even 'Dear Chris', all tell me far more than the note itself does. And I suppose I've got to come to terms with that.

To help me do so and despite, or maybe because of, the fact that I'm already drunk, I decide once more to take advantage of the shop's eight-cans-of-Stella-for-six-pounds deal.

Inside the shop I make a minor social *faux pas*, which, ironically, I do in the name of forging better relations with the staff. 'Can I have that on the tab, then?' I say, hoisting two four-packs of Stella up to the counter.

Behind the counter, the woman's eyes move nervously. 'Sorry,' she says, managing to make the word sound neither like a question nor an apology.

'Credit,' I say jocularly, indicating the handwritten notice behind her that says, 'Do Not Ask For Credit', although I could be pointing at the one that says, 'Examine Change Please, Mistakes Cannot Be Rectified Later', or the one that says, 'Two Schol Children Only At Once'.

'Sorry,' she repeats, and she's now assumed a look that you see shopkeepers in American films adopt just before they foolishly go for a gun hidden beneath the counter.

'It's all right,' I say. 'Just a joke. Your notice . . .'

The penny drops. 'Ah, credit.' She smiles a little uncertainly, enough to tell me that she hasn't got the joke, or doesn't think it's funny, or has got it, and doesn't think it's funny and doesn't really want to join in. 'Sorry,' she repeats for the third time. 'Six pounds.'

I hand over the six pounds and leave, feeling stupid.

Once I get home I put seven of the Stellas into the fridge – in full, triumphant view – and take one into the lounge, placing my fags and lighter beside it. Then I go through to the spare room where my hand hovers over the box for *Danny Baker's Own Goals and Gaffs* (which actually contains *Sandy and the Students*), but decide that tonight is not the night, and instead choose *Star Wars*, a fitting tribute to my father. I watch it until I fall asleep. It's a pleasant way to spend a Sunday night.

Except, of course, it's not.

I wanted civilised and pleasant and some kind of return to normality. What I get instead is me. And try as I might, civilised and pleasant just isn't my default setting at the moment. So what happens is this.

At four cans, I'm feeling extremely civilised and pleasant, and I decide some corn-on-the-cob would be nice, so I fetch some from the freezer and put a pot of water on to boil. While I'm waiting for that to happen, I decide it would be extremely civilised and pleasant to drink some more lager, so I do.

After six cans, I remember the boiling water, which has now boiled dry, so I put another pot on to boil, and this time I put the corn-on-the-cob straight in. What the fuck? I think. What the fuck difference does it make? I set the microwave timer so I won't forget about the corn-on-the-cob.

After eight cans, I decide to have a quick 'watch' of *Sandy and the Students*, then I go to the shop for more lager.

After nine, I decide to ring Sam. I can't recall the exact details of the conversation, but I remember screeching, 'I am *not* drunk,' down the phone. I am, of course, very drunk, and quite rightly, Sam puts down the phone. Presumably, at some point during a period in which I repeatedly phone her mobile, keep getting her voicemail and either redial or scream increasingly abusive messages, the microwave pings to tell me the corn-on-the-cob is done.

At ten cans, I am opening the kitchen window to try to get rid of the stench of burnt corn-on-the-cob, which has filled the entire flat. I throw the blackened husk, complete with charred saucepan, straight into a black bin liner.

At eleven cans, I sit on the sofa and clear the coffee table, placing my father's shoebox on it and drunkenly inspecting his gun. I put the gun to my head and pretend to be Robert de Niro in *The Deer Hunter*.

At eleven and a half cans, I decide it's time for bed and make my way down the hall to the bedroom. I get there, but I don't get as far as undressing. I pass out face down on the bed.

Which is where I wake up at exactly seven fifteen on Monday morning.

I know what time it is because our alarm clock bleeps to say so, and I wake with a sudden start, feeling unaccountably fresh apart from a racking cough that seems, nevertheless, to kick-start my system into life.

For a moment or so – the clock still bleeping – I lie there wondering why Sam's head isn't resting on the pillow next to me. First I think, She's away on business. Then I remember and I reach to turn off the alarm clock, which isn't 'our' alarm clock any more, it's 'my' alarm clock.

I roll off the bed thinking, stupidly, Cool. Already dressed, and then I wander through to the lounge, sniffing the thick, sticky, burnt air, wondering why the flat smells so bad.

Then, with a jolt, I remember the corn-on-the-cob and it's just the first of a series of memories that line up to take punches at my head: the phone call to Sam, the voicemail messages . . .

A car beeps in the road outside.

It's obvious that the night involved at least one other trip down to the shop. There are cans of Stella everywhere: on the floor, on the mantelpiece, on top of the stereo, everywhere apart from one place – the coffee table.

The car beeps again and I hear the baby start crying next door.

The coffee table is completely clean. There is only one thing on it, and from my position in the middle of the lounge I stare at it now, feeling the beginnings of worry gnawing at my stomach.

In the middle of the coffee table is the gun.

I remember now, looking at the gun last night, putting it to my head.

The car beeps a third time, long and insistent.

I look at the gun; wish I could use it to blow the driver's fucking brains out.

Taking a deep breath, I banish murderous thoughts and wrap the gun back in its tea-towel, stowing it in a cupboard – you never know who might come round. Then, shakily, I take a bath and imagine the water realigning all my organs, trying, by sheer force of will, to think myself into a state fit enough to go to work. I shave using Sam's Mariah Carey CD as a mirror (well, Sam, if you will take the mirror . . .), and I'm pleased to scruff the shameful grit from my skin.

I chug two garlic capsules and chase them with boiling black coffee. Burp once, twice, three times a lady.

I iron a white shirt with extra-special care and I even pull out the Shine-on to give my shoes a touch of polish. A smart appearance can hide a lot of deficiencies, I think, knotting my tie, scraping my eyebrows into shape and using my hands to brush my hair flat. Just a smart-dressed gent who had a few too many over a curry last night, that's all. That accounts for the breath, and the sweat that constantly accumulates along my top lip. For insurance, I douse myself in aftershave, even rehearsing, 'Yeah, bloody well spilt it, didn't I?' in preparation for the inevitable, 'Fucking hell, Chris, you smell like a whore's boudoir.' Better to be a spastic with a bottle of aftershave than an alcoholic, I reason.

Lastly, I go tonto with the eyedrops – another of my top tips for the heavy drinker. They don't exactly banish the problem of having peepers like the proverbial pissholes in the snow, but they mask it. You can maybe get away with claiming a touch of mild conjunctivitis.

And all the time I'm taking deep, steadying breaths, and

trying to ignore the state of the lounge and my own emotions slopping around inside me, which are constantly threatening to spill over on to the outside. And I can't let that happen.

I just about manage it, I reckon. When I'm ready to leave I think I've made a fairly good fist of my preparations. Hardly fresh as a daisy but surely good enough to pass muster. A little rough around the edges, perhaps. But I'll hide it well, I always do.

CHAPTER NINETEEN

Shortly after Christopher Sewell was sentenced to life imprisonment at Larksmere Prison in Leicestershire, Prison Officer Jack Barker was summoned to the governor's office there.

As Jack arrived, the governor was sitting at his desk talking to another man seated to the side of him. The two were drinking tea, and not out of mugs either, not the way Jack and his colleagues drank their tea, in long slurps followed by satisfied sighs. They drank from teacups, holding saucers below them. They didn't drink tea, they 'took' tea.

The second man in the office was Dr Joshua Oakley, the prison psychiatrist. Dr Oakley wore waistcoats and was occasionally seen striding through the corridors of the prison deep in thought and carrying large files under his arm. Jack had barely spoken to him before now, and the short nod he gave him as he took his seat was an indication of the status of their relationship. In return, however, Dr Oakley smiled warmly and openly at Jack. He and the governor had a favour to ask of him. Warm, open smiles were therefore the order of the day.

'Jack,' said the governor, smiling warmly and openly at his visitor. 'Please, take a seat.'

Jack was already sitting. 'Thank you, sir,' he said, wishing he'd waited.

The governor waved away his awkwardness. 'Tea, Jack?' he said, more warm and open than Jack had ever seen him. There was something about the scene that added to his discomfort: the two men had clearly been talking as they took tea together, and now they both regarded Jack with welcoming smiles painted across their faces like ill-fitting hand-me-down clothes. To Jack they looked like two ageing but murderous landladies who kept the bodies of dead guests beneath the floorboards of their Scarborough guest-house.

'No, thank you,' said Jack. Aside from his unease, he wasn't quite sure he was ready to make the leap from 'drinking' tea to 'taking' it. Not just yet.

'Fine, well, I think you know Dr Josh, don't you?' said the governor, indicating to his side, where the portly Dr Josh sat with a biscuit crumb clinging to his bottom lip.

Dr Oakley was not fond of being referred to as Dr Josh, he felt it undermined his intellectual authority, which he liked to cultivate at all times. When he was spotted by the likes of Jack, striding through the corridors apparently deep in thought and distracted, that was exactly the image he planned. He might well have been deep in thought, but it was unlikely he was concerning himself with weighty psychological matters. In fact, he was probably musing on how he might gain a lasting name for himself in the world of psychology and beyond. A name that would find him no longer striding the corridors of Larksmere Prison wearing loud waistcoats, but striding the corridors of the BBC wearing loud, and more expensive, waistcoats.

His role model in this endeavour was Paul Britton[18], who had begun his work in Leicestershire – he might well have worked at Larksmere – but who had become something of a famous name thanks to his books and television appearances. Dr Oakley also planned to write books and appear on television, an authoritative and avuncular voice. And who knows? Perhaps his predilection for vivid waistcoats might catch the eye of a producer with, say, a breakfast television programme. Perhaps he, Dr Oakley, could be the resident psychiatrist on *GMTV*, helping people with their problems, like TV's *Frasier*, or maybe giving a 'psychologist's view' on

---

[18] Forensic psychologist Paul Britton helped to pioneer offender profiling and has written two books on the subject, *The Jigsaw Man*, and *Picking Up the Pieces* (both Corgi).

celebrity gossip of the day – a slot they might call 'Shrink Rapping'.

Of course, if that happened, he supposed he'd have to get used to being called Dr Josh. No doubt *GMTV* would insist upon it – so much more approachable and friendly for their viewers. Dr Josh and his waistcoats – a 'shrink rapping'. Yes, he could live with the undermining of his intellectual authority if that were the case.

But first, this.

Under his very nose, Dr Josh had the one patient the whole country wanted to see on the couch: Christopher Sewell.

Had Christopher Sewell submitted himself willingly to Dr Josh's examination, he would not have been sitting in the governor's office smiling warmly and openly at a slightly overweight, fidgety-looking prison officer called Jack. He would be writing his eagerly awaited paper this very second.

But Sewell had resisted all overtures, stubbornly refusing to talk about his state of mind, the murder, anything. This irked Dr Josh. This breakthrough case, the psychological paper, the documentary teams and the phone call from the people at *GMTV*. So near, yet so far.

Happily, Dr Josh had an ally in the governor. For whatever reasons – but in fact they were not too far from his own – Sewell was a nut the governor was just as eager to crack. Both he and Dr Josh, it seemed, were as keen to escape this prison as most of the inmates.

Now the governor leant forward in his chair to address Jack, his expression moving from warm and open to serious and complicit. It suited him better.

'Jack,' he said, 'there's something the doctor and I would like to discuss with you.'

'Sir?' replied Jack, thinking, It's about Chris. This has got to be about Chris.

'It's about Sewell,' said the governor. 'Now, I think I'm correct in saying that you're very close to Sewell. Is that right?'

'That's right, sir. Yes.'

The doctor and the governor exchanged a glance, each at that moment thinking himself a Machiavellian genius.

On the other side of the desk, pinned by the twin glare of the two men's attentions, Jack braced himself for the inevitable.

It was true, he had rather attached himself to Christopher Sewell, become his unofficial minder, if you like. So far, nobody had said anything, but now it looked like that was going to change. Presumably the governor was about to haul him over the coals for being star-struck by the prison's most famous inmate and neglecting his other duties. In his defence he could argue – truthfully – that he hadn't been neglecting his other duties. But had he been paying too much attention to Christopher Sewell? Well, yes, your honour, yes, he had.

But the expected roasting did not come. Instead, the governor simply smiled, saying, 'Good, good ... Now, Jack, as you know, Sewell has continually resisted any attempts to talk about himself and his crime. Our psychological information on the man,' here he nodded at Dr Josh, who acknowledged the gesture with a nod of his own, 'is limited to observation only. Are you with me, Jack?'

Jack thought so, but he wasn't certain. He nodded anyway.

'And this is a situation we'd like to change,' continued the governor. 'We feel it would be beneficial for Sewell, and for future cases, if we were able to build up a thorough psychological profile of the man. Are you with me, Jack?'

Jack thought so, but he wasn't certain. He nodded again. He wished the governor would stop asking if he was with him.

'Clearly, Dr Josh here,' they did the nod-return-nod thing again, 'is the best man to draw up this profile, but first he needs an "in" so to speak. In order to draw Sewell out of himself, he needs to be pressing the right buttons. Which is where you come in.'

Suddenly Jack understood what the governor was getting at. 'Sir,' he said, 'I think I get you, sir. But the thing is, I'm only friendly with Chris – with *Sewell* – on a certain level, sir. I've never had the impression that he would open up to me, sir.'

He felt himself reddening as he said it, as if he'd spoken out of turn.

'Quite,' said the governor. 'We'd considered that. So we have a plan, so to speak.'

Dr Josh took up the story, leaning forward in his seat to speak to Jack. 'Our friend Sewell,' he said, 'has let it be known through his solicitor that he'd like to give an interview to a journalist. Just one. And we're going to let him have it.'

'Isn't that against prison policy, sir?' said Jack, blushing again.

The governor and Dr Josh shared another look.

'It's, um, *irregular*, Jack,' said the governor.

'Justified,' added the doctor, 'in this case, by what we hope to achieve.'

'You see, Jack,' took up the governor, 'if Sewell is talking to a journalist, then he can also be talking to us, giving us just the ammo we need to unlock him. Are you with me, Jack?'

'I suppose so, sir.'

'Listen, this one interview is all anybody gets. And what the hack does with it is none of our concern. It's going to be like finding Willy Wonka's golden ticket for whoever gets it but as I say, none of our concern. The journalist will be made aware that they can't reveal how they came by the information, but they'll go away happy. Sewell will be happy because he's given the interview he so desires and we'll be happy because we'll have the information we need. In other words, everybody will be happy. Are you with me, Jack?'

'Absolutely, sir.'

'Now, what I'm asking you to do is in no way underhand, illicit or illegal. Understand?'

'Sir.'

'But here's the rub. It must be kept quiet for the sake of propriety. If it becomes common knowledge that we're granting lifers media interviews all hell will break loose. Which is why I'm choosing you, my man on the landing, as it were.' At this the governor smiled, as if he had just conferred a knighthood upon him. Jack smiled wanly back.

'You are to stick to Sewell – just as you have been doing – and you are also to oversee the visits of whoever gets the golden ticket. Inside this prison only you and I and Dr Josh will know exactly why they're here. We'll be doing the visiting orders under the guise of legal visits. The journalist will be allowed a tape-recorder but absolutely no other equipment, and you are to sit in on all of the interviews, which will be conducted weekly and for no more than ninety minutes at a time. Understood?'

Jack did understand, and was now growing to like what he heard, his initial worries dissolving into nervous excitement.

'And after each session, you will have a chat with Dr Josh – a debrief, if you like – where you will be able to tell him what was said. How does that sound?'

'Fine, sir.' Jack paused. 'Just one question?'

'Yes, Jack,' said the governor uneasily. He had been hoping it would be subject closed, that he could leave Jack and Dr Josh to get on with it and he could go back to dreaming of a cosy job at the Home Office, which would be impressed with his ability to achieve progress with even the most difficult inmates. Something in prison admin, perhaps.

'Well, what if someone was to find out the real reason for the journalist's visits, sir?'

'Good question, Jack,' said the governor, relaxing again. Beside him, Dr Josh also did a mental stand-down. 'The answer is, the Simms O'Brien judgement. Heard of it?'

'Can't say I have, sir.'

'Jolly good. It's a ruling that allows prisoners to see journalists in cases where they're appealing about a miscarriage of justice. God knows, that's not going to happen with Sewell – the bugger seems to like it here – but nevertheless that's the umbrella under which we can shelter if it should get out. You don't worry about that, Jack. All you need to worry about is keeping the whole thing shipshape and Bristol fashion.'

The governor leant back in his seat, glanced across at Dr Josh who looked equally pleased, though in a more corpulent way, the governor was happy to note.

'So, do we have your support, Jack?'

'You do, sir. You can rely on me.' Jack could hardly keep the smile off his face. No worries at all now, only excitement. He had just been given licence to spend a great deal more time with Chris. And if the governor was prepared to take certain risks in allowing journalists into the prison, well, that was his look-out and he obviously had his own reasons for doing so. Nothing to do with Jack. 'Ours not to reason why, ours but to clean the sty,' as Fletcher said in *Porridge*.

'Thought so. That's why we chose you.'

Liar, thought Jack. You chose me because I know Chris. But he nodded deferentially anyway, standing at the same time.

'You're excused, Jack,' said the governor.

'Thank you, sir,' and Jack let himself out, nodding goodbye to Dr Josh as he did so.

Walking away from the governor's office and back to the landing, there was a certain spring in Jack's step. He didn't give a fig for the governor or Dr Josh and psychological evaluations. What he did care about was Chris Sewell, for two reasons.

First, he genuinely liked the man, whom he had come to think of as part-friend, part-responsibility. It was clear he was a man with problems, but he had certainly adapted to prison society well, seemed to welcome the regimented life, enjoyed the attention from the other prisoners and the scrutiny of the outside world. He certainly got enough post. And the canny bastard – one interview, indeed. Like he was bloody Madonna or something.

The second reason he cared about Chris was because Jack had a very special collection. His collection of celebrity-prisoner memorabilia. Up to now it had been a raggle-taggle assemblage, and so far he'd collected little of interest to other enthusiasts, usually prison officers like himself. In fact, all self-delusion aside, he had collected precisely one thing.

But he had attached himself to Chris, and now, with this new responsibility, he would be able to amass a minor gold mine of souvenirs, and easily enough to attract the attention of other collectors. Indeed, he concluded, Chris would provide the backbone of his collection. He would gain a name for himself as the world's leading resource for Christopher Sewell prison memorabilia.

He clapped his hands with a sound like a gunshot in the concrete corridor of the prison. I'm all right, thought Jack.

Later, Jack met the journalist Chris Sewell chose to conduct the interview. And once again he thought, You canny bastard.

CHAPTER TWENTY

It's almost half past nine by the time I get to the tube, meaning I'm going to be late again but what the hell? I'm the boss, it's my prerogative to be late occasionally.

Are you late a lot?

I'm late whenever I get pissed the night before. So, yes, I'm late a lot. Anyway, on the platform, other passengers seem to be casting looks in my direction, but I'm used to the paranoia of the morning-after, so I put it down to the drink. It's only when I get onto the train – after I've changed at Finsbury Park, actually – that I realise why, and that it's not the drink at all.

I realise because I take a seat and rest my hand on my chin, and absently scratch at my beard.

Funny, I think, remembering Mariah Carey, the bath, a very clear memory of pulling a razor over my skin. I move my hand surreptitiously to the other side of my face.

Which is smooth.

Back again. Scratchy and beardy.

This is bad. It seems I have shaved only half of my face.

Clearly, then, people have every right to stare. *I* would be fascinated by a man with one half of his face shaved clean, the other untouched since – when? God, since Friday morning. That's three days' stubble. That's a lot.

I run through possible reasons why the casual observer might think I've only shaved half of my face. A bet. Or perhaps they'll assume I've done it for charity. And with this in mind I begin to return the looks of the people staring at me, adopting an expression that says, 'Yeah, I know. Look a bit of a wally, don't I? Still, all for a good cause, eh?' This expression seems to involve lifting my eyebrows a lot, and before I know it I'm peering around the carriage like a spastic Roger Moore and people are looking quickly back at their books when they catch my eye, seeing me half-shaved, my eyebrows wobbling around on my forehead. They look away because that's what you do when you see a weirdo on a train.

Get a grip, Chris, I think, controlling my shaking eyebrows. The charity explanation only seems plausible if the beard is shaved cleanly half and half, and I can tell from touch that it's not. Batting away at my face like a blind man meeting himself for the first time, I feel that one side is definitely hairier than the other, but there are patches of escapees all over. A hillock here, a tuft there, a copse beneath my chin. Best to just tough it out, pop into a chemist for razors and find a toilet where I can finish the job. Still, how on earth could I have shaved just half my face? Mariah notwithstanding, it seems a peculiar error. The kind of mistake someone might make if they were a bit simple, a bit doo-lally. Not all there.

But I am all here, thank you very much. All my bits are present and correct. The most obvious explanation is that the alcohol has taken its toll, left me ragged and forgetful. Let this be an early warning to you, I think. Be grateful that you're aware of your depleted faculties and take measures to avoid more humiliation.

Meanwhile, I hide the unshaved side of my face in my hands and keep my head down until Oxford Circus, while three Numskulls in the Ablutions and Hygiene Department are flogged to within an inch of their skinny, stupid, neglectful lives.

Thank God for Boots and disposable razors and sampler-size cans of shaving foam. Thank God also for the space-age pay-as-you-go toilet cubicle on Berwick Street, into which I let myself now.

Looking in the mirror, it becomes apparent that my earlier preparations were not as successful as I'd thought. Or perhaps they had been, but the combined force of the alcohol and embarrassment has sent them awry. Sweat has matted my hair to my head and left my face with a sickly, oily sheen. And somehow I've wrenched at my tie as well, because it's now twisted so far over to one side it might have been worn by my Siamese twin.

Once again I thank my lucky stars I've spotted my mistakes before it's too late. I take it as a good omen. Fate is on my side. Leaning on the basin, I take several deep, balancing breaths, and then I open the pack of razors to finish shaving.

When I step into the lift at work I thank God it's mirrored and use the opportunity for a swift double-check. Just as I'm doing so, a beautiful blonde woman I recognise from Editorial steps in, stopping the doors expertly with her foot. She's holding a cup of coffee from Starbucks and she ignores my wan attempt at a smile. I have my revenge, though, because as the lift pulls to my floor, I dredge a silent belch from the pit of my stomach and exit the lift with the stench of Stella and garlic hanging behind me like an evil spirit. Stuck-up cow.

When I approach the *Sass* section of the sales floor I have a heart-stopping moment. Like when you were leaning too far back on your chair at school and you thought you were going to fall, but you caught yourself just in time. It's like that.

In this case it happens because, for some reason, I suddenly think I see the man who blew snot all over my coat. He's sitting in the chair next to mine as if waiting for my arrival, perhaps to empty his other nostril. He's wearing a suit, but all the same, I'm convinced it's him and I take four quick, angry strides over to the desk, ready to confront him, recapture my pride, confident on my home turf.

My mistake, of course. It's not him. The man who looks up at me, slightly taken aback by my swift, aggressive arrival, is not the snot man. His looks are in the same ballpark, it's true. And from behind you could be forgiven . . . But still. Not him. Wishful thinking on my part.

'Whoa, steady on there,' he says, his face wearing a look of amused surprise, slightly derisive at the same time.

I gather myself, regain my composure, which seems to be in short supply this morning, saying, 'Sorry. And you are?'

I'm standing. He's sitting. He reaches up a hand to shake mine – doesn't stand up. Surely he should stand up? Isn't that what you do when you meet people? Don't you stand up? Look them in the eye?

'I'm Luke,' he says. 'The new jackeroo.'

I wonder whether he was wearing that earring at the interview.

'The new Jack who?' I say. Adam and Graham are staring at me over the tops of their computers. They seem as confused as I am. I give them a look that says, 'We've got a right one here, lads,' but they don't respond. If anything they look more confused. 'I like your tie, Graham,' I blurt.

'No. Jackeroo,' explains Luke, also glancing across at Adam and Graham, his look also seeming to say, 'We've got a right one here, lads.' 'Sorry mate, I've been in Oz for the last six months. It's an Australian word. Means a newbie. Someone learning the ropes in the bush. Like a cross between Jack and a kangaroo.'

'I see,' I say, not seeing at all, thinking he's probably making it up. Clearly, Graham and Adam don't see either, judging by the way they're looking over at us, and I give them a conspiratorial smile, which I hope is reassuring too.

'The new ad-sales rep?' says Luke, again glancing over at Graham and Adam. 'We spoke on the phone. I'm the new boy. Are you Teacher?'

'Right. Yes. Of course. Welcome. I see you've found your desk. Good start. I tell you what, let me get a cup of tea and we'll go and see Geoff—'

'I've seen him actually,' interrupts Luke. 'He said, could you take me to Human Resources? Get me sworn in or something?'

There's that derisive look again, as if he expects me to rejoin with some kind of comment about how rubbish our personnel department is. I'm sure to give him a look in reply that suggests we take our personnel responsibilities very seriously; that they're not to be mocked. Indeed, that his visit to the Human Resources department is of the utmost importance. Even at this stage it's clear that Luke Radley's attitude leaves something to be desired.

'Right. Yes. Well, I tell you what. I'll get my tea after I've taken you to Human Resources.'

'Great,' replies Luke, still with a mocking edge to his voice. 'By the way, mate,' he adds, pointing up towards his nose, 'did you know you've cut yourself shaving?'

It's Luke Radley's fault that I make the biggest mistake of my day. Even, in retrospect, more calamitous than forgetting to shave one half of my face.

If he'd been slightly shy and a little lost, like Adam, or professional and businesslike, as Graham is, then he wouldn't have put me off my stride quite so completely. I knew the second I met him that he was wrong for my team. That earring, for a start. I would have to have a word with him about that. Then his mobile phone rang as I was preparing to take him to HR, and I had to tell him that we have a rule here on *Sass* magazine and it's that mobile phones have to be switched off – there are perfectly usable land lines for taking calls. To which he replied that he'd noticed someone on another magazine using theirs. To which I responded, fine, but this isn't that magazine, this is this magazine and the rule on this magazine is no mobile phones, OK? To which he replied, sure, but would it be too inconvenient if he kept his on for a couple of days, just until he'd given out his new work number? See, there was a problem on some rent owing on his old flat and he really needed to stay in touch. To which I reluctantly said yes, and, in a bid to take some kind of upper hand, congratulated him jokily on his negotiating skills, adding, 'We'll make a salesman out of you yet.'

And he said, 'Great,' with that same dollop of scorn, before asking me impertinently if I'd been 'on the sherbets' last night.

To which I replied, 'We work hard and play hard on *Sass* magazine.' At which point all remaining Numskulls in the Shame Management department were sent to the gas chamber and their families tortured to death.

Which all goes some way to explaining, or at least mitigating, my behaviour some half an hour later, when at last I go to fetch myself a cup of tea, which I'm telling myself will sort me out, put me back on the straight and narrow, and I find the kitchen in the most disgusting state – teabags in the sink, dirty spoons left out, cereal bowls piling up. And I stomp straight back to my desk and write this:

Put the Fucking Teabags in the Bin!

Which I stick up above the sink where everyone can see it, and which obviously comes from me, because later in the day Geoff Clarke calls me into his bloody office and asks me in no uncertain terms to take down the notice at once and stop concerning myself with matters in the kitchen and start concerning myself with issues such as sales targets and why L'Oréal have pulled an ad. And what do I think of young Luke Radley, got potential, yes?

I hate Luke Radley. As I go back to my desk, Adam and Graham are laughing at something he's said.

'I'm with you, mate,' says Luke to me. 'First thing I noticed when I got here. I said to myself, "That kitchen's in a terrible state . . ."'

As I take a seat I feel my hands shaking, and glance up at the clock, wishing lunch-time would hurry up.

There's another sales report I need to read in the pub.

That was you in the lift, wasn't it?

I think it may have been, yes.

It was. I remember. You clearly don't.

I'm sorry, Chris, not that particular occasion, no.

You don't even remember my special burpy present?

I'm afraid not, no.

Something tells me you'll remember me now.

Of course.

That was a line from *American Beauty*. The bit where his wife rolls up to the drivethrough with her boyfriend. Funny . . .

What's funny?

No, it's funny. It's a funny bit.

I see.

CHAPTER TWENTY-ONE

About two weeks before the sensational and shocking murder of the pop star Felix Carter, a shopfitter named Phil Coates was having a drink with four mates in a pub just off Tottenham Court Road.

They sat looking for all the world like a group of shopfitters who had just finished work, as if frozen into a satirical sketch, one in which an actor would appear from the left of the screen wearing a comedy anthropologist's beard, saying, 'And here we have the yellow-fingered shopfitters, glimpsed here in their natural habitat. First they will drink. Later they will feed.'

As with any other species, yellow-fingered shopfitters exhibited their own characteristics and these were never more visible than when they gathered in a flock. In summer, for example, the shopfitters liked to eat their lunch sitting outside whatever shop they were working on. They sat in a row on the pavement with their legs stretched out in front of them, clutching polystyrene cups of coffee and looking like a line of Bonfire Night guys. They looked incongruous among the smart shoppers and office workers hurrying past, but that's how they liked it. They took pride in being a greasy thumbprint on the window of the day.

From their sunny pavement vantage-point, the shopfitters liked to watch the world go by, liked it even more if the world was wearing the bare minimum, had tits like two puppies wrestling in a sack and didn't mind the odd playful comment in her direction. If this was the case they'd make growling sounds in the backs of their throats. Sounds like, 'furrr' or 'wurrrr'. And they'd follow up with a comment that would ideally achieve one of three purposes:

1. It would make the assembled group laugh.
2. It would make the victim feel uncomfortable or flattered, depending on whether she was 'a stuck-up bitch', or 'game', and elicit a suitable response from her, thereby making the group laugh.
3. It would draw attention to the mammoth size of the speaker's penis.

Thus, the shopfitter was mainly concerned with his relationship with his peers, with women, and with his own penis. In fact, this did not make him too different from the office workers who hurried past – the male ones at least – each of whom had similar preoccupations, and were probably admiring the wrestling puppies with just as much ardour. Only they did it privately. While the shopfitter, in his gang, lets his eyes roam greedily, the office worker steals his glances. There was no difference between the two sets of men: the shopfitters merely lifted the manhole cover off the sewer and let women look inside, that was all.

But they were only able to do so because they moved in a group. Like ants they were relatively benign individually. It was together that they were powerful. And, like ants, they looked to their leader for the codes that would define their behaviour.

In this particular group – the one sitting in the pub off Tottenham Court Road – Phil Coates was at the top of that hierarchy. He was their leader. At heart Phil was a bitter man and a natural bully. The bitterness tended to manifest itself in the guise of his hectoring, unpleasant personality, which he was fond of projecting loudly, and at length, in a manner as offensive as his huge beer gut and the tattoo of what might have been a bluebird that crept up his neck.

Like many unpleasant people, Phil was able to exert a great deal of influence over his mates who, in fact, were not mates at all but fellow workers. They'd come to the pub for a drink after work, after a hard day of shopfitting and listening to Phil's unremitting bile. Today's topic had been Pakis (smelly, money-grabbing), yesterday's was gays (unnatural, diseased), tomorrow's might be blacks ('But not you, mate, you're all right. It's the others I'm talking about').

It was a nice pub, the one they sat in, but it would have been a lot nicer without Phil Coates in it.

Individually his mates all hated Phil but, crucially, had not told each other. Sitting around the table, all guffawing loudly at Phil's loud, nasty comments, each assumed that he was alone in finding him objectionable. As a result Phil's behaviour was not only tolerated but seemingly approved of. The others were held hostage by him, frightened of saying or doing the wrong thing – anything that might make them the target of his abuse. They smoked the right brand of cigarettes ('Silk Cut? Silly cunt, more like. Fackin' poof's fag'), drank the right beer, ('Cooking lager?[19] Fackin' poof's drink. Get yourself a Stealth Bomber,[20] mate'), enough of it and at the right speed, and only ever left the pub early if they had a cast-iron excuse to do so. They brayed with laughter at each thing he said, made the right noises during his obviously fabricated stories of cheating on his wife with a woman called Laura, of getting into fights and menacing Jewish people in his van.

In other words, they were frightened of him. To the outsider they would have seemed the same. They all laughed at the same jokes; they all used the F-word with the same regularity: as a comma (f'ckin'), for definition (fackin'), or for emphasis (far-kin'), and they all looked the same. But they weren't. They were different. And the thing was, they couldn't quite put their finger on the reason why. After all, when it came down to it, Phil *was* the same as them. Hardly angels themselves, they weren't exactly full of praise and support for minorities, nor did they have a great deal of respect for women, whom they

---

[19] Any brand of lager that is lower in alcohol than a 'fighting lager'.
[20] Stella Artois.

generally preferred naked and staring at them from the pages of a magazine, or wandering past on the pavement, ready for a well-placed 'furrr'.

There was just something about Phil, something not quite right. It was as if he was driving on a different motor from the rest of them.

For example, when one made a comment about the barmaid, about her tits to be precise, Phil waded in with, 'Fackin' slag, mate. Cunt like a Grimsby welly, arse like a wizard's sleeve.'

And there was something about what he said, something accusatory, malevolent. It wasn't like they were averse to the colourful imagery used to compare a woman's private parts to a Wellington boot, or Phil's other favourite, a gutted rabbit. They were shopfitters, not social workers, after all. It was just that Phil took it too far. Something about what he said and the way he said it made them flinch. Inwardly, of course.

Still, they sat, courtiers at the table of King Phil. They drank the right beer with him and they smoked the right fags and they tried to push his tyranny to the back of their minds. To admit distaste for Phil, they imagined, was to admit they were different. Like most people, they were scared of being different.

But they weren't nearly as scared of being different as Phil was. And he was very, very different indeed.

It was shortly after the Grimsby welly comment that Phil felt something familiar buzzing against his backside. Almost immediately he stood up, ostentatiously adjusting himself at the same time. 'Right, lads,' he announced. 'Best go siphon the fackin' python. Big job. Could be a while. Don't any of you ladies get any ideas about following me in there, all right?'

Yeah, they all thought, grinning up at him as he stood. Yeah, right.

Then, just as he turned to go, he reached to the table and gave his mobile phone a spin, leaving it circling as he walked off to the toilet. It was almost as if he was trying to draw attention to it there on the table.

He was. The buzzing he felt in his back pocket was his *other* phone. The phone he used solely to speak to one person, the person who had just texted him.

He moved to the toilet as quickly as he dared, banging the door open in true Phil style. Once inside, however, his demeanour changed and he looked about quickly before reaching into his pocket for the Motorola. He pulled it out, opened it up and was scrolling to the message even as he slid into a toilet cubicle, locking the door behind him.

'Call me,' it said. There was no name to accompany the message: Phil had never entered one. He didn't need to because only one person in the world had the number. Not quite true: he got the occasional text message from BT Cellnet telling him about special offers. But other than that, just one human being in the world.

Eric, his lover.

Which tells us a lot about Phil Coates. A man so conflicted and in such denial of the fact that he was a homosexual that he spent most of his waking life insulting gays. A man so terrified of discovery that he had bought a pay-as-you-go mobile phone to keep that aspect of his life as far away as possible from his shopfitting, pub-bigot guise. A weak and frightened man, he was the thing he hated most in the world: a fat poof. Turns out Phil is not the shopfitters' king, he's their queen.

But he couldn't help himself. Now, his hand was shaking as he pressed the button for Eric's number. His guts churned and sweat prickled along his hairline. He kept one ear out for the toilet door as the number rang.

'Eric,' he said to the voice that answered, his voice low and urgent, 'what the fack are you on? I told you, no calls. Just texts.'

'I cannot use text messages,' whined Eric, from the other end. He was the other thing Phil hated most in the world: a camp poof. 'It's boring.'

Despite, or maybe because of, the other man's whingeing, Phil felt a stirring in his trousers. The python awakening. He reached to touch it through his jeans, squeezing his eyes shut with shame as he did so.

'Eric,' he whispered, hoarse, 'what do you want?'

'Well,' said the voice from the other end, full of the casual power its owner wielded over Phil, 'I thought we could get together tonight.'

'Yes,' said, Phil, registering his lover's insouciance and finding it both exasperating and unbearably sexy. Perhaps, he thought, he would be rougher with Eric tonight than usual. Time to show him who's boss.

'I've moved, darling,' said Eric, with the air of someone who moves a lot. He did. Being a rent-boy, he was moving all the time. 'I'm working in Islington at the moment.'

Phil hated being reminded that he paid for sex, and therefore paid to feel like shit; hated the knowledge that Eric was probably calling because he was low on cash and that his was a situation unique to commerce – one in which the vendor had all the power. And yet, and yet . . .

'Where, then?' he said, still listening for the door, wanting to hasten the conversation before the lads outside became suspicious.

'Oh, God,' said Eric. 'I can't be bothered to go through it now. Come to Highbury and Islington tube and call me from there.'

'Text you,' insisted Phil, sharply.

'Whatever,' replied Eric, sing-song style. 'See you later, lover.'

He rang off, and Phil stood there feeling turned on, disgusted with himself, hating his lover or, more precisely, hating the hierarchy of his love. Unconsciously, he rubbed at the tattoo on his neck, which might or might not have been a bluebird.

Then he began to write a text message, but not to Eric. This was to himself, to his other phone, which sat innocently on the table at the other side of the toilet door.

'Baby,' he wrote. 'Can you come over straight away? I want to suck your cock. Laura. XX.'

And outside in the pub his mobile phone bleeped. In a second or so, he'd return to the table, pick up his phone and announce loudly, 'Right, lads, old Coatesy is on a promise tonight.' With that, he'd drain his pint and, with his Motorola tucked safely in his back pocket, he'd take leave of his mates, on his way to see Eric.

Ideally, Phil would have liked to sprint to Warren Street tube. In the event he settled for a fast, waddling walk, his guts still churning, but with excitement, not nerves. He paid for a ticket and made his way to the Victoria Line. It was home-time for London and the crowds had started to build up. Aware of pickpockets, he occasionally touched a hand to his arse, just to check the Motorola was still there. Then he was on the platform, pushing through the crowds, using his huge girth, the unpleasantness that dripped off him, to barge on to a train then shoulder his way past a ragged-looking man carrying a briefcase just as he was about to sit down. With the seat successfully his, he met the man's baleful look with a smirk, stretched himself out and ignored the tuts of the woman sitting next to him. He closed his eyes, thought of Eric. Then stopped himself when he felt the python get hard.

At Highbury and Islington he pushed his way out again, squeezed from the doors of the train like toothpaste. But he didn't stop to roar, 'Fuck off,' in the direction of the people tutting in his wake. Instead, he was making his way down the platform to the exit, touching his arse to check for the phone.

Which wasn't there.

He stopped. Checked again. For a moment or so he looked like a man spanking himself as both hands flew to his back pockets and he searched frantically for the phone. He patted at his front pockets and had a mild feeling of relief when he touched something phone-like until he realised it was a phone, but the other one.

The Motorola had gone.

And, being an unpleasant man, Phil did not consider for a second that the phone might have slipped out of his pocket as he sat down, and that the ragged-looking man carrying the briefcase might have sat on it when he took the seat. No, he assumed he had been pickpocketed, probably as he was making his way down the platform. Pickpocketed by a black kid.

However, the rage he felt at the theft was swiftly displaced by another, more disquieting feeling. The Motorola had been where he stored Eric's number. It was a number he'd only keyed in once, when he'd added it to the address book. Other than that, well . . . although he'd stared at it many times on the screen of the phone, there was no way on earth he could remember it. And, of course, Eric had moved.

Had he been a less unpleasant man, Phil might have been able to retrieve his phone and find Eric. As it was, he never would.

And funnily enough, as he stood on the platform of Highbury and Islington station, doing the spanking-man act, he was experiencing another bit of bad luck back in the pub on Tottenham Court Road.

There, one of his mates had made an off-colour comment, to which another had replied, 'Fackin' hell, that was a Phil thing to say, that was.'

That was all it took. It was the start of a tentative conversation, after which none of Phil's mates felt they were alone in disliking him any more. As far as Phil's tyranny went, it was the beginning of the end.

CHAPTER TWENTY-TWO

I find a phone on the tube on the way home.

Have you been to the pub at lunch-time?

Of course. No doubt you were lunching at the Ivy, interviewing some film star. Me, I go to the Shakespeares' for three pints. And after that I go back to the office and stare at my computer screen for a couple of hours, then pack up my stuff and go.

As usual I get on at Oxford Circus and as usual I'm not feeling my best, so I'm looking forward to getting home. I've got good intentions for tonight. I've decided to tidy the flat, make myself a proper meal and enjoy, perhaps, just four tins in front of *The Empire Strikes Back*. At some point I'm planning to call Sam to apologise for all the calls last night, let her know I'm OK.

See, I'm aware that I've let things slip since she left. I think it's understandable, given the circumstances. I've had things on my mind – I've found a gun for one thing. But now I have to concentrate on winning Sam back, got to change my thinking. Simply put, I need to stop the bad stuff becoming worse and make the best of the good stuff.

I stand and bask in the breeze from the tunnel, announcing the oncoming train. Someone pushes past me, dangerously close to the edge of the platform. An arrogant, ambling youth, who thinks that walking close to the edge of the platform makes him cool. Momentarily, I fantasise about pushing him in front of the train, thinking how much fun it would be to watch his expression change from insolence to terror as the train bears down on him, thinking how fulfilling it would be to rid the world of one more dog-end.

But then he's gone, off to menace other passengers. And I

catch sight of myself, reflected in the train as it pulls into the platform. What I see is a man in a suit holding a briefcase. A man with a lot to lose who still, thankfully, hasn't lost it all yet. I see a man with a job, and a good one at that: one with responsibility attached, good prospects and a decent wage delivered in an intricate and difficult-to-open envelope at the end of each month. I see a man who still, touch wood, has a wife who will, touch wood, return to him to build a better and stronger relationship than ever before.

I feel like the hero who falls off the cliff. He's falling, falling, falling and, oh no, he's going to die. But then, at the last possible moment, his grasping fingers find purchase on the cliff-face and he dangles dangerously over the chasm before gradually pulling himself up, painful inch by painful inch, to defuse a ticking time bomb with just half a second to spare.

I'm him. That's what I think as I board the train, and I'm so galvanised by my resolution that I forget to be angry with the other passengers (the ones who barge on to the train while others are still trying to get off; the ones who don't move down the centre aisle, making use of all available space; the ones who refuse to move, making life difficult for people who get on; the ones who let a child take up a seat when they should have the child on their lap – no, I don't let them worry me at all).

And I'm so galvanised that I don't even get angry when I'm about to take a seat but some fat bastard builder-type shoves in front of me and sits down before I can. I don't even let it bother me when he smirks up at me with a look of self-satisfied triumph across his face. I'm above all that now, I think, looking down at him. Maybe the old Chris would have become worked up about it, but the new Chris has achieved a Buddhist-like inner serenity.

No doubt it's the fat bastard builder-type's phone that I find. And because of my new-Chris resolutions I immediately decide to return it, rather than keep it.

I find it when I finally get a seat, which is just as the train is pulling out of Highbury and Islington and the fat bastard builder-type hops up and wobbles off. Since I'm standing above him, I instantly nick in and grab the seat, and just as instantly feel something digging into my backside. With that sinking feeling you have when you realise you've sat on something, I reach behind me and feel for it, steeling myself against whatever horror could be lying on the seat on the Victoria Line.

But it's just a phone, one of those tiny, slinky phones with a flip-down mouthpiece. It's about the size of a cigarette packet, much better than mine, which is brick-like in comparison.

Remembering where I am, I make a point of holding it up to study it, doing all I can to draw attention to it, short of standing and asking whether anybody has lost it. But the other passengers look away. They adopt the sort of expressions you imagine people were wearing in news stories about girls being assaulted on crowded trains and nobody helping. I even turn to the woman sitting next to me reading a magazine and say, 'Sorry, this isn't yours, is it?' but she looks at me as if I'm holding a big shiny black dildo instead of a tiny mobile phone, so I give up and, with an exaggerated shrug and the Roger Moore raising of the eyebrows, I slip the phone into my inside jacket pocket.

Maybe the other passengers will think I'm going to steal it, but I'm not, I'm going to give it back. So I don't care what they think: I'm given sanctuary from their suspicion by righteousness.

I'm about to light a cigarette to celebrate my safe passage through the estate when I decide to go to the off-licence instead. Give the local shop the night off, I think, ward off any mounting notions they might have about my Stella intake. If that's the reason behind their failure to embrace me as a regular and valued customer, then a spot of retail adultery can't hurt.

Inside, I waver over the usual eight, but instead resolve to take just four, then light a cigarette once I get outside. Almost immediately I think a spot of Stella would go down nicely with my Marlboro, and after hesitating just long enough to decide that it's a pretty scummy area anyway, and nobody's really going to turn a hair to see a weary businessman enjoying a tin of Stella on his walk home, I pop the first can.

It goes down quickly – old habits dying hard there – so I pop the second one, still smoking and feeling a good deal more sprightly for the first, nevertheless deciding that I'll savour this one, sip it rather than gulp it down. Alkies gulp. And, anyway, I've only got four: I want to make them last.

Then, suddenly, I feel a thumping in my chest, and my first thought is, Fuck, heart-attack. All these years of heavy boozing and smoking, my father's death, Sam leaving, the guilt, the gun, Luke Radley – it's all come to a head and I'm having a heart-attack right here in the street.

And then I realise that it's not a heart-attack at all, because the feeling isn't coming from inside my chest: it's coming from my inside pocket. And, if I'm honest, it's not really a thumping either. It's more like a polite vibrating sensation, and it's coming from the phone I found on the tube.

Weird, I think. Fat bastard builder-types tend to have loud novelty rings on their phones, designed to draw maximum attention to themselves. This one's set to vibrate. Maybe it doesn't belong to the bloke on the tube at all, but to someone else entirely.

Either way, this, I think, is likely to be the owner calling to locate their lost mobile, and I feel a surge of nobility as I remember my Good Samaritan intentions.

Because I've got a tin of lager in one hand and a cigarette in the other, I have to stop on the pavement, put down the can, stick the fag in my mouth and fish around in my inside pocket for the phone, all the time fretting that it'll transfer straight to voicemail.

But it doesn't, and at last I flip down the mouthpiece, vaguely registering how cool that action feels, and maybe I should upgrade my own and, hey, perfect opportunity what with me deciding on a new start and all . . .

And I press the green button and say, brightly, 'Hello?' anticipating the sound of a grateful voice, expecting to share a few moments of laughing relief and then, perhaps, a meeting later, in a pub, say, where the appreciative owner – whoever it turns out to be – will buy me a beer or two to thank me for my honesty. Who knows? Maybe we'll spark up a little friendship before both going our separate ways, comforted that there is such a thing as values in this cold, cruel world of ours.

But that doesn't happen.

'You fucking cunt!' bellows a voice from the other end. Except, because the owner of the voice is clearly a London boy, born and bred, the words come out as 'You fackin' cant.'

My mouth tries to say something, but no words come. My speech capabilities are paralysed by shock and, anyway, the Cockney – obviously the fat bastard builder from the tube – is already in full flow.

'You fackin' light-fingered cant. I 'ope you're fackin' pleased wiv yourself. You cant. I 'ope you catch fackin' cancer and die, you fackin' cant.'

Momentarily confused by the cancer comment I catch myself looking at the cigarette in my hand then glancing around, as if it's not the phone's owner at all but some anti-smoking fundamentalist across the street. That's how caught off balance I am. But then, like waking up to the doorbell, it dawns on me what's happening.

How do you describe the fury? They call it a red mist and with good reason. All I know is that my inner serenity is suddenly destroyed, replaced by a torrent of rage; a bitch's brew of injustice and hurt filtered through two cans of Stella. Not only did this bloke nick my seat, now he's accusing me of stealing his phone.

'Fuck off, barrow boy!' I scream into the phone, holding it right up to my mouth, surprised by my own anger. 'Fuck off!'

If he's saying anything in return I don't hear him. The phone is up to my mouth like a microphone. I'm spitting at it as I scream: 'You want your facking phone! Here's your facking phone!'

And with that I take it away from my mouth and I throw it as hard as I can at the pavement, a real slam-dunker of a throw.

Given the velocity with which I hurl it at the concrete, it's not surprising to see it smash into a lot more than two pieces, four at the very least, bouncing off the pavement, some of it flying into the road where the pieces join broken glass and wrappers from Perfect Fried Chicken. One large bit of silver plastic remains on the pavement and I stamp on it – 'Fucker!' – then kick it, sending it skidding down the road.

With nowhere else left for my fury to go, no more plastic bits to mutilate, I stand and take stock, shaking and trying to control my anger as if fighting the urge to vomit.

'Fucker,' I spit. 'Fucking bastard. Fucking Cockney cunt. Fucking ungrateful cunt.'

There's a teenager walking up the other side of the street towards the estate, regulation baseball cap and earring. He doesn't need to shout, 'Weirdo!' but does anyway.

'Fuck off!' I yell back, anger adrenaline still racing around my veins. He gives me the finger back, and I wonder what happened to the good old V-sign. He walks on and I notch up a minor victory.

I'm surprised by my anger, but more surprised to find that it's a pleasant surprise: I feel good, cleansed.

It's not like I've saved a handicapped child from a burning building, or donated to Comic Relief, or even given a pound to a homeless man squatting by a cash machine but, still, it's a personal good feeling. Like I've achieved something, but just for me.

And when at last I pick up my briefcase and can of Stella, which I drain in one long and deeply satisfying gulp, and carry on walking towards home, I have the words of Travis

Bickle from *Taxi Driver* looping round and round in my head.

'Here is a man who *would not* take it any more. Who *stood up*.'

By the time I come to the shop near the flat, I have just one can nestling in the bottom of my crinkly plastic bag.

There's no decision to make. I ditch the bag in a bin, stick the remaining can out of sight in my coat pocket and step into the shop, intending once again to benefit from its eight-cans-for-six-pounds offer.

Only the offer has ended.

Naturally, I don't realise this until after I've lugged all eight cans to the counter, a manoeuvre that takes two trips to the chiller cabinet and back. Before, the offer had been explained by a handwritten piece of card (they're big on handwritten signs in this shop), which I'd taken for granted so failed to notice its disappearance. Stella, it turns out, is now being offered at 99p a can, with no concession to the bulk-buyer.

But I don't know this yet, and I'm holding across my six pounds – a five-pound note and a one-pound coin – wondering why the shop assistant, the same one who failed to get my joke about credit the other day, is taking so long to punch in the numbers on the till.

'Seven ninety-two,' she says, and stretches out her hand. Our two hands are held across the counter towards one another but, in a fine analogy of our relationship, failing to meet.

'Six,' I reply, firmly. 'Eight cans. Six pounds.' The adrenaline from my earlier show of assertiveness has yet to fade away and it's left me feeling jumpy, on edge. Not confident, necessarily. More . . . brittle.

'Offer close,' she replies, dead-eyed. 'Seven ninety-two.' And she uses her other hand to point at the back of the till and the little window displaying the amount owed: £7.92, it says.

Not: 'Actually, the offer has closed but I'll make one last

exception because it's you, and you come in here, oh, *every day*.'

Not even: 'I'm terribly sorry, that offer has closed, but we are now selling six cans of Foster's for five pounds if you want that instead.'

I think: Temper. Control. I do not want to shriek, 'Don't they have manners where you people come from?' because that would be a racist generalisation and I was not brought up to be a racist. I was brought up to be polite, kind and even-tempered. And, after all, if they want to stop the Stella offer that's their prerogative, I'm as much to blame for taking their (*fucking stupid*) sign for granted, even if I do have the nagging and, let's face it, ridiculously paranoid feeling that the reason they've stopped the Stella offer is because I buy so much of it, and one easy way to make more money from me is to put the Stella up in price.

'I see. Right,' I say, and pull away my coat to dig in my trouser pocket for change. There's another pound coin, that makes seven pounds. And a 50p piece, and a 20p and a ten and some coppers . . .

Somebody behind me tuts; a car blaring Eminen passes outside.

I can only cobble together seven pounds eighty-nine pee. Threepence short.

'I've got seven eighty-nine,' I say holding it all out.

'Seven ninety-two,' she says, her hand still outstretched, like a beggar, making no move to take my money.

'I'm only three p short . . .' I offer.

'Seven pounds ninety-two,' she says, her eyes darting now, that 'trouble looming' look. She's got that same gonna-go-for-my-gun expression she had the last time.

It's a Mexican stand-off. Until at last I say, 'Look, I come in here almost every day. I'm a regular customer, and should therefore be a valued customer. In this instance threepence is an extremely small sacrifice to make in an effort to keep me happy and retain my custom . . . Moreover, if you take into account the fact that I regularly invite you to "keep the change," then in fact *you* owe *me* money, easily enough to cover the threepence deficit here.'

Only I don't say that.

I will say it – later, over and over to myself. But instead what I say is, 'Well, I'll have to put one back,' and, as a small act of insurrection, don't *actually* go and put it back, just leave it there on the counter for someone else to replace, and exit the shop, barging past a huge tutting black woman, the fury returning.

We had Mr Watts for Commerce at school. I sat next to Toby Thorpe, who had 'Gene Loves Jezebel' written on his pencil case and 'Sisters of Mercy' stencilled ornately on an army-surplus-style schoolbag.

We sat behind Kim Crawford, whom we both fancied. In fact, if I remember correctly, the whole school fancied her, but she was kind of off-limits on account of her going out with Tom Barnes who had left school but was to be found outside the gates at the end of each day, smoking and lounging against his motorbike, waiting for Kim.

Apart from fantasising about spunking up the back of Kim Crawford's neck, I learnt something in Commerce. I learnt the difference between the various kinds of retailers, and the advantages and disadvantages of each.

Mr Watts told us, and we duly wrote it down, that the disadvantages of the sole trader – which is what my local shop would be classed as – was the lack of choice and the expense of the goods compared to the chains of supermarkets.

The advantage, though – and I remember this very clearly as I walk home boiling with fury, injustice again, impotence – was the friendly, *personal* service. I seem to recall him mentioning something about credit as an example of the friendly and personal service offered by the local shop.

I'm thinking about Mr Watts and his bald patch, and the back of Kim Crawford's neck and whether or not she was the first girl at school to get her hair bobbed like that, and of Leicester and so, inevitably, of my father . . .

But most of all, as I get back to the flat and pop another tin of Stella, I'm thinking of what Mr Watts told us about the sole trader and how that information has turned out to be false. And I'm thinking how desperately *unfair* that is. And I wish that I could do something to make that feeling go away for good.

CHAPTER TWENTY-THREE

About two weeks before the sensational and shocking murder of the pop star Felix Carter, a television researcher called Russ Phillips spent his first proper pay-cheque on a PlayStation 2 and a copy of the game *Metal Gear Solid 2*.[21]

Metal Gear Solid 2 was a sequel to *Metal Gear Solid* on PlayStation 1, which was Russ's favourite game of all time. You controlled a character called Solid Snake and, unlike the majority of games (at least until *Metal Gear Solid*), success was based not on a quick trigger finger and a deadly arsenal, but on stealth, guile and cunning. It also boasted a storyline that would put most movies to shame, and a plot almost as advanced as his other favourite games, the *Final Fantasy* series. The combination of action, stealth and story had proved irresistible to Russ – indeed, to most gamers – and he'd therefore been looking forward to the sequel with a mix of high expectation and trepidation. That his financial straits had forced him to wait before buying a PlayStation 2 had only increased his ardour. Now, as he switched it on and watched the advanced processing power of the machine at work, he felt something like a great calm wash over him, a sense of coming home, of completeness.

Russ had installed his new PlayStation 2, which came in black, in his bedroom. He lived in a communal flat in Fulham with four other lads of around his age (early twenties) who all had similar media-orbiting jobs and were all slightly differing facsimiles of one another. Central to their life was the house PlayStation (the original grey colour). It provided a basis for

---

[21] Published by Konami.

many of their group activities, established a hierarchy within the house and encouraged a healthy sense of competition between the boys, who were all young pups, as enthusiastic as Teletubbies about their lives.

None, though, was as serious about their games as Russ, which was why he felt no compunction about squiring his new purchase straight to his room and staying in there with it. Selfish as it sounds, it was not a miserly act on his behalf. Indeed, he was a very giving young man. The other lads knew and understood, and they were in the front room now, loudly playing ISS Pro and listening to the Aphex Twin, the way young men in their early twenties breaking into the fringes of London's media scene do. Anyway, the old grey PlayStation they were using belonged to Russ so, quite frankly, he could do what he wanted.

However, despite his newly purchased feeling of completeness, Russ found his mind wandering from the gorgeous-looking graphics leaping around his television screen. He found his mind wandering back to work, his new work at Bottom Drawer Productions where he was a junior researcher with a Monday tea-time entertainment show called *Happy Monday*.

Specifically, someone at work: Fiona Wallace.

Fiona, or Fi as she was called, had started on the same day as him, also as a junior researcher. She, too, had not long left a media-studies course at university. She, too, lived with a group of young, excitable friends in a similarly affluent area of London: Chiswick. Russ doubted whether Fi and her friends spent their evenings crowded around a PlayStation, but the similarities were already enough to bewitch him. And if the similarities didn't, then Fi's looks did – blonde, compact, really well dressed, slight, a sexy plum in the mouth.

He was a very giving young man, as we've said. And he'd have loved to give Fiona one.

In place of having Fi in his room, ready and willing to be on the receiving end of 'one', Russ decided to do the next best thing, which was to have a wank. So he paused his game, and with stealth worthy of Solid Snake, moved his chest of drawers just enough to block the door to his room. Of course, the lads knew they all masturbated. They regularly borrowed each other's magazines, and there were communal DVDs, which were, no doubt, used on the rare occasions when any one of them found himself alone in the house. But, still, it wouldn't do to be caught in the act, so to speak. The piss-take would be endless. So, not only did Russ take precautions to block his door, he also turned down the volume of his Kruder and Dorfmeister CD before reaching beneath his bed for an old copy of the Media *Guardian*, already the repository for several previous masturbatory encounters. Not that he found the Media *Guardian* erotic or stimulating in any way – he wasn't sick. Instead, he closed his eyes and summoned the image of Fi.

First he located her walking along a corridor at the Bottom Drawer studios, a clipboard hugged to her chest. She was wearing a tight cropped T-shirt above baggy trousers and she looked good – great, in fact. Even so, the clipboard against the chest wouldn't do. So, having located her image, he took away the clipboard and then, just for good measure, took off the T-shirt too.

Next he moved her into his bedroom where he had her remove her trousers, slowly unbuttoning the fly and looking down at herself as she did so. With the trousers off, and Fi naked – no knickers, wow – Russ moved her to the window-sill, which he widened for her benefit, and she sat there, smoking a cigarette and regarding him with seductive eyes.

Russ sensed movement on the landing outside his room and stopped, the image of Fi on his window-sill evaporating in a puff of cigarette smoke. He steeled himself against the sound as he heard, who? Was it Tom? Someone, anyway, moving to their own room, singing, rummaging noisily for something, then exiting the room, banging the door loudly behind them and taking the stairs two at a time. Russ let out a slow breath and started again, trying to recall the same image of Fi.

For a moment or so, he struggled, then he had her back on the window-sill, smoking, seductive eyes. Her legs, crossed – painted toenails, wow – dangling over his PlayStation 2. He kept her there for as long as he needed, which was not long. Just until he came with three wet splats on to the pages of the Media *Guardian*.

For a second or so he proudly regarded the topmost splat – quite a shot, he thought – which had landed right on an advert saying, 'Help me, I'm drowning!' then put himself away. He went back to his PlayStation 2, wishing that Fi's painted toenails really were dangling above it.

Trouble was, Fi didn't much like Russ. In fact, at the exact moment she had been sitting, smoking and naked, on his window-sill, in reality she was telling a friend all about him, in not exactly glowing terms.

'He's a spod-boy,' she said, over coffee in the kitchen of their communal Chiswick flat. 'He's got all the right clothes, but you take them off and he's a geek-o-zoid underneath.'

'So?' said her friend, Sarah, who was doing work experience at *Zest* magazine and was madly jealous that Fi had a proper job, and in television as well. The cow. God, what *she* would do for a job in TV.

In this way, the girls' house really was a mirror-image of the boys'. They were all snapping at the heels of a job in the media, either just starting out, in the case of Russ and Fi, or trying, like Sarah, via work experience, where they imagined themselves at the heart of whatever discipline they had chosen, even though they were principally used to make tea.

'So?' repeated Fi. 'Well, he's just a spoddo. He's always saying stuff like, "Oh, that's just like *Final Fantasy*." And, you know, it's like the other guys in the office know what he's talking about. It's, like, *soooo* annoying.'

The way she was talking, Sarah thought maybe Fi really did

want to remove his clothes and find the geek-o-zoid beneath, but she kept her mouth shut on that one. Wisely.

Fi was in full stride. 'The thing is, right, he's so in competition with me. That's what it is. I've put my finger on it now, that's why he's winding me up like this. Sorry, I'm really using you as a sounding board, aren't I?'

'No, that's all right, I don't mind,' replied Sarah. She did mind, really.

'Always trying to impress the producers, always coming up with ideas. And whenever he does – say, at a meeting – he always looks across at me. He's got this triumphant look on his face. If only, if only I'd started there before him . . . It's probably because I'm a girl. He's probably got this real lads' club thing going on where they can all talk about video games and stuff.'

Sounded fine to Sarah, she quite liked video games. Sounded better than doing work experience at *Zest* magazine, at any rate. 'Look,' she said at last, breaking Fi's largely nonsensical train of thought, 'you're great. You're really clever and talented and gorgeous-looking. You don't need to worry about him. He's probably not in competition with you, he's probably trying to impress you. And if he's looking at you, it's probably because he fancies you.'

'Ugh,' replied Fi, swatting imaginary flies away from her arm. 'Ugh.'

Sarah chided herself mentally for going down the old ego-boost route. Didn't seem to have worked, anyway. 'You've got this awards thing tomorrow night, haven't you?' she said.

That was true. The next evening the staff of *Happy Monday* were decamping to Alexandra Palace for a low-level TV awards ceremony. The *Happy Monday* host, an ex-radio DJ called Hughie, was the compère.

'Yeah?' said Fi.

'Well, you know, that's your chance. Glam up. Be Kool and the Gang. Show 'em what you're made of.'

Fi looked at Sarah as if she didn't quite know what the other girl meant. Sarah sent her a knowing look of her own, as if she did know what she'd meant, which she didn't. Well, she did. What she meant was: just fuck the guy and get it over with. But she didn't dare say that.

CHAPTER TWENTY-FOUR

Here's another piece of advice for the heavy drinker: of all the alcoholic drinks available, vodka is the only one – at least, the only one I know of – that leaves no trace on your breath. Did you know that?

No, I didn't.

Well, it is. And this is what I'm thinking, standing in front of an open kitchen cupboard, eyeing a gift pack of Absolut vodka miniatures inside. Five little bottles of vodka, each a different flavour – Citron, Mandrin, Peppar, unflavoured and Kurant – all tastefully presented in clear plastic packaging. I can't remember where they came from, probably a Christmas present or office raffle prize. Neither can I remember how long they've been there, but they've obviously been there for some time, just gradually blending into the geography of the cupboard, up there on the top shelf with the 'things we don't use much', like little glass dessert bowls for Angel Delight and melon balls, a packet of cocktail sticks, some paper cups still in their Cellophane, and some Tupperware that Sam's mum gave us even though we didn't really want it – we just took it to be polite.

The miniature vodka bottles might have remained hidden in plain sight were it not for the fact that I was in desperate need of Alka-Seltzer.

When I'd woken up on the sofa I'd registered three things at once: first, I had slept in my clothes again, something of an everyday occurrence at the moment; second, I was in dire need of immediate medicinal help; third, I had two cuts on the back of one hand. Drinking wounds. God knows where they had come from.

I'd sat there on the sofa for a few moments waiting for my memory to return, bracing myself against whatever horrors I'd got up to last night in my cups. But nothing came – nothing to explain the cuts on my hand – and eventually I pulled myself up from the sofa, peeled off my trousers and shirt and went in search of something to help me feel like a human being.

My hunt for Alka-Seltzer had proved fruitless. But here are those five little bottles of vodka winking at me, and I know that (a) drinking one would help me to feel normal again, and (b) my breath would not smell of fresh alcohol if I did.

I once read an interview with a heroin addict who described the pain of cold turkey. Cold turkey, he said, was like having the worst flu of your life, to which the interviewer had replied, OK, but surely a week with the flu was a small price to pay for kicking a habit that was swiftly killing you. The addict had responded, yes, that was true. But imagine having a really bad dose of the flu, some kind of fierce gastric strain. And imagine you could take one pill that would make all that discomfort go away in a matter of seconds. Wouldn't you take it?

It's him I think about as I stand in front of the kitchen cupboard.

I'm fully aware that, when it comes to drinking, downing a bottle of the vodka will put me into a whole different tax bracket. And I know that by drinking it I'm not waving goodbye to the payback for ever, just banking it and letting it gain interest for another time. But, still, that vodka can open my eyes for me, it can banish the mustard gas clouding my head, it can take away the headache, it can turn me from the living dead into someone who's ready to go to work and face the day and the whole process of getting their life back together.

So I grab the box, unstick the flap and let the five bottles slide out into my hand, and then, without thinking about it – deliberately not thinking about it – I do a lucky dip grab and end up with the Kurant vodka, which I down in one. It tastes nice, a bit like Ribena. And, of course, they're very trendy, these Absolut vodkas. Expensive too. Hardly the sort of thing you'd expect an alkie to be guzzling.

Me and the heroin addict are both right. I feel better almost straight away.

I have a bath, using Mariah Carey once again as a mirror for shaving, but this time I'm extra careful to make sure I shave the whole of my face. And when I've finished I use the bedroom mirror to check I've done a thorough job.

Next, I raid Darth Vader by pouring the contents of his head on to the lounge floor. He's mostly filled with bronze, but shifting around the pennies I find enough twenties and tens to get myself a pick-me-up from the shop with minimum embarrassment.

And all the time I'm doing this, one half of me is thinking, It's not bad, this vodka lark, while the other half looks on disapprovingly. I wait until the disapproving half's back is turned before I stuff the other miniatures into my coat pocket to take to work.

There's a lot of activity at the shop as I approach. Getting nearer, I see a parked van with the words 'Hackney Glass (domestic & commercial) 24-hr – No call-out charge, "The Clear Favourite",' written on the side. Workmen are doing something to one of the shop's front windows. The displays of fruit are absent, and two men wearing gloves are picking shards of broken glass from around the window frame. On the pavement is more broken glass and one of the assistants I recognise from the shop is sweeping it up, simultaneously gesturing to passers-by to walk round.

I think that 'Hackney Glass – "We Love the Sound of Breaking Glass"' would be a better logo. Although maybe not. Perhaps that might suggest they take some kind of pleasure in their customers' misfortunes.

What about 'Hackney Glass – "In a Glass of Our Own"'? Or 'A Glass Above', or 'A High Glass Service', 'Glass War'? No, not that last one – it sounds a bit confrontational.

I'm amusing myself with the glass/class puns as I go into the shop where, in a show of Blitz spirit, they're continuing to trade, albeit draughtily, and choose a bottle of Purdey's and a small one of Fanta.

When I take them to the counter to pay I want to ask what's happened to the window, but last night I promised myself I would cease all friendly advances with the shop after the threepence episode and, anyway, the assistant is shouting something through the broken window to the broom man as she's taking my money so it's not really convenient. I walk away none the wiser, still thinking merrily about glass puns and enjoying the top-up benefits of my miniature bottle of vodka.

I drink the bottle of Purdey's, burp up a fizzy mix of alcohol, garlic capsules and health-giving fruit drink then toss the empty into a bin before starting on the Fanta, taking just two good-sized gulps before – but only after checking nobody can see me – pouring two miniatures of vodka into it, giving it a swirl around and gulping for a third time, savouring its added bite. God knows what flavours I put in – tastes like there could be a bit of Peppar in there.

Then I replace the cap on the bottle and carry it in my hand as I walk to the tube: just a thirsty businessman enjoying a bottle of Fanta on his way to work.

All of this happens before I have a sudden and not-at-all-welcome flashback from last night.

Actually, it's not really a flashback at all, more a simple case of addition finally attended to by my booze-fuzzed brain. It involves my last accounted-for emotion – Mr Watts, that feeling of something being unfair – added to the two mystery cuts on the back of my hand, plus the broken window of the shop. To equal?

Suddenly I don't feel so good and I take another gulp of the Fanta, my hand almost shaking the bottle out of my lips.

On the train I find an elastic band in my coat pocket. I roll it up like a tiny firehose, press it together so that the rubber sticks and then let it go, watching it slowly unfurl. Once it's uncoiled itself all the way and resembles an elastic band again, I roll it up another time.

Comedians, they say, are prone to bouts of self-doubt and depression because they cannot trace their talent to its source. They open their mouths and funny things come out but they have no idea how or why. And what eats them up is that they never know if or when that invisible well of talent will dry up. Where does it come from, all this funny stuff? When will it end?

I find myself thinking the same thing. Where is it coming from, all this funny stuff? The only difference is, comedians are worried that the funny stuff is going to stop: I'm worried that it's not.

'Chris, I think it's for the best that you take some more time off,' says Geoff Clarke.

My first thought is, Shit, rumbled. Like at school, when you've been sitting carving your name into a desk and the teacher suddenly stops talking and you think, Shit, rumbled, only to look up and see that, actually, he's not staring at you, he's just double-checking something in a textbook.

So that's my first thought. I immediately jump to the conclusion that Geoff's somehow aware that I'm drunk. Or not drunk exactly – certainly not drunk by my standards – but not entirely sober either.

If he had guessed I'd take my hat off to him. Apart from a mild stagger that I disguised by pretending there was something on my shoe, I'd managed to appear totally sober. In these situations you have what I guess counts as an element of surprise. Since it's only nine forty-five in the morning, nobody is expecting you to be drunk and that conclusion is therefore the last one they'll jump to. You, meanwhile, can excuse any instances of erratic behaviour on a bad night's sleep, or some minor disturbance on the tube that's left you out of sorts.

That one small stagger aside, I made my way across the

potential danger area – the walk from the lift to my desk – with no mishaps, pretending to be lost in concentration, all the time successfully willing myself in a straight line.

When I got there, the boys looked at me, then quickly looked down again, pretending to be working hard just because the boss had arrived. Then I noticed Luke Radley wasn't wearing a tie, and rather than let it wait I thought I'd better tell him straight away. 'Oi, Oz-boy. What are you – where's the – where's *your* tie?'

Smirking, the boy replied that he wasn't wearing one, he didn't know it was the rule.

'We wear ties,' I said.

To which he replied, still smirking, that others in the office didn't wear them.

'I don't care what *others* do, here at *Sass* magazine we wear ties. What if you have to – what if you need to see a client?'

And he said, smirking even more, that he wasn't seeing a client today, and that if he had been seeing one, he would have worn a tie.

'Look, I don't care what you did in fucking . . . Melbourne,' I said, wishing I could wipe the smirk off his face, and giving it serious consideration. 'Just wear a fucking tie, all right. That's the rule.'

To which he replied, with an even larger smirk, then why wasn't I wearing mine?

And my hand leapt to my throat, only to find that I hadn't put my tie on, and I remembered stuffing it into my suit pocket intending to do so while I was on the train. I pulled it out like a magician's handkerchief and made a great show of putting it on, saying, 'I've *got* my tie, just make sure you have yours tomorrow,' but feeling defeated all the same.

A short time after that, Geoff had rung me and asked me to come to his office where I now sit, thinking how hot he keeps this room, and how he's sitting there all acclimatised and cool, and I'm wiping a film of sweat from my brow.

And I'm getting over that feeling of being rumbled. Realising as he's talking that he hasn't twigged I'm drunk. Instead, he just thinks I need some extra compassionate leave. 'I think perhaps you need a little extra time after your, um, father's death.' he says. 'The last thing we want is for your work to suffer. Give it a week or so, eh? Just take some, er, time to yourself, get yourself together and we'll see you back fighting fit when you're, um, ready.'

Which seems like a great idea, I think, especially kind of him, considering he doesn't know about Sam leaving. I'm already thinking that I can take a few days to get myself straight, perhaps ease off on the drinking, get the flat together. It'd be nice to write some thank-you letters to those who came to the funeral. I can write one to Sam's mum and dad and they'll tell Sam, who'll think I'm at last getting myself together. I can begin stage one of getting her back, whatever stage one is. And she'll come back and things can return to normal. I still have my job. I still have my wife.

'So, er, Chris, what do you say to that, mate?' says Geoff, into what's been a long silence.

'Yes. Yes. I mean, yes. Maybe you're right. Maybe I could do with a little more time to, you know, sort things out. I'll spend the day putting stuff in order and perhaps we can meet again later, so I can go through with you about the – you know, what the state of play is.'

'No need, mate,' says Geoff. 'No time like the present, eh? You get yourself off home. Graham's on top of stuff . . .'

(He is, is he?)

'. . . and young Luke seems to be fitting in well . . .'

(Oh, he is, is he?)

'. . . so all told, I think everything's taken care of here. I say just grab your stuff and we'll see you when you feel you're ready to return.'

'Well, why the fuck couldn't you have told me all this on the phone so I didn't have to drag myself into work, only to turn around and go back home again,' is what I *should* say. But I'm fairly taken with the idea, so instead I go, 'Great, great,' stand, and lose my balance slightly, reach to the back of the chair for support, which, because it's an office chair, swings around before I regain full control of my legs.

I'm a hair's breadth from falling to the floor of Geoff's office, but when I glance at him, ready to excuse my imbalance with a line like, 'Monday morning . . .' he hasn't noticed, is absorbed with something on his desk, so, thanking God, I let myself out of the office.

Graham is finishing something he's saying to Luke, 'So if you could get that done by the end of the day that would be very useful,' and looks at me as I return, then down at his desk.

'Right,' I say. 'I'm not going to be around for a few days, so you'll have to cope without me.' Nice, I think. 'Not going to be around for a few days' sounds like I'm away on business somewhere, been called into Geoff's office and given an important assignment, something I can't really go into with the staff.

They're all busy getting on with their work and don't answer me. I look over across the rest of the ad floor and other teams are looking our way with undisguised interest.

'Guys?' I say. 'Graham? Are you going to be OK in my, ah, absence?'

'I think so, thanks, Chris,' says Graham, looking me straight in the eye. 'I reckon I've got things covered here.'

And Luke Radley turns to stare at me with a mocking smile. 'I just hope we can cope without you, *boss*,' he says. And it's all I can do not to pick up my briefcase and swipe him across the head with it. If I caught him with the hard metal frame it could really hurt, open up a nasty gash.

Then I collect my stuff and leave, walking to the lift and out of the office. I don't know it then, of course, but it turns out to be the last time I'll ever see them.

On my way back to the tube I stop in at Oddbins to replenish the miniature bottles of vodka I'd taken from the kitchen earlier. I've no intention of drinking them, I just want to make sure they're there, ready for when Sam gets back. Don't want her thinking I've been guzzling them while she's been away. In the event, I can't find the right brand, and not in a presentation box, but I buy another brand anyway and shove them into my coat pocket. Maybe she won't notice the difference.

While I'm waiting for my connection at Finsbury Park the platform's almost deserted, so I take a seat on one of the benches and, since there's no one around, I drink one of the miniatures. The Fanta bottle's long gone, and I'm beginning to flag, so it seems like a good idea until I can get home, get some rest then wake up refreshed and ready to rock.

Trouble is, the vodka has the opposite effect and when I close my eyes for a moment, just to rest them, I don't open them again, not for a while at least.

Eventually I wake up to find a member of the London Underground staff standing over me. Dressed in a fluorescent orange tabard, she has a bag of litter in one hand and in the other she's holding a long metal grabber. She says, 'Hey,' for what may be the second or third time, but it's the first time I hear it at least. 'You can't sleep here.'

'Gurgh,' I say, my throat dry, grabbing for my briefcase: just a tired businessman nodded off on the platform, probably up all night working on a presentation. You know how these media types are, always burning the candle at both ends.

But my briefcase is gone.

'Gurgh,' I repeat, and the litter-picker – whose job title is probably something like Waste Disposal Operatives Team Leader – takes a step back, looking uneasy.

'My briefcase,' I manage. 'Have you seen it? It's gone.'

'I haven't seen no briefcase,' she says, with that exact amount of boredom – the sort all servants of the public sector have. 'I been up and down.'

'I'd like to report a stolen briefcase,' I say, with all the sudden authority of a drunkard.

'Station manager's office is up top,' she says. 'You'll be lucky.'

'There are cameras,' I say, gesturing to the end of the platform.

She harrumphs, 'Not that work,' and walks on.

There wasn't much in my briefcase, not much to show for a life. In fact, I can't think offhand of a single item in it. But, of course, that's not the point. Some toe-rag's walked off with my briefcase. Some fucking cunt. A cowardly fucking thief.

Some day, I think, a rain will come and wash all of this scum off the streets.

Speaking of which, guess who I see on the way home, when I've eventually shaken the all-enveloping anger, pulled myself on to a tube train, made the one stop to Manor House without nodding off, and begun the walk to my flat?

It's the dog-end, the youth who blew his nose on my shoulder the night that Sam left me. And this time it really is. No illusion, no mind playing tricks on me. It really is him.

I don't see him to speak to, as the saying goes. Instead, I spot him inside his house, on the opposite side of the road to me, where I'm walking past a row of shops.

His house is in a terrace of three just outside the estate, at least one of which is condemned and surrounded by corrugated iron with 'Keep Out' raggedly painted on it. His is the one on the end, perhaps a squat – badly kept, a patch of concrete at the front covered in trash: mattresses, a toilet, old kitchen units. He's in what seems to be his front room, and I'm able to see him through the window because he doesn't have curtains or a blind, or anything that ordinary, decent people have. Typical, I think.

As I hover outside the shops, near the door of the off-licence, I watch him cross the floor of the lounge and then, a moment later, slide out of the front door, slamming it behind him and glancing around with a patented 'I'm up to no good' look, before setting off in the direction of the tube station – that same arrogant walk, like he's unleashed himself to intimidate the world.

The thing that strikes me most about his exit, apart from the torrent of disgust I feel upon seeing him again, is the sound the door makes as it closes. It's a clinking noise that I remember from my safe, safe youth on the Groby Road in Leicester. The sound of a key on a string, ready to be pulled through the letterbox and used to open the door. The sound of it hitting the door as the door closes. Clink-clink – like that.

There's that trade-union threat, isn't there? 'We know where you live.' It isn't actually a threat, more a statement of fact, but all the more chilling for it. And I now know where Dog-end lives. And, even better, I know how to get in.

Before I carry on home I tip another miniature down my throat, and since I'm outside the off-licence anyway, in I go. Good news: they have the same vodkas I found earlier . . .

CHAPTER TWENTY-FIVE

Russ and Fi began kissing at around one a.m.

The TV awards ceremony – a midweek event – had started to wind down around them, and they were the only people left at the *Happy Monday* table, which was a picture of post-meal, boozy desolation. Not that they cared. And if the official part of the night was reaching its end, Russ and Fi were only just getting started. The champagne and cocaine saw to that.

It was a great kiss, they both thought so. Sometimes a kiss simply reminds you of an ex-boyfriend or -girlfriend and how well your mouths used to fit together; sometimes a kiss can be an entirely new adventure, one that wipes out all memories of previous relationships, dumps you in a warm and sticky now. This was one of those kisses. And even as the music ground to a halt around them, they could not stop kissing, coke and champers fizzing around their hormones. They grabbed their jackets but barely came up for air. They left the hall of Alexandra Palace, clinging tight to each other, and stopped twice for more passionate kissing. Then, when they were outside, they fell into a mini-cab and Russ said, 'Fulham,' and Fi didn't argue, and then they kissed some more, and this time the hands started to wander as well.

All this time they didn't speak. Not true. Occasionally they broke apart and one or the other would say, 'Oh, my God' – an expression of what-are-we-doing? surprise. Or one would say, 'Christ,' just to register the passion they both felt – partly down to the drugs and drink, of course, but only partly.

By the time they reached Fulham there was no question that they belonged to each other and that what was about to happen was a certainty. When she took his hand and placed it between her legs in the cab, he knew she was game. She knew he was game because, well, because he was a bloke, and she'd never met one who wasn't.

But Fi would surprise Russ with just how sexually upfront she was. When they reached his bedroom (and he gallantly resisted the temptation to take her into the lounge where at least one of the lads would still have been up smoking a spliff) she marched to the middle, swung to face him, then pulled her top over her head. He gaped. She reached behind herself and unclipped her bra, which fell to the floor, and he gaped some more.

'How do you want me?' she said, and all Russ's Christmases came at once.

'All ways, every ways,' he said, feeling like a guy in a film. She was looking at him coquettishly, seductively – just like the wank fantasy.

Yes, just like the wank fantasy, he thought, and said, 'Take off your skirt, so you're naked. I want to see you sit on the window-sill and smoke a fag.' He was surprised to hear himself say the words. Without the booze he would never have dared, and as they left his mouth he braced himself for a gale of derision, such an obvious male fantasy. Girl like Fi wouldn't pander, surely.

But she raised her eyebrows, as if to say, 'Kinky,' and did as she was asked, sliding down the skirt, peeling off her knickers, her eyes never leaving his as he watched, his trousers tented.

'Help me up,' she said, and he walked forward, his breath catching, held her round the waist and lifted her to the window-sill, which was just – only just – wide enough to accommodate her. And she crossed her legs.

'Bring me a cigarette,' she commanded him.

He did so, lighting it for her and passing it to her. She rested her elbow on her knee and smoked, regarding him, just like the fantasy.

OK, he thought, not quite like the fantasy. Her tits were

bigger in the fantasy, and she didn't have a tummy, and her toenails had been painted.

But otherwise just like the fantasy.

They watched one another, she casually flicked ash to the carpet and he had a mild twinge as he watched it drift dangerously close to his PlayStation 2. But only very mild. He was too turned on, could happily have stood there all night, watching her. In fact, he actually considered pulling out his dick and knocking one out right there. But that would have ruined the moment. Instead, he said, 'Stay where you are. I'll be back in just a second.' And he turned and hobbled to the bathroom, his erection briefly giving him the look of a Neanderthal, which, in effect, he was.

In the bathroom, he looked at himself in the mirror and saw a Russ on the verge of sleeping with a gorgeous blonde girl. He liked what he saw. But no time to waste, he thought, and he slid down his trousers and pants. He wanted to give his knob a wash. He wanted to be clean for Fi.

Meanwhile, in the bedroom, Fi finished her cigarette, looked around for somewhere to stub it out and spotted an empty lager tin on the other side of the room. She jumped off the windowsill.

And landed on Russ's PlayStation 2.

Which buckled and crunched. She was only a small girl but, nevertheless, PlayStation 2s aren't built to withstand the weight of a jumping, naked blonde.

In the bathroom, Russ was blissfully unaware. He had soap beneath his foreskin and it was stinging a little. Actually, he realised, it was stinging *a lot*.

In the bedroom, Fi looked down with horror at the PlayStation 2 beneath her feet. Both feet. Not one foot on, one foot off. No, she'd landed on it squarely with both feet. Despite herself, she laughed. And then she thought of Russ in meetings, saying, 'It's just like *Final Fantasy*,' in that voice of his, which rose at the end, making everything sound like a question.

So she jumped on it again. The devil in her made her do it.

In the bathroom, Russ was painfully unaware that, having destroyed his PlayStation 2, Fi was now grabbing her clothes and fishing for her mobile to call a cab. It turned out he'd been far too generous with the soap and his eyes were watering, even as he frantically splashed cold water beneath his foreskin. He didn't even register Fi on the landing, then tiptoeing down the stairs and letting herself out of the front door, closing it softly behind her.

He just kept splashing cold water on his foreskin.

'You killed my PlayStation,' he said, at work the next day.

She had rarely seen a sorrier state in her life. He looked like she felt. It was one of those unique occasions when she thanked her lucky stars that she was a woman and could use makeup to hide her sins. A multitude of sins.

'Did not,' she said reflexively, more as a tease than a genuine defence. She felt like she'd recovered a lot of ground in the period between sitting on Russ's window-sill and now.

'Your feet marks were on it,' he said flatly.

'Oh.' She looked at him, chewing the inside of her cheek. Yesterday he would have found it unbearably sexy. Today she had killed his PlayStation and left him high and dry just when he thought he was on for the sexual conquest of his life. Hell hath no fury like a geek-o-zoid spurned.

'Oh, what?' he said, his words pregnant with repressed anger.

'Oh, sorry?' she replied.

'How about . . .' He stopped as someone passed them in the corridor, then with his voice low '. . . how about sorry, *very* sorry, and here's the cash so you can buy a new one.'

'How much are PlayStations?' she asked, smiling sweetly.

'A hundred and ninety-nine pounds,' he hissed.

'No way!' She laughed. 'My brother got one for under a hundred. I'm not paying all that. If you paid that then more fool you. They saw you coming.'

His mouth twitched as he fought to control his temper. 'Yes, but mine was a PlayStation 2. Your brother probably got a PlayStation 1. The two are alike in name only. Well, apart from the fact that the PlayStation 2 is backwards-compatible.'

She almost lost it then. Once a spod-boy, always a spod-boy, she thought, but said, 'OK, Russ, I'll bring you the money as soon as I can.' And with that, she left him in the corridor, smiling to herself as she walked away. It was fun being a bitch, she mused.

As she walked away he called after her, 'One more thing, Fi. From now on, it's war, OK?'

'Fine,' she called back, thinking, Sure, and you can beg for that money.

And war it was, for Russ at least. So when he spotted a potential Felix Carter lookylikey wandering around Paperchase, quite by chance – and just what they needed for the next show – it was a shot across the bows, as far as he was concerned.

CHAPTER TWENTY-SIX

Things get hazy around this point, I'm drinking an awful lot. **I can see that.**

Let's see. What I get up to is this, but not necessarily in this order:

1. I go to the supermarket to try to put my life in order. I fail miserably.
2. I miss Sam, and I torture myself for not appreciating her when she was here. What do I mean? Here's an example: the door to our flat is draughty, so we have a sausage that Sam's mum made for us to keep the draught out. Just a fabric thing, probably filled with old T-shirts or something, but it does the trick. Of course, having it along the bottom of the door makes getting through the door tricky: the sausage drags along the carpet, gets stuck underneath the door, and you have to either pull the door back for another go, or reach down to free the sausage manually. The thing is, if Sam was in the flat first, sitting on the sofa watching, say, *EastEnders*, then she'd always leap up, saying, 'Hang on,' and grab the sausage for me, helping me into the flat. One day she confronted me with the truth: 'Have you ever noticed that I always help you with the sausage when you're trying to get in, but you never, ever help me? I can't remember a single occasion when you've got up to help me with the sausage. You just sit there with a beer, don't you? Blissfully unaware that I'm having trouble getting in . . .' I used that blustery non-defence where you just come out with crap, saying (untruthfully), 'But you're always in before I am!' or (equally untruthfully), 'God, selective memory!

I've helped you with it loads of times.' We both ended up laughing because of the comedy inherent in arguing over helping each other with the sausage, but she was right. I never did help her with the sausage.

3. I drink a lot of vodka, cry a lot, watch detective programmes on TV.

4. I spend time wishing I'd taken more notice of her. If we'd spent the night slobbing on the sofa over a takeaway curry and a bag of Maltesers she'd get the guilts just as we were going to bed, moaning, 'God, I feel so fat,' and end up doing a half-dance, half-exercise around the bedroom while I lay in bed, staring around her at the portable TV. Why was I staring around her? Why not at her? How could I pass up any opportunity to see the woman I love at her most natural? Watching the fucking television instead. Perhaps, if I was more rational, I might reason that if I had been watching her, she wouldn't have been at her most natural, probably wouldn't even have done it at all. But who's rational?

5. A researcher for a television programme approaches me in the street and asks me to appear on the following Monday's show as 'a Felix Carter lookylikey'.

6. See 3.

7. I start writing thank-you letters but never finish the first.

8. I break into Dog-end's house and shit on his bed.

9. I look at my dad's gun, hold it, load it and unload it. One time, I point it at the sofa and dry-fire it. I like the feeling of pulling the trigger so much that I do it again. I imagine that the sofa is Dog-end, or the person who stole my briefcase. I tuck the gun into my trousers. On one occasion I go to the shop with the gun tucked into my jeans, and even though it's not loaded, I meet the stares of the youths who hang around outside the shop. I want them to say something, to try to have a go. I want to pull the gun on them, watch their faces. I want them to know how it feels to be intimidated and frightened.

Erm . . .

No, don't worry. I know there was an awful lot there that deserves further explanation. Shall we start with number one, the trip to the supermarket?

Please do.

It's seeing her handwriting that does it. It has the effect of snapping me out of something. Or snapping me into something. Whatever, it has the effect of making me go to the supermarket.

The reason I go to the supermarket is because the example of handwriting I suddenly come across, as I'm searching in a kitchen drawer for a packet of Nurofen I was sure we had there (and, actually, where the fuck has it gone?), is a shopping list. There it is, staring at me from a bed of kitchen crap in the drawer – spent batteries, film canisters, a deck of playing cards, some Uhu glue. And this shopping list.

It's just a crumpled bit of paper from one of those 'Don't Forget!' pads, one that's clearly already survived a trip down to the supermarket and back. But it went down there and back probably stuffed into the pocket of her jeans. And before she went she sat in the flat, most likely in the lounge – in cleaner days – making the list and furrowing her forehead as she tried to remember what we needed. And then when she got back, she'd have been putting stuff away, checking the receipt as she always did, and somehow, probably absent-mindedly, the shopping list found its way inside this drawer; the sort of drawer that is a kind of spiritual home for lists like this. In other words, this list: it's a little piece of her.

It's just a little list of some stuff we needed. It says, 'milk, Fairy, eggs, wash powder, drain stuff, squash, bananas, lightbulb 60W', and one last thing that might be suntan lotion, but more likely sultanas. And the thing is, seeing it makes me go to the supermarket. Maybe if I'd found a note she'd written reminding herself to pay the gas bill, I would have paid the gas bill, or one saying, 'remember Mum's birthday', I would have remembered her mum's birthday. (What if I'd found one saying, 'Chris, can you stop drinking?' What then?) As it is, I go down to the supermarket.

Before leaving the house I down some vodka then tie my shoes, shrug on my jacket and I'm out of the door. I go right then remember right is the wrong way, call myself a dozy twat, turn and go left, up the hill, towards Safeway.

I'm about half-way there when it dawns on me that I have something in my shoe, which is giving me grief and that ignoring it doesn't seem to be helping it go away.

You know how you lie in bed for ages before you finally admit defeat and go for a piss? You lie there, and even though you know you won't get back to sleep until you've had a piss, you put it off for as long as possible. It's a denial thing. You think, If I ignore it, it might just – this once – go away.

It's the same with stones and shoes, only stones have a greater chance of disappearing than urine has of siphoning itself out of your bladder. Still, they never do. Like this one. I'm walking along, gradually becoming aware that there's this stone knocking around in the bottom of my shoe. And it lodges under the ball of my foot and it hurts; it's an irritant. So when I pick up my foot each time I have to throw it forward slightly to dislodge the stone from beneath my sole to the toes.

As walks go, it's not a very cool one. It looks as though I'm walking down the street shuffling to a silent song, or maybe kicking an invisible can, and I become increasingly self-conscious until it occurs to me that perhaps I'd look less stupid kicking a real can. I spot a litter bin, and discreetly pop one out to kick along. Only I'm not very good at kicking and I'm quite drunk, and soon I'm having to dart all over the pavement to control the can, which just makes the foot pain worse.

I leave the can, feeling vaguely guilty that I've created litter, especially when someone else had been public-spirited enough to bin it in the first place. But I'm concentrating too hard on trying to minimise the pain in my foot, before finally deciding – that same slow morning-piss realisation

– that I'm going to have to undo my shoe to get rid of the stone.

I stop and bend down, planning on a quick shoelace release, slip off the shoe, give it a shake, back on and continue. But perhaps because I'm slightly embarrassed about bending down in the pavement, so I'm all haste and no speed, or perhaps because I've been kicking my feet around and inadvertently tightened the laces, or perhaps because I'm too drunk (and have you ever tried undoing your shoelaces when you're drunk? It's not easy), whatever – I can't undo my shoelace. And my fingers do the clawing thing, and I find myself biting at my knee with rage, unable to get my suddenly obese fingers around the tiny lengths of tied-together lace. At one point – laughably – I even try to raise my shoe to my mouth so that I can work at the knot with my teeth. I'd have done it too, if I'd been more flexible. But I don't get my foot as high as I need it and can't stay balanced on the other. I lose my balance, then jump up as though I've seen a rat and carry on my way.

The stone is still hurting and now I can feel it digging into the top of my foot. I change my walk slightly, incorporating a wiggle into the kick, a flex-the-foot and loosen-the-stone in one movement, and I'm still walking like that when at last I enter Safeway.

It's only a five-minute trot from our house to the supermarket, but somehow I feel like Jesus probably had it easier when he carried his cross to Calvary. And at least he didn't have problems finding a trolley when he got there. I, of course, do. The trolleys are stored at the far entrance to the shop, not the one I've used, so I have to wiggle-kick my way along the back of the checkouts and past the newspapers to the snaking rows of trolleys parked outside. Now I'm beginning to sweat as the vodka's influence weakens and I realise, with a sinking heart, that I haven't brought any emergency supplies with me. At least, I think, I'm in the right place to get some. So, with only the briefest pause at the fruit during which I look at some bananas, I wheel my way round to the drinks section, still wiggle-kicking my foot.

There, I place two full bottles of vodka and one half-bottle in my trolley and immediately feel calmer, keeping my eye on them as I wheel to the top of the aisle, thanking God it's not too busy. Just need to get a drink, I reason, then I can have a proper walk around the shop, buy some supplies like a normal human being: Fairy liquid, tea, coffee, milk. I can stock up the fridge like it used to be when Sam was at home, cook myself a nutritious meal (my stomach turns, but I shush it down), begin to order my life again.

I take out Sam's list to check it. I had thought of buying all the items she had, but the things listed are for another day, another expedition, and if I'm going to prove to myself – and to her – that I can function normally, I need to go solo. Feeling like Luke Skywalker training to be a Jedi, I symbolically put away the list. I decide to feel the Force.

But first a drink. The baby-food section will be the least busy, I think, so I do a scan of the overhead signs and begin to wheel my trolley in that direction. The plan is to make a show of searching for the right brand of nappy while surreptitiously taking a single swig from the half-bottle, replacing the top then paying for it as normal. Just the one swig, mind. Just to tide me over.

With a carefully casual air, I wheel – the wiggle-kicking second nature now – down the baby-food aisle. I was right: there's not a soul in sight. In fact, I'm the only person on it. And if anybody does see me? Just a caring new man, picking up nappies for his newborn. Obviously throwing a party at the weekend, too – all that vodka's probably for some punch.

I stop by the nappies, which strike me as comfortingly squidgy-looking, but I restrain the urge to give them a squeeze. Instead, I do a quick look up and down, whip out the half-bottle and bring it in to my stomach as I squat down, pretending to study the packets of nappies. Of course, I'm doing nothing of the sort. I'm concentrating on getting the top off the bottle, which I manage with a sharp twist, doing another quick up and down look before bringing the bottle to my lips and taking a good long gulp.

But when I do my quick look, I don't really look. Or I do but my brain takes a second or so to process the information. So I've actually taken my gulp before the data filters down: there is somebody else on the aisle.

It's a young woman, pushing a trolley with a child in the seat. I recognise her and again my brain reacts slowly, scrambling around trying to place the features, until—

It's Becca, the woman from the drink group on Holloway Road.

Like one of those comedy moments in sitcoms where someone takes a swig of drink just as another character says something outrageous, I nearly spit vodka all over the nappies. As it is, I choke on the swig and vodka goes up my nose and into my throat. 'Down the wrong hole,' as we used to say when we were little. But even as I'm coughing, and my eyes are watering and my nose begins leaking vodka-flavoured snot, which I snort up, I'm frantically replacing the bottle top and straightening, turning away at the same time so she won't see me. Then, still coughing and spluttering, I reach behind me for the trolley, swinging it round to my front in what feels like a dangerous arc and quickly pushing it in the opposite direction. My eyes are watering and I dab at them, not caring if people think I'm crying. Who knows? Maybe they'll think I was overcome with emotion at the thought of impending fatherhood. Let them think what they want. My priority is to get at least two aisles' distance between me and Becca, booze convert *extraordinaire* – me with two and a half bottles of vodka in my trolley and nothing else. I ask you.

I sniff and get more vodka, which seems to speed to my brain in super-quick time. No wonder – isn't snorting vodka one of those trendy drinking games? The sort of thing someone like Luke Radley might get up to at the weekend. Maybe I shouldn't be so embarrassed now that I've inadvertently joined the in-crowd.

At last, gathering myself together, I push-wiggle-kick to the checkout where I unload the bottles of vodka on to the conveyor belt and wait for the woman in front of me to finish rooting in her purse for money-off vouchers she probably doesn't have so I can pay and get the hell out. And then I feel someone at my back, joining the queue, and who should it be but Becca.

She recognises me, no doubt about it. Just my luck. Reformed drinker – of course she's going to have a memory.

She looks up at me, and though the eyes tell me she knows me, she says nothing. Thank God for small mercies. But then her eyes travel down to the conveyor belt and she sees the vodka. Very deliberately she looks back at me. *Déjà vu.* Like the time at the group when I excused myself for a phantom toilet visit and never returned. She saw right through me then, and I'm even more transparent now.

There's something on the tip of my tongue to say, but I don't say it. Almost, but then the conveyor belt starts shuttling my vodka to the spotty teenager on the till, and the words are lost as I turn to attend to them.

I was about to say, 'I need help.'

I don't look at her again. I pay and I sweep my carrier-bag away from the till and leave the shop without a backward look. Then I walk home with the half-bottle in one hand, the carrier-bag in the other, wiggle-kicking my way up the road. I walk home looking exactly what I am.

Sometimes I think that booze is like the Mafia: every time you try to get out it pulls you back in.

Number five, then. The researcher. A very nice man named Russ Phillips.

It's another day, and I'm enjoying the feeling of freedom that comes from wandering along Tottenham Court Road on a weekday. I'm not sure what day of the week it is – if I wanted to, I could work it out easily, but it doesn't matter. It's a weekday, that's all there is to it.

And I'm walking along in my civvies: jeans, T-shirt, jumper, jacket. No briefcase (obviously), just carrying a bottle of Fanta, watching people scurry busily past, watching drivers hoot at each other angrily, pleased to be outside the shape of their day.

It's like being a tourist, or an alien visitor. And even though it's not sunny, it feels like it should be. I even stop at a pub for a pint, just to underline this feeling of glorious aimlessness.

I stand at the bar to drink my pint (which, come to think of it, might be a vodka and tonic or two) and while I'm there I hope I might strike up a conversation with the barman, or perhaps a fellow floater, someone else happy to stick two fingers up to the turbulence of an average day and while away a few moments shooting the breeze. It would be nice, I think, to meet an old man and spend a couple of hours with him. I could buy him drinks in exchange for entertaining stories about life just after the war.

But, sadly, I don't meet anyone to talk to (maybe it's just as well: post-war stories are usually dull) and instead I go back out on to Tottenham Court Road where I remember that I do have a purpose for being here after all: I have come to buy paper so I can write my thank-you letters.

To be honest, I'm not even sure of the protocol surrounding thank-you letters following funerals, but I'm hoping this will lend the gesture a touching authenticity. People will see it as genuine desire on my part to thank them for their support, will think, What a nice young man, his father would be proud. His mother too. And that's all I want, really – for my father to be proud, he who'd sat me down and made me write thank-you letters to grannies and aunts, expressing my gratitude for book tokens and pairs of socks. The thank-you letter is an honourable tradition in our family and I'm helping to keep it alive.

Plus, of course – and slightly more Machiavellian – Sam's

parents will get one and be better disposed towards me as a result. A small positive to help balance the many negatives they'll have been given by Sam in justification for her sudden, badly timed departure. I wonder what she told them when they asked why she was not at home with her grieving husband. I bet she had more to say than 'He never helped me with the sausage.'

Because I bump into the door as I go into Paperchase, I form the impression that the man who seems to be following me is a store detective. Understandable: somebody who cannot enter a shop without bumping into the door deserves to be watched. If I was in charge of the security team I'd be keen to watch me. Nevertheless, I want to tell him to fuck off. Nearly do, in fact, as I'm trawling through the posh notepaper, trying to find something suitable for thank-you letters, and see him peering at me over the top of the aisle opposite. He averts his eyes swiftly when he realises he's been rumbled but, still, I feel like marching over to ask him why he's not following the *real* undesirables. The ones who no doubt come into Paperchase all the time.

Eventually I find the right notepaper, which looks like a scaled-down version of the old woodchip wallpaper and will be a bastard to write on and fold, but looks good. And I find envelopes to go with it, which mystifyingly don't have lickable adhesive on, like you're supposed to drip candlewax on them or something. And I take the lot to the counter to pay.

But when I try to leave the shop, he's there, right in front of me, and I instinctively hold up my Paperchase bag, as if to say, 'Look, I've paid, all right?'

Only, it's immediately apparent that he's not a store detective at all. My experience of store detectives may be limited to documentaries about shoplifting, but I imagine them to be failed security guards, one rung below the useless specimen at work who won't even say hello to me. They don't wear nicely branded American skateboard clothing as this one does. Nor are they young and friendly, as he obviously is.

'Sorry, hello,' he says quickly, holding out his hand, which I shake. 'I'm Russ Phillips?'

It's not actually a question, but he has one of those voices that rises at the end, the kind of voice I seem to remember Stephen Fry consigning to Room 101 when he was on the programme. Typical posh liberal, Stephen Fry – expects us all to accept everything he is, detests the difference in everybody else. Therefore, because I hate Stephen Fry and he would dislike Russ Phillips, I like Russ Phillips.

I like Russ Phillips even more when he says, 'Sorry, look . . . I couldn't help but noticing, but . . . Well, do you know that you look quite a lot like Felix Carter?'

He's not wrong. I do look a bit like Felix Carter. Clearly not a great deal because I don't have women falling at my feet and he fucks supermodels. But it's been remarked upon before, my similarity to him: Catweazel, the other day, for example. To be honest I've always thought of myself as looking like a fat Felix Carter but, then, one happy by-product of Sam leaving has been a remarkable decrease in weight – only this morning I had to tighten my belt to an unused hole. So, hey, maybe I don't look like a fat Felix Carter any more, maybe I just look like Felix Carter, which is ironic considering how similar our appetite for alcohol is, how we both loved the Specials when we were young, how we both love *Star Wars*, how we are both consumed by guilt over our misdeeds, only to repeat them. Like *The Man in the Iron Mask* or something – twin brothers separated at birth, one of whom achieves great things while the other languishes in jail.

So I say, truthfully, 'Well, it has been mentioned before . . .' wondering what he wants, but also pleased to have somebody to speak to. He might have better conversational ammo than tales of rationing in the forties.

'Well, look,' says Russ Phillips, 'I'm a researcher with Bottom Drawer Productions. We do *Happy Monday* on Monday nights . . .' and I get the impression that he doesn't do this sort of thing often, that he's new to the researching game and

I'm some kind of short-term coup for him. 'Do you know the programme?' he says, interrupting my mind's stroll.

'Sorry, no. I don't think I've seen it.'

'It's in the teatime slot on Channel Four. Similar sort of format to *TFI Friday* . . .'

'Yes, yes, I know.'

'. . . sort of like a cross between *TFI* and *The Priory* . . .'

'Right, right.'

'Yeah, and the thing is, right, we've got Felix Carter in on Monday.' He gestures towards me. 'He's our main guest. And we usually like to have a bit of fun with our guests, you know? And one of the ideas on the table is to get some Felix Carter lookylikeys in the studio, do a line-up or get them involved in a sketch or something.'

'OK, I get it.' I can see where he's going with this now.

'So. Um, well, the million-dollar question: would you be willing, and are you available to appear on next Monday's show?'

'Yes,' I say, 'absolutely,' and I'm more than happy to help Russ increase his standing at work. I imagine his superiors patting him on the back, saying, 'Well spotted, Russ. And you talked him round, did you?' And I wouldn't even mind if Russ builds up his part a bit, says, 'Yeah, well, he took a bit of persuading but, you know, we got there in the end.' He seems a charming and enthusiastic young man, and I'm just about to suggest we go for a drink to talk it through and already hoping he doesn't reply, 'Yeah, a coffee would be great,' when he disappoints me by digging into the side pocket of his combat trousers and producing a business card.

'Here's my name and contact number,' he says. 'If you give me a call on that number, I can arrange for a car to pick you up on Monday morning.'

'Ah, right,' I say, thinking, Shame, it would be good to find out more about him. Perhaps ask how he got into television and whether there are any openings for someone like me. There can only be, what, five years between us? Who knows?

Maybe Bottom Drawer Productions could use a Felix Carter lookylikey on a full-time basis?

'Monday morning . . .' I repeat, staring hard at the card and finding it difficult to focus on the exact words.

'Will that be OK?'

'What day is it today?'

'Ah, Wednesday.'

'Monday it is, then. I'll call you.'

'Great, great. Yeah, give me a call tomorrow. Any time. I'm around all day,' then with a cheeky, kind of hopeful smile that I like, adds, 'I don't suppose you were thinking of getting your hair cut?'

'I could. Why? Would it help?'

'Well, you know, his is very short at the moment. I don't suppose you've seen it? On the cover of his new album?'

'No problem,' I say, running a hand through my hair, wondering when I last washed it. 'Probably needs a cut anyway.'

'Great,' he replies, beaming. 'Well, look, I've got to shoot. But we'll see you Monday? Give me a call, yes? Tomorrow's good.'

'Will do,' I say, waving the card at him as he retreats.

As he goes I'm thinking how nice it is to meet someone so open and friendly, but then resent how quickly he took control of the situation, and as I leave Paperchase I scold myself for not capitalising on my position. After all, he needs me more than I need him. He approached me. So why do I have to ring him, and not the other way round? And why did I agree to get my hair cut? The presumption – I might like my hair this length. Anyway, don't they have people at the studios to cut hair? Great, so the man in the street has to drag himself off to a hairdresser while *Happy Monday*'s hairstylists – probably the sort of woofters you see on daytime TV – will be busy with the heads of the real stars, like Felix Carter.

I curse myself for being so quickly and easily seduced by the lure of TV as I take a swig of Fanta and wander back out on to Tottenham Court Road.

On the other hand, I think, I *do* need a haircut. And if getting it cut makes me look more like Felix Carter, what's wrong with that? It's slowly dawning on me that my appearance on *Happy Monday* might be just the opportunity I've been waiting for: the first stage of my campaign to win Sam back.

But there are some things I need to do before that.

The first is to go to the Virgin Megastore to see the new Felix Carter album. Because I'm a bit worse for wear I accidentally walk past Virgin and end up in HMV where I discover the album's called *About Time Too*, and indeed features a picture of a very short-haired Felix on the front. A number-two or maybe three crop if my guess is correct. Fortunately for me, it's a fairly standard crop – nothing fancy about it, and I should be able to get a barber to do it without brandishing the album cover at him. But I buy the album anyway, even though I won't need it as a visual reference. And, taken by the idea of being his TV lookylikey, I buy the previous three too.

'Bit of Felix Carter, eh?' says the man behind the counter. 'Looks like you're trying to do some catching up here.'

'That's right,' I say, grinning at the assistant, thinking what a pleasant change it is to meet a friendly one. Strangely, though, I can think of nothing else to say, so instead I just continue smiling at him.

'Well, I'm not a big fan myself,' he says, 'but it's a bit better than all this fucking garage we have to put up with.'

'That's right,' I say, signing then taking my card and bag. I have another swig of Fanta and set off for home, feeling pretty good.

There's another thing I need to do, and I'll get round to that presently.

CHAPTER TWENTY-SEVEN

It was the highlight of Jack's week, no doubt about it. Escorting the Mystery Blonde for her interviews with Chris, taking her through the prison to the legal rooms where she set up her tape-recorder and sat listening to Chris's recollections, while Jack had the opportunity to sit and watch her, to marvel at just how beautiful this woman really was. Oh, yes, it was the highlight of his week, no doubt about it.

Not that he ever told her. He afforded her the utmost respect and courtesy and, in essence, gave himself the responsibility of being her minder as well as Chris's, loudly admonishing any prisoner who saw her and wolf-whistled, shushing the odd off-colour comment as she click-clacked elegantly through the corridors behind him. Christ, she was gorgeous, though. Who could blame a man starved of female company for the odd innocent whistle?

To her credit, she hadn't made the mistake many women did when they visited the jail's inner sanctum. She wore feminine but not revealing clothing, which Jack had primed himself to advise her on. No need, as it turned out. Neither did she wear perfume, another no-no – possibly she was aware of the wrought-iron bond between a man's nose and his penis. In all ways, she was a model visitor.

One day, as they walked through the prison for her weekly interview, Jack dropped back to walk beside her. 'Ma'am?' he said. 'What do you plan to do with your interview when you've completed your sessions with Sewell?' He referred to Chris as 'Sewell' when he talked to the outside world – it didn't do to appear too friendly with the prisoners.

'I haven't decided yet,' she answered simply, pleasantly. 'I'll see when I've finished.'

'I'm right in saying you're not allowed to reveal that you've spoken to Sewell, aren't I?' he said.

'It's a condition of me being here, yes,' replied the Mystery Blonde. 'I can't quote him verbatim, but I can use what he tells me providing I don't reveal my source. Like chefs, good journalists never reveal their sources.'

Jack didn't get the joke, but ploughed on regardless. 'Will it be for a newspaper perhaps, ma'am?' he prodded, motioning her through a gate, which he locked behind them.

'Doubtful,' she replied.

Her answers might have seemed monosyllabic and uncommunicative, but they didn't come out that way. Not to Jack at least, who thought her voice was sweeter than any music he'd ever heard, including Charlotte Church. And that was sweet. Still, he nodded thoughtfully as they continued along the grey artery of the jail. 'Ma'am, sorry, ma'am, but what, then?'

'I think,' she said, taking him into her confidence, 'I may write a book.'

'I see.' They reached the legal rooms, and Jack opened a door, allowing the Mystery Blonde to enter. She pulled a chair from beneath a table.

'I'll fetch Sewell now, ma'am,' he said, left her alone and made his way to the landing.

As he walked along, he thought about how the Mystery Blonde had seemed to take him in on a secret. In fact, it didn't matter to Jack one bit what she planned to do with her interviews. She could use them to wallpaper her spare room as far as he was concerned. But her tone had suggested that she considered Jack close enough to tell him something of importance to her and that, he felt, signified something of a change in the nature of their relationship.

Over the past few weeks, he had been escorting her to meet Sewell, sitting in on the interviews as they took place, and it was clear to him that a bond had developed between the man and the journalist. Now it felt as if the circle had been opened to allow him in. And that fitted his plans perfectly – his plans for his collection of celebrity-prisoner memorabilia.

His collection had begun about two years ago, when he picked up a used phonecard signed by Winston Silcott[22] from the prison floor. Another officer mentioned in passing that some sad bastards collect stuff like that, other officers in other prisons. 'What? Phonecards?' Jack had said, turning Silcott's card over in his hand.

'Yeah, but not just phonecards,' said the other officer, 'famous prisoners' stuff. Stuff made by the prisoners, you name it. Tell you what, I know a bloke down south, retired now, who'd probably pay you for that.'

So Jack had taken the bloke's number and contacted him. His name was Joe Brooks and the two men had corresponded regularly by e-mail, becoming quite friendly in the process. It turned out that Joe had accumulated a respectable collection. He had a work shirt signed by Peter Sutcliffe, some of Reggie Kray's drawings, an embroidery made by Charles Bronson,[23] and the banner used by Michael Hickey,[24] one of the Bridge-water Four, during his rooftop protest, which, funnily enough, had taken place at a Leicestershire prison, Gartree.

It was an impressive collection, thought Jack. It beat his Silcott phonecard by a country mile.

Joe described himself as an esoteric collector. Ignoring the

---

[22] Silcott's conviction for the murder of PC Keith Blakelock during the Tottenham riots of 1985 was quashed and he was awarded £50,000 compensation in 1999. However, he is currently serving a life sentence for another murder.

[23] Often described as Britain's most dangerous prisoner, Bronson has spent over twenty-six years in jail and has committed a number of offences while imprisoned.

[24] Imprisoned in 1979 for the killing of Carl Bridgewater, the Bridge-water Four – Jim Robinson, Michael Hickey, Vincent Hickey and Patrick Molloy – had their convictions quashed in July 1997 after the longest appeal in English legal history. Patrick Molloy died in prison.

vagaries of the market, he tended to concentrate on items involving subjects he was interested in – older ones, in general – and he was especially proud of his Hickey banner. He was on the lookout for any John McVicar souvenirs but, other than that, was more than happy with what he'd got. As a rule, he didn't trade.

However, he did point Jack in the direction of other like-minded prison warders, who'd be more than interested in getting their hands on Christopher Sewell memorabilia and would trade Jack prized goods in return. Maybe, he hinted, something owned by the Soho nail bomber David Copeland[25] – after Joe's time but, nevertheless, a highly collectable inmate. Or even something belonging to Robert Maudsley,[26] the UK's own Hannibal the Cannibal who, as legend had it, lived deep in the bowels of Wakefield prison. Whatever, Jack was sure that once he had picked up enough stuff belonging to Sewell he would not only build a reputation as an expert in that area but also be in a position to trade up for other collectable inmates. At the thought, it was all he could do not to rub his hands with glee. And now that the journalist appeared to have taken him into her confidence, well, the possibilities were surely endless

He decided to put that trust to the test, and on the next visit he was sure to have a copy of *Sass* magazine about his person, an old one his daughter had fished from the depths of her bedroom cupboard. On its credit list (the journalist had told him it was called a 'flannel panel') he saw both their names, under features editor and advertising manager.

---

[25] David Copeland is serving six life sentences for the Soho nail bomb, which killed three people, as well as bombs in Brick Lane and Brixton.

[26] Robert Maudsley, imprisoned for garrotting a man, has become a serial killer while in jail, murdering three more men behind bars. One of his victims was discovered with his head cracked open, a spoon hanging out of it and part of his brain missing. Maudsley has spent almost twenty years in solitary confinement.

He chose his moment, the three of them alone in the room as usual, and proffered the magazine with the request that they both autograph it beside their names, careful to look bashful and faintly embarrassed at the same time. He held his breath as his request hung in the air. The journalist hesitated, said, 'This is just for your private collection, Jack, yes? Just for your eyes only?' And he assured her that it was before she signed and passed the magazine to Chris, who scrawled his name without a second thought. He retrieved the magazine with a shy thank-you, and immediately popped it inside a plastic folder for safe-keeping. He gave himself a mental round of applause as he did so.

To this souvenir, he added several visiting orders, signed by Chris and with her name on. He also collected Chris's phonecards, a discarded prison shirt he had asked Chris to sign, and examples of woodwork from the workshop.

What he really wanted, though, was a photograph. As his collection grew, Jack felt that not only was it a valuable heirloom in its own right, it was also a personal record of his time spent with Chris and the journalist. To mark that, he wanted a picture of the three of them together. He planned to use his camera – the one with the self-timer – and set it up to take a picture of the trio in the legal rooms. Since Chris and – more importantly – the journalist had been more than happy so far to help him, they'd surely raise no objection to one more favour.

But when he asked, Chris said no before the journalist had a chance to answer. Well, he didn't quite refuse point-blank. Instead he said, 'Tell you what, Jack, not at the moment, eh? Not just yet. I'm sure the time will come, but not just yet.'

At which the journalist looked quizzical, and Jack replaced his camera grumpily in his pocket.

CHAPTER TWENTY-EIGHT

The next day I call Russ and we talk quickly. Well, he talks quickly, I was prepared to chat for longer. And after I've put down the phone to him, I go back to my preparations.

Sorry, have I missed something? Preparations?

That's right. Preparations. Do you remember number eight on my list? I break into Dog-end's house and shit on his bed? An operation like that requires preparation. You don't think I've forgotten about him, do you? Well, I haven't. He's unfinished business.

I'm sitting on the sofa, watching the television. *Oprah* is on, but Oprah's not on it. Instead, a psychologist is talking to a rape victim about her guilt.

She feels guilty because she incorrectly identified a man who went to jail for the crime, but was later released on appeal. Now, on top of the trauma of the rape, she has to deal with the psychological repercussions of sending an innocent man to jail. She's a bit of a mess. Luckily, she doesn't look it. Whether *Oprah* is filmed through a special anti-wrinkle gauze, or they employ the world's finest makeup artists, both she and the psychologist appear to be made of cream-coloured Plasticine. Even when I look carefully at the balding psychiatrist's face, I can't see a single line or wrinkle, not the slightest hint of bags or shadows, or even the tiniest trace of stubble. He's probably at least twenty years my senior, but his appearance is in direct contrast to my own haggard, worn look.

However, I won't worry about that now. Sorting out my appearance is something I need to attend to, but I'll do it at the same time as getting my hair cut, and I'm doing that when I've done this one more thing.

Looking at the psychiatrist and the rape victim, I wonder again about my own TV appearance. Come Monday, I'll be in the Bottom Drawer studios doing something – what do they say? – 'to camera', and I'll see a big box, the camera, with a winking red eye on top of it. But who will be on the other side? How many people will see me? How many people I know and once knew will suddenly spot this familiar face on TV and think, I know him, don't I? before clicking, 'It's Christopher Sewell'?

Old friends, old teachers, ex-girlfriends, family, workmates, ex-workmates, the woman who works down the shop, Toby Thorpe, Kim Crawford, the security guard who never says hello, Tom Barnes, the blonde girl in the lift, Geoff Clarke, Uncle Ted and Auntie Jean . . . they might all see me.

But the person I most want to see me is Sam. I want her to be sitting having her tea, watching *Happy Monday* and already thinking of me, what with Felix Carter being on, and the fact that I look a bit like him.

And then, just as she's biting into a mini-chicken Kiev, on I come, and she gasps, the piece of chicken suspended midway between plate and mouth, maybe a bit of tomato ketchup about to drip from it.

No, not the ketchup. She doesn't like tomato ketchup.

Just the Kiev, then, and she sees me, gasps, sees me smiling, happy, looking good with my hair cut and – this is very important – *in the context of looking like Felix Carter*, a recognition of that fact on national TV. And she wants me back. Simple as that. Like one of those grandiose Valentine's Day gestures you read about in the newspapers: a billboard on Piccadilly Circus, or a plane trailing a banner with a marriage proposal. *She wants me back*.

You don't do my job without knowing something about the value of advertising. You don't spend your days convincing clients of the strength of the *Sass* magazine brand without learning a bit about the importance of environment and context. So I'm fully aware of just how great an opportunity this is for me – the kind of advertising you really can't buy.

First, of course, I have to ensure that she sees *Happy Monday*, but I think I've already taken care of that. When I arrived home, I listened to each of the Felix Carter albums and chose a particularly touching song – a track from the new album called 'Love You (To The Nth Degree)'. I taped the song – just that one, bit of a waste of a C90 tape, but there you go – and put it in an envelope with a note written on my new Paperchase paper: 'Sam, please watch "Happy Monday" on Monday night. You'll know why. All my love, Chris.' And I posted it to her work, first class so she'll get it on Friday.

It's hardly an exact science, and I did toy with simply telling her: 'Dear Sam, I'm on "Happy Monday" on Monday night,' but decided the surprise is so important that it's worth the risk. I don't like to think what else she may be doing on Monday night, don't even know if she'll be home in time to see *Happy Monday*, but I'm banking on the note – and the tape – being enough at least to warrant setting the video. And if someone else sees it in the meantime and tells her, well, that's not so bad either. The important thing is that she watches it, registers that all-important context, is aware of a subtle act of rebranding on my part, then decides to buy in. If Clarks and Lucozade can reinvent themselves into the cultural *Zeitgeist*, then why not me? Surely the same marketing processes can work for my marriage?

I wonder if Dog-end will see it. I wonder.

As well as watching the Plasticine psychiatrist and the Plasticine guilt-ridden rape victim, I'm also loading my father's gun. I cleared the coffee table for this purpose in the old-fashioned way by sweeping off all my rubbish in one go. On to the floor goes the detritus of my current lifestyle, a lifestyle that's about to change: empty lager tins, Absolut bottles and an ashtray tipping butts on to the floor. It's a mess, but it's my mess, and it won't be around for much longer.

Now, though, I pop the bullets into the chamber and snap it shut, put the safety catch on, stand and put the gun into my belt. I snatch it out in a draw. It feels good. It feels like a film, like TV, not like reality at all.

I put it back in my belt and try it again. It snags. I work out the best way of having it holstered in my belt and try it for a third time. Clean draw. Then again. Smooth again. Satisfied, I walk into the centre of the lounge, doing a kind of rolling-hips walk, a Dirty Harry walk, just to get the feel of it at my waist. It feels good.

By the way, I want you to know that, at no point here, or during any other time when I'm admiring my father's gun, do I pull it out and say, 'You talkin' to me?' like in *Taxi Driver*. That would be a cliché. What's more, it would be unprofessional, and if there's one thing my preparations are, it's professional.

For instance, I test the gun at my waist by making sudden movements, as if I've been attacked from behind, just to make sure it stays in place. It does. Then I try walking around the house with it. It's not particularly comfortable – the barrel digs into my left inner thigh when I take a forward step – but it'll do for the short walk between my flat and Dog-end's house.

I put on my jacket to check for tell-tale bulges and it shows, so I try my coat, which is, ironically, the same one he sneezed on, and you can't tell it's there, not unless you were to touch it.

Good.

I take off the coat and remove the gun – not quite ready yet – to assemble what else I need. From the kitchen I take a pair of washing-up gloves. They are the yellow Marigold type, and I put them on the coffee table beside the loaded gun then go to the spare room where, after some moments of searching, I find a clipboard. I take it to the lounge and place it on the coffee table.

Next, I go into a small cupboard where we keep old clothes – 'decorating clothes' – and stacks of old shoes, which I hunt through now, searching for a pair of never-worn penny loafers that I bought in a sale without trying them on, confused by the difference between English and Continental sizes and finally buying a pair that were two sizes too small.

They hurt when I put them on now, hurt even more when I walk around the lounge in them, but they'll do. I can withstand the discomfort between my flat and Dog-end's house. Good.

Then I take four miniatures of vodka, drink one and put the other three on the coffee table, beside the Marigold washing-up gloves, the clipboard and the loaded gun.

Finally, I locate an old pair of sunglasses: the Ray-Ban Wayfarer type, though not genuine Ray-Ban, of course. Taking out the lenses is more difficult than I expect, even though they're a cheap petrol-station copy, but at last I manage it and I put them on, check myself in the rear of *The Very Best of the Jam*. I look like Michael Caine in *The Ipcress File*. Up close you can tell I'm a man wearing sunglasses without lenses, but the casual observer will simply register a man wearing glasses, and this is the effect I want. Good.

I'm ready. Stage one can begin.

I take the Marigold gloves and I clip them, fingers first, into the clipboard, then I tear some pages from a magazine and clip them over the top. If I hold the clipboard right I can disguise the bulge. Then I put the miniatures into one coat pocket, the lenseless sunglasses into the other and roll the coat around the clipboard. Last, I tuck the gun into my belt then leave the house, holding my bundled coat close to my waist. It might look slightly awkward to the casual observer, but I think I can get away with it.

I'm past the shops and get to the end of the road before I put on the coat. I have to do it awkwardly so as not to show the gun, but I'm confident I carry off the illusion: just a man feeling the chill putting on his coat. Now, of course, I'm a man carrying a clipboard, but that's exactly the impression I want to create.

It's late afternoon, deliberately the same time at which I saw Dog-end a few days before, and to the watching eye

I'm someone employed by, say, London Electricity or British Gas. Maybe someone selling double-glazing – hardly anyone suspicious.

I wait until I'm on the next road before I put on the glasses, even giving them a quick pretend-clean for my unseen audience. I mime misting them with my breath and giving them a wipe before putting them on: just a man thinking, Oh, must put on my glasses. If someone passes me, I will put my head down in case they notice the lack of lenses, but nobody does.

All this planning and preparation, this careful but subtle disguise – you'd have thought I'd know what I was going to do when I got there. The truth is, I don't. When I arrive at Dog-end's front door, painfully aware that here of all places there may be watching eyes behind me – shop assistants, their customers, people staring idly out of windows in the flats above the shops – I don't have a clue what to expect, or what my next move is.

To a certain extent, this is deliberate. I feel that I've prepared for the two possibilities, either that he's in or out, but beyond that I have to let the situation guide me. Hardly perfect, but there you go.

I hold my clipboard at an angle from my body, like a true clipboard pro. Anybody behind me will see it and register my innocent motive for rapping on the door, but once I've banged – once, twice, three times – I unbutton my coat and slip my hand to my waist, touching the butt of the gun. Ready.

Nothing.

There's no sound. No doors slamming and footsteps on stairs, or a voice calling, 'Coming!' Just silence. I try to regulate my breathing, aware of my heart hammering below my ribs, always conscious of the invisible witnesses behind. I knock again.

Still nothing.

This time I lean down to the letterbox. Nothing wrong with that, just a persistent caller checking to see if anyone's in. And

I call, 'Hello?' for a double-check and to reinforce the image for anyone watching. But I'm not really looking through the letterbox. My hand is in the way, reaching for the string I know will be there, pulling the key back to my side of the door.

Using my body as a shield, trying not to let my back betray the actions of my hand, I put the key in the Yale, twist left. Wrong way. Twist right, and the door opens. Then – deep breath – I step in and close the door quickly behind me.

Shit.

For some reason – and thinking about it, stupidly – I had assumed Dog-end had the run of the house. But clearly, just like my own home, it is divided into flats – two, by the look of things. I'm in a communal hall. Ahead of me is a locked door, which leads, no doubt, to stairs and the flat above. To my right is a second door. The same type, another Yale lock, and this I deduce is the front door to Dog-end's flat.

I wait. Somebody might be upstairs. Heard me knock. They might have been on the toilet, or fucking, or right in the middle of a complicated stew, tutting, wiping their hands on a tea-towel, undoing a pinny, making their way to the door . . .

But nobody comes.

I'm breathing hard. The silence of the house closes in on me. I feel my bladder heavy and my arse is pulsing like I need a shit. I take a miniature from my pocket (lucky dip – I get Mandrin), unscrew the top and down it in one gulp, feel a bit better immediately.

Still, I'm fucked, basically. I'm going to have to turn round and go. Unless . . . And I step forward and use my elbow to push at Dog-end's door.

Which swings open on squeaky hinges.

I feel a rush of fear and excitement, a bit like going for a job interview but times a hundred. I don't move for a moment.

Again, I'm waiting for someone to come. Dog-end, perhaps, zipping up his jeans and ready to confront whoever dares let themselves into his flat.

But nobody comes, so I unclip the Marigold gloves and put them on. Then I turn and yank at the key, once, twice, until the string snaps and it comes free in my hand and I pocket it before going through to Dog-end's flat and pushing the door to behind me.

It stinks. Of course. It smells not like a home but like a hidey-hole. It smells of too many fags and greasy food and windows that have been painted shut and stayed that way for years. I wouldn't have expected anything less.

The front door opens straight into the lounge and inside there are no pictures on the wall, just a decades' old, off-white paint job; cobwebs in the corners, stains where the rain has come in. The only thing not rank with age and abuse is a wide-screen television and video in one corner of the room, the only pieces of furniture are a brown, rotting two-seat sofa and a glass coffee table scattered with Rizla packets, torn cigarette butts and empty tins of Red Stripe.

I don't think it's his flat. It may be his home, clearly it is. But it's too temporary, even for scum like him. If you ask me, it's a squat, and that would account for the fact that, on closer inspection, there's no catch for the Yale on the inside of the door. Kicked off probably. Done drunk, perhaps, but more likely on entry to take possession of the flat.

I sway slightly, becoming aware of the window on to the street. As I'm just inside the door, I'm not visible from the outside, but if I'm to progress any further, they'll see me just as clearly as I saw Dog-end the other day. Fortunately, my initial appraisal of his curtains situation has turned out to be incorrect. There *are* no curtains as such: instead there are wooden shutters, and I move to my right, nudge one closed so that half of the window is covered. Then, with maybe just the briefest appearance at the window, I close the other, throwing the lounge into stinking darkness.

Right. I finger a miniature in my pocket. Think not – there's a first – then have second thoughts and down one anyway. I move through the lounge to the single doorway and find myself in a tiny hall. At the end is a bathroom, the door open, pea-green bathroom suite; the sort you see when you're looking around houses to buy and say, 'God, that bathroom!'

Next to that is a second door, which must lead to the kitchen. Must do, since the bedroom appears to be on my right.

All I know about breaking into houses I have learnt from TV and books. Television – all those detective programmes coming in handy now, see? – has taught me about fingerprints (hence: Marigolds), footprints (hence: shoes two sizes too small) and nosy neighbours who tweak their curtains and see the suspect (hence: cunning Michael Caine-style disguise). From books, specifically James Bond novels read beneath the light of a dying torch in Groby Road, I know that intruders nearly always need to relieve themselves once they've broken in. James Bond marks his cistern so he can tell whether opposing agents have searched his hotel room in his absence. And, like the shadowy agents of SMERSH, I now find myself in need of a piss. I'm about to head for the bathroom when I have a better idea, one that crystallises a plan in my head.

I sweep my coat out of the way, unzip and have a piss on Dog-end's hallway carpet. Really bright orange, strong-smelling, alcohol-abuse piss, steaming off his carpet. I arc it around, laughing, enjoying myself at last. The relief. The freedom. I replay him snotting on my coat. I piss all I can. I shake the last drops on to the wall. Then I snort all the phlegm I can, which is lots, bring it into my mouth and gob it on the wall.

I go through to the kitchen, which is just as I'd expected from the lounge: the kitchen of a scumbag. There is no furniture in it, just filthy worktops, a sink piled high with dirty dishes, a cat bowl with dried food chunks in it, a centuries-old washing-machine and a fridge with a Quiksilver sticker across the front.

I open the fridge and pull out the contents: a box with three eggs in it, half a pint of milk, a tin of Red Stripe, a tub of cheap margarine, a block of cheese going yellow at the edges, two large tomatoes, a bottle of tomato ketchup (the squeezy plastic sort), an onion and a jar of Marmite.

Apart from the tin of Red Stripe, which I open, and the tomato ketchup, I put the lot in the washing machine, then start looking in the cupboards, finding little else apart from a box of Rice Krispies (gets poured into the washing-machine), instant coffee (ditto), a box of dried cat food (ditto), two cans of baked beans and sugar (ditto, ditto). Under the sink I come across some obviously never-used Vim, which I pour into the powder tray of the washing machine, and some washing powder, which I tip all over the floor. Taking the tomato ketchup and slurping from the tin of Red Stripe, I go through to the bathroom.

I'm breathing heavily now, but it's with excitement. With release. With *power*. I'm making it up as I go along, thinking how creative I can be, imagining him seeing my face on TV, on *Happy Monday*, and half recognising it. What a shame he'll never fully know . . .

In the bathroom I take a bottle of own-brand shampoo, some soap, shaving-foam and razor blades and then find – great – some bleach. Back to the kitchen and I shove the contents of his bathroom into the washing-machine drum, pouring bleach to mix with the Vim in the powder tray.

Then I make my way to the bedroom, holding the bleach, ketchup and the Red Stripe tin. His bed is a mattress covered in a sheet but I leave that for the moment, looking around me. Again, there is no furniture in here, nothing to suggest a human being lives here. There's no wardrobe, but his clothes are stacked neatly in a corner, a little pile of branded sportswear topped off with a baseball cap.

I can fit about half of the pile – including the cap – into the washing-machine, and with it full I add a bit more bleach for good measure before setting the washing-machine to a hot wash, kicking around washing-powder as I move through the rooms. Doesn't matter – shoes are two sizes too small, remember?

Back in the bedroom and really in my stride now, I kick around the rest of the clothes and spray them with the last of the bleach before turning my attention to a ghetto-blaster and a stack of CDs in another corner. I open the CD drawer of the ghetto-blaster and squirt ketchup into it. Then I open the two tape-decks and do the same thing. The CDs I collect up and dump in the bath before opening the hot tap and squeezing in the last of the ketchup for good measure. I finish the Red Stripe and throw the tin into the ketchup-CD soup and leave with the bath still running, but not before blocking the overflow with some wadded tissue paper.

Back through to the kitchen now. Washing-machine's on. Good. It's making a racket – the tins of beans, probably – but otherwise fine. Now I hunt through drawers and find a large kitchen knife, which I take through to the lounge and use to slash open the cushions of his sofa. I hawk and gob a big greenie on the wall as I go back through to the bedroom and I'm about to start on the bed when I have a better idea. I need to answer a call of nature anyway.

This time I take off my coat. Lay the gun carefully on top of it, but within easy arm's reach. Then I unbuckle my jeans and, with my hand on the floor for support, squat with my arse hanging over Dog-end's bed.

I need to go, but it doesn't come as easily as I'd expected, perhaps as a consequence of the nerves. So I close my eyes, try to relax and push.

And push.

And finally, with that sense of relief that's up there with orgasms and sneezing, I feel a turd nosing its way out into the world, dropping and coiling itself comfortably on Dog-end's bed, for all the world like a sleeping pet.

Talking of which, guess what should wander in to have a look just as I'm crapping on Dog-end's bed? Of course: the box of cat food. I hadn't actually reckoned on there being a real-life cat hanging around the place, but here it is, staring suspiciously at me but probably quite excited to find out that – at last – you *can* shit on the bed if you want. I make a kissing sound at it, 'Puss puss,' finishing my shit before realising with horror that I don't have any toilet paper and the last thing I want to do is wipe my arse with Dog-end's sheets. Probably diseased.

The cat scarpers as I edge forward, half pull up my jeans and shuffle precariously towards the bathroom in search of bog paper. It's where I left it, but have you ever tried to wipe your arse wearing washing-up gloves? I can tell I've made a hash of it when I feel rubber on my arse and realise I've poked my finger through the tissue. Still, I finish the job and rinse the shit off the gloves under the running hot tap. I'm just about to pick up the paper and chuck it into the CD-ketchup soup, which is filling nicely, when I have a better idea (I'm full of them this afternoon): I walk through to the bedroom, daintily throwing the shit-stained tissues on to the bed where they join a small heap of stinking turds. The final insult to you, I think: your bedsheets were so foul I couldn't even wipe my arse on them.

Except not the final insult. Because I have a sudden flash of inspiration. A vision of me on *Happy Monday*, the Felix Carter lookylikey. And I'm saying something that isn't scripted and leaves the presenter bemused and blurting, 'Er, right. OK. I won't ask what that's all about.' And moving swiftly on to the next item. And Dog-end leaping out of his slashed-to-fuck seat, suddenly, sickeningly, knowing exactly who did this to his flat. And why.

Because what I said, smiling as I did so, was, 'How's the cat?'

Into the bedroom and I reach for a pillow, strip off the pillowcase. Then, holding the case and the kitchen knife, I go in search of the cat. 'Puss puss,' I say. 'Here, puss puss. Come to Daddy.'

It's behind the swanky TV and video, which I'm leaving

intact for obvious reasons. I can see it staring at me over the top of the video.

'You little furry fucker,' I say, smiling at it. 'Come on.' And I drop to my knees in front of the TV, holding the pillowcase loose and open in one hand and the knife in the other. What I want to do is frighten the cat out from behind the TV and into the pillowcase where I can stab it to death with minimum effort. So I reach forward like I'm trying to hug the television, poking with the knife and shaking the pillowcase as if to suggest that there are some tasty treats inside.

But it's not working. The cat simply moves out of reach of the knife-point and stays well clear of the pillowcase, and I don't have the reach to cover both sides of the TV at the same time.

I crawl round to one side of the TV, forgetting the pillowcase for a moment and stab forward, sending the cat shooting out of the back and through the door to the hall with me in hot pursuit.

We race past the gob and piss and bypass the CD-ketchup soup, straight through to the kitchen. There I see the cat bunched up and poised as if to jump, and see that it's heading for the kitchen window, which has been left ajar, presumably so that it can come and go as it pleases.

The cat is condemned by its inability to make the jump quickly. If it had been able to run-jump in one motion, who knows? It might have made it through the window to safety and I would have accepted defeat gracefully, silently applauded it as a worthy adversary.

As it is, I'm quicker than the cat. I stride forward and pull the window shut just as it jumps, makes it to the window-sill, realises the exit has been closed off and sees the knife sweeping towards its head.

But cats don't have cat-like speed for nothing and, miraculously, it avoids my blade, launching itself from the worktop and back to the floor where it skids on the washing powder, regains balance and hares back through to the hall.

In the hall I witness a moment of indecision as the cat almost races into the bedroom before thinking better of it and heading for the lounge again.

I drop to a walk, and enter the lounge. 'Come to Daddy,' I say, confident of victory now.

It's not behind the TV and video. It's the first place I look and one of only two places it can be.

Is it a stray? Probably. I can't quite see Dog-end trotting off down to the pet shop to get himself some feline company. Most likely it appeared on his window-sill one day, mewing for food, and Dog-end recognised a fellow scavenger and offered it some milk. Almost nice of him, I think. If only he accorded the same respect to his fellow man, then his little companion wouldn't be about to meet its end. I almost feel sorry for it, thinking it had found warmth and shelter here, only to find death.

It's under the sofa, of course. Another irony of its owner's lifestyle is the limited places it has to find sanctuary. And under the sofa really is no kind of sanctuary, since all I have to do is whip off the cushions to expose the grotty webbing below – just a few bronze coins, an ancient till receipt, a stick of Juicy Fruit and a bump where the cat hides, shaking.

I get to my knees in front of the sofa and raise the knife two-handed, like a high-priest in a Hammer horror.

And bring it down as hard as I can, right into the centre of the bump in the sofa.

Had you going . . .

I beg your pardon?

I can see the look on your face. You think I'm that far gone? That I'd kill a cat? Well, I'm not. It's true, I do consider it. I do chase it round the house and I do find it beneath the sofa. But as far as killing it goes, of course not.

You consider it, though, don't you, Chris?

Well, yes. Briefly. But only briefly. I'd had this idea, you see, about saying, 'How's the cat' on *Happy Monday*. Just so Dog-end would have known exactly who'd wrecked his flat, and why. I wanted him to see my face and know that there is justice in this world. And for a moment or so, the life of a cat in exchange for justice being served? Well, it seems like a fair trade.

Thing is, I'm pretty sure my father had that gun hoping that one day he might meet the man who ran down my mother. He was a man with a keen and noble sense of what's wrong and what's right. Fair play and all that. And, what's more, I think it was the injustice that killed him. Or, at least, his impotence in the face of that injustice. So I think he would have sympathised with me *wanting* to kill the cat. But would he have approved of me doing it? No. So that's why I don't. That's why I leave the cat cowering below the sofa and I stand, feeling good and merciful, and then I leave, gobbing one last greenie at the wall for the sake of 'Auld Lang Syne'. Even so, as I'm walking home it does feel like a shame that Dog-end will never know who shat on his bed. You go to all that trouble . . .

CHAPTER TWENTY-NINE

On Thursday, 30 October 2003, Felix Carter had just under a week to live; Christopher Sewell was breaking into the house of the man he called Dog-end; and psychiatric nurse Tony Simpson had the day off in lieu of hours worked. He had been looking forward to it for some time, planning it carefully to coincide with when his girlfriend, Gemma, would be away for the night, attending a marketing conference.

At first she had been annoyed by this, expecting him to organise his day off to correspond with one of hers, so that they might go shopping together, perhaps take a long weekend – she'd always wanted to go to Stratford-upon-Avon, for instance. But Tony had a winning way about him, and he explained that he'd reserved the day (and the night) to indulge himself in his two favourite activities: reading and watching videos. 'To take a swim in Lake Me,' he'd joked, using his phoney American accent, which always made her laugh. So she'd concurred, and secretly found his plans delightful and charming – so simple and unsophisticated. So boyish. So cute. She'd packed her bags and left for Brighton with a kiss on the lips, saying, 'Enjoy your swim.'

Tony hadn't planned his day off to the minute, but he had a basic structure in mind. He'd get up – at his leisure, but not too late – skip breakfast and take the tube to Oxford Street where he intended to visit, first, Borders, the huge bookshop along there, then HMV, almost opposite.

From Borders he would buy one, maybe two novels, preferably in the hard-boiled crime genre, and from HMV he planned to get some videos, none in particular, the only caveat being that they were something Gemma would normally refuse to watch, then proceed to Burger King (Gemma hated Burger King), and eat a Bacon Double-Cheeseburger meal, return home, close the curtains, read his book, and, as day turned into night, get royally stoned while watching his new films. Sorted, he thought.

Borders went fine. He chose a staff recommendation from the crime section: *King Suckerman* by George P. Pelecanos,[27] as well as an Elmore Leonard novel he had yet to read, *Be Cool*.[28]

Thanks to a sale at HMV, he found a Sex Pistols theme developing. Having picked up the *Sid'n'Nancy* video for £4.99, he was reminded that he had so far missed *The Filth and the Fury*, and bought that too, adding *The Great Rock'n'Roll Swindle* (seen, but ages ago) to his purchases.

Having watched these three films, he assured, he would be feeling all 'punk' so he took the escalator downstairs where finally, after all these years, he bought *Sandinista!* by the Clash. Already he was looking forward to formulating his own opinion on an album that divided critics into detractors, who thought it was a white elephant, and supporters, who fervently believed it to be a lost classic. Secretly, he'd already half decided that he was going to join the lost-classic camp, but one thing was for sure: no longer would he have to fall quiet or fake it when pub conversations turned to *Sandinista!*. That in itself was a good thing, especially since he and his friends were lapsed punks, to a man, and could happily while away the hours discussing the relative merits of the Adverts and Johnny Moped.

Finally – and what the hell? – he picked up *Raw Power* by Iggy and the Stooges, a CD that counted as an upgrade since he already owned it on vinyl, but his copy was so scratched as to be virtually unlistenable. As he paid, and the assistant congratulated him on his choice, 'Bit better than all this fucking garage we have to put up with,' he added four AA

---

[27] (Serpent's Tail).
[28] (Penguin).

batteries, Duracell, to power his CD Walkman so he'd be certain not to run out of juice on the way home. He intended to listen to *Sandinista!* straight away.

Happy with his choices he set off for Burger King, where he enjoyed exactly the meal he'd planned then departed for the twenty-minute tube journey between Oxford Circus and Shepherd's Bush.

It was just twelve thirty and there were only four other people sharing the carriage on Tony's train, so he settled down into an end seat, fished out his copy of *Sandinista!* and began to read the accompanying booklet. He hardly noticed when the tube train stopped midway between Bond Street and Marble Arch.

It's not uncommon for trains to stop between stations – in fact it happens quite frequently; certainly nothing to get worried about. Delays of up to five minutes or so occur all the time. So Tony paid it no mind. He looked at the adverts above the seats opposite him: one for a pregnancy-testing kit, the other for vitamin supplements. He flicked through his *Sandinista!* CD booklet as he listened to the album.

Because he was wearing headphones – and, being a conscientious sort, he had bought a pair that allowed him to listen at high volumes without annoying fellow passengers – he missed an announcement by the train driver. He was aware of it outside the music, but chose not to listen, reasoning that the driver would be apologising for the slight delay and assuring passengers they would be on their way in due course.

Which, in effect, he was, only with a turn of phrase that those passengers not listening to the Clash found vaguely disquieting.

'Ladies and gentlemen,' he said, over the Tannoy. The driver had a habit of stretching his words when he was making announcements but, fortunately for his family, it wasn't a vocal tic he carried into everyday life. Indeed, at home it was the kids' treat for Daddy to use his 'speaker voice' in normal conversation – 'No football till you've tidied away your PlayStation' became 'No football-ah . . . until you've tidied away your PlayStayshun-ah . . .' He dreaded the day the kids no longer thought it was such a treat, perhaps even found it embarrassing.

To be exact, then, what he said was, 'Ah-ladies and gennermen-ah . . . Do you want the good news or the bad news-ah? Okay, the bad news-ah: we've been asked to hold on here for a few moments more-ah . . . I haven't been informed as to the exact nature of the problem, but as soon as I know, you will too-ah. In the meantime, sit back, relax and think about the good news – it's raining outside-ah, so at least you're in the dry-ah.'

Despite the light-hearted delivery, which made the passengers smile, the two pieces of information they found mildly worrying were that (a) the delay would last 'a few moments more': 'a few *minutes* more' and they wouldn't have worried; 'a few *moments* more' meant nobody knew how long it would be. And (b) the driver didn't know what the problem was, which meant either (i) he did know, but didn't want to tell them for fear of worrying and/or panicking them, like perhaps there was a largish stream of molten lava proceeding down the tunnel towards them, or (ii) he really didn't know. And if the driver didn't know, then who did?

Some minutes later the driver made a second announcement, during which he repeated that the train was being held for a few moments – again, that word – and that the unidentified problem was being attended to that very moment, and that he was very sorry if their day's shopping was being interrupted but remember to thank London Underground when their credit-card statement arrived. Some of the passengers smiled, two old ladies turned to one another and one said, 'Quite jolly, isn't he?' but others – those who were now worrying about missing appointments or being late back from lunch – found his jocular tone slightly irritating.

Meanwhile, Tony Simpson sat listening to the Clash. Having finished with the small print of the booklet, he slid it carefully back into its case, replaced it in his bag and took out his George P. Pelecanos novel. He was soon engrossed in it.

CD one of *Sandinista!* had almost finished before Tony Simpson's head jerked up. He had suddenly realised they had been sitting still for an awful long time now.

He looked around him but the other passengers sat sullen, and made no effort to communicate with him. However, their demeanour suggested that there was nothing to be concerned about. A delay; a long one, for sure, but just a delay. Mentally he shrugged, and went back to Pelecanos and Strummer.

The next time the driver made an announcement – his fourth since the train had stopped – Tony lifted his headphones. The driver explained that the train was being held in the tunnel indefinitely while engineers worked to fix what appeared to be an electrical fault. London Underground apologised for the delay, but requested that passengers remain patient, the problem *was* being attended to, and the driver would pass on any new information as soon as he had it. Not that it helps, added the driver, but he had a cup of coffee going cold at the terminus.

Tony smiled at the driver's joke. He noticed that none of the other passengers did. Miserable buggers, he thought, and went back to his book.

The next time he stirred from the dual attentions of Pelecanos and his Walkman was when *Sandinista!* ended. *Sandinista!* is a famously long album, hence the white elephant tag, around two and a half hours long, in fact. And Tony had listened to all of it stuck on a tube train midway between Bond Street and Marble Arch. Some day off, he thought, although he was not unduly bothered. He was in no immediate discomfort, the passengers around him were obviously agitated but otherwise well behaved, and he was enjoying the book. Moreover, he now had *Raw Power* to relish, the full CD experience. So he switched CDs, and Iggy sang, 'I'm a street-walking cheetah with a heart full of napalm.' Tony went right back to school.

Every now and then the driver would make another announce-ment, and mostly Tony would listen, but became bored with the driver's poor attempts at humour and his bingo-caller voice, which made each announcement take twice as long as it should. Still, the novelty of listening to *Raw Power* hadn't worn off, and he found himself amazed when the CD didn't jump, as his vinyl always had, right in the middle of the title track.

At one point another passenger, a man of about his age, moved past him in the aisle, mouthing something as he went. Tony lifted his headphones and bent his head forward: 'Sorry?' The man looked ashamed. 'I'm really sorry about this. Can't hold on any longer.' Then he opened the door at the end of the carriage and, as discreetly as the circumstances allowed, had a piss. Tony felt sorry for him; didn't watch. He wrinkled his nose at the smell of urine that filled the carriage but it was soon gone, the door closed and the man back in his seat and, really, if that was the worst this delay had to offer, then fine.

Soon *Raw Power* had finished and he fancied another crack at *Sandinista!* so he put that on again. He stopped listening out for the driver's announcements, reasoning that he'd be able to tell the news from the other passenger's faces. Mainly they slept, or read like him, or talked if they were in pairs. They'd long since stopped bothering to tut or roll their eyes or harrumph and study their watches ostentatiously. In other words, they dealt with it. When the driver made his increas-ingly unwelcome announcements they shared their disapproval at his inappropriate banter by making faces at each other. They didn't spark up relationships as such, but they were comforted by their joint inconvenience. Ironic, really, that such a classic example of the old Blitz spirit in action should be conducted in its birthplace – the Underground. But Tony didn't think about that, he just kept on reading and finding different things to admire in *Sandinista!*.

Above them, of course, the shit was hitting the fan. A train stuck midway between Bond Street and Marble Arch meant the Central Line was effectively out of action, which meant passengers were forced to use alternative routes, which meant those routes became overcrowded – and it was not even rush-hour. Soon, all lines were experiencing delays, which usually only occurs during some kind of service-wide action, such as a strike. Presently, those 'delays' were upgraded to 'serious delays' as the system struggled to cope.

The word soon passed from those whose job it was to compile the travel news to those whose job it was to compile simply 'the news'. A tube train stuck underground for near-on four hours became an item of news in itself, to be treated at first as an example of the deepening crisis faced by London's transport system. But as the day wore on, news teams from radio, TV and the papers were dispatched to the area, ready to greet the passengers of the stranded train when they surfaced, and when their story could be exploited for its human angle, which, after all, always provides the spine of any compelling news story.

At the time of their despatch, the journalists and photographers had no idea what that angle might be, but they were under orders from their news editors, who knew, from their own time in the newsroom, that the human angle would be there, *had to be there*. It was simply a case of finding it.

A train stuck in a single place for four hours, for example. One of the following was likely to happen:

1. Passenger A has an epileptic fit. Passenger B, a nurse on her day off, is there to provide medical care.
2. Passenger A goes into labour. Passenger B, a nurse on her day off, is there to provide medical care.
3. Passenger A is drunk and aggressive and assaults Passenger B. Passenger C does 'what anyone would do' and subdues Passenger A, finally delivering him into the hands of the police when the drama is over.

4. Passenger A has a heart attack. Fortunately Passenger B is on hand.
5. Passenger A asks Passenger B to marry him. Passenger B says yes and they invite Passengers C to V to the wedding.
6. Passenger A gets talking to Passenger B, only to discover they are related.
7. Passengers A to Z all die.

Any or all of the above might or would be happening in the ground below the media's feet as they gathered, not sure whether to assemble at Bond Street or Marble Arch, but following each other and the bits of misinformation that came their way.

There was not a great number of them, this was only ever a local news story (unless number seven turned out to be true), but there was enough to make their presence felt. They set up camp and intermingled in that strange mates-who-stitch-each-other-up way that is almost peculiar to members of the news media.

And they waited.

And, below ground, the passengers waited too.

And finally London Underground got its act together – although it never actually got round to admitting exactly what act it was they got together – and, some four and a half hours after Tony Simpson had first boarded the train at Oxford Circus, he emerged into fading daylight at Marble Arch.

He was yawning, slightly stiff, but otherwise unconcerned. Some time into the wait, the 'four-hour ordeal', as more than one newspaper would later describe it, he had reasoned that had he been at home he would have been sitting reading anyway, and despite the lack of basics such as tea and a toilet, he was really quite comfortable, and if he'd needed a piss, well, the other chap his age had proved it could be done with minimum loss of dignity.

So when he was asked about his experience he was accordingly upbeat – an attitude at odds with that of his fellow passengers who shrugged off their Blitz spirit like rain-soaked overcoats and began huffing and puffing, loudly proclaiming their intention to demand compensation and grovelling apologies from London Underground, with more than one 'slamming' the lack of information given during the wait and drawing particular attention to the 'irritating prat' of a driver.

Fortunately, at least for the self-esteem of the driver and his family, these last remarks were never reported. Poor chap, he would have been mortified. He felt his friendly commentary had helped ease the situation for the passengers, whom he had come to see as being in his care, and later, when Tony Simpson came to the forefront of the story, even appearing on *Happy Monday* with Felix Carter, for God's sake, he felt slightly hurt that his efforts hadn't been given more attention. After all, what had Tony Simpson *done*, except say . . . 'It was all right, really. I had a good book and a fresh set of batteries for my Walkman.'

Because that was all he did say. Not quite true. To that he added, when he was asked his name and address. 'Er, Simpson. Tony Simpson. With a Y. S-Y-M-P-S-O-N. Nobody ever gets it right. Sorry, from? What, in London? Oh, from Shepherd's Bush.'

I wake up in the hall of my flat. Or should that be I wake up in the *hell* of my flat? Who cares? Either applies. In any event, I wake up.

This is the morning after you break into the guy's house?

Yes. But, naturally, I don't remember that straight away. I just hear the rustle of the demons' wings, and they'll tell me what I've done in a moment or so. They'll torture me with it, in fact. They'll say, *'Look what you went and did. Look how low you've sunk.'*

Luckily, I know just the thing to see them off and there, on the coffee table, is a tiny bottle of magic anti-demon potion, which I reach for now. It's Citron flavour. Lemon fresh for the morning. Just the thing, and it goes down a treat.

Well, if you consider coughing and gagging and almost throwing up a treat. Which, in the present circumstances, I do.

I feel slightly better at once. Not better enough, though, and I cast around for another. There's the little plastic presentation box they come in, and scattered around are several empties, a Peppar (very hot, the Peppar – you'd think twice, even in my condition), an unflavoured and a Mandrin. No, two Mandrins. There are also many, many cans of Stella. I kick one, it rolls and turns out not to be completely empty, so I pick it up and swig, my dehydrated body glad of the fluid even if, as I well know, alcohol is dehydrating and by drinking it I'm only making myself worse. Hey, as the man said, isn't that the point?

Still, it doesn't feel like worse. I wander through to the kitchen, my grip on the day increasing as the alcohol worms its way hotly into my grateful bloodstream. In lieu of more vodka, the lager will do, and I brace myself against a kitchen worktop, stare out of the window into the tiny backyard behind our flat. Just room enough for a barbecue, which we had once, using one of those disposable foil efforts you can get from Safeway.

I'm piecing together the events of last night. Straight away I remember breaking into Dog-end's house and shitting on his bed. As far as I can recall, Dog-end's is the first bed I've ever shat on, certainly in my adult life. I'm sure that as a youngster I shat on a bed or two, and maybe I'll be shitting on beds in my dotage, but as far as deliberately, and with malice aforethought, Dog-end's is my first. My shit-bed cherry gone, just like that.

Something inside me – a demon – whispers that shitting on a bed is a bad thing, but something else replies: How can it be a bad thing? Since when is justice a *bad thing*? Against the law? Not my law. That's the way the world should be, I think: someone snots on your coat, you shit on their bed – a simple exchange of bodily fluids. I can hardly kid myself that Dad would be proud. After all, there's a world of difference between doing toilet and gunning down the man who killed your wife, but I think he'd understand. The gun proves that.

And, luckily for me, that voice is louder, more persuasive than the whisper, gets louder and even more persuasive as I finish the can of Stella. Very lucky for me. It allows me to stand straighter against the worktop, and to think, think, *think*.

Remember that episode of *Friends* (favourite of Sam's; I took the piss) where Ross has cheated on Rachel? He's terrified that Rachel will find out and goes to Joey, who tells him to take care of 'the trail' – the trail of information that might lead back to Rachel.

Ross hadn't shat on Rachel's bed – that kind of thing doesn't make great comedy – but, for me, the principle is the same.

Let's think, then. I'm confident that my preparations before the event were sound, and I remember being careful to let myself in and out of the flat as unobtrusively as possible, both times wearing my door-to-door salesman disguise of clipboard and reading glasses. So what I need to do now is dispose of any evidence that might lead back to me, and that means dumping the glasses, the coat, the clipboard, the Marigolds and the shoes. Good.

All the evidence is already inside the flat, so all I need to do is gather it up and get rid of it, as far away from here as possible. It's not like I expect the police to call in the DNA experts, and I've never been fingerprinted, haven't got a police record, so the chances of the trail ever leading back to me are very slim indeed. In addition, will the police really care about a scumbag like Dog-end? Not likely. You can't tell me that he wasn't already known to them – probably a repeat offender. Coppers will be hanging out the bunting when they find out what I've done, and if they did catch me they'd probably shake me by the hand and send me on my way, turn a blind eye like at the end of *Death Wish*. But, still, I'm not taking any chances. I'll get rid of the stuff just in case.

And then, as planned, I'll get my hair cut, to look more like Felix for my TV appearance – or *advert*, as I'm now thinking of it – and also to look a lot less like the bloke who went in and out of Dog-end's flat, just in case someone happened to be watching.

OK, so I feel like shit, and I haven't tidied the flat as I intended, but so far so good. And I wonder if Sam got her tape, and whether she's planning to watch *Happy Monday*.

As I go back to the lounge, the TV is trailing a documentary that's showing later. It's called *Being Felix Carter*. 'Unprecedented access to the life of Britain's biggest star,' shouts the voiceover, as footage from the programme flicks across the screen. Here's Felix, sitting at a kitchen table with an older woman, perhaps his mum, one of his songs playing on the soundtrack. Then he's on stage, the camera panning back over what seems like endless, endless people, all of whom appear to be holding cigarette lighters in the air and singing along to another of his songs. They adore him. Every single one of them is transfixed by the bloke on stage who looks like me.

Next Felix is sitting in what looks like his lounge: in stark contrast to my own, his is clean and trendy, but he's talking about drinking, saying, in a trailer soundbite, 'Booze. It's like women. I can't live with it, can't live without it. Other people have cars, I have a wagon, and I'm either on it, off it, chasing after it or running away from it. But I tell you what – it's always there.'

And then it cuts to him in the studio, then talking to some fans, more fans who love him, gazing adoringly up at him as he signs autographs – a bit of easy banter as he does so.

After the advert's finished I stand in front of the television for some moments, then put on *About Time Too* as I collect together my evidence, ready to go out and get my hair cut. He looked quite tanned and muscly in the advert. No time to get muscles, but I could go and get a quick tan somewhere. That'd make Russ a happy researcher.

I shouldn't really, I should go the long way around, the route that bypasses Dog-end's house, but a mixture of curiosity and Dutch courage gets the better of me, and when I walk to the tube station, I go past his house. My one concession to caution is that I walk by on the other side of the road, glancing across as I do so.

It looks the same, of course. To see the house from the outside you would never know what havoc I wreaked in it. It's even possible that my presents have remained undiscovered. Perhaps Dog-end has that pleasure to come. He's spent the night elsewhere, blissfully unaware that his flat is slowly flooding, that a festering turd lies on his bed and that his washing-machine has clanked its way to self-destruction, his clothes ruined, his CDs destroyed. It's all I can do not to laugh, and I feel a guilty, shameful thrill as I head towards the newsagent for a bottle of Fanta.

Outside is an A-board holding an *Evening Standard* bill, which says, 'Crime In Hackney – can you help?' and I think, I already have, as I push open the door and catch sight of the policeman standing at the counter.

For a second or so I feel totally sober. But then, almost as quickly, I realise how drunk I am and I have to remind myself that although it may be anti-social, being drunk in the morning isn't a crime. Either way, I can hide it well. I always do.

On the other hand, while being drunk in the morning isn't a crime, breaking into houses is, which makes me a criminal. And we criminals get nervous when we encounter policemen. Especially when we're carrying a rucksack full of evidence linking us to the crime. Coming into the shop to buy Fanta suddenly seems like a bad idea. Up there with taking this particular route to the tube. I curse the Dutch and their stupid courage, not to mention their lager.

I've been pausing at the door, dazzled by the navy of the policeman's back, but as he turns to look at me I gather myself and step inside, my heart hammering, sweat dripping from my armpits. Reasoning that a sudden about-turn might incriminate me, I affect a look of nonchalance, simultaneously trying to hide my guilt and my drunkenness, and make my way to the drinks cabinet, where I pretend to be lost in the indecision of which soft drink to buy.

The policeman turns back to the shop assistant. 'This would have been between the hours of, we think, two p.m. and seven p.m. yesterday,' he says. 'You would have been open?'

'I was, yes,' says the shopkeeper.

I open the door to the drinks cabinet, knowing that I've inadvertently stumbled into the investigation of my crime, calling on the god of vigilantes to help me keep it together. He's a fucking scumbag, I think, hard enough for the policeman to hear. You're not supposed to care.

If there was any justice in the world the police wouldn't give a hoot. No, if there was any justice in the world I'd be able to step inside this drinks cabinet and it would transport me to another dimension, anywhere but here.

'And you didn't see anything suspicious?' continues the policeman. 'None of your customers mentioned anything to you?'

I take a bottle of Fanta, unable to justify delaying any longer. I close the cabinet door.

'I'm afraid not,' says the shopkeeper. 'Look, I wouldn't be able to see across the road from here anyway.' He points forward, out of the door and across the road towards Dog-end's house. Both the policeman and I follow his arm, and he's right: between the Lottery adverts and personal ads in the window, the view is limited at best. Thank God for that at least.

'And nobody's said anything to you?' says the policeman. He says it to the shopkeeper, but to me as well. I raise my eyebrows and sort of shrug at him and he turns back. I feel like I've just had electrodes attached to my testicles.

'Sorry,' replies the shopkeeper, 'I'll keep an ear out, though.'

'Thank you, sir. Let me give you this card. With the publicity this is getting, we're hoping someone's going to come out of the woodwork, so if you do hear anything, can you contact me on this number?'

'Will do.'

And then, at last, the policeman leaves, giving me a nod as he goes, which I return with a nod that's more like a nervous twitch. Actually, it *is* a nervous twitch. When the door's closed behind him, I put the Fanta on the counter, steel myself and say to the shopkeeper, 'What was all that about?' Because, of course, I would. Not to ask would look strange, as if somehow I already knew what the policeman was enquiring about.

'Woman across the road got broken into,' says the shopkeeper, ringing up the Fanta.

Woman?

'Police are doing their high-visibility bit because of this . . .'

There's an *Evening Standard* open on the counter between us and he twists it round so that I can read it. It's open to a double-page spread. A strapline at the top says, 'Criminal London. Day Five: Hackney' and below it are up to ten stories: 'Gang beats youth', 'Car crime figures', 'Arson attack' – a sorry collage of the area's criminal activities. Below the stories is a second strapline that says, 'Can You Help? Call Crimestoppers' and a number. But it's the biggest story on the page that the shopkeeper points at, his finger hovering above the newsprint. Alongside the story there is a picture of a forlorn-looking woman, about my age, looking like life has taken her round the back and beaten her up. She's standing in front of the door to a house.

I recognise the house, of course I do. It's the house I broke into last night, that until about, oh, thirty seconds ago, I'd thought was Dog-end's house. But the shopkeeper had said 'woman', and here she is, in black and white. Beaten-up-looking, hardly the kind of woman you'd take home to meet Mother, but a woman all the same. Emphatically not Dog-end.

I catch my breath, control the shakes, and say, 'God, how awful,' as though I've scanned the story, which I don't need to do because I already know what happens. 'I'll take one of these as well,' I add, indicating the *Standard* and renewing my pleas to the god of vigilantes – Get me out of this shop without breaking down. Please.

He does, and I hurry away, out of sight of the shop and Dog-end's house and up the road towards the tube where I open the paper and read:

POLICE HUNT 'VILE' RAIDERS![29]

Police are appealing for witnesses after the home of a Hackney woman was raided by vandals in what has been described as a 'vile' attack.

It is the second time jobless Colette Carew (28), has been the victim of raiders in the space of a week – last Friday burglars took money and jewellery from her Stoke Newington home.

Nothing was taken in the latest break-in, which happened some time in the afternoon yesterday (Thursday), but in a catalogue of destruction, intruders

- left excrement in Ms Carew's bed
- deliberately flooded the home
- destroyed clothing and property
- vandalised stereo equipment

'I am stunned,' said Ms Carew last night. 'I will never get over the shock of coming through the door and seeing what they had done to my home.'

'An attack of this nature is always distressing,' said Det. Insp. Trevor Harvey of Stoke Newington Police. 'But this was particularly vile. The human excrement left in the house leads us to believe we are dealing with something worse than simple vandalism. The people who did this are obviously disturbed and we are anxious to catch them before the nature of their crimes escalates further.'

Police are appealing for anybody who has seen anything unusual in the area around the time of the raid to come forward.

Did you see anything? Call Crimestoppers on the number below.

---

[29] From the *Evening Standard*, Friday, 31 October 2003.

Last Friday.

She was burgled last Friday.

Last Friday, when I stood and watched Dog-end let himself out of her flat, thinking it was *his* flat. Assumed that his furtive glances were simply his way of putting on his low-life coat. But they weren't. He really *was* checking to see if anybody had seen him, checking because he'd just finished burgling Colette Carew. God, no wonder she looks so beaten up: she's been burgled twice in the space of a week. And on the second occasion by me, gloriously losing my shit-bed virginity.

And to think I stood and I watched Dog-end leave the scene of the crime. I chortled to myself like some kind of arch-villain planning my next fiendish move, when in fact I had him *there and then*. I could have followed him. Picked up the phone and called the police. Been the hero. The Good Samaritan who helped in apprehending a burglar. I might even have been in the papers. A good deed in this day and age, worth a little story, surely? Something for Sam to see. That and the *Happy Monday* appearance might have done the trick.

Buffoon. Idiot. Instead of being the good Samaritan, the hero, the man of whom my father really would have been proud, I'm now the person the police want to catch. Want to catch really badly, by the sound of things. Forget Dog-end, he's small fry compared to me. It's me they'll be saving the bunting for.

Oh. God.

I lower the paper. Vaguely I think how helpful it would be if all my drunken episodes could be so formally documented – 'Warnings over corn-on-the-cob blaze', 'Rogue shoes in loose stones probe', stuff like that – but it's the vodka talking, and it's forgetting that, right now, I'm concerned with this. Concerned with the pincer attack that guilt and paranoia are staging in my head.

Right, let's deal with the fear first. I need to get rid of this stuff, need to get my hair cut, need to feel I've scuffed enough dirt over the trail between me and Colette Carew before I can even afford to be motivated by guilt. We'll come to that in a bit.

Still, try telling the demons that. And I slurp some more anti-demon potion. Sharpish.

CHAPTER THIRTY-ONE

'It was all right, really. I had a good book and a fresh set of batteries for my Walkman.'

It played at the end of the local evening news. Tony Simpson. Good-looking, personable young chap. Likeable smile. The sort you can imagine giving up his seat for an old lady. His headphones around his neck, his Pelecanos held up for extra emphasis. The personification of the much-missed Blitz spirit but given a noughties shine. All he needed was his book and his Walkman and he was happy. A simple man.

And the world, at least the United Kingdom bit of it, likes a good-looking young man of simple tastes who smiles his troubles away. And his quote was a mundane enough quote, but that was its brilliance. It fired the imagination.

It fired the imagination of the *Guardian*'s literary editor, who thought the god of ideas had smiled down upon her and immediately commissioned a piece on 'the power of a good book', asking the writer to lead in on the quote from Tony Simpson.

It fired the imagination of an advertising creative who worked on the Sony account – a quick-hit instant newspaper campaign. Tony Simpson. The Walkman. Copy along the lines of 'If only the tube ran on batteries'. Genius.

But first it fired the imagination of a national newspaper editor who was new to the job and keen to establish his ideas quickly.

Peter Bryant had established his reputation on a series of high-profile local newspapers where each time he had presided over increasingly impressive sales figures. Each time his newspaper's circulation figures had gone through the roof he was poached: first for another title within the group, then to the group's flagship title, then by a rival group to their flagship title and finally by the nationals. The biggest national there was: the *Sun*.

His success was based on combining two journalistic ideals. He was first and foremost an old-style news warhorse. His shirt was never tucked in, his tie never less than half-mast, and he believed in good old slowly dying-out principles like investigative journalism, building up contacts, getting stories in the pub, things like that.

To that ethic, however, he brought an attitude that was positively New Age in the newspaper world and it could be summed up by his two favourite slogans: People Stories, and Positive Angles. Hardly rocket science, but they had served him well in the local-newspaper world and now he was to find out whether or not they would translate to the national arena.

The basis of his principles was a celebration of people, the readership. Too often readers opened a newspaper only to find themselves awash with bad news, swamped by issues they didn't understand. In Local Land he wanted each reader to feel good about themselves and the area they lived in (very important), not terrified that it was a crime-ridden dump where their neighbours were about to fleece them of all their worldly goods. And no, he argued to the older, cynical members of his editorial team, that didn't mean ignoring crime stories, ceasing council reporting or any of the other things that provided the meat of everyday journalism. Instead, it meant a shifting of the news agenda, prioritising the positive upwards, moving the bad news down the page and bringing the good news upwards. Make people feel good about themselves and the area they live in, that was the key.

And it had worked. He put his success down to the application of those values: a minor alteration in news values, the highlighting of the feel-good factor. Not, he was keen to stress, by shrouding the bad news – it happened, it had to be covered

– but by hunting out positive angles, celebrating good work, and shouting about readers' achievements.

A happy side-effect of his news policy was a breaking down of the barriers between public and paper. As the public no longer feared opening his newspaper in case it made them terrified to step out of the door, they came to see it as a supportive friend, instead of a rather forbidding head-teacher. And to that new relationship, the readers brought their own stories, making his newspaper first choice when it came to picking up the phone – and every newspaper in the world relies on people picking up the phone. So his newspapers quickly began to stuff the opposition, scooping the major news stories each time, and the readers not only gained a trustworthy and loyal friend, but also a friend with the best gossip.

Now, as the new editor of the *Sun*, he believed there was no reason why these local-news values couldn't be applied to a national newspaper – the area was bigger, that was all. Otherwise, his new constituency had exactly the same desires as the old one. It was simply a matter of the careful and gradual introduction of a slightly new agenda.

Note 'careful and gradual', and for his first two weeks into the job he'd let things run as they had under the previous editor, waiting for the right opportunity to arise.

And with Tony Simpson it had.

Tony Simpson, he'd decided, was to be the first recipient of the new 'Nice One, *Sun*!' award.

There was no physical award as such – though there was no reason why there couldn't be in the future: instead it was a badged story. A weekly – and hopefully, eventually, daily – tale that celebrated the bulldog breed of Britain: bravery, generosity, a Good Samaritan act and, in this case, stoicism.

His ultimate aim was for the 'Nice One, *Sun*!' award to be as readily identifiable with the paper as Page Three (his view, incidentally: had to stay). And while at first the copy would be an existing story assigned the 'Nice One, *Sun*!' tag, as the idea gathered momentum the piece would be purpose-written by a reporter dedicated to the task. Moreover, by flagging the story in this way, it clearly set aside a section of the paper with which the public could identify. Before long, he reasoned, they would be picking up the phone and ringing in, responding to the sign-off: 'Do you know someone who deserves a "Nice One, *Sun*!?" If so, give us a call. Don't worry about the cost, we'll call you straight back.'

Oh, yes, 'Nice One, *Sun*!' was his baby, so when Tony Simpson, his Walkman and a good book appeared on Peter Bryant's radar, he grabbed the opportunity with both hands, explaining to his evening news team that he wanted Tony Simpson found, he wanted a picture of him re-creating 'the pose' and he wanted an interview with him that pitched him as an ordinary, decent bloke who didn't whinge and whine and run for his solicitor when bad times came a-calling, but who made the best of a bad situation. And, oh, play down the fact that he's a psychiatric nurse. Make him just a nurse, and make sure we get his pittance of a wage in there as well. And stress that this was his first day off in months, and even though he spent it locked up in a stuffy tube train he's kept a smile on his face.

And he wanted it all for the following day's paper.

To design, he placed an order for a Nice One, *Sun*! flash that would run as page furniture in the top left-hand corner of the story. Something in a medal shape perhaps, with the red of the newspaper masthead edged in gold, but you're the experts I'll leave it to you. Just remember, this is going to become a regular fixture so make it something timeless.

And with that done, he sat down to write an accompanying editorial that would introduce the concept of the Nice One, *Sun*! award, and explain why Tony Simpson was its inaugural recipient. He began with the headline, 'That's the Spirit!'

Are you warm enough? It can get a bit chilly in here. I'm not sure there's much I can do about it – even I can't control the heating in here, but perhaps we can sort you an extra layer.

Actually, I'm fine, thanks.

Right. Now where am I?

You're disposing of your evidence. The things you think can link you to the break-in.

That's right, I am. And I'll say this much, I'm methodical. I use the vodka, don't let it use me. I take it to sharpen myself, give myself an edge.

In addition I chase the fear and guilt into a back room and lock them in there, and even though I can hear them banging on the door, I zone out the sound. I need to, so I can concentrate.

First, I dump the newspaper. Casually toss it into a bin as I go past – just a man who's finished with a newspaper, nothing unusual in that. Meanwhile, my hair feels like a big neon guilty sign on the top of my head, and I'm itching to get it off, but first I have to chuck the evidence.

Previously I'd intended simply to dump the whole rucksack in a bin, but not any more – not now that the stakes have been raised. I'm no longer someone who dispensed a bit of rough justice on a known criminal, I'm now a 'vile raider' with a 'disturbed' mind. And where the police would previously have turned a blind eye, *Death Wish*-style, now they'll probably beat me half to death just for being vile and disturbed. Yes, the stakes have gone up, but I raise my game in response.

Next go the sunglasses with no lenses. I get rid of them just before I reach the tube, tossing them into some bushes. They're not what I'm most worried about. The really damning bits of evidence in my view are the shoes and the gloves. The police would have been able to take footprints from the mess in the kitchen, and while they're now looking for someone two sizes smaller than me, if I'm found in possession of these shoes, that's me done for.

The gloves are less of a worry. Can you match gloves to glove-prints? Can you even take glove-prints? I'm not sure, but I think I've seen it done on TV. The sooner I get rid of the gloves the better as far as I'm concerned.

I unload the clipboard on the tube, leaving it wedged into the seat behind me when I get off at Oxford Circus. I make sure not to get rid of it until I've changed at Finsbury Park: that way it could have come from anywhere between Brixton and Walthamstow Central, and even though it's not a key element of the evidence I'm mentally accumulating against myself, I'm still ensuring I don't get sloppy. Not now, not at this stage.

I get off at Oxford Circus and fish around in the rucksack for my sandwiches (imaginary sandwiches – but to anyone looking, I'm just a man searching for his sandwiches) but it's not sandwiches I pull out and decide they're unfit to eat before casually tossing them into a nearby bin – it's the first of the two shoes.

The second shoe goes into a litter bin on Regent Street as I look for my sandwiches a second time.

I wish that I worked in a school, or a factory, or anywhere they have furnaces in a spooky, deserted basement that I could use to burn the entire rucksack in one go. Because by the time I've got rid of everything in it, I've looked for imaginary sandwiches in Leicester Square, Soho and Tottenham Court Road. I dump it in a litter-bin on Great Titchfield Street.

I breathe a careful sigh of relief as I do so, looking down the road with X-ray eyes and seeing my evidence scattered over a section of central London measuring a good three square miles. Good. These litter-bins must be emptied all the time, probably by different people, and soon the incriminating bits will be separated and scattered even wider. And if a homeless person sees my coat in the bin and decides he can make good use of it in the nasty weather, all the better.

I feel a weight lift from my shoulders, and go in search, first, of more vodka, and then to a cheap and cheerful barber's for a number-three crop. We'll see about the suntan after that, but for now I hear the demons fluttering and hurry towards an Oddbins.

I lucky-dip the vodkas almost as soon as I get out of the shop and for a bit of extra fun I don't look at the bottle before I down it, see if I can guess which it is. Secretly, I hope it's Kurant. I like the Ribena taste. Reminds me of Groby Road. I've got the quick, furtive downing of miniatures almost perfected now, like those old lags who can roll up a fag one-handed. I unstick the box, roll out a single bottle into my closed fist, then slide it base first up my sleeve with just the tiny neck protruding. Like a magician's sleight of hand, like Spider-Man's web-shooters, only filled with vodka.

With the standard miniatures, you need two hands – at least, I do – to get them open, one to grip, the other to twist. But there's something about the design of the stubbier Absolut bottles that makes it possible to open them one-handed. And by using my method, I can have the bottle in my palm and unscrew the cap without ever bringing it into public view. When that's done, I have an open bottle of Absolut ready to dispense, literally up my sleeve.

Once the vodka is safely open and up the sleeve all the hard work is done and I have several drinking options. Favourite is the theatrical yawn, head tilted back, hand up to cover the mouth, vodka into an open throat and look out, Bloodstream, here she comes.

Then there's the cough, which is tricky because you have to get your timing right or risk spluttering precious vodka into the street and drawing unwelcome attention to yourself. I've even done the hand scratching the ear, which you can do while simultaneously holding a fag, but you need to make sure there's nobody on the other side of you. On this occasion I plump for the yawn – I've been careful not to see accidentally which flavour it is, and it turns out to be . . . Kurant! Hurrah! Things are surely looking up.

In the back room of my mind, Fear has quietened down, but Guilt's making enough racket for two, shouting to be let out. Fortunately, the vodka hushes it, but not for long.

I'm in the pub when it occurs to me that I should buy new clothes to look more like Felix for *Happy Monday*.

I don't know why it hasn't hit me before, me with my big ideas about advertising and presentation, but since I've had my hair cut in the right style, I might as well go the whole hog.

That's one reason I think about clothes. The other is because I do genuinely need some new ones.

I'm sitting at the bar, and I'm thinking how nice it would be if a woman sat down next to me and struck up a conversation. She'd have to be on her lunch-break, of course, I'm not sure I'd want to chat to the kind of woman who hangs around in pubs all day. I'd want this one perhaps to be clutching a paperback novel that she'd intended to read in a few quiet moments. She'd be blonde, smartly but not overbearingly dressed. She'd be in her late thirties or early forties, pretty but worldly-wise, and she'd smell of perfume or hairspray, whatever, but mixed with cigarette smoke. For a moment or so she'd sit reading her book and sipping her drink, which would be a gin and tonic or a white wine spritzer, and then after a few minutes she'd ask me to pass her the small bowl of nuts sitting on the bar in front of us.

Shame, there are no nuts in front of me.

In that case, she'd ask for a light, but only after digging around in her handbag for some time. Digging in it noisily, loads of things rattling around in there: a mobile phone, lipsticks, miniature bottles of perfume, compacts, pens, cheque books – all that stuff women carry around with them. She'd be ferreting around in it for so long that she'd draw attention to herself, glance up and at me. 'I'm sorry. Do you have a light?'

And I'd light hers first, then mine, just like in films. From there, we'd begin talking. I'd buy her a drink, she'd buy me one back, check her watch and realise she was late for work but not care. And after an hour or so talking she'd sense my vulnerability and, as I raised my glass to my lips, she'd place her hand on my drinking arm, softly now, and say, even more softly, 'You know, you really should stop drinking. I can help . . .'

But there's no way this will happen, and the main reason is because I'm so poorly dressed. Women don't start conversations with badly dressed men in pubs because a badly dressed man in a pub by himself in the middle of the day is probably an alcoholic. Let's face it, who wants to spend their afternoon speaking to a needy alcoholic? Not the sort of woman who would care enough to ask him to stop, that's for sure.

So I drink the rest of my drink and leave the pub with no saviour in sight. My leg's gone dead and when I stand up I lose my balance – must have been sitting in an awkward way.

CHAPTER THIRTY-THREE

'It was all right, really. I had a good book and a fresh set of batteries for my Walkman.'

The picture of Tony Simpson, his Walkman and a good book appeared in the newspaper on Friday morning. That same morning, in the Bottom Drawer offices, the *Sun* was one of a number of papers spread out on the table in front of the *Happy Monday* production team, who were right in the middle of a barnstorming meeting.

It was not a barnstorming meeting in the sense that it was going well, and delegates would say to one another afterwards, 'That was a barnstorming meeting, eh?' rather it was the *Happy Monday* version of a *brainstorming* session, a device beloved of the creative media who buy coffee from Starbucks then sit around sparking ideas off one another in the hope of coming up with something truly sensational. *Happy Monday* had bastardised it into a *barnstorming* meeting, because that was the *Happy Monday* way: their aim was to put their own unique spin on to everything they did, from what appeared on the screen right down to the way they conducted their meetings.

Take the Felix Carter interview, for example. Most programmes would be content with simply having Felix on, asking him some questions, showing a clip from the film, letting him plug the new album and probably getting him to sing a song from it. Not *Happy Monday*. They'd got hold of three Felix lookylikeys – two from tribute acts, one who'd been spotted by Russ in Paperchase – and were planning to incorporate them into the interview. The joke was that Felix was 'everywhere' at the moment. The host would point this out, then say to Felix, 'Look, you're here, but you're also in the audience,' and the camera would cut to a Felix lookylikey sneaked unobtrusively into the audience, who'd wave.

Then cut back to Felix, and the host would say, 'And you're picking your nose over there,' and in a corner of the stage would be the second lookylikey, engrossed in the activity of picking his nose, ignoring the camera.

And lastly the host would say, 'And you're even in the toilet,' and they'd cut to a lookylikey apparently relaxing backstage on the toilet with a copy of a newspaper. Take that, Parky.

This particular barnstorming meeting was being held to decide sketches for the following Monday's show. The engine of the programme – interviews, band performances, an outside broadcast – was already in place and had been for some time. The aim of this meeting was to discuss how to give the show its contemporaneous edge. *Happy Monday* was in the habit of taking topical items and giving them a satirical spin, hence the presence of the day's newspapers and the request at hand: 'Ideas, people, please.'

However, this meeting was not going as well as usual, thanks mainly to the behaviour of two researchers.

Sitting at the top of the table, the producer, Grant, reflected that Fi and Russ had seemed to be getting on very well together when they started. Indeed, there'd even been idle talk of the two of them becoming an 'item', certainly they'd seemed close at the awards. Lately, however, the pair had been at each other's throats. Grant had nothing against a bit of competition within the team, but these two were taking healthy rivalry to extremes.

Now they were snarling across the table, giving one another 'Manson lamps', as Tony Soprano might say. The problem was that Russ had just reminded the group – or, more specifically, reminded Fi – that it was he who had come up with the idea for the Felix sketch and subsequently found the third Felix in Paperchase, and what had Fi contributed to that week's programme exactly?

It was fighting talk, Grant knew. Shows like *Happy Monday* lived and died on the quality of their ideas, as the demise of *TFI Friday* had shown. Indeed, above him on the wall was a sign that read, 'There Are Never No Ideas,' and this was something of a motto to the production team. True, it was open to abuse, when an innocent 'I've no idea,' in response to a query about the whereabouts of Sellotape would elicit a pedantic chorus of 'There are never no ideas,' but in the main it held fast. The show lived and died on its ideas, and so did its people. So, by challenging her apparent lack of them, Russ was going for the jugular.

Grant had no idea why. But he wished he had a Blofeld-like button that could pitch the warring juniors into a pool of piranha fish below. Now there, he thought, was an idea.

Until Fi suddenly had a better one.

'All right,' she said, drawing herself to the table, looking from Russ's Manson lamps to the rest of the group. 'What about this?' And the idea she went on to describe was a good one. They all (apart from Russ) agreed it was something of a doozy. It was this: a running gag throughout the show, introduced in part one, then appearing immediately ahead of each ad break. We cut to this guy Tony Simpson, and he's sitting on a sofa somewhere in the studio, Walkman on, nodding to whatever he's listening to and apparently engrossed in a book.

In rushes a member of the production team, all flustered and panicking, who says, breathlessly, 'Oh my God, Tony! The studio's sinking!'

Or: 'Oh, my God, Tony! Felix Carter hasn't turned up!'

Or: 'Oh, my God, Tony! The bar's run dry!'

And each time, whatever the nature of the emergency, Tony Simpson simply looks up, all casual like, and says, 'It's all right. I've got a good book and a fresh set of batteries for my Walkman . . .' Genius!

They loved it, apart from Russ, who was simply disconsolate. It was cool, it was funny, and it was topical. Tony Simpson was a good-looking bloke, very telegenic, and best of all, he fitted with the profile of the *Happy Monday* viewer. He could be found easily – the *Sun* would happily give up his contact details in return for a quick plug for their Nice One, *Sun*! award – and what's more he was almost certain to be willing to appear. After all, if he was OK to be the *Sun*'s mascot, he was *bound* to want to appear on *Happy Monday*.

There was one minor problem, and it really was just a minor problem. Live television programmes are planned in terms of 'units', and by adding the Tony Simpson sketch, they were squeezing too many units into this particular show – this was swiftly pointed out by the *Happy Monday* production assistant.

Not that this was unusual, it's standard practice to have too much material in case of unforeseen circumstances – the running order is fluid right up to and during the broadcast. Still, they would rehearse all they had, and if something had to go when they went live, so be it. It would probably be the Felix lookylikeys gag, they decided. After all, it wasn't *that* strong.

'Hear that?' said Fi to Russ under her breath, as they trooped out of the room. 'The Felix idea's not *that* strong.'

'You owe me for the PlayStation,' was his only reply as he stalked off, thinking, Fucking Tony Simpson.

CHAPTER THIRTY-FOUR

Have you ever had a change of image?

Well, yes, I suppose I have.

Ever tried to dress up as a famous person?

Um, well, for fancy-dress parties and things.

That's not what I mean. I mean, have you ever seen a famous person then wanted to be like them?

No.

You move in different circles, though, don't you? You move in the same circles as they do. You probably wouldn't understand.

What wouldn't I understand?

That . . . That you see a famous person and they can be just like you. You can look like them – maybe people will tell you, 'Hey, you know, you look like so-and-so,' – and you can even share their characteristics, but somehow . . . See, I looked similar to Felix, and we both had a drink problem. But he was him and I was me. Do you see? He had what he had. I had nothing. And when I get back from my shopping trip, get dressed in my new clothes and look in the mirror, that's what I think.

I think, The man staring out at me from the mirror looks like Felix Carter, but he's not. And that kind of nags at me.

On the positive side, I may not be Felix, but at least I've made a decent job of being his lookylikey for the show. My hair is short, like his, and I'm wearing the sort of clothes he wears; certainly the sort of clothes he was wearing in the photo-shoot for *Phonic* magazine. It didn't seem too complicated: a pair of baggy jeans, dark T-shirt and a denim jacket and I was in business. I had to use guesswork for the trainers, but the ones I got were the most expensive in JD Sports, and even though I'm positive Felix wouldn't go within a mile of JD Sports, they certainly go with the outfit. At least, an assistant assured me they would.

As for a tan, I never got round to it. I got as far as the door of a tanning salon, looked at the girl behind the desk – tight white uniform, perfectly made-up – and decided I wasn't ready to enter her world. Besides, I felt the beginnings of an erection so, all told, I felt it better to cut my losses and leave at once. If I'd had time tomorrow I could have worn my Felix clothes and gone, but I won't have. As Russ explained yesterday, a car is coming for me at eight a.m. I'm needed for rehearsals.

I say that to myself in front of the bedroom mirror: 'My car's coming at eight. I'm needed for rehearsals.'

I like the sound of it, the way it rolls off the tongue. I like what it suggests – a doorway into a different and altogether better world. One where people are dispatched to collect you.

I say it with a sigh in the middle: 'Yeah, my car's coming at eight,' *sigh*, 'I'm needed for rehearsals.'

Then I say it casually: 'Yeah, you know, I'm needed for rehearsals.' *Yawn.* 'Got a car coming at eight.'

I'm still saying it when the phone rings. Because I'm lost in the fantasy, it takes me a moment to realise what the sound is. And by the time I've worked it out, it's rung three times.

Our answer-machine kicks in at seven so I dash to the lounge and I'm about to answer when it occurs to me that it might be Sam: I reach to the stereo, which has been playing Felix's album, flick it to track three for 'Love You (To The Nth Degree)' and turn it up before answering.

'Hello?' I say, out of breath, a slight slur in my voice – I must check it next time I speak, I think. The music's loud. Too loud. In my haste I've whacked the volume knob right up. Even so, there's no mistaking Sam's voice.

'Hello? Is that Chris?'

'Sorry,' I say. 'Wait a sec.'

I put the phone down right next to the speaker, I take a step away and wait for Felix to sing, 'I lo-o-o-o-ve you . . .' before reaching to the stereo and turning it down.

'Sorry about that,' I say, noting my lack of slur with gratitude.

'Don't worry. Is that Chris Sewell?'

It's not Sam.

'Yes.'

'Right. Hi. My name's Betty, I'm with Costumes at Bottom Drawer.'

'Oh, I see.'

('Yeah.' *Sigh*. 'Got Costumes on the phone.')

'I just need your measurements. For tomorrow?'

'What, for a costume?' There was a slight slur there, the last word came out as 'cosjewm'. But for the moment I'm more worried about the costume – the concept, not my pronunciation of it.

'What cosjewm?' I say. An image of me dressed up like *It's A Knockout* floats in front of my eyes, complete with bucket.

'We need to give you something to wear, love.'

That's nice, I think, she called me 'love'.

'Well, I mean, you don't have to, because I've been out today and bought some clothes.'

'Ah . . . Well, bless you, darling, but you didn't really need to. We'll be kitting you out when you get here.'

'I had my hair cut as well . . .'

'Yes, well, we would have, er, done that too. In Hair and Makeup. Sounds like young Russ doing his fly-by-night bit again. Did he not tell you I'd be calling?'

'I don't think so.' Curse of the drinker. No trust in your own memory.

'Typical. OK, well, have you got your measurements?'

If she'd asked me the same question earlier in the day I wouldn't have been able to answer. Sam normally takes care of that kind of stuff. I abdicated responsibility for memorising clothing sizes to her. Happily, I've spent the afternoon hopping around in changing rooms, so I know all my sizes and I'm able to give them to her, just like a regular person would.

'Thanks,' she says finally, impressed. 'We'll have you looking like his twin by the time we've finished with you.'

Great, I think, putting down the phone. 'Looking like Felix's twin', cars to pick me up, Costumes on the phone, Hair and Makeup – I can handle all this. Oh, yes, things are surely looking up. Taken care of this way, I can concentrate on getting Sam back.

I'm on the road now, I think. But only after I've done this next thing.

And the thing is? I need to chase away the demons.

To do that I need to visit Colette Carew.

I go through to the bedroom and take off my Felix clothes, carefully laying them across the bed I've hardly slept in since Sam left. From the cupboard I take my special suit worn just twice in the last two years: once to a wedding of one of Sam's friends at which I got drunk, knocked over the cake and called the bride a fat bitch *et cetera*, *et cetera*, and then to my father's funeral. I put the suit on the bed while I have a bath and carefully shave in Mariah Carey's backside, remembering to do the bedroom mirror double-check afterwards.

When I'm dressed in the suit I dither over whether or not to take the gun. I've become used to carrying it around with me. It gives me a confidence boost. But the suit isn't heavy enough to disguise it at my belt, so reluctantly I leave it behind, pick up the rest of my things – fags, keys, mobile – and set off for, first, a bank, then Colette Carew's house. But only after lucky-dipping and coming up with . . . Citron. Not bad. Tangy, sharp, refreshing. Just the ticket for the job at hand.

I'm a salesman. It's my job to be persuasive. Therefore, I think, I should be ideally suited to the task ahead. Still, when I bang on the front door, I find myself shaking with nerves, wishing I had time for another lucky dip.

I'm keenly aware of the eyes burning into the back of

my head, just as I was the other day. What if someone recognises me? The hair, glasses and coat are all different, but who's to say some highly observant disabled person doesn't sit at their flat window day after day, like James Stewart in *Rear Window*? And at this very moment they're squinting at me through a pair of cheap binoculars, brow furrowed in recognition, before setting down the binoculars on a window-sill and wheeling themselves over to the phone.

When she answers the door, saying, 'Yes?' I make it my first job to get inside the house as quickly as possible.

I've never done door-to-door selling before but the principle must be the same. After all, they're still the same discipline. You have to win over the client as quickly as possible, get their confidence. Start by . . .

Smiling, I say, 'Ms Carew?'

'Are you the police? I'm sorry if you are, like, but I've had it up to here with the police.'

If I was expecting Colette Carew to be a wounded, vulnerable victim then I was wrong. The only sign of her recent ordeal is a weariness that begins behind her eyes and spreads to her lower face, slackening her mouth.

Naturally, though, she's suspicious. That's fine, the client always begins the meeting from a position of natural reluctance and cynicism. It's up to the salesman to relax them.

'No, you'll be pleased to hear.' She's smaller than me, which means I'm talking down to her. Not perfect. But I smile as openly as I can, ensuring the smile reaches my eyes, which hold hers, establishing trust.

As I speak, I'm nodding almost imperceptibly. A new trick. The thinking is that as she sees me nodding, her brain fools her into thinking she agrees with me. Wily, aren't we? Bet you didn't realise we do all this sort of stuff on your behalf?

'I'm a local businessman,' I continue, nodding and smiling. 'We read about your terrible burglary – well, your *two* terrible burglaries – and we were wondering if we could help.' Hands open, giving the impression of honesty. Body language is very important in establishing a rapport with the client, especially when you consider that only seven per cent of human communication is verbal. Once upon a time we were taught to mirror the client's body language to put them at ease, but it's a practice that's currently out of vogue. Nowadays the thinking is simply to be as open with your body as you can, resist putting hands in pockets, crossing your arms, that sort of thing.

Her face is a picture of hope mixed with suspicion. She wants to believe me, but life's snatched away the giving hand too often.

'Perhaps I could come in?' I offer, desperate to be away from the disabled and their prying binoculars.

'You might as well,' she says at last. 'Every other fucker's been in here.'

I'm not sure whether I'm supposed to laugh, so I don't. Instead I nod thanks and step inside the door, which she holds open, then breathe a mental sigh of relief as it closes behind me.

Inside, I remind myself that I've never been in this house before so I don't know which doorway belongs to her, don't head straight for it.

'Through here.' She turns away and pads through to the lounge with me behind her, takes a seat on the slashed-up sofa and reaches for a packet of Peter Stuyvesant on the glass coffee table.

The lounge is just as I remember it. Stinking. Only more so now, of course – Colette Carew's intruder pissed in the hallway and the whole flat wears the odour of his stale urine. Well, I think, at least the fact that the stink is part mine makes it easier to bear. Thank God for small mercies.

The window shutters are closed and I'm grateful for that, but she hasn't turned on the overhead light so I study her in the dusk of the lounge.

She's about my age, almost attractive. But in that kind of beaten-up way I'd noticed from her newspaper picture.

Her hair's unwashed and tucked behind her ears. She wears a white sleeveless top – hint of bra-strap – and a cream, seen-better-days skirt.

Sitting on the sofa, she seems to make herself small, picks out and lights her cigarette with small, flighty, but well-practised movements, tossing the Clipper lighter back to the coffee table when she's done. Her knees are tight together and she draws her arms close to herself to smoke, sucking at the fag noisily, exhaling even more loudly. It strikes me that her face is a perfectly evolved smoking mechanism. Her lips seem to have grown into a protruding O-shape to meet the cigarette all the more quickly, her cheeks hollowed and high. I cast a glance around for the cat, like it might saunter in, recognise me and raise the alarm. There's no sign of it and I suppress a shudder at what I almost did to it.

'So you read it in the paper, right?' she says at last. No offer of tea. No invitation to sit. Not that there's anywhere to sit anyway.

I feel a slight irritation, which I fight. After all, if my motives for being here *were* purely philanthropic, I'm being treated pretty badly. But they're not, so down, Irritation, down. Even so, it's hard not to feel disgust for her and I decide quickly that I want to be away from here as soon as I can.

'Yes. It sounds terrible.'

'Yeah, well, I didn't say what they put in the paper. I bin misquoted. Can I do anything about that? Take 'em to court?'

My disgust levels rise, unchecked this time. The ungrateful bitch. A local businessman has seen that report and come to help her, and all she can do is complain about being misquoted.

'I don't know. Would you want to?'

'They put words in me marf, I didn't say none of what they put. I 'ad a reporter come round but I didn't say none of what he said I did. I didn't say I were stunned.'

'Oh. Um, I think they're allowed to quote you if you kind of agree with what they say.'

You'd know more about that than me. Was I right?

Yes. You can put something to somebody and if they say yes, then you can quote them.

Like, 'Are you a complete tosser?', 'Yes,' becomes, 'I am a complete tosser,' said Christopher Sewell.

Pretty much.

'Well, it ain't right,' says Colette Carew. 'Fuckin' papers. They never write the truth, do they?'

'I wouldn't know about that.'

I need to be out of here now, and I've lost control of the meeting. First rule of sales: take the reins, steer the meeting.

'Well, er, listen, Ms Carew. Our company, we'd like to make a donation to help you in what must be a very difficult time for you.' I reach into my jacket pocket and take out a wad of notes I've just withdrawn from the bank. Three hundred pounds to be exact.

'What's the catch?' she says, seeing the money in my hand. Her eyes narrow to wary slashes.

I try to ignore the ingratitude; the fact that she makes no move to stand. 'No, no catch. We have, um, a fund at work to help, er, people like you and it'll come out of that. Well, perhaps one catch, if you can call it a catch – we'd like to remain anonymous. Obviously, you know, if others find out about our fund we'd be inundated by people wanting handouts.'

She's looking at me warily, but with more interest. 'You high up in this company, are you?'

'I am, yes.' I take a step towards the coffee table, brandishing the money. 'I'm the finance director.' If I'm hoping that she'll make a move to accept the cash from my hand, I'm disappointed. She acts like the subject of an FBI surveillance video, as if taking the money incriminates her. Instead I'm left holding it towards her.

'Would three hundred be a help?' I say.

'Thirty pence would be a help.'

'OK. Three hundred it is.' And, with no sign of her taking

the money from me, I reach down to the coffee table and place it just beside her packet of Peter Stuyvesant.

'You're leaving that, are you?' she says.

'That's for you. We just ask that you keep it to yourself, that's all.' Should I add for her not to tell the police? Part of me thinks so, but another part thinks it might ring suspicious bells in her head.

And then her hand reaches for my crotch and she begins to massage my balls.

I look at her, there's something like triumph in her eyes. I'm stiffening under her hand and she has hold of my cock now, massaging it as it rises in my trousers.

I gasp.

'You don't have to go now, if you don't want to,' she says. But there's nothing coquettish, nothing inviting about her words. It's just a simple statement of fact she makes as her fingers find my zip and pull it down.

At first it feels like I'm going to let her continue. Little Chris is making his presence felt. But then I pull away, suddenly seeing myself like an out-of-body experience, suddenly seeing her and realising what she is: that she represents the chasm between where I've come from and where I want to be.

I don't mean to go 'Eurgh,' as I pull away, but I do. She lets go and the triumph fades from her eyes, replaced by something more like defeat. Her face hardens.

'I'm sorry,' I blurt, 'I didn't mean – I mean . . . I'm married,' and I wave my wedding ring at her, using my other hand to do up my flies. 'See? Really, all we want to do is help you out financially.'

She reaches forward for her Peter Stuyvesant and the lighter from the coffee table. The manky, dirty coffee table.

'Well,' she says at last, long overdue, 'thank you. There aren't many like you about.'

'No,' I say, trying not to let the irony of what she's just said creep across my face. God, if only she knew.

'I guess I shouldn't judge everybody by me own standards,'

she says, setting flame to her cigarette. She throws the Clipper back to the coffee table.

'It's not that,' I say, taking a step back towards the door. 'You're very . . .'

Very what? Very beaten-up-looking? I change tack.

'It's just that . . . I'm married.' And, once again, I show her the wedding ring. It's as if I'm giving her the finger.

'You're a good man,' she says, as I reach the door.

'Thank you,' I say, almost choking on the words. I pull the door closed behind me. There's still no catch – Dog-end must have bust it open when he burgled her a week ago.

I leave. Away at last. Away from what I did to her house, away from the smell and away from the old me. Then, standing outside her front door, I gather myself together, allow myself a smile because, after all, I did an honourable thing in there, perhaps the first really good thing I've done in weeks. I owe myself a drink, I think. A drink to celebrate. Thankfully, there's the off-licence opposite where I buy a bottle of vodka and some tins of Red Stripe, on which I make an immediate start.

'Who am I?' says Felix to the interviewer, whom we can't see.

He's sitting on a snooker table, which, we've been told, takes pride of place in his house. He's already shown us his collection of *Star Wars* toys, a kitchen he claims to never use, his CD collection, a baseball cap he says he 'rescued' from the set of *Enemies*, a photograph of him with his arm around Jeremy Irons. 'A great actor. Just such a learning experience working with him.'

Now he's sitting being interrogated by an interviewer.

We're about half-way through *Being Felix Carter*, and I'm most of the way through my bottle of vodka. I'm wearing my Felix clothes in honour of the occasion.

'Who am I? God knows. I mean, can you ever say what one person is like? You're like this in one situation, like that in another. You can't just grade people like apples. Is it apples? I don't know. Like potatoes, then.'

I stripped off when I got home, let my suit fall to the lounge floor and went through to the bathroom where I sat in the bath with a can of lager thinking of my TV appearance tomorrow, getting excited by it. I wonder if Sam will be watching. Hope, hope, hope that she is. I don't want to think of the alternative, that she might miss me altogether and all of my efforts will have been in vain. Instead I concentrate on her seeing it and plot myself into the future. A future that includes her coming back to the new me, the flat tidy, me going back to work and heading up my team, tackling Luke Radley and taming him.

Then, a baby perhaps. Sam's mum and dad coming to visit their grandchild, proud parents standing by. Not unreasonable dreams. Neither are they unobtainable. Not if everything goes according to plan.

So, feeling lightheaded and happy, I got out of the bath, pulled the plug and let Colette Carew drain out my life. In the bedroom I put on the Felix clothes because they're clean and new and they suited my mood. And then I sat on the sofa, ignored the mess, and watched *Being Felix Carter*.

'Yes,' he says. 'I do have a problem with drink. Look, I was there at the beginnings of rave culture, right? When all that mattered was having a good time. That's what we lived for. Then all of a sudden I'm in the charts, I've got *Smash Hits* asking me what I had for breakfast. And I'm – what? – twenty years old, still a young lad, really. And all of a sudden you're given everything you want. I mean everything. You have no idea. You're like this money-making machine. You're making money and everyone around you is making money off you. So you service the machine, right? You keep it happy. And if it wants oiling, you give it oil. And, yeah, I need a *lot* of oil. Ha ha.'

He picks up a packet of cigarettes and takes one: Marlboro Lights, same brand as me. I reach for my own.

'I could do with a drink now actually. Want one?' he says

to the interviewer, but, of course, the interviewer is sitting behind the camera, so it's like he says it to the camera, says it to me.

'Cheers, Felix, don't mind if I do.' I raise my vodka bottle to toast the screen.

'Are you drinking at the moment?' asks the interviewer.

He does a comical look around him. 'No. Why? Have you got some tinnies?'

'Got a couple in the fridge, Felix,' I say. Although, of course, I haven't. I've drunk them all.

'I'm having some time off for good behaviour,' he says. 'The thing is with booze, it's like women. I can't live with it, can't live without it. Other people have cars, I have a wagon, and I'm either on it, off it, chasing after it or running away from it. But I tell you what – it's always there.'

I nod in agreement.

'What sort of a drinker are you?' says the interviewer.

'Ha! Mouth open and in it goes,' I say.

'Ha! You know, I do it like this,' says Felix, making a drinking motion with his hand. He goes on to say more that I don't hear because I'm laughing so hard at our combined joke.

'Do you drink alone?' asks the interviewer.

'Oh, all the time . . .'

I cheer a little, raise the bottle in another toast.

'Drinking alone, Felix,' I say to his talking head on the TV, 'it's the only way, mate. It's the only way you can be sure of good company, isn't that right?' But I'm not sure if I believe that.

'You once said that people didn't believe you had a problem. Why was that?' says the interviewer.

'It comes down to how you handle the drink,' he says. 'It's like it completely tears down all of your psychological defences, and even stuff like just how unfair the world is gets me down. I call them the demons, man. The demons come, and sometimes the only way to get rid of them is to start drinking again.'

He says this last bit directly to the screen. Directly to me. I feel a shiver. Felix knows the demons.

And then this portion of the programme ends and we go to a break. After the break there is footage of Felix in concert and I find myself unsteadily copying his on-stage swagger around my lounge, using the bottle of vodka like a microphone.

I feel different. For the first time in weeks I feel happy. Like I'm not alone, and like everything's going to be all right.

CHAPTER THIRTY-FIVE

About two weeks before the sensational and shocking murder of the pop star Felix Carter, his minder, Frank, was musing over a problem he had.

The problem was not that his employer, the drink and drugs wild man Felix Carter, was being pestered by a stalker called Brian Forsyth, or that his employer, the singer-cum-movie star Felix Carter, had a habit of going AWOL and was in constant need of being saved from compromising situations, being saved from himself.

Those were problems that Frank, as a professional celebrity minder, ex-army, Tae Kwon Do expert, chess player and Everton supporter, was trained and experienced in dealing with. In fact, the problem was far closer to home. It was the squatters who lived two doors down the road.

Frank didn't know for certain that they were squatters. They might not have been. And since he didn't have access to their rent books and bank statements it would be impossible to know. But there were clues. Every single one of the rabble he saw going in and out of the house – men and women – had dreadlocks, for example. Most seemed to be just as fond of piercings as they were of dreadlocks. They wore colourful, flowing clothes. Outside their house, and sometimes outside Frank's, much to his annoyance, there was a bloody great green van with stickers in the windscreen. Stickers that said things like, 'Glastonbury Green Fields pass,' and 'Womad Festival pass' and one that said '*Non, merci*' to nuclear power, like saying it in French made it more urgent.

Well, if they weren't squatters, they were doing a good impression of squatters. And Frank saw through them. Spoilt rich kids, he thought. No respect for money, society, themselves or other people. He was too intelligent to let his thoughts wander down the Army-would-sort-them-out route, but every now and then he put a mental foot on the path. He couldn't help it. He was a disciplined man. Ex-army, black ops, very hush-hush. Then a Tae Kwon Do instructor before a career as a doorman at a top London club. Then head doorman, and then, thanks to the associations and trust he built up with the celebrity clientele, a minder. And now he was Felix Carter's minder, which made him one of the top minders in the country.

It was a position to which he'd risen by being one of life's problem-solvers. If there was a problem, Frank solved it, and he solved it quietly and without fuss, without publicity. He could tell a story or two, and who knows? Maybe one day he would. He wouldn't be the first celebrity bodyguard to release his autobiography, that was for sure. And he solved his problems, first, by using his head. If that failed, he used his fists, or perhaps the telescopic baton he kept permanently in his trouser pocket. And if that failed, well, he knew people. Dangerous people. People from way back, whose lives he had saved, or careers he had rescued. People who owed him favours.

But the problem he had now? This was a new one, and its proximity to his home seemed to render it insoluble. He was perplexed. Moreover, he was frustrated by his impotence in this matter.

He didn't know quite when the parties had started, but he guessed at around the same time that the green van had arrived. Perhaps it was a new intake of squatters, a more rowdy, hedonistic bunch than the last lot, just got in from Goa, or wherever squatters live when they're not in the UK. Either way, the parties had started.

At first they hadn't been unduly disturbing. After all, they were two doors down and the thump of the bass was irritating but bearable. He and his wife slept in a room at the rear of the house and could easily fall asleep with the bass in the background. More importantly, their two-year-old daughter, Jessica, who slept in the room next door, had not been disturbed at all, one room removed from the noise. Yes, the army officer in Frank had pursed his lips in annoyance, but the chess-playing Tae Kwon Do expert rose calmly above it, redirecting the anger to a more serene, productive place.

But then the bongos had arrived.

The introduction of bongos appeared to take the squatter's parties to a new dimension, specifically, outside. Now, it seemed, they liked nothing better than to throw open the back door to the house, light a fire in the garden and play the bongos in time to the music from inside the house. They also enjoyed accompanying the rising crescendos with loud whoops and yells, indicating their pleasure at the bongo players' prowess.

What on earth the people who lived directly on either side of the squatters thought of all this, Frank didn't know. What he did know was that he was Frank, by name and nature. And Frank knew that problems only got worse if you didn't nip them in the bud, so on the first night the bongos started, when he, Mrs Frank and Jessica had been rudely awakened, he decided to go round there to talk to the squatters.

First, he prepared himself mentally, approaching this problem like any other. A big man, in his professional life he used his bulk as a tool of intimidation, finding that 99 per cent of potentially explosive situations could be resolved with his presence alone, usually accompanied by a low, controlled tone of voice.

Here, though, his instinct told him that this would be the incorrect attitude. From what he knew of these people they prided themselves on being on the outskirts of society, their enemy was 'the man'. And if Frank was to go round there adopting his most familiar bearing, then he would surely come across as 'the man' and his overtures would be ignored. Indeed, he might simply inflame the situation, providing the squatters with a common enemy, namely him. He knew countless men who would simply go round there with strong-arm tactics, stand imposingly at the doorway and offer up veiled threats. But that was the wrong way, he told himself. He would do it with brains rather than brawn.

So, no heavy stuff, not even a hint of it. What, then?

Well, from what he knew of these people they were simply hippies at heart, the nuclear-power sticker bore testament to that. That being the case, they would surely respond to an appeal to their better nature. An appeal that comes not from 'the man', but simply 'a man'. A man who wants to provide the best for his family, who is a victim of the society from which they have so fortunately escaped. In other words, he decided to go for the sympathy vote.

It was an approach that went against everything Frank stood for, but he believed it was the best in the circumstances. He had thought it through, tackled it like a chess problem, and this was the best move. So he chose his clothes carefully, an old gardening T-shirt and a pair of jeans, trying to look as dishevelled as possible; anathema to poor old Frank, who normally prided himself on an immaculate appearance. He thought, How would 'the man' dress?, then tried to pitch his own look as far away as possible. He even stood before the bathroom mirror and mussed his hair up so that no trace of his usual neat side parting showed. He practised a wearied, hang-dog look in front of the mirror, then left the house.

In the street he could hardly hear the bongos, but the bass rattled the windows of the house two doors down. He banged on the door, wondering if anyone would hear him, but dropped his shoulders anyway, ready for the door to open, remembering to look weary, tired and conciliatory. Basically, trying not to look like Frank.

The door was opened by Catweazel, though Frank was not to know that that was his name. Neither was he to know that Catweazel was rarely to be found without cider in his grasp, nor that wherever there was a free party involving people with dreadlocks and piercings – certainly in the north London area – Catweazel was never far behind. He was not to know, either, that Catweazel harboured a certain admiration for his boss, Felix Carter, or that Catweazel had recently sat in a pub with a man named Christopher Sewell, who bore a resemblance to his boss, Felix Carter, and whom Frank was soon to meet. The two men were to remain eternally ignorant of how closely their destinies were aligned.

All Frank saw was a dreadlocked man in an Ozric Tentacles T-shirt clutching a two-litre bottle of Strongbow.

All Catweazel saw was 'the man'.

'Yeah?' said Catweazel. Behind him the bass vibrated through the air of the house, which Frank could tell was full of people. People with dreadlocks and piercings, no doubt. The smell of dope smoke and alcohol reached his nostrils.

'Hi,' said Frank, who never said hi. 'Hi, look, I was just wondering. I have a small daughter just down the road, and she can't get to sleep because of the bongos. It's her birthday tomorrow and everything, and I was just wondering if you could perhaps lay off the drums for her? I mean, the music's OK. It's just the drums, outside and all . . .' He gestured around him and Catweazel looked upwards in response, as if expecting to see flying saucers in the sky.

Frank thought, Fucking space cadet, and cursed his luck in getting this one. Still, the lie about Jessica's birthday had been a doorstep innovation and might just do it for him, providing the space cadet had an ounce of human compassion.

'Shit, man,' said Catweazel, who suddenly felt a blind-ing flash of love, not for the man, but for his daughter, perhaps down to the three ecstasy pills, several litres of cider and four spliffs he'd had. 'Shit, man. Her birthday, right?'

'That's right.'

'What's her name, dude?'

The last thing Frank wanted to do was give this hippie his daughter's name, so the second lie came easily. 'Hannah,' he replied.

'Well, look, man,' drawled Catweazel. 'I'll see what we can do for little Hannah, OK? You leave it with me.'

'Thanks, man,' said Frank, who had never in his life called anyone 'man' before. 'I appreciate that. Enjoy the rest of your party.'

'Wicked,' said Catweazel, and the door closed.

Frank took a deep breath. Well, he thought, that had gone all right. He felt bad for jettisoning the day-to-day Frank to achieve his objective. He felt bad for lying about Jessica's birthday. In all, he felt as if he'd sold himself out. But then, he reminded himself, he'd thought the problem through, and if the problem was eliminated then it was down to his tactics. We shall see. And with that, he made his way back to his own house, let himself in, undressed and climbed into bed beside his wife who was still wide awake.

'What did you say?' she enquired.

'I just asked them to desist,' said Frank.

The bongos continued, but that was OK, thought Frank, it would take the space cadet a few moments to calm them down. His plea wouldn't have fallen on deaf ears.

But they continued.

And then, after a moment or so, they heard singing over the bongos, indistinct at first, but soon the words carried over to them.

'Happy birthday to you, happy birthday to you,' sang the squatters, from two doors down.

'Well, at least we know why they're having a party,' grumbled Frank's wife from the other side of the bed. 'It's obviously someone's birthday party.'

'Happy birthday, dear Hannah, happy birthday to you,' sang the squatters.

'Yes,' said Frank, through gritted teeth. 'That'll be it, then.'

CHAPTER THIRTY-SIX

'Oh, look, it's me.'

They're the first words Felix Carter says to me. Even though it feels like he's been speaking to me for some time now, they're the first words he actually addresses to me.

Where is this?

Sorry, this is at the TV studios. He comes over and says, 'Oh, look, it's me,' when I'm sitting in an over-large easy chair in the foyer of Bottom Drawer Productions in south London, waiting for a car to take me home. A car that is clearly never going to turn up.

The fact that the car has not turned up and is showing no signs of turning up is no mere inconvenience to me. I need to be home as a matter of some urgency. I need to be home because I am already having difficulty, as Mick Hucknall would say, holding back the tears.

And that is because the day has not, by any stretch of the imagination, gone to plan. You'll forgive the pun, but it's been a very unhappy Monday for me.

You see, if Sam had switched on the television to watch *Happy Monday*, or set her video to record and watch it later that night, she might well have wondered why my note asked her to. She would have been more than justified in doing so, because I never appeared.

My day has gone like this.

I woke up on the sofa to the sound of . . . Of noises. The television, the door buzzer, a thumping in my head. A searing, outward pulsing, destroying all but the most immediate thought in its blast radius. I touched my head.

The buzzer went. I said, 'No. Stop,' weakly, then remembered the day, the TV studio and the car that was supposed to be picking me up at eight a.m. 'Eight on the dot,' as Russ had said cheerily on the phone, some days earlier. At the time, I'd hung up and resolved that, whatever happened, the last thing I must do the night before *Happy Monday* was get hideously drunk.

Of course, the last thing I did the night before – what I'd done all weekend, in fact – was get hideously drunk.

I pulled myself from the sofa, slowly, like a man using wooden legs for the first time, groped my way to the front door and yanked at the door phone, which clattered to the wall away from my grasp.

'Hello,' I said, pulling the phone to me by its cord.

If he was disorientated by the clatter, he didn't show it. 'Car for Chris Sewell to Bottom Drawer,' came a disembodied voice. I imagined a driver wearing a cap on the other side of my front door.

'Can you give me five minutes?' I managed.

'Sure. Take your time, mate. I'll be in the car when you're ready.'

'Right.' I put the phone back, sliding it into the holster at the second foggy attempt.

For a moment or so I steadied myself against the wall, wondering if I was going to be sick, deciding yes, then no, yes again, then – finally – no. And I loped to the bathroom, looked in the Mariah Carey CD.

OK, I thought. Rude awakening. Bit of a shock. But we can handle this. We've handled this situation a thousand times before. It's always been my opinion that a hangover is more effectively dealt with by giving it a challenge to rise to – keeps the demons' wings from fluttering too loudly. And what bigger challenge is there than an appearance on *Happy Monday* – my Felix Carter advert – my chance to get Sam back? Better to have five minutes to freshen up than hours to spend waiting and getting nervous. Make the hangover work for you, that's the trick.

So I splashed the coldest cold water on to my face, and then I splashed some more. After that, I took off my new, now slept-in T-shirt and washed beneath my armpits, spraying deodorant on before replacing the T-shirt. I had some stubble but didn't think that was a problem: Felix often had stubble and, if I remembered correctly, was sporting a five-o'clock shadow during last night's documentary. My hair's too short to bother with and, after giving my teeth a thorough clean, I felt I looked good enough to face the world.

Perhaps three minutes had elapsed and I was ready. Almost. Before I left, I threw on the denim jacket and fished in the pockets, found three miniatures, one of which was empty and I tossed on to the sofa. Two left – Kurant and Peppar: I gulped the Kurant greedily, waited for the whoosh, relished the fruity flavour, then stuffed the other bottle back into my pocket.

Last, I looked at the gun on the coffee table, then just as quickly forgot about it. Probably not a good idea to be wandering around a TV studio with a gun tucked into my waistband.

Now I was ready. From comatose to out-the-door in just over three minutes. Not bad at all.

The car was a Lexus, the driver not as I had imagined him. He wore a grey suit – no cap – and sat silently in the front as I rested in the back and let him take me over the river, watching the city, fighting the nausea and the banging head, glad of the vodka snaking its way warmly around my body. And no, it was not lost on me, sitting in the back of the car, dressed like Felix Carter, battling with my hangover – not lost on me at all.

The Bottom Drawer studios are in the middle of what appears to be an industrial estate just the other side of the river.

'Here you go,' said the driver, pointing to the entrance. 'Through there is Reception. Someone'll take care of you.'

In the event, Russ was there to take care of me, passing through Reception as I entered. He approached when I caught his eye, looking exactly as I remembered him. Only the clipboard was new.

'Ah,' he said. 'Great. You're the last of our Felixes to arrive. Except the real one, of course. Did Betty get in touch?'

'Er, Betty?'

'Costumes? Did Costumes ring you at all?'

'Oh. Costumes,' I remembered the slightly slurring conversation with the woman who wasn't Sam. 'Yes, they did, thanks. I gave her my measurements.'

'Wicked. Well, listen,' he gestured towards an easy chair opposite the reception desk, 'why not take a seat here and I'll run you through the day and then we'll get a floor assistant to show you to your changing room?'

'Changing room?'

'Yeah, you get a changing room. Just like the real stars.'

I smiled despite myself and despite Russ's condescending attitude ('real' stars, indeed). I get my own changing room – cool.

'OK,' he said, as we sat. 'Have you done any live television?'

'No.'

'Any TV at all?'

'No.'

'Right. Well, here's how the day goes. We're doing a camera run in about, ooh, forty-five minutes, and you'll be needed for that. It's like a rough rehearsal, really, so we can get all the shots right, rehearse the autocue, get the band rehearsed and whatnot, and you'll be needed for that. What I suggest you do is not bother changing until after the camera run. We'll break for lunch and shortly after that we'll do a dress rehearsal, for which you'll be needed again – in costume this time, please. You'll need to go into Hair and Makeup before that. Now, once we've done the dress we'll break the crew and you can either wait in your dressing room to be called for the actual show, or Hospitality will be opening a green room and you can sit in there, have a drink and watch the show on the ring main. What you can't do is go out into the studio, I'm afraid. We'll be bringing in the audience shortly after the dress and obviously if they see you that's the joke spoiled.'

'The joke?'

'Yes. Your part in the show. It's kind of a gag and it relies on you not being seen by the audience. The director will go through all that on the camera run, OK?'

'Yes.'

'Right. Now, once you've done your bit, please don't bugger off. We'll need to do what we call a "clear", which means no one can go until we're off air, I'm afraid. Just to cover our backs, you know? However, once we're off air we'll break the studio, start the de-rig and there's normally a bit of a get-together in the green room to which you're more than welcome. Now, how does all that grab you?'

'It sounds like you've made that speech before.'

He looked at me strangely. 'I'm sorry? It sounds like what?'

'I said, "It sounds like you've made that speech before."'

'Ah! Yes, well, I have. Many times. The thing to do is not to worry. Just relax, enjoy the day, pay attention to what people tell you and you'll be fine. It's chaos, but it's organised chaos. OK?'

'Yes.'

'Are you sure you're OK?' He looked concerned.

'Yes. Bit of a cold, that's all. In fact, I don't suppose I could lay my hands on some Nurofen or something, could I?'

'No worries. I'll get it sorted. In fact, here's just the person. Fi!' he called to a small blonde girl hurrying through Reception with a clipboard hugged to her chest. She stopped, grimaced, and came our way.

'Yes, Russell,' she said, her forced smile indicating she didn't much like him. A shame. I liked Russ a lot. I was looking forward to chatting with him later, perhaps at the green room get-together he'd mentioned.

'Yes, Fi. This is Chris, one of our Felixes, the one *I* found in Paperchase.'

'Right,' she said, turning to me. 'Gosh, we have heard *a lot* about you. Why, Russell hasn't stopped going on about you.'

'Well, Fi,' said Russ testily, 'we needed a Felix lookylikey, so it was probably fortunate I was able to find one.'

She gave me an appraising look. I wondered if she knew – those antennae that women have – that I was drunk, hung-over, whatever I was.

'Spitting image,' she said, not without sarcasm.

Russ shot her a look. 'Would you take him to his dressing room? Get him settled and ready for the camera run?' he said. 'Oh, and could you sort him some painkillers?'

'Painkillers. Ah,' she said, in a that-explains-it voice, then, 'Russell, you seem to have confused me with a floor assistant. We have floor assistants to take guests to their changing rooms. I'm a researcher, same as you, remember?'

'Yes, Fiona, I know,' said Russ, his voice strained. 'But there are no floor assistants around at the moment and there really is no time to waste, so I wondered if you might do it.'

'And why should I have to do it?' said Fi, her smile forced. 'After all, Tony Simpson is due to arrive shortly. You remember him, don't you? The really strong idea I had.'

Russ glared. 'Well, Fiona, as you're so useful with your feet, I thought you wouldn't mind. Especially as you owe me, so to speak.'

For a second or so they stared at each other like two cats about to fight, before finally Fi seemed to back down, saying to me, 'Right, want to follow me? Sorry, what did you say your name was?'

'Chris,' I said, standing and trotting after her towards some lifts, our trainers barely making a sound on the stone floor. As I followed, waving goodbye to Russ, it occurred to me that I liked the world of television so far; liked the organisation of it. It seemed as if everything knew its place in this world, where you would be told what to do and have someone take you there to do it. I felt protected, cared for – so far, at least. This, I thought, is the world of Felix Carter, and here I am, as close as I'll ever come to being him. Do heads turn as we make our way across Reception? From a distance, do people see me and think I'm him?

In the lift, perhaps because we'd left Russ behind, Fi seemed to thaw. Maybe there's some kind of history between them, I mused. A furtive snog at the Christmas party and then some accidental loose talk afterwards. Shame if there was, I thought. They could make a nice couple.

'It's my lucky day,' she said, her eyes on the blinking light panel of the lift. 'Four Felixes in.'

'Do you think I pass muster?' I said.

'Pardon?'

'I said, "Do you think I pass muster?" Sorry. Cold.'

'You're cold?'

'No. I've got one.'

'I see. Hence the painkillers, yes?'

'That's right.'

The lift arrived and we stepped out.

'Well, don't worry about that. I'll sort you something out when I've got a moment.'

I was fingering the bottle of Peppar-flavoured vodka in my pocket, waiting for the opportunity to drink it, but worried also. Just one bottle of vodka. Was that going to be enough to last the day? The green room couldn't open soon enough for me.

'Right. What have we got here?'

The director's name was Gavin and what he had here, standing in front of him, were three blokes who looked vaguely similar to Felix Carter. We were standing on the stage where, a floor assistant assured us, 'it all happens'.

Behind us were the sofas where the *Happy Monday* host greets his guests, to the left another stage where a band was setting up, occasional blasts of feedback and noise drowning out the conversation.

Gavin was noticeably older than either Fi or Russ, but in

all other respects almost exactly the same, right down to the trainers and clipboard. He wore headphones around his neck and, as he spoke, his eyes darted above our heads as if there was something he'd much rather be doing: talking to the 'real' stars, perhaps.

He consulted his clipboard. 'Sorry, you're . . .' pointing at me.

'Chris,' I said. 'Chris Sewell.'

'Ah, you're the chap Russ found in Habitat.'

'It was Paperchase, actually.'

'And you're . . . ?' pointing to the Felix at my right.

'Hi, Gavin, I'm Tim. Actually, we've worked together before.'

Gavin looked up sharply from his clipboard, his face softening instantly. 'Tim!' he said, moving forward to shake the man's hand. He hadn't shaken mine. 'Um, um, don't tell me . . . *Stars In Their Eyes*!' Tim nodded vigorously, ridiculously pleased at having been remembered. But, then, can you count that as remembering? I don't think so. Neither does the Felix to the right of him, judging by the look he gives Tim.

'Well, well,' said Gavin. 'You know, we thought you were robbed.' Then, shouting to a member of the crew, 'George! Look, it's Tim. He was Felix on *Stars*. We thought he was robbed, remember?'

'Too right!' bellowed George in reply. 'Fucking Celine Dion . . .'

'Excuse George,' said Gavin, to the three of us. 'Gets a bit carried away. Well, how's things, anyway, Tim? Much luck after the show?'

'Quite a bit, thanks, Gavin, I'm on the nightclub circuit now. Doing very well out of it too.'

'Great, great. Well, you're a bit of a live TV veteran, then. Won't need to tell you what to do.' Tim beamed with pride, the Felix at his side glowered.

'OK,' continued Gavin, to the third Felix this time. 'So you must be Stuart.'

'That's right,' said Stuart, full of Cockney.

'You're the Felix tribute act, then?'

'Yeah.'

'Ah,' said Gavin. 'So you must be in competition with him?' pointing at Tim.

'S'pose,' said Stuart, looking sideways at Tim who, already taller than the rest of us, seemed to rise a couple more centimetres.

'Right,' said Gavin, judging the mood. 'Well, we're all friends together today. OK, let's run through what we're going to be doing tonight.'

He explained that the joke was that Felix was doing so much promotion for his album and his film that he seemed to be everywhere, and *Happy Monday* wanted to 'take the mick a bit, kind of make a virtue of the fact that it's not an exclusive interview'.

One of us, that would be Tim, would be sneaked into the audience, and at a certain point during the interview, the camera would cut to him. His cue would be, 'Look, you're over there.' When Tim heard that, he simply had to look like a member of the audience, only bored. No smiling or acting up for the camera. Just look bored. Easy. Job done.

The next cue would be 'And you're over there,' and the camera would cut to Stuart. Stuart would be backstage, and his job was to pick his nose on cue. Again, just pick his nose. Look bored. 'Perhaps inspect your finger as well, Stuart, like you've just dug one out.' Simple.

Next, the third cue. 'And you're even there!' which would be my cue and I would be . . .

'Sitting on the toilet.'

'I'm sorry?' I say.

'You'll be on the toilet, reading a paper, and . . .'

'What?' The other two Felixes were looking along the line at me, neither of them having much success hiding their smiles.

'Yeah, um . . .' Gavin looked worried, as if it had only just occurred to him that I might not want to be filmed sitting on the toilet. It probably had. 'Did Russ not tell you?'

'Tell me what?' I say.

'That you'd be sitting on the toilet with your trousers around your ankles, and . . .'

'My what?' I say.

Gavin looked fed up, like he had a million other things he needed to be doing, half of which needed doing now, none of which included massaging the ego of an uppity guest, especially not when there were a dozen more important egos in need of a more urgent rub-down.

'Look,' he said, sighing, talking as if he were addressing an old person, 'the gag is that you're sitting on the toilet, and, yes, you will have your trousers around your ankles – you can keep your pants on – and you're reading a paper. The camera will cut to you, and you're reading this paper, right? And you kind of look up, like you've been disturbed, and angrily shut the door in the face of the cameraman.'

The drink rose in me, angrily. 'I'm not fucking doing it.' I snapped.

But any sound was lost, drowned by a sudden and deafening blast of feedback from the band.

'Jesus Christ!' yelled Gavin, taking his hands away from his ears. 'Stevo! Will you keep it down over there, for fuck's sake!'

A disembodied voice came over the microphone. 'Yeah, sorry about that, Gav. Rock'n'roll, eh? Rock'n'roll.'

Looking more besieged than ever, Gavin turned back to me. 'Chris,' he sighed, 'are we clear?'

I searched for drink's helping hand, found it had been withdrawn. 'Yes, Gavin, clear.'

Just then, Fi approached, another man in tow.

'Gavin, hello. Can I introduce Tony Simpson?'

Gavin turned, shook the hand of the newcomer, who smiled broadly and warmly in return.

'Hi, Tony,' said Gavin. 'First time in a TV studio?'

'It is, yes,' said Tony, looking past Gavin and smiling at us. We shuffled and smiled in return.

'OK. Well, I'll go through with you what we're expecting from you. Nothing too taxing, I promise. Fi, let's get the AD to take these guys to their positions, and we're ready to roll. Ah . . .'

Up strolled another man. I recognised him as Hughie, the show's presenter, in the bright Hawaiian shirt that was his trademark. Like a lot of fat people he wore gaudy clothes to disguise his huge gut. Better informed than Gavin, he ignored the group and pointed straight at Tim, saying, 'You were robbed on *Stars In Their Eyes*, mate.' Tim glowed proudly.

'Fucking Celine Dion!' chimed George, from over the way.

'Fucking Celine Dion!' bellowed Hughie, as if in competition, his huge chest inflating even further as he barked the words over our heads. It wasn't a conversation, it was a takeover. We were smothered by his personality, as attention-grabbing as his shirt.

When he'd finished with us, I watched as he commanded the production team, striding around the stage, interspersing questions and commands with loud, raucous jokes; watched as he created his own world around which other, smaller, planets orbited eagerly, watched in awe.

In a few moments, another man, Tom, also armed with headphones and a clipboard, joined us and took us off ready for rehearsal. 'We'll find a newspaper for you in a minute,' he assured me, leading me to a toilet backstage.

Later, what seemed like a long time later, I finally had a drink.

During the preceding hours, I had sat on the toilet for two rehearsal sessions. Trousers not around ankles and no newspaper the first time; trousers around ankles, with a newspaper and *in costume* the second time.

The costume consisted of a pair of slightly flared, tailored pinstripe trousers and a tight black T-shirt. I thanked God I had lost weight; mused that it was, indirectly, Sam's doing that I'd lost weight, then remembered why I was here in the first place. There was some kind of self-perpetuating circle, or a self-fulfilling prophecy at work, but I couldn't be bothered to work out what it was, or what it was called – I was flagging somewhat.

Having downed the Peppar earlier that morning I'd been left all day without a drink and my body was beginning to rebel. By about four o'clock my eyelids were struggling to meet, and on more than one occasion I felt myself nodding off for good – once during the dress rehearsal when I was supposed to be engrossed in a newspaper on the toilet.

What's more, because of my role in the show, I'd seen very few people. Just a floor assistant, who had called me to and from my dressing room for the rehearsals, a makeup girl, a cameraman – his job: to have the toilet cubicle door shut in his face by me – and various people hurrying down various corridors.

When I was not needed I had sat in my dressing room, reading that day's copy of the *Sun*, which I was careful not to spoil, since it also doubled as my only prop. I waited, and I looked forward to the promised hospitality. First because I needed a drink. Badly. And second, because I needed to talk to Stuart.

The green room opened just after the dress rehearsal, and it was there that I found Stuart.

I suppose, subconsciously, I had expected the green room to be green. It wasn't. A long room, with rows of orange stick-together sofas at one end, a table filled with food and a man serving drinks at the other, it was in fact painted cream. In one top corner was a single monitor. This, Russ had told me, was the ring main, where guests could watch the show from the comfort of hospitality.

By the time I got there – and I got there quickly – there were already people in it. The band, who, I'd discovered, were called the Grobbelaars, were sitting with their manager, looking nervous but excited. Tony Simpson was chatting to a girl holding a clipboard. He waved. None of the show's big stars was anywhere to be seen, but Stuart was sitting by himself, nursing a Coke and holding a plate of canapés. There was, thankfully, no sign of Tim. I waved to Stuart, made a motion like I'd join him in a sec and strode to the bar.

'Vodka and tonic, please,' I said, to the man behind the bar. He wore a bow tie and looked to all intents and purposes like Jeeves, the Internet butler, although less helpful.

'We've got beer and wine only,' he said. I weighed up my options, decided beer; no, on second thoughts, wine.

'Glass of red, please.'

He motioned at some filled glasses set out before him. 'Help yourself.' So I did, and, ignoring the canapés table, went back to join Stuart, gulping from the wine as I did so. I felt the booze wash through my body, blessed it.

'Costume fits, then?' I said, by way of conversation as I sat next to Stuart. He looked me up and down. We were both wearing the same outfit. Two not-quite-Felixes.

In real life, two men sitting side-by-side on an orange sofa wearing the same clothes might have attracted the wrong kind of attention. But this was not real life, this was television, and apart from the one wrinkle I was enjoying myself. Now, if I could just get that wrinkle ironed out . . .

'How did your rehearsal go?' I said, twisting in my seat to face him.

'It was all right.'

Stuart was not the chattiest vegetable in the patch, but I soldiered on. 'You nervous, are ya?' I said, unconsciously aping his accent.

'Not really. Don't have to do much. Be honest wiv ya, I was hoping for a bit more, like. Thought it might be good for me club work.'

There was a bellow of laughter from the side of the room. Looking up, I saw that Tony Simpson and the clipboard girl had joined the Grobbelaars, forming a single group. Them on one side of the room, me and the moody Stuart on the other. Great.

Nevertheless, I'd seen a window.

'Well, look, I don't mind swapping if you want?'

Stuart looked at me. Disconsolate Felix regarding hopeful Felix. He began to laugh. Not quite the huge guffaws coming from the Grobbelaars' end of the room, more of a low snicker. I found myself not knowing whether to be pleased that his miserable face had at last cracked, or offended that he found my suggestion so laughable.

'Well,' he said, after laughing for some moments, 'I don't fink *that*'s going to be very good for me club work, do you?'

'It might be.'

'I want people to take me seriously, mate. This is my living, you know.'

'Go on,' I said, holding out my copy of the *Sun* to him – like that was going to change his mind. He stared at it as if I was offering him a bag of vomit.

'Er, no, mate. We've rehearsed and everyfink. I'm sticking to what they've told us, thanks.'

'Go on,' I repeated, already aware that appealing to his better nature was getting me nowhere.

'Look, mate, no offence like, but I don't know you from Adam. Why should I swap wiv you? What's in it for me?'

I held out the *Sun* to him. He refused to take hold of it, even when I shook it enticingly.

'OK,' I offered. 'What if I give you fifty quid?'

He looked at me, then past me, like he was considering making a quick dash to the Grobbelaars' side of the room.

'Nah, mate, leave it, orright?'

'One hundred?'

'No.'

I batted his arm with the *Sun*. 'Three hundred, then?'

Three hundred quid. Currently my get-out-of-jail figure.

He looked testily down at the spot on his arm where I'd

hit him with the paper but, still, he seemed to consider it. Perhaps the figures were now getting so large it seemed foolish to continue resisting.

'Three hundred notes? Just for swapping?'

'That's right. Look, I want my wife to see me on the show. It's kind of a surprise, right? And I just want it to look really good. And I'm worried if she sees me on the bog, right, she'll just think I look like a twat.'

That seemed to decide him. He shook his head and I cursed myself for reminding him of the net result of appearing on the toilet on national television.

'Look,' he confirmed, 'I'm sorry, no.'

'Three hundred fucking quid!' I shouted, swiping him hard on the arm with the paper at the same time. He recoiled sharply, the level of my voice – the anger – bringing a sudden spark of fear to his wary eyes.

Over on the other side of the room the Grobbelaars' laughing conversation died abruptly. They looked in our direction.

A beat. Stuart looked imploring. I smiled semi-apologetically. For a moment they stared quizzically at us then, like a motor starting, the conversation spluttered back into life and they turned their attention back to each other.

I took a deep breath, thought, Control. Control, and, with exaggerated care, placed the *Sun* on the sofa beside me. Stuart regarded me the way a cat watches a dog – a mixture of fear and disdain.

'Look,' I said, my voice low and reasonable again. 'The toilet thing? It's a laugh, innit? I mean, it's the bit people are going to remember. It's the big finale to the gag.'

As I said this, it occurred to me that I was right. It *was* the bit people were going to remember. My gut instinct had been that if Sam were to watch the show, suddenly seeing me with my trousers around my ankles was hardly the pantie-moistening turn-on that I'd imagined it to be. But that was based on my earlier feeling that she would be seeing me in a certain light; as a Felix lookylikey, and therefore a talented sex-god with a cheeky public persona. Well, maybe all I needed was a simple shift in my thinking. So what if I was not to be paraded in such a complimentary light? I *was* still going to get the biggest laugh, the bit of the joke people would remark upon afterwards. And, after all, wasn't that just as endearing? Take Felix, for example. Isn't his sex-appeal at least partly based on his tendency to make the opposite sex laugh? Maybe I was being too hasty.

Whatever, it looked like I was going to have to live with it. Stuart was having none of the toilet idea, three hundred pounds or not. He looked relieved when Tim appeared, asked if he could join us, then sat down and sank into an uneasy silence, watching the Grobbelaars' crowd enviously. For a few moments the three of us Felixes sat in a line watching the other crowd before I offered to get the drinks, welcoming the change of scene when I strode the length of the room to the bar.

Later, I was back in the green room, more people in it this time. The programme had finished, the de-rig begun, the production team and guests all seemed happy – another good show.

Only, there were three guests who weren't too happy. The three Felixes – now reconvened in the green room – had missed their moment of fame, thanks to time constraints, thanks in no small part to Tony Simpson.

For my part, I had spent half of the show – from just before the Felix interview to just after it – sitting on a toilet backstage with my trousers around my ankles.

The wine I'd drunk in the green room had massaged away any of my earlier tension, but the disadvantage was that I now needed to go for a piss. My arse was telling my head that it was sitting on a toilet, and my head was relaying chocks-away information to my bladder.

'Excuse me,' I said, to the cameraman who stood in front of me. His name was Cram – or Gram – and it was his job to give me my cue before, obviously, filming me.

The idea was that he'd count me down and, on 'three,

two ... ONE,' I'd pretend to look up from my paper, give an irritated look that I'd practised in front of my dressing-room mirror, then reach and push the door closed, right in Cram's face.

'Excuse me,' I repeated. 'Have I got time to go to the toilet?'

Cram, who clearly felt he'd drawn the short straw in being stuck in a backstage loo for a minor sketch, sighed. 'Can it wait, mate? We'll be on in a sec.'

'S'pose,' I replied, sending abort, abort messages to my bladder. The wine had given me a kind of Dutch courage, and the day was surreal anyway, so I felt no nerves from sitting there – just a mild discomfort from the need to urinate. And I waited, watching Cram who seemed too absorbed with events in his headphones to make much conversation; feeling disengaged from the programme going out live just a few yards away from me.

And then, as I sat there, it became clear that something unexpected was going on out front.

'Felix has been introduced,' said Cram at first, and the pair of us mentally readied ourselves for our cue.

Then, 'He's taking his time reaching the stage for some reason. Looks like he's gone AWOL. Typical.'

I held up the paper in front of me, ready, trying to picture the scene out front – Hughie standing with one arm outstretched as Felix bounded from backstage to front. But what was he doing now? A bit of horseplay with some members of the audience, perhaps? Going over for handshakes and kisses with female fans?

'He's still not reached the front,' said Cram, frowning. 'Wait a minute. He's gone back again. Ah, now he's got that chap with him.'

'What chap?' I asked.

'That Tony Simpson chap. The headphones bloke.'

'What's he doing?'

'Dunno,' said Cram, distracted. 'He's not supposed to be on now. Bill, what's going on out there?'

Cram listened. I sat, trying to ignore the pressure in my bladder.

'Oh, it looks like Felix has dragged on the Tony Simpson bloke, sat him down,' said Cram at last. 'It's unscheduled. Dunno what's happening. Director's in a paddy.'

We waited for another few minutes, then, 'Right. It looks like we've been dropped.'

'Oh.'

'Yeah, but we've got to hang around until the end of the item. Just in case. Sorry, mate. You can go back to the green room afterwards, eh?'

'Right.' I sat and looked down at my trousers around my ankles, trying not to think of Sam, wherever she was, sitting in front of a television, wondering what she was supposed to be seeing, disappointment creeping numbly up my body. Everything over the last few days had been building up to this moment. And, just like that, it had been snatched away.

Cram drifted back into headphone-monitoring mode, and I sat absorbing the shock, unable to either have a piss or pull my trousers up or find Tony Simpson and pull him into an empty sideroom, throttle him to death and leave him there. Until, at last, Cram seemed to snap back to reality.

'OK,' he said, shouldering his camera. 'Stand down. As you were. We're all done here. Hey, at least you're in the right place for the toilet. Enjoy your dump.'

'Actually,' I said, 'it's not a dump. I just need a piss.' But he didn't reply. He'd already turned his back and was carrying his camera away.

So, a few moments after that, I joined the other two Felixes in the green room, both wearing the same disgruntled face I no doubt bore. And we waited for our all-clear so that we could go home.

I didn't know about them but, free booze or not, I had decided that home was where I wanted to be. I needed to put as much distance between myself and this place as possible. Thinking of the effort I had gone to, the emotional time I had invested in being here, I now felt used and degraded, like a prostitute. Worse, it seemed as though the other people in the green room were laughing at us, three pissed-off Felixes sitting on a sofa as the crowd built up around us.

And then I managed to collar Fi and ask her to organise a car, and she promised me she would and if I waited in Reception for it to arrive it would be there presently. But it wasn't, so I went to find Fi again, and this time she seemed to be in deep conversation with Russ, a low but heated conversation that I didn't want to interrupt. So I went back to Reception, and still the car didn't arrive.

And then Felix Carter walked into Reception, the first time I had seen him all day.

'Oh, look, it's me,' he says, wandering over to where I'm sitting.

CHAPTER THIRTY-SEVEN

Not to put too fine a point on it, Frank was embarrassed. He was embarrassed that he had this seemingly intractable problem. He was embarrassed that his first attempt to solve it had met with such miserable failure. He was embarrassed because the parties had continued, and with them the bongos and the sleepless nights, and each time he had seen, or, at least, imagined, the looks on his wife and daughter's faces that told him, 'Do something.'

He was too embarrassed to call the police. Frank had never had need of a policeman in his life and he certainly wasn't going to start now. Sorry, but policemen needed Frank, not the other way round.

He was too embarrassed to go round again, because he was so ashamed of trying to be something he wasn't the first time. Especially ashamed because it hadn't worked. He could go over there doing his Frank-the-minder bit and they'd only have to say, 'How's Hannah?' and he'd be humiliated.

For God's sake, he'd faced down terrorists, slit throats at dead of night, picked off the enemy with a sniper's rifle, and now he was foxed by a bunch of crusties down the street? It just wasn't . . . Frank.

He was embarrassed to be embarrassed.

Frank was too intelligent to let his thoughts wander down the Molotov cocktail/night-time incursion route, but every now and then he put a mental foot on the path. In fact, more and more lately his thoughts had been returning to some form of direct action. A final solution. Which was another reason he had not returned to the squatters' doorstep. If he was planning to do something, he didn't want to be the first suspect. If, if . . .

As the parties continued, and so did the drumming – two or three times a week – it became less of an 'if', more of a 'when', until one day he found himself wondering if he could still remember how to make napalm the way he used to, out in the field. He stopped himself short. For Christ's sake, he thought, listen to yourself. You are a family man, one of the country's top celebrity minders, probably a best-selling book in front of you. You have too much to lose.

So instead he gave Grey Dave a call.

Frank and Grey Dave met one night in an almost empty pub in Crouch End. The two men had not seen each other for many, many years, but they had seen a lot of each other before that; seen too much together, the kind of things that form a bond between men that time can't break.

That was the way it should have been, anyway. That was the way Frank thought it would be.

Only Grey Dave seemed to have forgotten about the unbreakable bonds of men in the field. Seemed to have forgotten about the times Frank had watched his back on black ops and vice versa. He seemed more interested in winking at the barmaid and he snorted derisively when Frank told him about the 'problem', murmuring it across the table like a teenager asking a pharmacist for condoms.

'For fuck's sake, Frank!' exploded Grey Dave, shattering the silence of the pub and shocking Frank back in his seat. 'Go over there, give one of them a good hiding. Kick some fucking manners into one of them.'

Funny, thought Frank, Grey Dave had been given the nickname 'grey' because of his shadow-like stealth in the field. The years had obviously robbed him of any natural tact he'd once had. He recovered his poise. 'Dave, my position. You know what I do. You know I can't afford to stick my neck out,' he said calmly, watching Grey Dave's eyes as he did so.

'And I can?' said Dave in reply, holding Frank's gaze.

Frank mentally surrendered his pawn. Dave had a good point. Why should he, Frank, assume that he had more to lose than Dave? He had done so because he had gone legit, and he was fairly sure Dave hadn't. If he knew Dave – and he did, very well – Dave would be up to his neck in something dodgy and, judging by the sniffing, the frequent trips to the toilet and sudden loud outbursts, that something had to do with cocaine. Still, it was an assumption. And what did assume do? It made an ass out of you and me.

'This is what I'm asking, Dave,' he said, keeping his tone measured. 'This is what I'm asking. I need a job doing. In the field, you were the man who did the jobs. Are you still?'

This appeal to Dave's ego seemed to have an effect. The other man picked up his pint glass and swirled the lager.

'Could be,' he replied at last. 'Depends on the job.'

'I'm thinking a fire,' said Frank. 'A non-fatal, but definitely bongo-destroying fire. Localised.'

'You could set a fire,' said Dave flatly.

'I can't because I'll be out of the country. I'm thinking of planning a holiday for me and the missus. I hear Menorca's nice this time of year.'

'What, November?'

'It's a figure of speech, Dave. Are you in?'

Dave regarded him across the table, saying nothing.

For a moment or so Frank mused that this job would be made a lot easier if, say, Grey Dave's wife and kids had once been killed by bongo-playing squatters. But since they hadn't, and the alliances of battle-scarred men seemed to have been forgotten, he would have to resort to . . .

'How much?'

'Two grand. And a favour.'

'What's the favour?'

'Your man Felix. Bit of a drug fiend, I hear. Got a nose for nose.'

'He's . . . Go on.'

'It's nothing, really. All I ask is that you mention me to him.

And perhaps that he'll mention me to his mates. And those mates to their mates, see what I mean?'

Frank let out an inward sigh of relief. Was that all? he thought. Well, then, thank God for that. 'Dave, that is not a problem. You just make sure you do the fire right, OK? No fatalities. Localised. I don't want to come back all tanned and find my house has burnt down. Here's the address.' He pushed a folded piece of paper across the table at Grey Dave, who took it with a practised swipe.

'And the money?' said Dave.

'Now, or on completion of the job, it's up to you.'

'Well, I'm a bit strapped . . .'

Frank shrugged. 'Then let's take a walk to the cash machine.'

Grey Dave drained his pint. 'And the favour?'

'It'll be done,' said Frank, standing. 'Don't you worry about that.'

'How will I know?'

'Dave, we have fought wars together. We've seen things together no man should be asked to see. If I say I'm going to do something for you, I'll do it.'

Grey Dave nodded, and the two men shook hands before putting on their coats and leaving the pub.

As they left, Grey Dave thought about the look he'd seen in his old mucker's eyes and laughed inwardly. Would he do that favour? Would he fuck. Was he going to take Frank's cash and let him start his own damn fire? Yes, he rather thought so.

Frank, meanwhile, also laughed inwardly. So he'd been wrong about the ties of old comrades. So what? He got rid of the bongos and he did it on his own terms. Grey Dave would never know whether or not he'd done the favour, which he had no intention of doing.

Not if he wanted a job when he came back from Menorca.

CHAPTER THIRTY-EIGHT

You've seen famous people before, of course.

Yes, many times.

Then you'll know the effect they have on a place. Like Felix, when he walks into Reception at Bottom Drawer. The room seems to stop and rearrange itself when he steps out of a lift and strides across the hard wood floor, a clipboard girl and a smartly dressed man hurrying behind him.

Everybody stops what they are doing – even if what they're doing is nothing – and all eyes turn towards him. Hardly tall in stature, he might as well be for the attention he commands. Receptionists straighten and preen imperceptibly as he crosses the floor; a man sitting in a chair beside me suddenly stops his mobile phone conversation then begins talking in an excited whisper; a motorcycle courier stands entranced, watching Felix as he absorbs the awe that descends upon him. Even here, in the reception area of Bottom Drawer, which must surely be accustomed to celebrities wandering its corridors, Felix Carter seems a peerless, almost celestial presence.

He's dressed exactly as I was before I huffily tore off my *Happy Monday* outfit and tossed it to the floor of my dressing room. Only he wears the clothes as if they were made for him – they probably were – as if they were born to shroud his lean, toned body. Try as I might, I can't imagine the same trousers puddled around his ankles, as mine were just an hour or so earlier.

Similarly, our hairstyles, though ostensibly the same – just a crew-cut, for God's sake – seem wildly different. Mine, a sheared number three, nothing more; his, a statement of style. Moreover, a statement of *his* style, an extension of his personality, the confidence that seems to drip from him as he strides through the reception area, all of us caught helplessly in his tail wind.

And then he stops, sees me sitting in my easy chair, waiting for a car that will never arrive. And he comes over.

'Oh, look, it's me,' he says, wandering over to where I'm sitting. Clipboard-girl and Suit-man turn on their heels to follow him.

He stands before me. 'Or is it . . . is it . . . a mirror?' And he pretends to do his hair – his perfect, sculpted hair – all the time staring at me, into me, like his own mirror image.

I feel lightheaded, unsure what to say or how to react: partly the butt of his joke at which his hangers-on and others in Reception begin to laugh, but partly the chosen one, the one person in the reception area who has intruded into the mind-space of Felix Carter.

At last he stops, smiles – *that* smile: that heartbreaking, friend-winning, whose-round-is-it smile – and holds out his hand to me.

'Hello, mate,' he says. 'Are you me? Or am I you?' Everything a surprise with him, off-centred. Even the simplest greeting is whipped unwillingly into his world, Felixised.

'I'm me,' I manage, to chuckles from Clipboard-girl and the girls behind Reception. I ignore them, all my attention tunnelled directly before me.

'Then who does that make me?' Still the smile, still the hand, which I take, late, after he seems to have been holding it out for some moments. But I think I've got the hang of the game now.

'You're Chris,' I say, with more confidence. 'Chris Sewell.'

'I'm Chris, am I? Making you Felix?'

'That's right, Chris. Pleased to meet you.'

'Pleased to meet you too, Felix.'

I should stand, but I can't. And the pair of us look at one another. Me smiling now, him grinning like this is the most fun he's had all day. That star quality they talk about, the ability to make you feel at the centre of their world. And I'm sucked right in. Fall hook, line and sinker.

Then, someone is at his shoulder. Hughie, clapping him heartily on the back at which Felix grimaces slightly, only I notice it – a moment shared between us – and turns.

'You bastard!' booms Hughie, in full takeover mode. But even he, even the chubby crown prince of Bottom Drawer, has no chance of stealing any of Felix's celebrity charge. The room belongs to Felix and the previously commanding Hughie is reduced to the status of courtier. I watch, fascinated, the hierarchy at work.

'Pull a stunt like that again and I swear . . .' Hughie makes a move as if to punch, all in jest, but Felix doesn't take the bait, smiling as he rises effortlessly above his host's bungling attempts to level the playing-field. On noticing me for the first time, Hughie uses me to try a different tack.

'And, my man,' he announces, to the increasingly bemused Felix, 'you owe this chap here an apology . . .' gesturing at me.

Felix looks down at me, looking at him. 'Do I, Felix?' he says.

'I'm not sure, Chris. Maybe . . .'

'Course you fuckin' do!' roars Hughie, seemingly unaware of the strange name swap that's taken place between me and Felix. 'It's all thanks to you that this little guy didn't get his five minutes of fame.'

Little guy. Little compared to you, you fat fuck. *His five minutes of fame.* I look at Hughie with undisguised contempt.

But his crass bid to create a no-guests-allowed celebrity circle has failed, because Felix looks down at me, that smile again, that same look, which seems to invite me to collude in his contempt for Hughie.

'God, did I?' His voice is so full of warmth I find my disgust for Hughie subsiding, my disappointment negated also, both drowned in Felix's charm. 'In that case I am *so* sorry. I can get a bit carried away sometimes. Forget meself, you know?'

'You can say that again!' pipes up Hughie, but Felix is all but ignoring him now and, frozen out of the conversation, Hughie gives Felix a last, still unwelcome, clap on the shoulder before announcing, 'Right. You take care, fella. I'm off to the green room. Things to see, women to do . . .' and leaves, carrying with him the merest acknowledgement from Felix like a piece of cake from a birthday party.

We watch him leave. Behind us, Clipboard-girl and Suit-man hover impatiently.

'He's right, is he?' says Felix. 'I fucked up your TV thing by being a prick?'

'I didn't see what you did,' I say, unsure what my reply should be but desperately trying to find the right one so the spell won't be broken.

'Ah, I was just pissing about. Always have to be pissing about, me. Did you come far to end up on the sub's bench?'

'From north London. I'm waiting to go back now, only my car hasn't turned up.'

'That settles it, then. I can make it up to you by giving you a lift home. That all right, Frank?' He turns to the man in the suit as he says this. 'We OK to give Felix here a lift back home?'

A look passes between them. Actually, it's more of a barely raised eyebrow from Frank who looks past Felix at me, then back again, as if to say, 'Don't like it. It's not procedure.'

'He's all right,' exclaims Felix. 'Aren't you? Look, Frank, if it makes you feel any better, tell yourself he's a decoy we're using in case of attack by Basque separatists.'

Felix fixes me with that conspiratorial look, 'Frank is my driver-stroke-bodyguard. Ignore him. He's a big man but he's in bad shape. Was it the SAS or the Paras you were in, Frank?'

'The Royal Marines, Felix.'

'Royal, eh? Then you should know all about manners, and the polite thing to do is to offer Felix here a lift home.'

'We didn't do manners in basic, Felix.'

To me: 'Frank's just pissed off because he's going straight home and we're holding him up. He's off on his holidays and he wants to be with Mrs Frank, isn't that right?'

'Bit of time off will be nice . . .'

'Then let's get going. Right.' He turns to Clipboard-girl. 'Rebecca, it's been business doing nice with you,' and she laughs uncertainly, shaking his outstretched hand as he continues his exit with whirlwind energy. 'We're off. Ladies and gentleman, Felix Carter has left the building. Come on.'

And with that, I find myself joining Frank and trotting after him, basking in the admiring eyes that follow the three of us through the doors and out into the evening.

'The idea, Felix,' says Frank firmly, edging past us to the car, which is parked directly outside the doors, 'is that I leave first. Therefore, if there does happen to be a nutter with a breadknife he meets me before he meets you. You have a stalker, remember?'

'Blah blah blah,' mimics Felix in return.

'Yeah? You'll be blah blah when someone's sawing off your hand for proof of captivity.'

'As long as it's not my wanking hand.'

'You? A wanker? My lips are sealed.'

'Good. Keep your lips sealed and your lisp thealed.'

'Ha bloody ha.'

I'm giddy with it. A sudden, nervous entrant into this quickfire, alien world of Army-trained drivers and their cocksure pop employers. Even off-duty, Felix is still the showman, full of banter, brimming with dynamo verve. How much is conducted for my benefit I neither know nor care, thankful simply of the opportunity to share the same air as Felix, drinking in the feel of his world and finding I like it – like it more than I could ever explain. Here I feel, not as if I belong exactly, more as if I'm protected. As if the world can't hurt me any more. I feel . . . I feel the same way I feel when I'm drunk. Only this is better, more pure.

Frank looks me up and down as I get into the car and I'm glad I don't have my gun, sure that he'd be able to spot it. Inside, the door thunks solidly shut and it's as if I've stepped into a different world again: Felix's car – a Mercedes – is even more plush than my Lexus earlier, the temperature perfectly controlled, soundproofing blocking all noise from the outside world. Our voices take on a different timbre inside its womb. Theirs do, at least. I haven't said a word since we left Reception, my head reeling.

'Right. Where to?' says Frank to his rearview mirror, looking at me.

'Drop me first,' replies Felix.

'Felix . . .' starts Frank.

'Frank, tell me, where do you live?'

'Muswell Hill.'

'That's right. And I live in Kensington. And our friend here lives in north London – where . . . ?'

'Stoke Newington.' They're the first words I say.

'Exactly, in Stoke Newington. So don't you think it makes perfect sense to drop me off first, drop Felix off, then go home to Mrs Frank where you can pack your trunks ready for Majorca?'

'It's *Men*orca and I'm not happy about it.' To me: 'No offence.'

I shrug it off, 'None taken,' not sure exactly how I might take offence.

'Look,' Felix leans forward in his seat, reaching right through to the front. I put my hand on the seat between us then draw it away, putting it into my pocket. 'Let's put it another way. I am your employer and as such I don't think I should have to drag all the way to north London and back again.' To me, piss-taking: 'No offence.'

'None taken.'

'Got it?'

Frank starts the engine, a low growl that barely penetrates the car's noiseless interior. 'You're the boss.' And we drive on, away from Bottom Drawer, heading for Felix's house.

Felix leans back, relaxing into the leather, his head right back on the head-rest. Then, twisting it towards me, he says, 'Fancy a beer?'

My heart skips a beat. 'God, yeah.'

He laughs and punches my arm at the same time. 'Nah, mate, I'm pulling your lariat. Have you not heard? I'm visiting with Mr Sobriety at the moment. Chris is a bad, bad boy. Me and drink, you know, we're like Richard Burton and Elizabeth Taylor – always fighting, always making up, falling out again. We love each other but we're bad for each other too. Fuck, you're not a journalist, are you?'

I don't know how he does it, but he seems to do it each time. The interview with him I read, the documentary – he has this knack of summing up how I feel each time, saying my words for me . . .

And suddenly I find myself wanting to connect with him more than I've ever wanted to connect with anyone, knowing somehow that he has within his grasp the power to set my life back on track, pull me away from the edge of the pit I've dug for myself. The realisation comes to me in a rush, but I check it, knowing that suddenly to blurt out my own troubles would be to frighten him off – he'd probably have Frank beat me up by the side of the road.

So, carefully, I say, 'With drink, it's like you're either drinking, or you're not, or you're trying not to drink or you're trying to drink less. It's always there somehow. It's this kind of unwelcome presence.' And I'm pleased with that comment, because I know he feels the same way – it is, after all, a regurgitation of his speech from the documentary about being on the wagon, but paraphrased – and I haven't actually personalised it, haven't directly stated that my own problems are the same as his. Instead, I've hinted at them, offered him a clue that he's invited a kindred spirit into his car.

'Aye, well, we're all prozzies, really. Just depends who your pimp is. Bring me a bottle of Jack Daniel's and I'm yours for a tenner. I guess there are worse things to be. Ronan Keating, for example . . .'

I laugh, perhaps too much, but I'm aware that he's walking the conversation away from the subject of drink, reluctantly watching my in-roads disappearing into the distance. But I don't want to lose him just yet, so . . .

'It was kind of a shame I wasn't on tonight.'

'Yeah, look, I'm sorry . . .'

'No, I don't mean . . . What I mean is, I was hoping my wife would see it.'

'Oh, yeah? She back in Stoke Newington, is she?' He points, as if pointing at our house.

'No. We're separated. I wanted her to see it because I kind of wanted her to think that I looked like you.'

'Oh, yeah?' He shuffles in his seat slightly. Am I making him uncomfortable? Maybe, but I'm aware that we only have this journey time together, and that if I want to form a bond with him it has to be done now.

'Yeah, I thought – you know – it would help bring her round.'

'Ah . . . Well, you probably had a lucky escape . . .' He has the good grace to prevent himself adding a comment about him being an ugly bastard anyway, adding instead, 'I mean, you know, you'd want her to come back to you because of you. You know, not because you look like someone else. Maybe the TV thing wasn't the right way to go about it, mate.'

'I suppose I'll have to think of something else . . .'

'I wish I could help. Tell you what, charm her with your winning personality. Never fails.' Then suddenly he pitches forward in his seat. 'Frank, put the radio on, would you? See if my song's playing.'

'What's your song?' I ask queasily, feeling a drop of perspiration run from my armpit to my waistband, but sensing another in.

'Not my song, *my* song. In the charts. "Love You (To The Nth Degree)".'

The radio goes on, something I don't recognise. Felix slumps back with a disgusted noise.

'They never play what you want, do they?' I say, weakly, losing him by the second. I could cry.

'No.'

'It's a good song.'

'Thank you.'

'I bought the album the other day.'

'Cheers, mate.'

'And the album before that.'

'Right. God, thanks.'

'I like that other song too – "Planet Of The Gapes". That's a good one.'

'Yeah, cheers. We're quite proud of it. It's about leading a life in the public eye.'

Felix is looking out of the window now, probably willing the buildings to slip past more quickly. Though he hasn't changed his posture, his body language seems to have changed. He's pulling away from me. From welcoming to defensive. Thinking of a drink, I wish, wish, wish he'd been serious about going for a pint. Sweat pools on my top lip, I brush it away surreptitiously.

'I sent my wife a tape. Of that song – "Love You (To The Nth Degree)".'

'You did?'

'I thought, you know, a nice romantic song. It's like flowers but more personal, you know?' Of all people, he should understand this, surely? My head has started throbbing now, I'm trying to control my breathing.

'Yeah, well, that song – "Love You (To The Nth Degree)"? It's not really a love song. It's, like, a piss-take of a love song. It sounds like one, but it's taking the piss if you listen to the words . . .'

'Really?'

'Yeah. And when I sing, "I lo-o-ove you", I'm kind of singing it in this sarky voice. That's also why, in the title, the words "to the nth degree" are in brackets. That's very important, that.'

'Oh.'

'Right. Here we are.'

Looking out of the car window, we turn into a quiet, leafy street and I see a street sign – Acacia Avenue – the road lined with shiny, expensive cars. Behind them, rows of well-kept townhouses with steps leading up to the front doors. Just across town from my own street, it might as well be on a different planet. Where are the mini-cabs insistently blaring their horns? The couples arguing noisily on the pavement, the kids kicking footballs at the cars?

And we stop.

And I'm trying to think of something else I can say, something that will prompt him to invite me inside, grant me further access to his intoxicating world, or make a date for the future – to chat, just to talk. Why not? After all, haven't I read of him saying that he has no friends to speak of? Why not choose me?

But my racing mind fails to find the right words. Really, what could I say? What can I offer him? Why on earth would Felix Carter want to be my friend? I've got nothing . . .

(although I have, of course)

. . . he could possibly want and, anyway, the moment's gone, because he's opened the car door, and the central locking clicks with an expensive clunk and he's already out and standing in the road, leaning in to say goodbye. 'You never know, mate, maybe she didn't listen to the words. Stick with it, eh? Good luck. Seeya, Felix.'

'Seeya, Chris,' is all I manage, finding myself part relieved the ordeal is over, failure or not.

And then he's stopping Frank getting out of the car.

'Frank, will yer stop acting like me mam? Just stay here, watch me inside and then get off home, will you? I don't need a fucking nanny, I need a driver. So drive.'

And then he's dashing across the road, doing an impression of a fast bowler as he goes, king of his street. Where moments ago his energy seemed to leak away into the atmosphere, now, outside the car, he appears to have found it again as he bounds up the steps to his front door, and digs in his trousers for his door key.

Which he won't find, because I have it in my pocket.

Sure enough, no key. He pat-pat-pats at his trousers with no success. Earlier in the journey his key, a single Yale-style affair on a Bart Simpson key-ring, slithered from his trousers to the seat between us and I picked it up and put it into my pocket. Now I have my hand on it, ready. I'm waiting to see what will happen, prepared to give the key back if needs be, if he insists that it's in the car somewhere and that we must all hunt for it, but not if I don't have to.

'What's wrong?' tuts Frank from the front, making to get out of the car, but Felix is already bouncing down the steps, quick look and across the road, pretending to machine-gun Frank as he comes. Unconcerned. Good.

Frank's window glides down and Felix's head appears in it, winking at me, saying, 'Frank, gimme your key.'

'Where's yours?'

'Dunno. In the house. And if you say I'd forget my head if it wasn't screwed on I'll call up a tactical air strike on Menorca.' He winks at me again in the back. I smile, my hand sweaty on his key in my pocket.

The engine goes off and Frank struggles with his keys, finally passing Felix a single Yale through the window.

He takes it, saying to Frank, 'Don't get burnt,' as he does so.

'What?' says Frank, sharply.

'In Menorca, mate. Don't get burnt.'

'Oh,' says Frank.

And off Felix goes again, this time with a simple 'ta-ra', his party trick now to run backwards and flick us the V-signs as he crosses the road. We watch as he runs up the steps, unlocks the door and lets himself in, a final V-sign his parting gesture as the door slams closed behind him.

Frank sighs. 'OK,' he says, his eyes in the rear-view mirror. 'Where to?'

'Stoke Newington, please,' I reply, as if to a cabbie. 'I'll direct you when we get a bit nearer.'

I'm sheepish when Frank pulls up outside my flat, such is the difference between my street and Felix's. Nevertheless, I find myself wishing the trip could have gone on for longer, so that I could have soaked up the experience more fully – sitting in the back of the car, gliding imperiously through the streets of London.

We haven't spoken for the journey, except for me to give him directions, and when at last we arrive I hop out of the car as quickly as possible. On the pavement I briefly enjoy the image of a man who looks like Felix Carter stepping out of his Mercedes and bidding farewell to his driver, and then he's gone, humming off up the street and I'm alone on the pavement outside my flat, my day over, Chris Sewell again.

I feel a loss. As crushing and as final as I felt when I put down the phone to Auntie Jean when she'd told me my father had died; the same sense of creeping injustice, that something has been unfairly snatched away from me.

As I take deep breaths, it dawns on me that I'm shaking, perspiring heavily, my mind soaked with the emotion of the day, my body crying out for a drink. So, turning, I wander to the shop where I buy a bottle of vodka and don't bother asking the woman behind the counter to keep the change.

Once inside the flat, stepping back into my old life, treading over the mess of my lounge, the depression hits me hard and I unscrew the cap of the vodka, gulp greedily from the bottle.

No messages on the home phone. No messages on the mobile. I pick up the handset and my finger hovers over the zero, ready to dial Sam's number, thinking, yes, I will, having second thoughts – what will I say? – deciding, finally, no. Instead, I turn to the coffee table and sweep off the debris, leaving just one object: the gun. I dig into my pocket, pull out Felix Carter's house key and place it carefully beside the gun: a grinning, colourful Bart Simpson sitting next to my dad's wartime revolver.

And then I put Felix's CD on the stereo, listen to the words of 'Love You (To The Nth Degree)'. Very important, those brackets. He was right about the words as well.

By the way, you'll never guess what?

What?

I saw a familiar face in here the other day. A new arrival.

Who?

Dog-end.

God, really?

Oh, yes. It was definitely him. The old memory's improved since I've given up drinking. Of course, he won't know me. Well, he'll know me, of course, everybody does, but he won't know that it's *me*, if you see what I mean. I thought I might pay his bunk a visit on the way to the toilet one day. Or perhaps I'll get someone else to do it for me. As I said, I've got a lot of respect in here, a lot of people look up to me.

I'm not sure you should be telling me this sort of thing.

Really? I thought you wanted the whole truth from me?

Well, I do.

Then you'll get it. Tell me, have you been to see Sam yet?

I'm really not sure I should say, should I?

Very well, but if you do, be sure to give her my love.

CHAPTER THIRTY-NINE

On her way to Bedford, the Mystery Blonde had been unable to put her finger on exactly why she felt so odd travelling to meet Samantha Sewell. An experienced journalist, she had interviewed a great many people – most of them very famous, very stylish and very glamorous – and was more than used to the attendant feelings: nerves, anticipation, professional pride and so on. But as she drove ever further up the A1 she became aware of a different emotion, one that she eventually deduced sprang from a feeling of involvement. A very specific feeling of involvement at that. Here she was, about to meet Christopher Sewell's wife (and she *was* still his wife, though a divorce was imminent and moving as fast as bureaucracy would allow), and she felt, not like a journalist about to meet an interviewee, but like a mistress about to meet a cuckolded spouse.

In many ways, she supposed prettily, she was Christopher Sewell's other woman. Certainly, as far as she knew, she had been his sole prison visitor not connected in some way to the legal process. Other journalists had tried, of course, but she was the only one to gain access, and though she had her suspicions that this had much to do with a residual desire to help *Sass* magazine on Sewell's part, it had still personalised the relationship to a certain extent.

She was, therefore, more nervy than usual. Being ice-cool and chic and beautiful, she did not show these nerves, but really she was like a swan: calm and serene to the watching eye, madly, messily paddling beneath the water.

Samantha Sewell now lived on an estate on the outskirts of Bedford. It was not an estate in the London sense of the word; not like the one Christopher and Sam Sewell used to negotiate on their way to and from work. Instead, this was a sprawling collection of detached family homes, each with its own sloping driveway, a garden with a path and, in most cases, a rotary washing-line.

It was a place she recognised from her own childhood. It reminded her of lawn-mowers and plastic buckets and spades and sandpits and slowly deflating paddling pools. It reminded her of the sound of Sundays when the estate would seem to be heaving with domestic industry. But most of all it reminded her of really, really wanting to leave, and it struck her as ironic that her future should be so closely allied to such a place.

The deal, struck with Samantha's solicitor, was that Mystery Blonde would be – once again – the only journalist to gain access to the home. It helped that she knew the solicitor. Indeed, she had introduced him to his wife while they were all still at Oxford together, and the relationship had now stood her in good stead, oiling the wheels of the process, removing the need to establish trust, which was the hurdle all other journalists had fallen at.

Even so, Samantha Sewell had been uncertain and cautious. The carrot offered by the Mystery Blonde was that Sam would be able to 'have her say', to 'set the record straight'. But it had been a clumsy and predictable play, and Sam had simply replied that she had nothing to say and that the record seemed fairly straight anyway. Or words to that effect.

There could be no argument with that second point. After Felix (obviously), Sam had emerged as the biggest victim of the whole affair, and even the most sewer-fixated tabloids had either failed or not attempted to dig up any information to alter that perception.

Her motives, then, when she eventually returned, via her solicitor, to say that, yes, she would agree to a meeting, remained a puzzle, and Mystery Blonde could only speculate as to her reasons.

Her best guess was what the Americans call 'closure'. As far as she knew, Samantha had been relocated to Bedford – just twenty minutes' drive from her mother's – shortly after the murder, and her whereabouts had been unknown ever since. She could change her name and she could alter her appearance, but short of plastic surgery she was always going to be Sam Sewell in some shape or form, and that meant there would always be someone to recognise her. From what she knew of Sam, the Mystery Blonde surmised that she would soon grow tired of hiding, would want to go on with her life – she had previously held a good job as a conference organiser.

Sam could not deny her past, but at least she could put it into some kind of perspective. Who knows? Maybe she simply wanted to speak to someone, anyone. And the Mystery Blonde just happened to be the person she chose.

The directions were good, and she found the house easily within the maze of the estate, parking her Audi TT in the driveway as had been agreed, making sure to hide all evidence of her journalistic purpose from the holders of twitching curtains: she pushed her dictaphone and notebook into the depths of her handbag and, pausing for a moment, switched off her mobile and thrust that in too – it wouldn't do to have the very persistent Aaron Bleasdale calling or texting her in the middle of the interview. And then she made her way to the front door, just like a sister – happened to be in the area on business, thought she'd pop in before making her way home.

Sam had closed the door swiftly behind them before the two women had had an opportunity to size each other up – the two women in Christopher Sewell's life. One, the beautiful, mysterious blonde journalist (but a swan), the other his ex-wife, considerably less beautiful but still attractive – Renée Zellweger to the Mystery Blonde's Claudia Schiffer.

If the suburban, sleepy Bedford estate seemed a million miles away from what had been the most sensational celebrity death since John Lennon's, then the Mystery Blonde knew immediately that it had taken its toll on Samantha Sewell. Like any good writer, she had promised herself she would steer clear of such prosaic clichés as 'hunted', 'haunted' or 'worn' in reference to the killer's wife, but here all those words seemed so apt. Later, when she compared press photographs of Samantha Sewell to the mental image of the woman she met, she would think of her as having been *decreased* by her experiences. Actually shrunk by her exposure to the eye of the storm. Her heart went out to her then, reinforcing her feeling of mistress-meets-cuckold.

'Did you find it all right?' said Samantha, though she was not interested in the answer.

'Yes, thank you,' replied the Mystery Blonde, aware that Samantha was not interested in her answer.

'Come through to the kitchen a minute. I'll make some tea.'

The house couldn't have been further away from the environment Mystery Blonde was used to. She found herself amazed that the glare of the media's eye could be reduced to this small and, truth be told, slightly shabby house on the outskirts of Bedford. It was clear that Samantha had done little to personalise her new home. There were no pictures on the wall, just discoloured squares left by a previous occupant. Coat hooks near the front door were empty. The house smelt musty, as though nobody had been living in it, although, of course, they had.

The kitchen did nothing to rid the Mystery Blonde of the impression she had formed: of transience, of a person suspended half-way between two lives. The worktops looked dusty and unused, the shelves were empty. The room's only concessions to life were a microwave, a toaster and a kettle that Samantha picked from its base and took to the sink, wordlessly filling it.

The Mystery Blonde mentally shook away her hesitancy. True, this interview was not being conducted in the plush suite of a London hotel, or over lunch at the Ivy, or relaxed into huge brown leather sofas at Soho House – all more natural habitats for the rarefied likes of the Mystery Blonde – but it was an interview all the same. An interview just like any other. And whether it was over cocktails at the Met Bar or in the kitchen of a seen-better-days Bedford estate family home, the principle remained the same.

Except this was harder.

The calibre of person usually speaking into her tape recorder was a media-sussed celebrity, micro-celebrity or wannabe celebrity, someone who actively courted the attention of the media and was keen to make the best use of their mouthpiece. In those circumstances she could switch on her dictaphone and it was as if she activated the interviewee at the same time, leaving them to regurgitate PR-approved soundbites ready for faithful transcription.

Samantha, on the other hand, while not an unwilling interviewee, was new to the artificial intimacy of the process. She had not employed Max Clifford or Freud Communications to coach her into media awareness – although no doubt she would have been approached by agencies. In fact, her experience of journalists thus far would have made her more than normally wary of them.

So it was to her post-grad journalism course with the Westminster Press that the Mystery Blonde's thoughts turned as she attempted to excavate memories of lectures in interview technique. Lessons that had long since fallen into disuse in the cosmetically enhanced world of the women's lifestyle press.

Establish a rapport. That was the first rule, and it was something she'd failed so far to do, letting the silence hang uncomfortably as Samantha, like a tired ghost, took two mugs from a cupboard and fished teabags from a box.

Then, at last, she seemed to remember herself, motioning at one of two chairs tucked beneath an empty kitchen table.

'Please sit,' she said, and the Mystery Blonde pulled at one of the chairs to sit at the table, dragging it across the vinyl floor with a noise like dinosaurs yawning. But if she had expected Sam's invitation to open the conversation, she was disappointed, and silence – dark, barren silence – once again washed thickly over the room.

'So. How are you?' said the Mystery Blonde, finally, into the vacuum. She said the words with genuine empathy, felt that any number of TV talk-show hosts would have approved of her soothing, matronly tones. Nevertheless, it wasn't a great question to begin with, and she mentally cursed herself for not making a more simple, banal enquiry – something to do wtih the area or the weather, the brand of tea. Anything.

The basic tenet of a factual, news-based interview (distinct, but not entirely different, from a personality interview) is to set up a reverse pyramid structure, beginning with a broad open question, which in this instance is defined as a question to which the subject cannot answer yes or no. Thus, 'How do you feel?' is an open question. 'Do you feel sad?' is a closed question.

The reverse pyramid structure works on the basis of the interviewer satisfying him or herself that the answers to the questions, Who, What, Why, When, Where and How have been satisfied – each in relation to the original question. Having reached the bottom of the upside-down pyramid, and therefore exhausted that particular line of enquiry, the interview can then move on to the next question.

It's not an exact science. The nature of any conversation means it's not always possible to control the interview to such an extent. But, still, keeping this process in mind aids the journalist to steer the conversation in the right direction, and if it jumps to the next topic before the first has been fully explored, well, that's what notebooks are there for: to make a little mark reminding the reporter to come back to that point later on.

The Mystery Blonde had her own notebook, of course. She dug into her expensive Orla Kiely bag for it now, pulling it out along with her dictaphone, which she placed on the kitchen table, firmly, as if announcing the purpose of her visit. Sam glanced at it and her head jerked slightly in response to its appearance, as though the Mystery Blonde had slapped a dead eel on the table, rather than a microcassette recorder, made by

Philips and purchased from Dixons along Oxford Street. Sam's response to the Mystery Blonde's clumsy opening gambit had, thankfully as far as the Mystery Blonde was concerned, been a simple shrug and a tired sigh, so it was to her notebook that the journalist looked.

Here, she had scribbled down some of her questions, memory-jogging sentences, all designed to help guide her through the interview as smoothly and as thoroughly as possible. Beginning, she had decided, with a simple enquiry: when did you last see Chris? Then tracking back, talking about their relationship together, asking whether or not Samantha had ever seen evidence of the man Christopher Sewell had become.

What was their relationship like? Had he ever shown violent tendencies? Been violent towards her? Was she frightened of him? How had his drinking affected her? Had he shown signs of frustration and pent-up rage – the classic symptoms of the sociopath?

Moreover, had he ever displayed any indication of an unhealthy attitude towards celebrities, and Felix Carter in particular? Had she known she was living with a killer?

This, she felt, was the backbone of the interview – Sam's thoughts on Chris. Of course, through her own extensive interviews with Chris, she already knew the answers to many of these questions, his side of them, at least (and she had no reason to doubt him); the purpose of today's exercise was to gather Samantha's perspective – of all the people in the world she had been closest to Christopher Sewell.

And now Sam set a cup of tea before the Mystery Blonde, then one for herself, pulled out a chair opposite and sat down.

The Mystery Blonde took a deep breath, ready to begin the interview.

'I know what you're expecting,' said Sam, before the Mystery Blonde could ask her first question. 'You're expecting me to say the kind of things that wives of these people always say:

"I had no idea. He was the model husband. Gentle and kind and nice to the kids. He led another life I had no knowledge of. He was not the man I thought I knew. He was leading a double life. How could I have been so blind?" Is that what you're expecting?'

The Mystery Blonde wanted badly to switch on her dictaphone, her hand on the table poised to creep towards it. But she left it alone, not wanting to draw Sam's attention to it, scare her away from her own thoughts.

'And if you said all that. Would that be true?'

'I'm sorry?'

'Well, I mean, did you know?'

'Know what?'

'What sort of man he was. Is?'

Sam looked at her tea, the liquid circling lazily in the cup. She raised her head and sighed, long and hard, then looked at the Mystery Blonde who saw tears in the other woman's eyes. 'I don't . . .' began Sam, choking on her words. 'I don't . . . know.'

The Mystery Blonde let the silence hang for a moment or so. A good interview technique. Not like normal conversation, with both participants eager to fill the dead air as quickly and efficiently as possible, the interview is one-sided, with the interviewer a conductor, a facilitator. And sure enough . . .

'Maybe I did.' She looked across the table, her eyes bright with tears poised to spill down her cheeks. 'Maybe that's why I left him when I did. His dad had just died. Do you leave your husband when his father's just passed away, no matter what kind of state he's in? At the time I told myself it was because he needed to get himself together. Now I look back and wonder just how frightened of him I really was. And, you know, when I think that . . . Maybe . . . I should have . . .'

She stopped again, her head hanging. Then, 'I don't know, you've met him, haven't you? What do you think of him?'

And, God, what did the Mystery Blonde think of Christopher Sewell?

Well, he was very lucid, quite charming, funny, even. Very self-aware, and confident with it. He was relaxed. There was a sadness to him, but it was a sadness with which he seemed to have come to terms. Indeed, far from being frightened and unnerved by him, she enjoyed being in his company and listening to him. More than once it had occurred to her that his words were seemingly at odds with the man who sat opposite her, as if the angry, frustrated person he described – the killer – was another man entirely. As if . . .

'He's changed, hasn't he?' said Sam, before the Mystery Blonde could answer the question, letting her off the hook. Sam gave a short laugh and stared out of the window into the unkempt garden.

'He's changed,' she repeated. 'You've got the better man.'

Maybe she had got the better man, thought the Mystery Blonde. Maybe Chris had changed. It was like he'd settled, as if he'd fought with his troubles and – not won necessarily but at least reached an *entente*. When she began her interviews with him her senses told her she was sitting opposite a killer and that, however human he seemed, that was what he was – a man capable of cruelly gunning down another man. Yet as the sessions had progressed that feeling had melted into the background. She'd found herself wandering into his world, at first expecting to be ambushed by the reality of what he was, always glad of the ever-present Jack. But the rude shock had never arrived. And now, forced for the first time to step beyond her professional self and question what she thought of him as a person, she found the answer was simple: she liked him.

The Mystery Blonde absorbed the shock her own admission had given her, her feeling of mistress and wife confirmed beyond all doubt. She allowed the ensuing silence to hang, to ferment, before finally letting out a slow, inaudible breath and reaching for her dictaphone.

'OK, Sam,' she said, pulling the other woman's attention towards her. 'We'll begin the interview now. If you don't mind.' Sam shook her head, the Mystery Blonde watched to see her tape turning.

'Why don't you tell me about the last time you heard from Chris?'

'It was the night he killed Felix Carter.'

'Was it?' said the Mystery Blonde, surprised.

'He rang me from the house.'

'Your house?'

'No, Felix Carter's house.'

Stunned, the Mystery Blonde snapped, 'I'm sorry?'

'He called me the night of the murder, from Felix Carter's house.'

A tip for the heavy drinker. Never get drunk then fall asleep wearing clothes you intend wearing the following day. Follow this advice and you won't do what I do, which is to nod off on the sofa wearing my Felix jeans, only to wake up and find them soaked in my own urine.

Nice, I think.

You obviously think so too.

Sorry, I didn't mean . . .

Never mind. Anyway, while the disadvantage of losing consciousness on the sofa is that you wake up with jeans soaked in piss, and you're given a sudden, rude and unwelcome reminder of the kind of person you've become, and you wake up with a start, shaking and coughing, your mouth dry, your head reeling with the promise of a headache to come, and, of course, the demons are circling above you ready to shit shame and guilt on your head, the advantage is that your next drink is always within arm's reach.

And so it is. My bottle of vodka, standing tall and proud on the coffee table before me. Other contents: one ashtray (overflowing), one packet of Marlboro Lights (three left), one cigarette lighter (disposable, generic), one firearm (loaded) and one front-door key (previous owner: the country's biggest pop star).

So it's for the vodka I reach, left with the top off – stupid, alcohol evaporates, everybody knows that – bring it to my lips, drink, cough, dry heave, but otherwise feel a great deal better, and I pull myself from the sofa and begin to peel off my soaking wet jeans.

My plan had been to set off for Felix's house in the early

afternoon, perhaps one or two o'clock, turn up at his house and produce the key, claiming I'd found it on the back seat of the car the night before and, since I knew Frank was off to Menorca, not bothered giving it to him – not even mentioned it, in fact – but thought I'd return it personally.

Felix, grateful for the return of the key he would since have assumed he'd lost, would invite me in, spying the bottle of Jack Daniel's I would be holding, which sparks a devilish look in his twinkling, pop-star eyes. On entering his lounge, I stop and enthusiastically admire his collection of *Star Wars* paraphernalia, especially his original movie figures, which I know line the shelves, and we begin a conversation about which is the best *Star Wars* film (mine is *The Empire Strikes Back*, but I'm fully prepared to fall in line with whatever film Felix chooses).

Now, though, the plan has to change. It's already coming up to midday and I know that you don't get a pair of jeans de-pissed and dried again in a couple of hours. Of all garments, jeans take their time drying, and if you think I'm wearing anything else but my new jeans to visit Felix Carter, then you've got another think coming.

So it's to the washing-machine that I stagger, feeling like the skinhead in that old washing-powder advert, the one who needed his white shirt washing and shouted, 'Aw, Mum!' when he spilled powder all over the floor. I find myself glad that I'm not Colette Carew, and that my washing-machine works, even if, like the skinhead, I'm not 100 per cent sure how to work it. But I do, of course, I'm not a retard. I even make sure the machine's set to 'time saver' mode and, after seeing to it that the machine's begun its cycle, I slope off for a bath, lugging my bottle of vodka with me. Felix would understand, I'm sure.

It occurs to me in the bath that I'm taking an awful gamble on him being in. He has, after all, just released an album and has a single in the charts and a movie to promote and is therefore likely to be right in the middle of a punishing work schedule. Do pop stars have Tuesday afternoons off? I don't know, but if the worst comes to the worst, and he's not in, I've already decided not to put the key through the letterbox. If he isn't in I can simply claim to be security-conscious and hang on to it until he is in, give it to him personally. Go back another day, in other words.

Then again, neither can I wait too long. If he assumes he's lost his key, even with his apparent disregard for his own safety, he might opt to get his locks changed, meaning he won't be nearly as pleased at the return of the original, won't feel so obliged to let me in. And I can hardly rely on Bart being of such sentimental value that a reunion with him will do the trick.

No, time is of the essence, the air of spontaneity para-mount. Just have to touch wood that he'll be at home and, obviously, alone.

Out of the bath and I immediately regret not putting my new Felix T-shirt in with my Felix jeans. It's more than a touch on the stinky side, so I get busy in the kitchen sink, tipping washing powder into a bowl of hot water and cleaning it the old-fashioned way, letting the rhythm of the washing-machine massage my booze-damaged head, enjoying the vodka as it works its anti-demon magic.

I'm feeling good now, stronger. Like last night, striding behind Felix as we left the Bottom Drawer building together. A little team of two. We could almost have been brothers. I bet at least one person who caught sight of us together, without any background knowledge, would have thought we were brothers. *At least one.*

T-shirt washed. I hold it up to my nose, do a satisfied 'um, meadow fresh!' look for the benefit of imaginary cameras and go through to the lounge where I drape it over the radiator, central heating already fired up and belting out heat in readiness for its denim test. In comparison to the jeans, the T-shirt will be dry in record time.

Next I go through to our spare room where we keep the books. Once the messy black sheep of all our rooms, it's now an exercise in minimalism compared to the state of the rest of the flat. Never mind, the mess is clearable, it's on my list. In the spare room I find the *A-Z* which I take through to the lounge and place on the coffee table, next to the gun and the key-ring.

By the time this stage of preparation is over the washing-machine cycle has whizzed its way to completion and I fish out my jeans, drape them over the lounge radiator next to the T-shirt. Then I change my boxer shorts, find a towel, which I spread over the piss on the sofa, and sit down to watch as much of the *Star Wars* trilogy as I can fit in before my jeans are dry and I'm ready to leave – call it homework. As the Twentieth Century Fox fanfare sounds on the first film, I check the video clock. It's one thirty p.m.

I'm methodical. I get up first to turn over the jeans when Luke discovers his aunt and uncle's bodies, then every twenty minutes after that. It's sauna-hot in the flat, but sitting in my boxer shorts I'm comfortable. I've finished what was left of the vodka but I'm feeling levelled-out so I don't search for more booze – the last thing I need is for my Dutch courage to turn into English-on-holiday. I'm pleased with my preparations and I don't want to spoil them. Not now.

It's about four fifteen when I decide the jeans are dry enough to wear, so I kill the central heating and wait for the flat to cool down before I dress – don't want to sweat. With my clothes on, I stride around the lounge, mentally and physically preparing myself, limbering up like a footballer before cup final, or like Felix before he goes on stage.

Ready now. I check the *A-Z*, find Acacia Avenue and locate the nearest tube, a short walk away. I tuck the gun into the waistband of my jeans and put on my jacket, reason that the gun won't be seen as long as I keep the jacket done up, slip the key-ring into my pocket. Fags, lighter, mobile phone, my own keys, a last check of the *A-Z* . . .

It's about four forty-five and nearly dark when I finally leave the flat, walk down to the shop, buy a bottle of Jack Daniel's and four vodka miniatures – not Absolut, no chance of a lucky dip, darn – relishing the feel of the revolver at my waist as the woman serves me, mentally daring her to be rude.

Then I make my way to the tube station, taking the long way round – the route that doesn't lead me past Colette Carew's house. As it's November, it's nearly dark.

During the tube journey I down two miniatures, one before King's Cross, the other shortly after, both times using my failsafe 'yawn' technique. Still, despite the nerve-chasing effects of the booze, butterflies are trampolining in my stomach. I'm jittery, excited, and the thing is, I'm not sure exactly why I'm making this trip, but certain I must, that at the end of it lies an answer, a resolution. And it lies with Felix, all roads seem to lead to his house. It feels like all the signposts of the past fortnight have been pointing in this direction and only now have I chosen to follow them. Still, exactly what I plan to achieve when I get there, I don't know. Like my trip to Dog-end's house, where my motives were slightly more sinister, I think that I'll only really know when I get there. I just have this feeling . . .

I just have this feeling that if I can talk to Felix, everything will be all right.

Nervous, I stand on the steps of the house at Acacia Avenue, with the bottle of Jack Daniel's in one hand and Felix Carter's front door key in the other. Old Bart Simpson, he dangles from my hand as I press the door buzzer; press it once, firmly, hear the buzzer sounding inside the house. And wait.

I arrange my face into a smile. Not the easiest thing to do, and what sort of smile? I want a smile that says I'm not a pest, not a pathetic, fawning fan, but an equal, just another guy, and one with a good and legitimate reason for turning up on your doorstep. What better reason than the return of a door key, after all?

From inside the house I hear movement, like someone

moving towards the door. I fix the smile as I hear the Yale turn and the door opens.

His head appears around the door, just his hair and eyes visible. There is no welcoming light in his eyes, no smile or greeting, just suspicion. Still, I pretend not to notice it, thinking, Good reason, I have a good reason, and smiling at him despite the sinking look across his face.

'Hello, Chris,' I say, desperately trying not to look too eager, too pathetic.

'Uh, hello, mate,' he replies, not playing the game, still only his head visible. I get the impression he's naked behind the door. He's using it to shield himself. His eyes dart to the road behind me, then to the bottle of Jack Daniel's. 'Um, what can I do for you?'

'I've got something for you,' I say. God, that sounds creepy.

'Um . . .' He looks uncomfortable, irritated at being disturbed, the sort of look I imagine Jehovah's Witnesses see all the time. But then, I tell myself, Jehovah's Witnesses aren't returning your lost property. In a few moments, when he knows why I'm here, his attitude will change. Then his face will break into a smile and he'll crack a Felix joke and invite me inside.

'Look, mate,' he continues, 'I've got a car arriving . . . soon. I've got to . . . you know, I can't stop and chat. What is it?'

'Well,' I say, 'I could come back another time, but I thought you might need . . . this.' And I hold up the key-ring, Little Bart swinging in front of his eyes.

He seems to relax slightly, but only slightly. He's still wary, *too* wary, really. Like, hello? I'm the Good Samaritan here. I'm returning your key.

'Ah,' he says. 'Where'd you get that?'

'You must have dropped it in the car last night. I found it after you'd got out. Thought you might need it, so here I am.'

'Why didn't . . . I mean, did you not think of giving it to Frank?'

God, what is this? Famous pop star too big for his boots to acknowledge a good deed? Come on, it's not like I'm expecting him to drop to his knees with gratitude, but still, a smile wouldn't hurt. I got a thanks just for buying his poxy album, but now that I've trekked all the way to west London he's treating me like a leper.

'No point in giving it to Frank, was there?' I say, aware suddenly of three things: my own irritation, the gun at my waist, and Felix's unease. 'Frank will be sunning himself in Menorca now with Mrs Frank – probably enjoying a welcome-party Sangria as we speak. He wasn't going to be able to return your key, was he?'

'Frank didn't let me know you'd found my key.'

'That was because I didn't tell him. No point in bothering him with that, he might have wanted to drag all the way back across London to return it to you. You wouldn't have wanted that, now, would you? Not when I could come over and give it to you personally. You know something? You really should be pleased.'

'Um, oh, God, mate, I am. It's just a bit . . . I'm just . . . Look, thanks a bunch for coming all the way over with the key. I'll just take it now, though, eh?' and he holds out his hand from round the door, reaching for it as I offer it to him. Bart's plastic feet almost brush his palm, but then, at the last moment, I jerk it up and his fingers close on fresh air. He looks foolish and knows it.

'Uh-uh,' I say. 'What's the magic word?'

'Don't piss about. Just give me the key.'

I hold up Bart in front of my face: 'Hey, don't have a cow, man.' A crap Bart impression. Never could do Bart, I'm more of a Homer man.

A shadow passes over his face. The wisecracking pop star is all but completely gone now – it's me who's inherited that mantle, at least for the time being – and in his place is a nervous homeowner, just the same as the rest of us. As vulnerable as Colette Carew, probably even more so.

He looks back over his shoulder, into the house, then back again, appearing to consider something, saying, 'Look, mate, tell you what – thanks for bringing the key over. I've got someone coming for me, like, really soon. So why don't I pop back in and grab the address of me management company? I'll let them know you'll be in touch, you can give them a call and we'll arrange some backstage passes for one of the Christmas gigs – you and a mate – as a thanks from me for going out of your way, all right?'

No invitation inside. No drink. No *Star Wars* bonding. Not even a cup of fucking tea. No, Felix, I think, it's not all right.

'Look, look,' I bluster quickly, at the same time remembering my salesman technique and nodding, only too much, overdoing it in my panic, nodding up and down at him like a spastic headbanger. 'We've got off on the wrong foot. Look, I've got your favourite,' holding up the Jack Daniel's, 'remember? Bottle of JD and you're anyone's for a tenner? Tell you what, I'll let you off the tenner. But why don't we have a drink on it, eh?' Nodding, nodding. Sweating desperation.

But my powers of persuasion are on holiday, and my speech only seems to strengthen Felix's resolve and he's saying, 'Er, no. Look, wait there, OK? I'll be back in a sec.' And before I can reply, he steps in, closes the door.

Closes the door right in my face.

The Yale clicking home.

The street, empty and quiet, my breathing, short and fast. In my head: despair, injustice, hurt, rejection, impotence – jumbling and colliding, sparking light before my eyes, refusing to form a whole until I can think no more.

Think: *concert tickets*. The big kiss-off.

Only, it's not even that, is it? Remembering the look that passed across his face, the glance backwards into the house . . .

Bending down, I place the bottle of Jack Daniel's on the doorstep. Then I reach to my waist, pulling the gun from my belt with my right, at the same time using my left to push the key into the Yale, twist, wrong way, then right way, the door opening.

And I step inside. I walk across the threshold and into the hall, finally, after all this time, passing into a place from which I can never return.

Uh, sorry, just a second.

That's all right. Take your time.

Jack? Jack, you know this photograph you're after? Well, I think we'll be in a position to give it to you today. Only there's a condition, mate. Yeah, well, it's your choice, hear me out. The condition is that you remain outside the door for the remainder of the session. You can be just outside the door, but I'd prefer it if you didn't remain inside the room. No, mate, there's no ulterior motive, it's just that I can feel myself becoming emotional and I'd prefer it if you didn't see me like this. I've got too much respect for you. Sorry, where are my manners? Is this OK with you? Jack will be outside. You'll be in no danger.

Um, yes, I think so, yes.

Is that settled? Why don't you run along and fetch your camera, Jack? Perhaps get yourself a chair while you're at it and we'll give you a knock when we're ready for the photo-shoot? Don't you worry about a thing . . .

OK, he's gone. Are you all right with this?

I am, yes. Tell me, that's not the real reason, is it? That you don't want Jack to see you emotional.

Very perceptive. No, it's not.

Then what is?

Because I have something to tell you that nobody else knows. First, though, I need your word that you will never tell anyone outside of this room. It'll be our secret. Do I have your word?

Before I give it, why?

Why . . .

Why trust me? I'm a journalist.

329

Have you seen *Indiana Jones and the Last Crusade*?

I think . . . I'm not sure.

It's the one where Sean Connery plays his dad. They're searching for the Holy Grail, and at the end they find a chamber filled with goblets, only one of which is the Grail. The baddie's there as well and he makes a grab for the most ornate goblet and glugs it down straight away. The baddie kind of melts horribly – big special-effects scene – and after he's died, this old knight who's guarding the chamber just says, 'He chose poorly,' like that, a real classic understatement. Then Indy has to make his choice, and he chooses right. When he does, the old guy guarding the chamber says, 'He chose wisely.'

The thing is, they don't know. When they're selecting which goblet they think is the Holy Grail, they don't know for certain if it's going to be a force for good, or do them terrible harm. They use intuition, but they don't know until they drink. And it's the same with you. With you, I think I've chosen wisely. Have I? Can I trust you?

You can, yes.

Then what I have to tell you is this.

When I let myself into Felix's house, he's not alone.

At first I think it's the booze playing tricks on me, like that ancient joke you see in films where something fantastical is happening and a nearby drinker does a comedy double-take. They use that gag on just about every James Bond film ever made.

Anyway, that's what I think as I walk through the door and into the hallway, taking a small step for mankind, a giant fucking long-jump for Christopher Sewell. I think, Shit, I'm seeing double.

Because I'm expecting to see either an empty hallway, or at the very least a hallway with Felix Carter in it. What I'm not expecting to see is a hallway with Felix Carter and another man standing in it.

I'm slamming the door shut behind me even as I'm squeezing my eyes tight shut, just in case it really is double-vision I'm getting. But when I open them again both men are still there, staring at me open-mouthed. One of them is Felix, that's for certain. The other man I don't recognise, but he commands my attention.

Probably because he's holding a gun.

And because he seems very highly strung.

'Who the fuck is he?' he's saying to Felix, his voice nervous and high-pitched.

Felix is holding out his hands in a flat-palmed peacemaker stance, one arm out to me, the other directed at the highly strung bloke. For a second he looks like he's directing traffic.

'Steady, guys, steady,' he says. My own gun is pointing down the hallway in their general direction, not really aimed at either.

Highly Strung Bloke takes a step away from Felix, moving slightly to try to cover both of us with the gun. I feel a vague pang of jealousy. This guy, whoever he is, seems to have a cooler-looking gun than me. It's certainly more modern. I can't be certain but it looks like the type where you push a magazine into the butt. It means he'll have more bullets than me. Could be important if we decide to have a full-on shootout right here in Felix's hallway.

But Highly Strung Bloke is screeching now. 'Who the fuck is he?'

I point my gun at him, unfashionable as it suddenly seems.

'Who are you?' I say.

'Guys . . .' says Felix.

'Who are *you*?' says Highly Strung Bloke, bringing up his second hand to hold the pistol in a two-handed grip. Again, I feel outdone. Now he's a got a cooler gun and he's holding it in a cooler way too. I consider changing my grip but decide that copying him makes me look weak. Suddenly, not looking weak is very important and I hope that Highly Strung Bloke won't twig that I'm drunk.

'Who are you?' I say.

We have each other dead in our sights. I wonder if he's a gun virgin too. Judging from the way he holds his, I guess probably not. And if it weren't for the fact that he seems to be holding Felix captive and Felix is standing there in just a pair of boxer shorts and is scared half to death, I would have assumed that Highly Strung Bloke was simply another bodyguard, a holiday stand-in for Frank. As it is, he's obviously not, but for the moment I can't think who he might be. Whoever he is, he isn't here to protect Felix, that much is certain.

I could jump to the conclusion that this is some kind of sex game Felix's playing, what with him standing there in his underwear. But, like I say, I'm a salesman, I read body language, and even if you factor out my presence it's clear there's no sexual chemistry in the hallway. No, I conclude, I got here just moments after this bloke arrived. Somehow he forced his way in while Felix was in the process of changing – there's a dress suit hanging in the doorway behind them. If I hadn't pissed myself in the night I would have been here first, the roles would have been reversed.

In the gloom of the hallway I can make out Highly Strung Bloke's features. He's younger than me, but only by a couple of years or so. He's shorter than both Felix and me and he has a small, squashed-up face to go with his stature. It's an unpleasant face if I'm honest. The kind of face that struggles to hide unpleasant emotions within. And although I've heard him say barely five words, I take an instant dislike to him. True, that might have something to do with the fact that he's aiming a gun at me, but even without the extraordinary circumstances, I don't think I'd like him. He looks like the kind of person people describe as a nasty piece of work.

A highly strung nasty piece of work.

God knows what he must think of me. Probably arriving at exactly the same conclusion. Whatever he thinks, it looks like he's worked out that I'm neither the police nor a bodyguard. Possibly the huge lanyard sticking from the bottom of my antique gun has given the game away on that score. I'm just another guy with a gun who's happened to gatecrash the party. Ghastly coincidence and all that, but there you go. And he seems to relax slightly. Or, at the very least, he takes control of his screeching voice.

'Who are you?' he repeats, only this time without the glass-shattering pitch. As he says it his squashed-up face seems to screw up even more. Insanely, he reminds me of a snooty shop assistant.

'I'm not the police,' I say calmly, amazed at my own composure. Surprising what a gun can do for you, I guess. 'I'm not a bodyguard. I'm just a guy. Why don't you tell me who you are?'

'I'm Felix's stalker,' he says, and as he passes on this information his chest seems to puff out with pride, in much the same way someone might look if they were telling you they were the Home Secretary, or starring in the new Tom Cruise movie.

But why not? Because, of course, I have heard of him. I've read about him many times in *Phonic* magazine, I've heard Frank refer to him. He's almost famous. Only nobody knows his name.

'What's your name?' I say.

'Brian Forsyth,' he replies, as if addressing an acolyte, and I feel a surge of resentment, suddenly coming over all playground.

'Well . . . I'm his lookylikey,' I say back.

'I've never heard of you,' he retorts primly, 'and, anyway, you don't look much like him.'

'Yes, I do.'

'No, you don't. None of them do. Especially not that *Stars In Their Eyes* bloke. He's even worse than you.'

'The point of *Stars In Their Eyes* . . .' says Felix, speaking for the first time in a good five minutes. It strikes me that this really isn't Felix's day. One nutter with a gun, fair enough, comes with the territory. But two? '. . . the point of *Stars In*

Their Eyes,' he continues, 'isn't that the contestants look like the star, it's that they *sound* like him.'

All three of us ponder this interruption, then Brian says to me, 'I thought you were going to be the bodyguard.'

'Frank?' I say.

'Yes, of course Frank,' he replies, his eyes darting, as if suddenly nervous at the thought. 'Frank's due here. He's coming.' Clearly, as Felix's stalker, he has prior knowledge of Frank and, having met him myself, I'd say he's got every right to be nervous.

'No, he's not,' I say.

'Yes, he is. He's coming to pick Felix up. He always comes in the house. I've seen him.'

I look over at Felix and see his eyes upon me, imploring. I get it now. Felix knows that I know Frank's not coming, that he's on holiday. But this is Felix's big bluff to Brian. He's using Frank as his ace card, and he's using Brain's carefully acquired stalker's knowledge against him, because Brian knows that Frank would normally come in. But he'd also know that a stand-in driver wouldn't, that a stand-in driver might not have the signals and codes a full-time minder like Frank has. Like I say, it's not Felix's day today.

Especially when I say, 'Look, calm down. Frank's on holiday. He's not coming, OK? He's gone to Menorca.'

Brain looks at Felix. 'You lied,' he says forlornly.

'I forgot,' says Felix lamely, giving me daggers.

Quite frankly I couldn't give a fuck what Felix thinks. I'd prefer a less jumpy gunman pointing weapons at me, thanks.

'There is a car coming, though,' says Felix. 'God's honest truth.'

'But the driver won't come in, will he?' I say, before Brian can have another thrombo.

'No,' says Felix softly, seeing steel shutters crash down in his mind's eye.

'And how long have we got before he comes?' I say. 'Bearing in mind it's probably not in any of our interests if you lie.'

'A couple of hours,' he says, his eyes dead now.

With that established, a kind of peace seems to break out in the hallway. At the very least, Brian appears to relax.

'OK, lookylikey,' he says finally, 'what are you doing here?' We may have reached some kind of stalemate, but our guns are still trained on each other. Felix, the third point in the triangle, is absolutely still. God only knows what he's thinking.

But it's a good question. What am I doing here? How did I walk into this godawful mess?

The most immediate answer is that I walked in because I was peeved about being palmed off with some concert tickets. But that's only half of the truth. The thing is, I'm not a Brian Forsyth, not a stalker. I'm not an obsessed fan. Up until a few days ago I didn't even own a Felix Carter record, my only connection with him being that people occasionally remarked upon my resemblance to him. I'm here because a window to his world has opened and through that window I've glimpsed some kind of redemption. I'm here because . . .

'I want help.'

They look enquiringly down the hall at me. Like, help what? Help changing a tyre? Help with your homework? Help what?

'I want help . . .' They both incline their heads forward, willing the words out of my mouth.

'Help getting back with my wife.'

There's an almost palpable relief in the hall at my words. Looking at it from their angle, it might have been worse, I suppose. I might have wanted help with some kind of nasty sexual problem. A bit of marriage counselling seems fairly tame, given the circumstances.

'Look, guys,' says Felix at last, and his tone betrays that he's suddenly remembered this is his house, and he's the star, and we're here because of him, and so what if we're holding guns? He's reconciled himself to that. Now he wants to take control.

'Look, guys, why don't you let me get some clothes on?

I've got some clothes through there in the lounge. I can get dressed. We can talk about this wife problem you've got. And then once we've done that,' he addresses Brian, 'we can talk about whatever it is you want. How does that sound?'

He's recovered his composure, all right. His voice is deliberately measured and soothing. I wonder, Do pop stars get training in how to deal with people like Brian Forsyth and me? Has Frank schooled him in crisis-situation techniques? Keep calm, reason with your intruder, find out his name, don't make sudden movements, don't show fear . . .

Like dogs, people like us can smell fear.

'Come on,' he adds calmly. 'Let me put some clothes on. I'm cold. You'd both be doing me a real favour here.'

That's a nice trick, I think, establish intimacy. I could have told him that. I'd do the same thing myself, if the roles were reversed.

'Yes,' I say. 'That's fine.'

'No,' barks Brian Forsyth. He says it with a wheedling, 'I was here first' voice. He might as well be telling me I can't play with his toys.

'Well,' says Felix to Brian, still calm, that reassuring voice, 'you're the boss' (nice: confirm your own place in the hierarchy. Must remember that one), 'but I've got a pair of jeans and a T-shirt in the front room through there,' he gestures to his right, 'bit of a mess, I'm afraid, but we could go through, I could put on some clothes and we could sit down and all,' he does an all-encompassing gesture around the hall, 'have a chat, find out what it is I can do for you both.'

I look at Brian. I'm not sure I like the suggestion that he's the boss. Let's not forget I have a gun too. But I let it ride. It seems as if we're going to take care of my business first, and that's good enough for the moment.

'All right,' says Brian, reluctantly. 'Lead the way, but very slowly.'

Felix does as instructed, turning slowly and walking through the door leading to the lounge. Brian steps back and seems unsure whether to cover me or Felix with the gun. I shrug, as if to say, 'I'm not a threat,' and Brian follows Felix, some kind of level ground established between us.

I walk into the lounge behind them, my gun now at my side, and it's just as I remember it from the documentary, only less tidy. Much less tidy. He doesn't quite share my own reckless approach to domestic order, but we're on the same page. From that, I take some comfort. Even more so when I spy the empty lager cans littering a table that sits flanked by the room's two sofas; both expensive white-leather jobs. The real deal.

'Where are these clothes, then?' says Brian.

'Over there.' Felix points, carefully and deliberately, at the other sofa which, indeed, is strewn with clothes.

I join Brian in the middle of the room and we both watch as Felix walks slowly over to the far sofa, picks up a pair of jeans, which he holds up for our inspection. Clever.

'That's an old-looking gun,' he says to me, pushing one leg into his jeans.

Brian snorts. Slightly derisively, I feel. Clearly he's feeling the gun envy at work here.

'Perfect working order,' I say defensively, aware that I'm not one hundred per cent certain of that fact but, knowing the old man . . .

'I know, I mean, I wasn't suggesting . . . Just looks interesting, that. What is it, some kind of wartime gun? Looks like one of those desert guns. Where did you get it?'

'Fell off the back of a camel.'

'Ha ha. Right.' He pulls a T-shirt from the sofa and, again holding it out so we can see it, pulls it over his head.

'It was my dad's gun,' I say.

'Really?' says Felix. 'You don't look old enough to have had a dad in the war.'

Brian is looking at me now, interested.

'He wasn't. I don't know where he got it from. I think he probably had it in the hope that he might one day meet the man who killed my mother.'

'Oh . . .' Pure fear darkens Felix's face as, dressed, he stands, pinned in place by Brian's gun pointed at his chest. 'I'm really, really sorry about your—'

'She was knocked over in the road by a driver who didn't stop. The police never caught him. I think the injustice of that situation tore my dad up, you know? And I think this,' I gesture with the gun, 'helped him get through it somehow. Maybe it was the hope. The thought that each day might be the day when he'd get his answer, and if he did, well, he was prepared.'

Brian stands silent, his gun trained on Felix, not participating in the conversation. I motion to Felix to sit.

'That's terrible, man,' he says, lowering himself slowly to the sofa. He's looking at me but he has one eye on Brian. I feel sorry for him, I really do. He probably has no idea who he should be more frightened of. 'About your mother, I mean. I can see how you feel. It's just not . . .'

'It's not fair, is it?'

'It's not right.'

'Do you think all this is fair?' I wave around the room with my free hand, at the *Star Wars* figures, at the two white-leather sofas, the pool table, the thousands of CDs neatly housed in designer stacking systems, the TV – bigger than any TV I've ever seen – and the equipment in the cabinet below it: video, DVD, PlayStation 2, Xbox, satellite. 'Is this fair?'

'I've been very lucky,' says Felix carefully, choosing his words like a man picking his way over a minefield. 'Look, is that what you want? Do you want money? Are you down on your luck? I can help—'

'No,' I say. 'You don't understand. What you have is above all this. You have something far more valuable.'

'You're special,' pipes up Brian suddenly, as if I'd vocalised something he'd been feeling. 'You're not like normal people. You're not like us.'

It's not quite how I would have put it, and I'm not entirely happy with the 'us'. Being lumped in with someone who was obviously bullied at school and has spent the intervening years obsessing over a pop star hardly does me any favours but, then, he does have a point. After all, who am I to put myself above Brian Forsyth? I've burst in here with a gun just the same as him. The fact that he probably has rooms filled with Felix posters and mine are filled with empty lager tins, well, it still doesn't make us all that different.

'I'm the same as you,' says Felix, to us both. 'I'm just a bit luckier, that's all.'

I open my mouth to speak but Brian jumps in.

And how.

His voice breaking with emotion, he says, 'You're luckier because people love you and they don't love me. You're luckier because people listen to you, and people have never listened to me in my life. You're luckier because you're rich and handsome and I'm poor and ugly, because every day of my life people treat me like shit and every day of your life people treat you like a god . . .'

(Shit, I think. I've opened a can of worms here.)

'You're luckier because you're talented and girls like you, and I've never had a girlfriend in my life. You're luckier because people think you're funny ha-ha, and they think I'm funny weird . . .'

His hand is shaking on the gun. I see the shine of tears in his eyes. I'm beginning to worry.

'You're luckier because you have fans and people just despise me. And you're lucky because you have a fan like me and you can afford to treat him like shit.'

And then he stops, runs out of steam at last.

Felix stares up at Brian from his seat on the sofa, his eyes wide with fear.

It occurs to me that Brian has asked me why I'm here – for 'help' – but I haven't asked him the same thing. What are Brian's reasons for being in this house? I wonder. What do stalkers do when they confront their prey?

But it's not the time to ask. Brian seems to calm himself,

some of his old blankness slowly returning. I stand there, surprised by the passion of his words but dimly registering that everything he said was right, and a lot of it I feel myself at some kind of primal level. A lot of it is why I'm here. Brian's right: Felix is in this mess precisely because he's special, because he's a star. And we're not. And we're pissed off about that.

It's just Felix's bad luck, really.

Just his bad luck that we're drawn like moths to his flame. I don't know why Brian is, he's got his reasons, no doubt. But I know why I am. Because I recognised myself in him, because I saw the other side to my coin.

Now Felix looks across the room at me, as if asking me for help. But he's looking in the wrong place. He's forgetting that I've crossed my own line and I did it when I stepped over the threshold to his house. He looks to me for help because he thinks I'm not as far gone as Brian is, but in my own way I am. You don't go charging into the home of the country's biggest pop star armed with a gun if you're in control of all your faculties. You just don't.

So don't bother looking to me for help, Felix. It's not like good cop, bad cop here, it's just two different levels of nutter. Which one's more scary? I don't know, take your pick.

Felix looks at me, I look at Brian, Brian looks at Felix. Three points of the same triangle, or three stages of the same evolutionary scale.

'Are you OK?' I say to Brian. Felix seems to deflate into the sofa as I ask. He's just seen his one potential ally consorting with the enemy.

'Yes,' says Brian, turning towards me, 'Yes, thanks.'

'Right, then,' I say, turning to Felix. 'A couple of hours before the car arrives. Plenty of time to test your real value. Time to show just how lucky you are.'

'How?' he asks, flat-voiced, not even looking at his two tormentors.

I glance around and see what I'm looking for: a telephone, one of those expensive cordless models. Just the ticket. I walk over, pluck it from the charger and go back to the middle of the room, showing it to him. 'You're going to use some of the famed Felix charm on my behalf,' I say. 'You're going to help me get back with my wife.'

Because that's what I want, really. That's all I want.

'Mate . . .' begins Felix, but I shush him. I'm struggling to hold the gun and get to grips with the phone as I try to dial Sam's mobile number.

Except I can't dial the number, because I don't know it. On speed-dial at home and at the office, stored in my own mobile's memory – with everything else remembering it for me, I'd never bothered. A minute or so passes as I plug away at the digits on Felix's cordless in the hope that Sam's number will come back to me, but it doesn't, and I'm just about to admit defeat when I remember that I am, in fact, carrying my own mobile.

With the gun trained on Felix still, I use my other hand to pat my pockets for the mobile. It's in the front of my jeans, only I can't reach it and keep the gun on Felix, because I'm already holding the other phone. So I stand and fumble, like the inept idiot I so obviously am.

'Here,' says Brian at last, walking forward, holding out his hand for the gun. 'Let me take that for you.'

I look up at him and our eyes meet. My immediate thought is, no, don't give up the gun, stick it out of the way in your belt. But there's something in his eyes, something about the reassuring nod he gives me that convinces me he's not a threat. After all, he's had ample opportunity to get the drop on me since we've entered the lounge. And the fact is, I can't use my own mobile because Sam's phone will tell her it's me, so the alternative is to stand around juggling phones and guns and, really, it's not a good look.

So, as a show of faith, of solidarity among nutters, I give him the gun. He takes it, aiming them both at Felix, a gun in each hand. I'll say this for Brian, he knows how to look cool with weaponry.

And then I go back to fishing out my mobile, calling up

Sam's number and dialling it into the cordless, talking to Felix as I'm doing so. 'I'm going to dial this number, and when she answers I'm going to give the phone to you,' I say. Felix looks apprehensive. 'When you speak to her, you're going to tell her who you are, and you're going to persuade her to come back to me. Brian's right. People listen to you, people treat you like a god.'

'How am I going to do that?' says Felix, his nerves etched across his face.

'You'll tell her that I have your support, and that you have been through exactly what I'm going through, and together we're going to get off the drink and I'm going to be a good husband to her from now on.'

'Look, er . . . Chris, I really don't think . . .'

I stop him with a raised hand. 'Well, you have been through it, haven't you? Mr Wagon-chaser, "The Man Who Would Be Clean". Penelope Keith not Keith Richards. Aren't you the expert? People listen to you, don't they?

'You said last night, you said,' I mimic his voice, ' "I'd love to help yer, mate. Charm her with yer winning personality." Well, now you *can* help me. Only you charm her with *your* winning personality. You've got a whole lot more winning personality than I have. There's your real fucking wealth, *mate*.'

The phone is ringing. Brian stands silent by my side, both guns still trained on Felix.

'OK, OK,' says Felix, 'Please, just keep calm. We don't need to get hot under the collar. I'll do all I can to help you, I promise. What's your wife's name?'

'Sam.'

'Sam. OK.'

I hear the phone pick up at the other end, hear Sam's voice say, 'Hello?' and feel my stomach do a little leap at the sound.

I toss the phone across to Felix, who catches it and raises it to his ear. He takes a deep breath.

CHAPTER FORTY-ONE

'I'm sorry?' repeated the Mystery Blonde. 'Just say that again
– for my benefit. He rang you from Felix's house?'

'In a manner of speaking,' replied Sam, thoughtfully, her
hand clasped around her mug of tea. All of a sudden, as
though reminded of something, she raised her head, a smile
playing around her lips. It wasn't much of a smile, tinged
with some sort of nostalgia as it was; still, it was the first
time the Mystery Blonde had seen a glimpse of the woman
Sam had been, and she checked her impatience as Sam said,
'Here, I've got something to show you. Pretend you've got an
achy neck.'

'Pardon?'

'I got Chris with this once. Pretend you've got an achy
neck.'

'If you're sure. OK, then – my neck hurts.'

'Ah, well, I may be able to help you with my healing
hands . . .'

Again, the Mystery Blonde resisted the temptation to urge
Sam on, stopped herself also reaching for the dictaphone and
switching it off to save precious tape, knowing that to do so
would be to break the spell. Somehow, this felt like therapy
for Sam and to join in, to humour her, helped ease the Mystery
Blonde's conscience. She knew that as a journalist – the kind of
journalist she wanted to be, anyway – it was her job to act as
a conduit between events and the public, and sometimes those
interests were not best served by being kind to her subjects.
There were always victims, and they were usually people like
Sam. Here, at least, she could do her best.

'Would you?' she said, touching her neck for Sam's benefit.

'It hurts just here. I think I must have cricked it on the drive up.'

'Certainly.' Sam pushed herself out of her seat, leaning across the table and reaching out a hand to touch the Mystery Blonde's beautiful neck, just below the ear.

The Mystery Blonde gasped in response, feeling a soothing, unnatural warmth from Sam's hand. 'Wow,' she said, genuinely impressed, as Sam removed her hand. 'How did you do that?'

Sam beamed. It was like the sun coming out. 'The tea,' she explained, pleased with herself. 'I had my hand around my tea-cup. Actually, I thought you might twig as I'm sitting just here. See, it's best to do it sort of secretively.'

'It's great,' laughed the Mystery Blonde, almost despite herself.

'It's nice as well, isn't it?' said Sam. 'Chris used to say it was. I do it on myself sometimes.'

For a moment or so, the two women sat smiling at each other across the kitchen table, and suddenly, inexplicably, the Mystery Blonde felt her eyes misting with tears. Then the moment was gone. Sam's head dipped back down again to study the table, and the Mystery Blonde cleared her throat.

'That was lovely, Sam, thanks. OK. Shall we . . . Well, do you want to tell me about this phone call?'

'Sorry, yes.'

'How was it "in a manner of speaking" that Chris called you?'

'Because it wasn't actually him who called.'

'I see. Then who was it?'

'It was Felix.'

The Mystery Blonde thanked her lucky stars she hadn't been taking a mouthful of tea at that exact moment. 'It was Felix?' Aghast, she repeated Sam's words back to her.

'Yes.'

'Um, I didn't know this . . .'

'There's no reason why you should. I told it all to the police, but apart from them – and my mum – you're the first person I've told. It didn't come out in court or anything . . .'

'OK. Talk me through it.'

'To be honest, he was lucky to get me. I was going to change my mobile, change the number and everything. You know how, if you've got the person's name in your address book, their name flashes up when they ring? Well, I'd been getting a lot of calls from Chris, usually at really odd times of the day – mostly in the early hours. I'd stopped leaving my mobile on overnight. If I did, I'd come back to it and there'd be, gosh, sometimes *forty* missed calls. And he'd leave messages, really long messages that I couldn't understand because he'd be so drunk. I just deleted them straight away, and if ever he rang during the day and his name flashed up, or his work number, I'd just let it go to answer-machine. But this time there was no name. They were calling from Felix's house, you see? From his phone. It just said – I can't remember whether it just said "call" or an actual number flashed up. It doesn't matter, the police knew it had come from his house anyway. So, OK – where was I? Oh, yes, so the phone rang and I answered it. Like I say, I wouldn't have done if I'd known it was Chris. And there's this guy, a voice I don't recognise, and he just says – I don't know – something like "Hello, is that Sam?" which was kind of odd, in a way, because most people – since college anyway – call me Samantha. See, you call me Sam, don't you? But that's because you've been seeing Chris, and that's what he's always, *always* called me.'

'Oh, I'm sorry.'

'No, no, that's all right. I'm just saying. So, anyway, that struck me as odd, that he called me Sam and not Samantha. But then he said something like "I know this is going to sound strange, but I'm Felix Carter, the singer Felix Carter." Well, then I just assumed it was one of the guys from work, you know? Messing about. They ring up and try to sell you double-glazing or something, string you along for a bit. It's sort of one of those bloke things, isn't it? They think they're all comedians. The blokes at work do anyway.

'So I played along. I said something like, 'Well, I'm sorry. I'm afraid I don't think I know anyone called Felix Carter . . .'

'No,' says Felix. His eyes are fixed on me, Brian's guns trained on him. He seems more nervous now than before, as if the sudden direction the situation has taken has thrown him off-kilter – Frank has not prepared him for this, obviously.

'You don't actually *know* me,' he says into the phone. 'I'm Felix Carter. I'm, well, *the* Felix Carter. You know? I've got a record in the charts . . .'

He's chewing the inside of his cheek, looking at me and shaking his head at the same time. His expression is telling me that Sam doesn't believe him. My face must darken because he holds up a steady-on hand, his eyes darting to Brian – my new dog of war – listening at the same time.

There's a pause as he listens, then . . . 'I'm sorry, love,' he says into the phone. 'You want me to what?'

'. . . "Sing it for me, then." I was playing along, you see? Thought I was, anyway. So I said, "Oh, I'm sorry, I only listen to the radio for the cricket scores," and that was sort of a joke, because it's like a running joke in the office that I hate cricket and during the summer it's all the guys in the office talk about. Cricket this, cricket that. So then I said, "Well, maybe if you sing it to me," and he said, like, "What?" and I said, "Go on, sing it for me, then," thinking I had the measure of whoever it was. And then I heard a hand go over the mouthpiece and that convinced me, like they were trying to control their laughter or something, you know? I was convinced then that it was a wind-up.'

He covers the mouthpiece with his hand. 'Mate . . . this isn't working. She wants me to sing for her.'

'Well, sing, then,' I hiss back, whispering, almost mouthing the words. 'Sing the hit. Sing the one in the charts.'

'That's what she wants me to sing.'

'Then sing it. Do it.' Beside me, Brian threatens with the gun. 'But sing it properly,' I say. 'Don't sing it sarcastically.'

'Sarcastically *is* proper – OK, OK. You're the boss.'

And then he starts to sing down the phone to her. The chorus of the song: 'I lo-o-o-ve you.' And it is . . .

'. . . the *worst* singing I've ever heard. I mean, I was thinking, they had the voice right. That was quite good. But the singing. You have to remember that I really thought it was a wind-up. I had no idea – and the singing just confirmed it for me, I thought he was singing it badly on purpose. And as he was singing, I was just laughing along with it, going, "Is that you, Dave? Is that you, Nick? Don't give up the day job," stuff like that. And then I heard this voice in the background. It was Chris, I recognised it immediately. He was saying something like . . .'

'What the *fuck* was that?'

'And that just did it for me. As soon as I heard his voice. I thought, Oh, God, like when – like when you put your hand in something nasty, you know? And you bring it up to your nose and you realise what it is and you just want to get rid of it as quickly as possible. It was like that. I thought it was the most horrible, horrible – not a joke, exactly, just a horrible, horrible *thing*. Not like I'd been raped. Obviously, nothing's as bad as that. But *like that*. Like I'd been taken advantage of. I suppose because I'd been laughing along, because I thought it was one of the boys from work, that sort of made it worse. That just made it all the more hurtful. It was as if he'd got together with some yukky mate he'd found in a pub, and they'd dreamed up this sick little scheme together. And they were laughing at me. That was how I felt. That, after everything he'd already done, he could go and do this. So I just cut them off. Just cut them off, switched off the phone and it was all I could do not to chuck it against a wall. And then I went and cried, and cried, and cried, and my mum came in and I told her, and she just went mad, she was calling him all sorts . . .

'But, you see, how could I have known? How was I to think otherwise? Obviously, when it all came out, I realised then that . . . that it really had been Felix, but at the time . . . That poor man. I've gone over it since. Over and over it. Thought, Did he try to give me a sign? Was there something he said that I missed? Was there *any way* I could have known what was really going on? Anything I could have done? I feel like . . . I feel like when I cut him off I signed his death warrant.'

And then the Mystery Blonde shot out of her seat and to Samantha's side, where she cradled the woman as she broke down, knowing that it wasn't Felix's life Sam had destroyed. She had destroyed her own.

'What the *fuck* was that?' I say again, looking over at Brian, who looks as shocked as I feel. Probably more so. After all, he's just heard his idol make a right bollocks of his own song. They say you should never meet your heroes, maybe this is why.

But Felix is not replying to me or even looking at Brian, although the guns have never wavered. He's shouting into the phone, which has clearly gone dead, shouting, 'No, don't, please – Hello . . . Hello! Sam?' Now he's looking up at me, his eyes wide with worry, the phone frozen in mid-air. He's small in the sofa, engulfed by the white leather. 'Please,' he says at last, holding out his hands. 'Please just keep calm. She's put down the phone.'

'Because your singing was shit!'

Forgetting himself, he shouts back, 'I was under pressure! He's pointing a fucking gun at me! Nat King fucking Cole couldn't do it like that!'

'Don't shout at me!' I bellow back. Beside me, the emotion of the situation seems to be getting to Brian. I register the guns shaking from the corner of my eye.

So does Felix, his eyes flicking from Brian and the guns back to me. Again, he holds his hands forward, a calming action. 'I'm sorry,' he says weakly to me, glancing at Brian.

Not nearly as sorry as I am.

First he fucks up my *Happy Monday* appearance by being over-flamboyant and attention-seeking and messing up the time-slot, next he serenades my wife with a voice like a strangled pet. Felix Carter may be a dab hand at getting stadiums full of fans to hold their cigarette lighters in the air, but as far as my marriage goes he's a wash-out. A complete fucking failure.

'Shoot him,' I say to Brian, standing next to me.

Except I don't, of course. But it occurs to me that if I wanted to, I *could*. And that if I did, Brian would probably obey.

In fact, it slowly dawns on me that there's been a power shift in this room, and that the three stages of evolution I noted earlier have changed. Now – in here at least – I am the person who has the power, who is listened to, who is protected.

I am the new Felix.

And in that moment not only do I experience what Felix feels all the time, but I realise that I have at last found the answer I came looking for and it's this – this feeling. It's a good feeling. I like it.

Just my luck, though, I don't get to feel it for long. Just long enough to register it, in fact. But long enough to miss it when it goes.

Because Brian chooses that moment finally to reveal his purpose for being here.

He takes a step to his right, flanking Felix and me. We both turn our heads towards him and watch. Watch as he tosses first his own gun to the sofa, then slowly raises my father's to his head.

Felix leans and snatches up Brian's discarded gun from the sofa. 'God,' he says, the gun in his hand. 'It's a – it's a toy.'

So much for the solidarity of nutters, I think dimly. He wasn't offering a helping hand at all – he just wanted a real gun. He wanted a real gun because he'd been intending to kill himself in here all along. And a bullet in the head is so much cleaner than what he'd presumably been planning – either slit wrists, or perhaps an overdose, Felix tied up and forced to watch as his stalker took his own life. But instead of his afternoon going to plan, I'd arrived – nutter-with-a-gun number two – and simultaneously thwarted and speeded up his plans. Another stupid-twat production from Christopher Sewell.

Now he stands before us with the gun held to his temple the Robert de Niro in *Deer Hunter* way. Much the same way as I held it to my own head the other night. Only that time I did it to see what it felt like. Brian's for real: the void behind his eyes tells me that.

'Brian,' I say, holding out my hand. 'Brian, don't.'

I don't see his finger whiten on the trigger the way you're supposed to. It's just a feeling I get that he's about to do it.

That, and the way he squeezes his eyes tight shut and lets out a little whimper.

I launch myself forward, seeing the hammer on the revolver go back and come forward again, watching my own hand reaching out to the gun but falling way short as the hammer slaps forward.

Turns out the old man wasn't infallible. Somewhere along the line he forgot to clean something, or check something properly. Or maybe he did, and that one bullet was too old, or just a dud. Either way, it doesn't fire. It doesn't even misfire. The hammer simply thumps home with as much effect as if Brian had been using his own toy gun.

He's in his stride, though. Just as I stop short, thinking, Thank God, a reprieve, he's pulling the trigger again and the chamber is revolving as the hammer comes back for a second time. Is this one going to misfire too? Could Dad really have lived with a crop of duds in his shoebox? I doubt it, so I'm grabbing for the gun, saying, 'Brian, no,' for a second time, trying to pull it away from him.

'Leave me!' he cries, trying to wrest the gun away from my hands, which are locked together around the grip of the pistol, the lanyard waving like an insane metronome beneath our grappling fists.

Suddenly, Felix is also with us, his hands joining the fight for the gun. And he's a strong lad, is Felix, those famous pecs earning their keep now as he pulls at the gun. One moment it's above our heads, the three of us grunting as we struggle for possession; the next, it's between us, sandwiched by our bodies.

Then, inevitably, it goes off.

No dud this time. The report of the gun, slightly muffled by our bodies but still loud in the room and very, very real.

The fight ceases. We all go rigid, each of us knowing that one of us will have been hit. Had to have been hit. The position of the gun made it certain.

I think, Maybe it's me. Maybe this is what it feels like to be shot: a numbing nothingness. And that maybe, in a second or so, my body will be on fire with pain as my central nervous system suddenly comprehends a massive trauma.

But then Felix takes a step away from our little group.

It's funny. All his life, Felix has been chosen first. I'm willing to bet that he never shuffled on the sidelines at school football, praying not to be picked last, never sat along the wall of the sixth-form disco, unable to find a partner for the final slow dance, the one where you always got a snog. In his adult life the public chose him as their idol, film-makers have chosen him to star in their film, he's been chosen all the way to the top.

So he can hardly moan when the bullet chooses him as well.

Felix steps back and takes a seat on the sofa, heavily. It makes a thump-whoosh sound, the way expensive sofas do. For a second or so, the exhaling sofa is the only sound in the room and then the gun drops to the floor and Brian and I look at one another wide-eyed, and then slowly – very slowly – we look over to the sofa.

There, Felix is watching a reddy-black stain creep across the front of his T-shirt. As we stare, he places one trembling hand against the ragged hole in his chest, then draws it to his face and studies his blood-coated fingertips. Looking up at us, his mouth quivers. His eyes flick open and closed, as if he's trying to prevent himself falling asleep. In effect, I suppose, he is.

'Whoops,' I say, as we watch his mouth quiver and his eyes flick, watch the pop star Felix Carter dying before our eyes.

Brian's squashed-up face twists into an 'oh-crikey' expression. I return with a face that says 'that's-torn-it'. Together we look like a couple of kids caught scrumping apples on Farmer Brown's land, not two men who have just killed one of the country's biggest celebrities. At least we have the good grace not to burst out in a fit of the giggles.

For a while we both watch until the quivering and flickering is over. Until it's clear that Felix is dead.

Again, the house is silent and Brian and I regard each other awkwardly, Felix's corpse by our side.

Finally, I say, 'Brian, what have you touched in the house?'

'Why?' he replies, looking up at me. He looks up because he's a good deal smaller than me, but he looks up for another reason also. Because I hold his future in my hands.

'We need to wipe your fingerprints from anything you've touched,' I say. 'So when the police arrive, if they take finger-prints, they'll only find mine.'

'I don't understand,' he says, and I think I see him retreating back into himself, fear I might lose him.

'Brian, listen,' I say. 'You're going to go. I'm going to stay. We don't know for certain which one of us pulled the trigger, but I'm going to say it was me and that I acted alone. There'll be no reason to disbelieve me. It was my gun. I'll have powder burns on me. I had his door key. Everything fits.'

'Why?' says Brian. 'Why are you going to take the blame?'

Why? Good question. Because I remember how it felt some moments ago when the roles in this room were reversed. Because then I wanted to be Felix Carter. And now I think that the next best thing to being Felix Carter is to be the man who killed him.

But I don't tell him that. Partly because I don't want him to arrive at the same conclusion, I suppose. But partly because I'm tired – really tired – and I can't be bothered to explain how I feel. At last, I finally know how I feel, and I can't even be bothered to explain it.

So we wipe up fingerprints together. I do all the remembering I can from the detective programmes I've watched and we do our best to cover any traces of the fact that Brian Forsyth was ever in the house.

Once we've done that, he goes, and as he leaves I wonder whether this incident will have put him off stalking for good, or will he just have some time off then get back to work making some other poor bugger's life a misery? Ronan Keating, perhaps. We'll see, I suppose. Perhaps one day you'll be interviewing him. Wherever he is, I just hope he's feeling a bit luckier now.

With him gone, it occurs to me that I need a drink, so I drink one of my miniatures. A little after that the door buzzer goes. The car, I assume. For a moment I dither over what to do, thinking that I don't want to be discovered just yet – I'd rather get myself together first. OK, if I'm honest, I think I'd rather get drunk first, get drunk in Felix's house – maybe play some PlayStation 2, watch one of his films on his big TV, play a little pool. Just hang around and enjoy the experience of being him.

The phone goes but I ignore it, let the answer-machine kick in, and then the buzzer goes again, but this time I strip off and go to the door where I tell the driver I'm ill.

I tell him I've been on the bog and that I've got the shits. He's a funny chap. Dead excited about meeting me. Makes me sign a CD cover he has in his pocket for his daughter. Has a pen handy and everything.

There's a bit of a scary moment – the Jack Daniel's is still on the doorstep, you see. But, as I say, he's a funny chap. Just points to it and goes, 'God, I wish I had your milkman.'

And I just say, 'Huh, probably a fan's left it there. We'll need to get it checked out before I can bring it in.' Like I have teams of security on hand to taste my food or something.

Anyway, he seems happy enough, and off he trots, and when the car's gone I go to fetch the Jack Daniel's, take a seat in the sofa opposite the body and have a drink. The next thing, the cleaner's coming in. I never got the chance to try out his TV.

I think you know the rest.

I think so, yes. Thank you.

Which pretty much concludes our business, doesn't it?

It does, I suppose. Just one thing, Chris. What you've told me, about Brian Forsyth.

Which goes no further.

No, absolutely not. But . . . are you telling me you didn't actually kill Felix? That you're in here for something you didn't do?

The gun went off, is what I'm saying. Any one of us could have pulled the trigger – Felix might even have done it himself. I just want someone to know that I'm not a killer. I never wanted to kill anyone. It's just that when someone died, I saw a way out, and all told, it's turned out for the best. Out there I was Chris, in here I'm Felix. Do you see?

I see, yes. And one last thing. Why choose me?

Because I can trust you, and as my biographer you should know the whole story, even if you can't use it all. That way you'll get closer to the truth about me. You know something? Not many people get the chance to read about themselves, in interviews and books. The old Chris would never have done. So I just want this book to be as good as possible. After all, there'll be another celebrity killer along in a minute, stealing all my limelight. It's a cut-throat business. I've got to make the most of it while I can.

Ah, look, Jack wants his picture. Are you OK to stick around for the photo-shoot?

Killing Felix Carter[30]
By Andrea Watson

List Price: £6.99
Our Price: £5.59
You Save: £1.40 (20%)

Availability: Usually dispatched within 24 hours
Category(ies): Crime, Thrillers & Mystery
See larger photo

Paperback – 352 pages new edition (1 June, 2004)
Dunsmure; ISBN: 0 340 82360 7

**Write an online review and share your thoughts with
other shoppers!**
Amazon.co.uk Sales Rank: 8

Average Customer Rating:*****
Number of reviews: 4

Editorial review
Andrea Watson, formerly a features editor with *Sass* magazine
(where Christopher Sewell also worked), and a regular feature of
the gossip columns (usually as a mystery blonde on the arm of a
celebrity) has earned her journalistic spurs with this study of Felix
Carter's killer, Christopher Sewell.

---

[30] From Amazon.co.uk.

Here she offers an unrivalled portrait of the man, charting his rapid decline from married career man to celebrity stalker, and drawing some fascinating parallels between the life of a star and the life Sewell now leads inside prison, where 'Christopher Sewell memorabilia' has become valuable currency.

To her own research and conclusions, Watson has added interviews with Sewell's ex-wife, Samantha, as well as ex-work colleagues, to craft a compelling, exhaustive and oddly sympathetic narrative, which, while shedding no new light on the murder itself, illustrates starkly how a seemingly normal man can become a killer. All too easily, it seems.

For fans of Felix Carter, true-crime enthusiasts or anyone who found themselves grimly fascinated by the murder, this is essential reading.

**** *An absorbing read!*

Reviewer: areader@hotmail.com

A man breaks into a pop star's house and shoots him. What made him do it? This is the question this book attempts to answer, and does so superbly. If you're looking for juicy gossip about Felix Carter, or even inside info on the murder, you've come to the wrong place. But if it's a serious look at why someone becomes a murderer, then look no further. Andrea Watson does not reveal where she got the majority of information for this book, but if it's a testament to her journalistic skills, then all I can say is, she was wasted on women's magazines!

* *Don't buy this book!*

Reviewer: katesutton@wherewereyouwhenfelixdied.com

You should be able to award zero stars. This book is a travesty! It is just someone trying to make money from the memory of the greatest-ever pop star. All REAL Felix fans should boycott this book!

**** *The author's a fox!*

Reviewer: lukeradley@hotmail.com

I knew Christopher Sewell and was interviewed by Andrea Watson for the book. Put it this way, it was worth having to put up with that guy just to meet her! Andrea, any time you fancy going out for a drink, you know where I am!

**** *Thank you, Chris*
Reviewer: Anon4689@anon.com
I also knew Christopher Sewell, but only for the briefest time. However, during that time, he was especially kind to me and I shall never forget him. Thanks, Chris, and if you're reading this, you'll be pleased to know that I'm no longer a big Felix Carter fan. I now like Ronan Keating better.